I0770206

pour decisions

AMANDA CHAPERON

Pour Decisions is a steamy small town romance full of explicit language and sexual content. To avoid—or locate—the open door chapters, please flip to the Dicktionary I've provided in the back. For the complete list of *Pour Decisions* content warnings, please visit my website at www.achaperonauthor.com.

To Mer, who laughed when I said I was writing a slow burn.
Guess what, bitch? I did it!
Thanks for always believing in me ;)

And to Joe Burrow. If you know, you know.

I LOVED A NICE set of tits as much as the next guy, but not when they repeatedly showed up on my security cameras.

Honestly, I'd seen enough nipples tonight to last a lifetime.

Scrubbing a hand over my face, my scruff scraping against my palm, I wondered how I'd ended up here. I was a night club owner, yes, but this wasn't a fucking *strip* club.

Most nights weren't like this. Generally, club goers treated my place with respect. Patrons reveled in the music and the drinks and the company. I knew tonight was out of the ordinary but...my god. What the fuck was going on? Why weren't these women deterred by the possibility of being arrested for public nudity? And didn't they realize how much trouble *I* could get in for these stunts? I was, admittedly, rich, but that didn't mean I wanted to be paying stupid fines out the ass for women who couldn't control themselves.

That two-for-one tequila shots special was proving to be an unwise decision. Surprisingly—and thankfully—the men were keeping their hands to themselves, and I hadn't yet witnessed any wayward cameras capturing footage of the half-naked women.

I was holed up in my office, dutifully pretending to work while really I kept an eye on things from behind the safety of a locked door. Even though I preferred to be alone, I liked being alone *here*, where if I was gripped by the sudden need for company, I could go downstairs and camp out behind the bar, slinging drinks and grinning for the masses that jockeyed for my attention.

But being on the floor didn't hold any appeal for me tonight.

Tonight, all I wanted to do was plan my next business move.

When I'd moved to Traverse City six years ago, I'd been running. Running away from the spotlight that followed me everywhere I went in Detroit. Running from the fans who stopped me on the street to say they were so sorry about my retirement—as if they were the ones who had to live that fucking nightmare. Running from the reminders of the career I'd had to give up.

Football had been my life...until it wasn't. Until one bad hit had dislocated my shoulder, torn my rotator cuff, and taken it away from me forever. I'd been in my prime, and it had all ended in the blink of an eye.

And I knew it was *only* football. I was still alive, healthy, and had all of my limbs. But losing football, for me, *was* like losing a limb. I'd spent over twenty years honing my craft, becoming the best I could be in order to play at an elite level. I was only thirty when I'd gotten injured—an injury, mind you, that shouldn't have taken me out. After the surgery to repair my shoulder, it healed fine. But *fine* wasn't good enough to get me back to QB1. Hell, after I finished rehab, I could barely throw for twenty yards.

I didn't have the long ball in me anymore, and I was faced with two choices: leave the game with dignity, on my own terms, or shuffle around the league playing backup to young up and comers until I was forced out.

It was obvious which door I chose.

I saw myself out with my legacy intact, and the rest was history.

God, I missed it.

Regardless, I'd settled into my new life nicely, despite the fact that it had greeted me several years earlier than I'd planned. I bought this place in cash, sight unseen. With the help of a local contracting firm highly recommended by an athlete friend from Detroit, I gutted and renovated the club on the main level, my offices on the second floor, and the apartments on the third. Back then, there hadn't even been *walls* up there. For several months, I'd slept on an air mattress in the drafty, cavernous space. Naming it after myself had definitely been a choice, but I liked to think that was what made Lawless such a success. In the five years since I'd opened the doors, the club had become a Traverse City staple.

Since then, I'd expanded into a restaurant—Birdie's, which I named after my mom—and a sports bar that was welcoming for all ages.

Now, I was ready to move onto my passion project: a distillery.

Well, it was less my passion and more a torch I carried for my dad. He'd always planned to open a distillery on our family ranch back in Idaho, expanding the Lawless brand beyond horses and cattle into spirits. It was something we'd dreamed about together, an endeavor we swore we'd take on once my playing career was over.

But that wasn't an option for Dad anymore, owing to the fact that he was no longer among the living, so it was up to me to see it through.

I knew exactly which spirits I wanted to distill and the names I'd give each of them. I knew my timeline and already had the contractor lined up to start work as soon as possible. And I knew where I wanted to build, but that last one was proving to be a bit of a challenge—mostly because I hated asking people for anything.

But this time, I was going to have to bite the bullet.

Normally, I'd call my best friend and ask him to be the go-between for me. Amara was, after all, his girlfriend. Unfortunately, Cal was off in the wilds of the Upper Peninsula, service-less on some self-exploratory mission before he headed to Door County to see his parents. Not to mention, the text he'd sent me before he left told me things between him and Amara were on shaky ground.

Cal: I got fired, and I'm pretty sure Amara and I are done. I'm headed to the UP and then to Wisconsin for a few weeks, so I'll be out of service the next couple days. I want to chat when I get back about that job you offered me a few months ago.

Instantly, my curiosity was piqued. Amara was—or had been—his boss, so shit had to have hit the fan in a major way. But that wasn't my problem.

Me: You have any free time this afternoon? I'd like to meet with you.

Amara Delatou: If this is about Cal…

Me: It's not, I promise. I have a business proposition for you.

Amara Delatou: Business I can do. I'm free whenever.

Me: Can I come up now?

Amara Delatou: Sure. I'm at the winery.

Me: Great. See you in 20.

Were my palms sweaty because I was about to go to Amara, hat in hand, and ask her to do me a solid? Or was it because I knew what the woman looked like naked?

Yeah, we were going with the first one.

I settled my ball cap on my head, stuffed my feet into my scuffed up Ariats, and headed out the door.

My house was on the northeast side of Traverse City, right on the shores of Boardman Lake, and about a fifteen minute drive from the winery. In the opposite direction, if I were to head into the city proper, I could reach any of my businesses in the same amount of time.

That's why the location for the distillery was so important. Land around here was a premium, especially on the northern half of Old Mission, where I desperately wanted to build. Naturally, the perfect piece of land was owned by Delatou, Inc., and I needed Amara to agree to sell it.

I couldn't explain it, but I had this inkling that building this distillery and getting the business up and running would change my life. That it would fill the hole in my heart, and was the piece my life had been missing.

On the drive up, I rolled the windows down in my truck, content to let the fresh air soothe my anxiety. A lot was riding on this meeting, and I could only hope Amara was in a good mood. I still had no clue what I'd be walking into in terms of her relationship status, and I hoped whatever issues she had with Cal at the moment didn't make me the enemy by proxy.

I'd been in the Delatou, Inc. offices at Chateau Delatou enough times to easily navigate my way to Amara's, so I parked in the employee lot and made my way in.

Not bothering to do more than wave and smile at the people I passed, I made a beeline down the long hall to Amara's door, knocking softly before moving inside. Amara greeted me with a hug and a kiss on the cheek, and instantly my nerves evaporated.

We'd had a brief fling the summer I opened Lawless, but it ended as easily as it began. I moved onto my next business venture, Amara went to Europe, and we remained good friends. We just didn't work as lovers. I was happy that my best friend and Amara had found each other.

"It's good to see you, kid," I said as I sat down on her cushy leather couch. She remained standing nearby, and I bit back a grin as her eyes narrowed.

"I hate when you call me that."

"I know you do," I said, letting the smile free. "Why do you think I do it?"

"You're not that old, you know."

I snorted. "Please. I'm pushing forty."

And I felt it every day. Years of football compounded by natural aches and pains that came with aging meant I frequently woke up with creaky knees and tight lower-back muscles.

"Thirty-seven is *not* forty," Amara said with an eye roll. "And let's be real, you look damn good for your age."

I quirked a brow, lips twisting into a smirk. "You hitting on me?"

Amara grinned as she approached the drink cart. "Just stating a fact."

It was too easy to fall back into this banter with her, and I had to get my shit together, to remind myself of the reason for this meeting. I wasn't here to flirt with my best friend's girl, innocent as it was.

"You want a drink?" she asked, gesturing to the spread of bottles.

"Bourbon," I said, knowing a couple fingers wouldn't hurt. "Whatever you've got."

Amara selected the bottle of Four Roses—my personal favorite, at least until my own was in production—and poured some into a tumbler, filling a glass of water for herself.

I raised a brow. The Amara I knew never turned down a

cocktail. "You're not drinking?"

"I can't," she said as she handed me my drink then sank down on the couch across from me.

My eyes narrowed. "Are you okay?"

"Fine," she said quickly, then deliberately settled a hand on her lower abdomen. "Great, actually."

I damn near spit my drink out. She couldn't possibly mean...

"Ho-ly shit. You're not..." I trailed off, hoping I was wrong.

"Just over two months," she confirmed.

I rolled my lips between my teeth, carefully considering my next words. I knew the chances of the father being anyone but my best friend were slim, but still I asked, "Cal?"

Amara simply nodded, and hurt flashed across her face at the mention of his name. "I'm assuming you've talked to him," she said.

"Yeah," I snorted, "but he didn't tell me about this."

I kicked one of my Ariats up onto my opposite knee and resisted the urge to squirm. God, this was bad. Obviously, I had no idea how Cal felt, but he was going to be a father whether he liked it or not. And finding this out on the heels of being fired? What a fucking mess.

"How is he?" Amara asked quietly, and I softened.

"Off in the wilderness somewhere," I said, waving a hand. "He was heading to visit his parents, but he went through the U.P., taking a few days to unplug."

"That's good," she said absently. "He needs that."

"After you fired him and ripped his heart out? Yeah, I'd say so."

Because honestly, what the fuck? Talk about kicking a man

while he was down. And what the fuck had happened that she fired him *knowing* she was pregnant with their child? I found myself suddenly irritated at the woman across from me.

"So he told you he got fired, but not that he got me pregnant?"

"We didn't exactly talk," I explained. "He sent me a text saying he got fired, that y'all were done, and he was going off the grid for a few days so I wouldn't be able to reach him if I needed to. And that he wanted to talk about the job I'd offered him a few months ago when he got back to town."

Amara perked up at that, clearly surprised. "What job?"

"I want him to manage my finances," I told her, dropping my foot back to the floor and leaning forward, resting my elbows on my knees. I didn't miss the way her gaze strayed to the tattoo on my left arm—my last name. I knew how much she'd loved that ink once upon a time.

"He'd be perfect for that," she said, seemingly reluctant to tear her gaze from my arm.

"I know," I said. "That's why I want him."

"Well, he's suddenly unemployed, so I think it'll be pretty easy to convince him."

I reclined on the couch again, the leather creaking with my movements, and folded my arms over my chest as I narrowed my eyes at her.

"There's no chance of him getting his job back?" I asked.

Honestly, I was thrilled by this new development. I'd been bugging Cal for months to leave the winery and come work with me, and it seemed like I was finally getting my wish. The circumstances were a little fucked up, but I'd take what I could get.

With a sigh, Amara simply shook her head, and I nodded in response.

"I'm not going to ask what happened," I said, "because quite frankly, it's not my business. I did, however, actually come here to discuss my business."

I'd had enough of the feelings talk. Now it was time to get down to the real reason for my visit.

"Lay it on me," Amara said after taking a sip of her water.

"I want to buy a piece of Delatou land."

Amara's brows rose toward her hairline. Clearly, that wasn't what she'd been expecting from me, and I succinctly launched into my whole business plan. I could tell she was impressed, and a little seedling of pride rooted and began to sprout in my chest.

"I'd also love to offer you a partnership opportunity," I said once I'd finished my spiel. "What you're doing here is impressive, and I'd love to work with you on this. Hell, maybe one day we could even branch out into spirit-based cocktails."

It was clear she liked the sound of that from the small smile on her face, and I could practically see the wheels spinning in her mind. Even so, when her face once again settled, I could tell she was going to say no. Call it that sixth sense for reading people I'd picked up as a football player, but Amara was not on board with a partnership. While I wanted to work with her—truthfully, I wasn't doing this thing *without* a partner—all I really needed from her was a deed to the land. As long as she could come through for me on that, I could find someone else.

Then, a little gleam appeared in Amara's eyes, and I mentally braced myself.

"Delia."

"Your sister?" I asked, confused. "What about her?"

"She's been begging me for a project for ages," Amara said, face brightening. "I think this would be perfect for her. She's a marketing whiz and has been looking for a way to become more involved in the family business. Right now, she manages our social media, but I can tell she's getting restless. This isn't quite what she had in mind, I'm sure, but I think you two would work well together."

"No."

It came out harsher than I intended, but there was no fucking way I was working with Delia Delatou.

Amara raised a brow. "No?"

"She's too...young," I said, wincing at the weak excuse. "And don't think I forgot about the shit she pulled at my cabin over Memorial Day."

I didn't fuck with people who fucked with other people for sport. In my eyes, Delia Delatou was a loose cannon, and I wasn't getting within fifty yards of that shit.

"She's only a year younger than me," Amara reminded me. "And that's all water under the bridge."

I snorted. It may be water under the bridge between sisters, but I couldn't forget the way Delia had dared Amara to make out with *me*, knowing our history, while my best friend and the man who was ass over boots for her sat right next to me. The whole thing left a sour taste in my mouth.

"I'm not doing it," I said firmly. "I'll find someone else."

Maybe Cal would want to be my business partner. Just go full send on working together.

"Just meet with her," Amara said. "Please."

"No."

"I'll sell you the land if you do."

"Are you...bribing me?"

The fucking balls on this woman.

"No," she said, though we both knew she was. "I'm making you an offer. Meet with Delia, and I'll sell you the land. I'm assuming you've got your eye on a particular parcel."

With a sigh, I shifted and withdrew the piece of paper from my back pocket, tossing it onto the table between us. Amara picked it up and unfolded it, studying the copy of a plat map of the other end of the peninsula, where I'd outlined the land I wanted in red. It was the perfect spot. High on a bluff but flat enough to construct the distillery and a parking lot. It'd offer a two hundred and seventy degree view of the water, and wasn't too far off the main road.

"How much?"

"I'll have to ask my dad and get back to you."

"See that you do," I said, rising to my feet.

"Get that meeting on the books with Delia and I will," she shot back.

"You drive a hard bargain, Delatou."

"I'm more than just a pretty face."

"Don't I know it," I murmured as I dropped a kiss on her cheek. When I straightened, I added, "For what it's worth, kid, I'd give Cal a chance to explain. When he talked to me about you, he was completely spun out, and that was months ago."

Amara perked up, clearly surprised. "He talked to you about me?"

I gave her a sad smile. I wasn't playing the go-between here.

"Just talk to him, Mar."

And then I was gone, pausing only briefly at Amara's assistant's desk to get contact information for Delia. As she handed it over, I was gripped by the sense that she was passing along my death sentence.

I NEARLY SPAT MY coffee all over my computer screen when I found an email from Owen Lawless waiting in my inbox Tuesday morning.

What the hell could *he* possibly want from *me*?

I even went so far as to rub my eyes and blink rapidly to make sure I wasn't seeing things. With a lingering hangover—and subsequent headache—from the Labor Day festivities of the day before, I wasn't exactly firing on all cylinders.

I set my mug down on a ceramic coaster and clicked the message open.

SATURDAY, AUGUST 30, 2025 (3:57 P.M.)
FROM: OWEN LAWLESS (OWEN@OWENLAWLESS.COM)
TO: DELIA DELATOU (DELIA@DELATOUINC.COM)

BUSINESS PROPOSITION

Dear Ms. Delatou,

I'm reaching out today at the request of your sister, Amara. I have a business proposition she informed me you may be interested in, and I'd like to set up a meeting. I'm available any day this upcoming week between the hours of noon and three p.m.

Please respond at your earliest convenience.

Sincerely,
Owen Lawless

I scrunched my eyebrows together in confusion. There was a lot to unpack there, and I hadn't had enough coffee to deal with it. Instead of attempting a response, I rose from my desk chair and shuffled downstairs, exiting the garage and padding inside to refill my mug. Then I passed through the front door and onto my screened-in porch. This far north in the state, fall was already peeking its head out from the blanket of summer, and I could not be happier. This was truly my favorite time of the year, when the leaves on the maple, oak, and birch trees fencing my yard began to yellow, when the air became crisper, when the breeze smelled of softly decaying things.

I dropped myself onto the padded swing, mug cupped in my hands, and allowed my gaze to roam around my neighborhood. I took my coffee out here whenever the weather permitted, loving the combination of the warm liquid and fresh air to wake me up. Across the street, the Millers were hustling outside—she ushered the kids into her SUV to take them to daycare while he hopped in his truck to head into Traverse City for work. Next to them, Mr. Tuggle shuffled out to his mailbox in his slippers and robe to grab the morning paper. The curtains on their front room twitched as Mrs. Tuggle peaked out, surveying the new day.

Across the street on the other side, the newlywed Mr. and Mrs. Rinaldi climbed into their van and headed downtown, in the direction of the grocery store his family had owned and operated for the last forty or so years.

And next door to me, Tanya Geralt sat on her own porch, a mug of something—most likely chai tea if I knew her—steaming in her hands. When I caught her eye, she waved and shouted, "Good morning!"

"Morning, Tanya!" I hollered back.

Tanya was the owner of Granny Smith's, the local bar and restaurant my grandmother had built back in the seventies. Her family's roots in this town ran nearly as deep as mine, and despite having been so young, I knew my family was pleased—if a bit skeptical—when she stepped forward to buy it in the nineties. She was barely twenty-four back then, but she'd made a success of the place. Between Granny's, Sydney's Diner, and Brie's Bakery, the townsfolk of Apple Blossom Bay were spoiled with good cooking.

And I was spoiled to live in such a tight knit community. My first winter in this house, Mr. Rinaldi taught me how to use a snow blower so I could clear my own driveway. Mr. Tuggle, who owned the local hardware store, taught me everything I needed to know about home improvement, giving me the skills to update this place myself. Anytime I was sick, Tanya would bring me a vat of her homemade chicken noodle soup to make me feel better.

I had my family nearby, yes, but there was something so heart-warming about being welcomed wholly by people who weren't genetically predisposed to love you. That was part of the reason why I'd bought a house in town instead of building on my land farther north on the peninsula. I loved Mom, Dad, and each of my four sisters dearly, but I wanted something that was *mine*. When I first looked at this house, even before stepping inside, I knew it was home.

It was an old farmhouse that formerly sat on the outskirts of town, the once vacant land around it now filled in with housing as the town expanded. Thanks to the diligent record keeping of our town officials, I even had a few framed photos of the house when it was new and surrounded by fields decorating my walls. Today, though, I was only a few streets off the main thoroughfare. I had a corner lot with a sizable yard and trees providing enough privacy in the back. Plus, there was room to grow if I had a family one day, and I loved having neighbors.

I'd known right away it would need a lot of work to modernize it, but I enjoyed the challenge. In fact, I relished it. The hard work was a good place to channel my anxiousness and energy that I would otherwise exploit elsewhere. I'd done all the up-dates—save the roof, siding, and some interior framing—myself, including tearing down and replacing every rotted board of the wrap-around porch I sat on now, gutting the kitchen to put in new cabinets and countertops, installing new laminate flooring throughout both levels, painting, and a plethora of other things. In the five years since I'd graduated college and purchased this place, I'd slowly but surely turned it from neglected to lived in.

As I'd documented the entire thing on my Instagram and TikTok accounts, I'd been surprised by the enthusiasm and rapid growth of my audience. I had dual degrees in marketing and business from Northwestern, but the updating of my home was my first true chance to put either of them to work, and I discovered how much I loved the social media aspect of marketing and branding.

Truthfully, I'd only gotten the business degree because Dad had begged me to, saying it was good to have something to fall back on if marketing failed. It wasn't that he didn't believe in me; he was simply a practical man trying to raise practical daughters. I heeded his advice if only because I wanted to make him happy. What I'd really wanted was to major in photography, but I had settled for a few courses in school and more online, mostly self-teaching. I've always loved photography, and had earned fun money in college by shooting special occasions for my contemporaries. I quickly learned social media photography was a whole different ball game, but one I enjoyed immensely. I really cut my teeth on it, and years of trial and error had gotten me to the place I was now.

All in all, things had worked out exactly as they were supposed to.

Happily, I inhaled deeply, drawing in a breath of fresh morning air and basking in the sounds of my neighborhood waking up and starting the day. I didn't know how Amara lived out on the peninsula by herself. The silence would drive me crazy.

Speaking of my big sister, I headed into the house and upstairs, scooping my phone off my nightstand where I'd left it and dialed her number.

"Morning, sunshine," Amara said, voice still sleepy.

"Morning, sissy. Did I wake you?"

"No, you're fine," Amara said. "I'm just always tired. This baby is sucking the life out of me."

I grinned at the thought of my future niece or nephew. I couldn't believe both of my older sisters were pregnant at the same time. I wasn't anywhere near ready for children, but I couldn't quite tamp down on the jealousy that panged in my chest. I was happy they were experiencing something so wonderful together, but I hated feeling left out.

It was that classic middle child in me. I wasn't truly happy unless I was the center of attention.

"How are you feeling otherwise?"

"Good! Really good. Cal's been taking good care of me."

Her tone was suggestive, and I gagged.

"Spare me the details," I said. "I'm just happy you guys worked your shit out."

It had been touch and go over the last few weeks—since Amara found out she was pregnant, then promptly fired Cal from his position as Delatou, Inc.'s CFO—whether or not she and Cal would work through their issues and realize how much they loved each other. When Cal popped up at the company Labor Day party yesterday, I knew things would be okay.

Amara deserved that, deserved to be treasured and for her baby to have its father in its life. They were going to be amazing parents.

"Me too," I heard Cal say in the background, followed by the smack of a kiss.

"So is there a reason you called?" Amara asked.

"Oh! Yes!" I said, remembering myself. "I had an interesting email from Owen Lawless waiting for me this morning. Know anything about that?"

"Took him long enough," Amara mumbled. Then, "Yes, I do. We met last week because he wants to buy a piece of land from us to build a distillery on. He also asked me to sign on as a partner, but I can't commit to that right now between the winery and pregnancy. So I recommended you."

"Recommended me how?" I said, gripped by inexplicable apprehension.

"I may have...bribed him a bit."

"With?"

"I told him I'd sell him the land if he agreed to meet with you. And before you go off on me, just listen. You've been asking for a project for ages. Unfortunately, we don't have anything new happening at the moment, and that won't be changing for at least the next year while I get through this pregnancy and the first few months of motherhood. This is your chance to have something that's just yours, Lia. All I did was get you in the door. I know you can do the rest yourself."

While I wanted to be mad at her for basically forcing Owen into this meeting, I softened. As always, my sister's heart was in the right place.

"A distillery?" I asked tentatively.

"Yes!" Amara said, quickly running through the plans Owen had relayed to her. I had to admit, I was impressed. Then again, the man already owned three thriving businesses in the area, not to mention being a successful brand himself, so I shouldn't be surprised.

Already, my mind whirred with marketing ideas, content strategy, and what exactly I could bring to the table to secure this partnership deal.

It seemed Daddy had been right: that business degree was about to come in handy after all.

* * *

TUESDAY, SEPTEMBER 2, 2025 (10:43 A.M.)
FROM: DELIA DELATOU (DELIA@DELATOUINC.COM)
TO: OWEN LAWLESS (OWEN@OWENLAWLESS.COM)

RE: BUSINESS PROPOSITION

DEAR MR. LAWLESS,

I TRULY APPRECIATE YOU REACHING OUT AND GIVING ME THE OPPORTUNITY TO MEET WITH YOU. I'M FREE AT 1 P.M. ON FRIDAY. JUST NAME THE PLACE AND I'LL BE THERE.

SINCERELY,
DELIA DELATOU

TUESDAY, SEPTEMBER 2, 2025 (11:08 A.M.)
FROM: OWEN LAWLESS (OWEN@OWENLAWLESS.COM)
TO: DELIA DELATOU (DELIA@DELATOUINC.COM)

RE: Business Proposition

Please meet me at my offices, which are located in the Lawless Club building. Park in the back lot and press the buzzer. Someone will let you in and direct you.

Sincerely,
Owen Lawless

Tuesday, September 2, 2025 (11:18 a.m.)
From: Delia Delatou (delia@delatouinc.com)
To: Owen Lawless (owen@owenlawless.com)

RE: Business Proposition

Dear Mr. Lawless,

See you then.

Best,
Delia Delatou

I spent the intervening three days between scheduling with Owen and the meeting itself either at the winery shooting content for socials—a job I was more than happy to do since it meant a lot of following Liam Danvers and his tattooed self around the vineyard as harvest commenced—and doing research on the spirits industry, forming a plan of attack in terms of branding and marketing and social strategies. When Friday rolled around, I was as prepared as I could be—which is to say, pretty goddamn prepared.

Still, my palms were clammy with nervous sweat as I pulled into the lot behind Lawless that afternoon. I'd never been here during the daytime, and it was disconcerting to see a space normally teeming with life looking so...desolate.

I knew he'd opted for us to meet here simply to knock me off my game. This was his turf, his home field advantage. By having us meet here, he was asserting his dominance, trying to prove that he had the upper hand. Showing me that he held all the cards, and he was merely doing me a favor.

And, okay, maybe he *was* doing me a favor at the behest of my sister, but I knew my worth. I knew what I was bringing to the table, and Owen Lawless would be a pretty shitty businessman if he didn't agree to partner with me.

Gathering my bag and keys, I stepped out of the car and approached the back door, reaching up to press the buzzer as Owen had instructed. A minute later, it opened to reveal a pixie of a girl.

"Can I help you?" she asked, bored.

"I'm Delia Delatou," I said. "I'm here for a meeting with Owen?"

"Right." She jerked her head. "C'mon, then." When I followed her in, the door shut heavily behind us, the hall descending into darkness. From ahead the girl said, "Head onto the floor.

There's a staircase at the far left. When you reach the top, take another left. His office is at the end of the hall."

She disappeared almost as quickly as she'd arrived, and I gingerly navigated through the dimness and out onto the main floor of the club.

If I thought it was strange to see the exterior in the daylight, it was nothing compared to the interior. All the booths and tables empty, no press of bodies jockeying for position and attention at the long bar, the DJ booth silent. It was almost like stepping into an alternate reality, one of those back room, liminal spaces where nothing was as it should be.

I made quick work of the stairs and long hallway, taking a fortifying breath before rapping lightly on Owen's office door.

"Come in," he said, and I pushed inside.

He rose from his chair as I entered, steepling his fingers on the surface of his desk, the silver ring on his pinky glinting in the sunlight as he watched me.

God, every time I laid eyes on the man, it was like being smacked in the face all over again. No one in their late-thirties had the right to look like that. Even without knowing him, it was obvious from one quick scan of his body that he was an athlete. You didn't get muscles like his from standard gym sessions. He was broad through the shoulders and chest, his torso tapering to a trim waist and flat stomach. His short-sleeved Henley clung to his washboard abs, the buttons open to reveal the tips of his collarbones and that strong, tan throat. The light jeans he had on molded to his thick thighs and looked soft and well-worn, clearly a favorite pair he'd put a lot of miles in. I couldn't see his feet, but I knew from experience that they were stuffed into dusty brown

Ariat boots. His signature ball cap was turned backward on his head, his slightly too-long dirty blond hair brushing his collar and flipping out around his ears.

It gave him a boyish air—the floppy hair, the casual clothes, the cornflower blue eyes that glinted mischievously, even though his overall expression was stern.

Owen Lawless was rugged and sexy, looking like a bad idea waiting to happen, living up to the legacy of his last name.

"Hello, Owen," I said, offering a little wave and sheepish smile.

"Hi, Delia. Thanks for meeting with me."

"I'll admit, I was surprised to hear from you."

"Your sister made a...compelling argument for giving you a chance."

I narrowly held in a snort. I guess that's what we were calling *bribery* these days.

"Yes, I understand you weren't exactly keen on the idea," I said slowly, "but I promise I'll make it worth your while."

Owen waved a hand, gesturing for me to proceed. "Let's hear it then."

I inclined my head to the coffee table and couches behind me, and Owen raised a brow. I didn't like having this giant desk between us, him wielding it like a bunker protecting his ass. I wanted us at least on the same level, and I wanted to spread all my work out on the table and let him see how much time and effort I'd put into this simple exploratory meeting.

Once we settled onto our respective couches, I launched into my pitch.

For his part, Owen nodded along as I spoke, attention fixed raptly on me, asking questions in exactly the places I anticipated he would. I couldn't help but grin each time I answered him flawlessly.

The man was putty in my hands.

My plan was simple: document everything. Every step of construction, from materials selection and framing to decor and interior finishes; each moment of distilling from the first, inevitably awful batch to the final product; interviews with Owen, behind the scenes videos, cocktail recipes and packaging reveals. The entire process from start to finish.

I'd learned with my house that people wanted to see everything, and they enjoyed the nitty gritty as much as they loved the highlight reel. With my experience and a face like Owen's, this thing was a slam dunk already.

Or whatever the football equivalent was. A chip-shot field goal? Sure, we'd go with that.

"This is...impressive," Owen said, clearly reluctantly, when I'd finished, leaning back against the suede couch and crossing his arms over that beefy chest. His muscles flexed in the most distracting way. I wanted to sink my teeth into them, to lick a path up his forearm along that tattoo of his last name and feel his coarse blond hair scratching my tongue, to swirl along the ink curling around his right biceps.

And, okay, what the fuck? I was about to—hopefully—get into business with this guy; I needed to also get into bed with him like I needed a hole in the head. Not to mention he'd already fucked my sister, so I *definitely* wasn't going there.

This was merely my inner chaos demon talking, wanting to come out and play with the paragon of masculinity sitting in front of us. In any other situation, I wouldn't think twice about it. I'd have already straddled his lap, slipped my tongue in his mouth and put a hand down his pants.

But this was *important*. Arguably the most important meeting I'd ever had. Opportunities like this didn't come around often, and I refused to allow the seductress within me, driven by her baser instincts, to fuck it up.

"Why do I sense a 'but' coming?" I asked, clearing my mind of those dirty images.

"I'm just not sure this is the best decision for me—business wise," he added quickly.

I raised a brow. "Why, exactly?"

"I don't think I need to remind you."

"Humor me."

Mostly because I have no idea what you're talking about.

"That shit you pulled at my cabin on Memorial Day with me, Cal, and Amara," he said. "I don't work with people who toy with me and the people I care about. It's one thing to mess with your sister. I get it. I'm the oldest of seven, so I know a thing or two about fucking with siblings. But to drag *me*, her *ex* into it? As well as Cal? When you knew full well that things with them were on those new, shaky legs? I didn't appreciate that."

Shame washed over me as those—albeit hazy—memories flooded back. The problem was, I had a habit of acting first and damning the consequences to hell, especially when I'd consumed large quantities of alcohol. That night had not been one of my finer moments, but I'd been so sick of watching Cal and Amara make eyes at each other all day. I knew daring my sister to make-out with Owen would effectively drive her into Cal's arms—and she'd proven me right.

Plus, it had all worked out perfectly in the end, so what was the big deal?

When I relayed this to Owen, he said, "The big deal is I'm not sure I can trust you."

"Look," I said, sitting back and mirroring his pose. "You don't have to like me to recognize that I'm going to be an asset with this business. What's it going to take to get you to agree?"

"I'm not sure there's anything you can do, Delia," he said slowly. "I agreed to a meeting and nothing more. Now that I've fulfilled my end of the bargain, Amara has no choice but to sell that land to me. That was the deal."

Panic clawed at my throat. This opportunity was slipping away, and my mind scrambled desperately for a way to hold on.

Then it struck me.

"We can use my land."

Owen's brows raised. "What?"

"My land on the peninsula. You can use it."

"Free and clear?" he asked, incredulous.

I grinned. "Of course not."

"Then what do you want?"

"Isn't it obvious?" I said, crossing one leg over the other and leaning forward, propping an elbow on my knee and my chin in my hand. "Equal partnership."

"Equal partnership."

I couldn't help it: I grinned.

I had to admit, Delia Delatou had a set of balls on her, much like her sister. Not to mention she definitely knew her worth. I'd fully expected this meeting to be a formality before I politely sent her on her way. What I hadn't anticipated was for the girl to come in here and surprise me with the careful thought and research she'd put into her proposal.

Honestly, I was impressed, and I couldn't deny I was genuinely contemplating partnering up with her.

But an *equal* partnership? That was a slippery slope. She was so young, so untested. Giving half of this business over to her had to be one of the craziest offers I'd ever received. I was dumb to even consider it...right?

God, I wished Cal was here. He'd know exactly how to handle her, to let her down easy.

Then again...he was as good as Delia's brother-in-law, so

maybe I'd be in the minority.

"You do realize taking your land for free but having to give you half the profits would cost me more money in the long run than just buying the piece of land I originally wanted, right?"

"Well, yes..." she said, trailing off. "But my land is better than that piece. Plus, if you don't take me up on my offer, all of this"—she swept her arm over the papers spread out on the table between us—"goes with me. Good luck finding someone better."

Honestly, she was probably right, but was taking her on worth the trouble of having to work side by side with her? I wasn't sure that was a fair trade.

Delia was a wild child. I could see it in her eyes. But there was something else there too. A hesitancy, for sure, as if she was holding a part of herself back from me—though I couldn't imagine what or why. And then there was her obvious competency.

The whole picture was confusing, the subject hazy and poorly developed.

I hated how badly I wanted to be the one to bring it into focus.

"I need to think about it," I said at last, garnering myself a chance to collect myself. "And I need to talk to Cal. See if he thinks it's a good idea."

Delia grinned widely. "Cal loves me, so I guarantee he tells you to partner with me."

"I wouldn't be so sure," I said slowly, trying to convince myself more than her.

Delia, who had begun shuffling her papers back together, only rose to her feet. I'd been studiously avoiding letting my gaze linger on any part of her too long, but I couldn't help myself now.

The girl was an absolute stunner. Model-long legs. Hips, waist, and bust curving and dipping slightly into a soft hourglass shape. She wore a pair of shiny black pants that molded to her thighs and ass and cinched at her ankles, a silky, long-sleeved blouse in a light blue pinstripe pattern, and gold jewelry on her wrists, fingers, neck, and ears. Her long, dark-brown hair hung down her back in waves.

But it was her eyes that were the real star of the show. Similar to Amara's golden hue but darker. Fiercer. Glinting with mischief. When the light slanting through my office window caught them just right, they lit up like a tumbler of really good whiskey on ice.

They were the kind of eyes you could get drunk on if you stared into them for too long.

"How about we agree to a little wager?"

"What kind of wager?" I asked skeptically.

"If Cal doesn't advise you to partner with me, I owe you a hundred bucks."

I snorted. "That's a drop in the bucket for both of us. At least make it interesting."

"A thousand then."

"Okay," I agreed. "And if he does, I'll give you the same."

I extended my arm, intent on shaking on our deal, but she slapped my hand away. Her touch lingered on my skin like a phantom, warmth creeping over my entire body.

"I don't need your money," she said, gathering her things and heading for the door. When she reached it, she looked back over her shoulder at me. "*When* he gives you the go ahead to partner with me, you do it. No questions asked. No negotiating terms or fighting either of us on it. We take a fifty-fifty split, and you sign on the dotted line."

I sighed, knowing there was no simple way to get out of this—and I wasn't entirely sure I wanted to. I had to hope Cal vetoed the idea outright so I could avoid whatever shit I was about to step into.

"Fine," I said. "I'll let you know by Monday."

Delia chuckled as she walked away, as though she was in on a joke I hadn't figured out the punchline to yet. Her laugh echoed through my office long after she'd disappeared.

I was so fucked.

Once she left, I wasted no time calling Cal and telling him to get his ass to my office. I had a lot to wrap up before the weekend, and I didn't want this potential partnership with Delia hanging over my head while I tried to unwind. For once, I wasn't passing my weekend holed up in this office, and I didn't want to spend a single second of my cabin getaway worried about work. The sooner I got Cal in here to discuss, the better.

Cal had only been working for me for about a week, but I had to admit, we'd fallen into a routine easily. I supposed it helped that he'd been my best friend for the better part of the last five years, and he was extremely good at his job.

By the time he knocked on my open office door, I was practically crawling out of my skin, ready to dump this on him and pray he agreed with me. I felt a bit like a child waiting for a parent to swoop in and make it all better.

"What's up?" he asked, dropping his messenger bag on the floor and sitting down on the couch—right where Delia had been a half hour ago.

I grabbed the proposal she'd given me and handed it over.

"I met with Delia this morning," I explained.

"The meeting Amara bribed you into?" Cal asked with a chuckle and a raised brow.

"The very same," I grumbled. "Anyway, she...surprised me. Came fully prepared with this, admittedly amazing, proposal. And offered to let us build on her land instead of the piece I was going to buy from Delatou, Inc., which is admittedly better. I checked. Still, I'd be stupid to turn her away, but I also think I'd be stupid to agree." I removed my ball cap and hooked it over my knee, dropping my head into my hands and burying my fingers in my hair. A slight tug at the roots had my scalp stinging, but I welcomed the pain. Welcomed the brief distraction from the turmoil in my chest.

"I need your help," I mumbled to Cal.

"Why, exactly, do you think you'd be stupid to partner with her?"

"Because she's...Delia," I said dumbly. "A total wildcard and not someone I should be getting into be—business with."

I almost used the colloquial "getting into bed with" but damn, I did not need *that* image in my head. Didn't need the thought of those long legs wrapped around my waist, her hair around my fist...

Goddamnit, Lawless. You had to go there.

I thought of all the ugly things I could. The photos of burn victims my brother Crew had shown me. Same with the car accident victims from Lane, the cop. The birth of calves on the ranch. The one time growing up when my dad attempted to cook chicken while Mom was out of town and tried to feed it to us with the center still raw.

The last one did the trick, and I swallowed down a gag as the blood diverted away from my cock.

"So what do you need from me?" Cal asked. "You can make your own choices, O. I'm not your keeper."

"I need you to tell me it's financially irresponsible to partner with her."

His brows rose. "And if it's not?"

"Just...take a look at the damn proposal," I said, gesturing to the papers in his hands.

With a slight shake of his head, Cal did as I asked. While he studied the figures and thoroughly examined everything Delia had brought me, a restless energy settled on my bones. Unable to sit still any longer, I stood to pace the length of my office.

I didn't do well with silence.

I'd spent too many years in locker rooms being hounded by teammates, coaches, and the press to feel comfortable in the quiet. Not to mention, I was the eldest of seven kids, including five younger brothers, so I'd never really known a moment of peace in my lifetime. That was largely why I spent my weekends locked in my office at the club instead of home alone.

I loved my brothers and sister, and of course all my teammates, but constantly being surrounded by people made it a little difficult for me to relax into any sort of stillness.

As I idly twisted my dad's wedding ring, which I wore on my pinky, I wondered what he would say if he could see me now, if I could call him up and hear his voice on the other end of the phone. Would he be proud? Offer advice on ways I could improve? Beg me to come home and take over the ranch?

I'd never know, because he'd taken up residence in the Lawless

Ranch Cemetery a long time ago.

At last, Cal looked up at and cleared his throat, expression unreadable.

"Well?" I prompted.

"I'm...impressed. But also not?" I raised a brow in question, and he continued. "I mean, I've seen the work she's done on the winery's social media accounts, so I know she's talented with this sort of thing. But these ideas?" He brandished the presentation. "I hadn't realized she was capable of *this*. It's well thought out, the budget is manageable, and the marketing ideas are, for lack of a better word, genius."

"So you're saying I should work with her."

"If you'd asked me that a few months ago, I would've told you no. But I'm officially the poster child for judging a book by its cover and it blowing up in my face."

I snorted. Cal *had* spent an awful long time choosing only to see the worst in Amara, even after multiple people had told him to give her a chance—myself included. It was nice that he'd finally come around to recognize the shrewd business mind and talented, intelligent woman she was.

But Delia and Amara were not the same.

The stupid, logical part of my brain argued, *But what if they were?*

If not the *same* then at least...similar. They were sisters, after all.

Fuck. My head hurt.

"Shoot me straight, Cal," I blurted, my exasperation with this whole situation getting the better of me. I didn't like feeling out of control, and somehow, in one short meeting, Delia had tilted my world on its axis. "Do you think this is a good idea, partnering with her?"

Cal sank back in his seat and scrubbed a hand over his face. "I understand your apprehension. But even as someone who doesn't give a shit about that stuff, I've seen the impact her marketing strategies have had on the winery's bottom line. And have you seen her personal content?"

"What personal content?"

"Brooooooo." Cal dragged out the world annoyingly, and I grimaced. He'd been spending too much damn time with me. "After she graduated college and moved back, she bought a fix-er-upper and documented her entire renovation process."

"What does that have to do with opening a distillery?" I asked.

"She's incredible with marketing, she's personable online, and she's definitely got an impressive flair for design. Amara told me she also has a business degree, and she's been successfully running her own business with brand partnerships and all that shit for years. You could do worse."

I leaned forward and rested my elbows on my knees. "I need a yes or no answer here, Cal. Make the decision for me."

I knew what I wanted to do. I *wanted* to work with her. What I couldn't figure out was *why*.

"In my expert opinion...yes, you should work with her. You'd be an idiot not to."

A lead weight sank into my stomach, but I nodded. I'd do it because I wanted to, and because I trusted Cal not to steer me wrong.

But I had a feeling I'd be an idiot either way.

Monday morning, after a relaxing weekend at my Torch Lake house where I'd managed to shake my melancholia and get my head back on straight, I reluctantly returned to the office. The first item on my agenda was a call to Delia. I'd promised her a response by today, and I was nothing if not a man of my word.

"Hello?" she said tentatively when she answered.

"Hey, Delia. It's Owen."

"Hi, Owen. What can I do for you?"

"Would you be able to come down to my office today? Whenever it works for you."

"I can be down in twenty minutes," she said quickly.

"I...yeah, that'll work. See you soon."

Delia arrived in record time, trimming the twenty minutes she'd promised me down to fifteen.

"Thanks for coming in on such short notice," I said when she stepped into my office. Her perfume enveloped me as she brushed past, the scent something warm and inviting, like cookies fresh out of the oven, and I stiffened.

I held my breath, waiting for the cloud to dissipate, then sucked in a lungful of fresh, clear, Delia-free air. I had to keep my wits about me, couldn't allow something as simple and innocent as her perfume to go to my head like this. I couldn't let my little head make the decisions where this woman was concerned.

"I take it you've spoken with Cal," she said, sitting on one of my couches and crossing one of her legs over the other. She wore some sort of stretchy pants today, the pale blue fabric pulling taut over her thighs with the position.

"I have," I said, "and he encouraged me to partner with you. So I'd like to officially offer you a deal. We use your land, and you sign on as an equal partner."

A slow smile unfurled on Delia's lips, and I fought the urge to match it. I couldn't indulge her. Not yet. I still wasn't entirely sure this was a good idea, and I needed to maintain some level of stoicism and professionalism in the face of this woman who, admittedly, had knocked me a bit off my game.

I mean, she was a knockout. The very definition of a smokeshow. She could give some of the models and actresses I'd tangled with in my early years in the league a run for their money. Particularly my ex, who had that old money, aristocratic kind of beauty. Delia's was less conventional, but far more intriguing and captivating. Her Greek ancestry bronzed her skin, and her hair was a deep mahogany. I'd learned through a perusal of her social media that she rarely showed her face in her content, and I guessed it had something to do with the creeps that left leering comments the few times she had. Personally, I'd like to find those men and shove their balls down their throat, but it wasn't my place to protect her. The fact was, this woman—she wasn't destined to hide. She was better suited for billboards and magazine covers than behind the scenes.

Which was why her competency had come as such a surprise. That line of thinking was incredibly sexist, but my personal experience with beautiful women had me wary of a pretty face that masked an intelligent mind. I'd been fucked over by gold diggers too many times not to be.

"I've taken the liberty of having my attorney draw up a standard partnership agreement for us," I said, moving to my desk and lifting the file folder off its surface, then walking it over to her. "Review it and let me know of any changes."

Ignoring me, Delia lifted her phone and tapped away at the screen. A moment later, a light tapping came at the door.

I opened it to find Logan Daniels standing on the other side.

"Hey, Owen!" he said brightly. "Good to see you again."

"You too, Logan. But what are you doing here?"

"He's my attorney," Delia said. When I frowned, she added, "You didn't think I was signing this without having a professional review it, did you?"

"I mean...no," I said slowly. "But I didn't think you'd be doing it right now."

Delia shrugged as Logan settled at her side on the couch. "No time like the present."

With a rough sigh, I moved to my desk and dialed my own attorney. Logan got on the line and explained what was happening, and the two men quickly devolved into a lengthy legal discussion, the bulk of which went right over my head. They barely spared me or Delia any attention, save asking if we were on board with one particular term or another.

Surprisingly, Delia had few hangups with the terms of our partnership, and I had fewer still. I would've given her anything she asked for if it meant we could start breaking ground as soon as possible, but she made it easy on everyone.

When all was said and done, Logan disconnected and clapped his hands together.

"He's sending over the updated version right now," he told us, then turned to me. "Can you get into your email and print it for me?"

Two minutes later, the contract was hot off the printer, my hand poised over the document, ready to scribble my name. Hesitating only briefly, I inked my signature with a quick jerk of my wrist, officially binding myself to Delia. A moment later, she did the same, Logan and Hugo, my head of security who we'd pulled in from downstairs, acting as witnesses.

"There's one more thing before we disperse," Logan said.

"What's that?" I asked.

From his briefcase, he withdrew a document printed on thicker, creamy paper, the logo for what I assumed was his law firm emblazoned in the bottom left corner.

"Delia needs to add your name to the title of the property. I've prepared a standard deed conveying the property from Delia's name as an individual into your partnership," he said, his fingers tracing the language in the "Grantee" section of the document. "Neither of you can sell or add anyone else to the title of the land without both of you signing off on it. It's already a two-and-a-half acre split off Delia's whole forty, so that's no longer an option. Understood?"

Delia and I both nodded. I'd completely forgotten about the land, and I was a little surprised but also impressed that she'd chosen to split a little piece off instead of signing half of the whole thing over to me. Honestly, I would've done the same. Plus, we didn't need that much land anyway. What she was signing over would be more than enough.

I was about to confirm Delia's desire to do this—to give me, *us,* this—to make sure she was truly all in, even with the ink on our partnership agreement drying on the table in front of us, but

Logan beat me to it.

"Are you sure you want to do this?" he asked her quietly, shooting a skeptical glance my way.

"I'm sure," Delia said, offering me a bright smile that would've made me weak in the knees had I not been seated.

Damn, I really needed to get laid. One look from this girl, one flash of her bright, perfect teeth, and I was half hard.

Quickly, she signed the deed, Logan notarized it, and that was that. As he gathered his things and moved toward the door, blabbing on about recording and copies and other legal bullshit, I held Delia back from following him.

"A word?" I asked.

"Sure," she said, then looked to her brother-in-law. "I'll see you up at the house for dinner this week."

Logan nodded and dropped a kiss to her cheek before disappearing.

Something was seriously wrong with me, because jealousy flared in my chest at that easy affection. He was her brother-in-law, for fuck's sake. And even if he wasn't, Delia wasn't mine to be possessive of. I needed to get my shit together.

When he'd gone, I cleared my throat and said, "I have a meeting with the architect tomorrow. I'd like you there."

"Well I would hope so since this project is half mine."

I fought the urge to roll my eyes, instead meeting hers, their caramel depths all smoke and mischief.

"Meeting is at eleven, Whiskey," I said, the nickname slipping far too easily from my tongue.

And the regret was instantaneous.

"Whiskey?" she asked, arching one of her perfect brows.

"Because that's the—" I bit off that train of thought, not voicing the words rolling around in my head.

Because that's the exact color of your eyes, I wanted to say.

Instead, I went with something no less true but in far safer territory.

"Because I'm still not entirely convinced you aren't a bad idea."

Delia nodded, the hint of a smile tipping up one corner of her mouth. With a mock, two-finger salute, she said, "See you tomorrow, QB," and left.

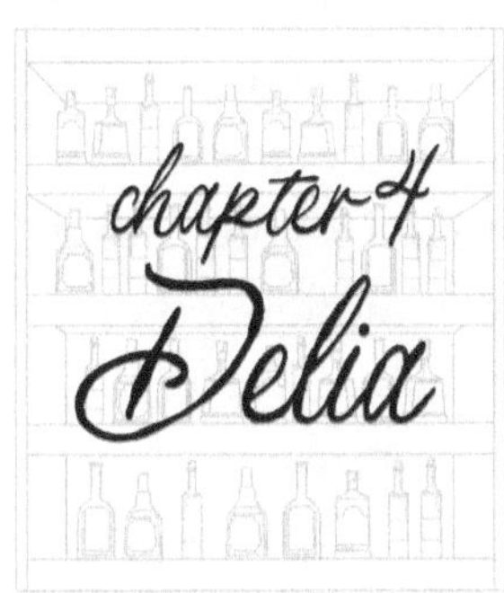

chapter 4
Delia

EXACTLY AS I DID most days, I woke up on Tuesday morning, got ready, and headed down to Brie's Bakery. This morning happened to be a special occasion as, for once, all of my sisters were free from work obligations and joining me for breakfast.

When I walked through the doors, the comforting scents of sugar and butter swept over me in the most perfect welcome. I found Ella already seated at our usual table in the corner. It wasn't surprising that she was the first to arrive given she lived above the flower shop that was only two storefronts down from Brie's.

"Morning, sunshine," I said when I dropped onto the chair across from her.

Ella's only response was a grumble, which was basically a jovial greeting coming from her. With her head tilted down, gaze intent on something on her phone screen, I took a moment to study her. She had changed so much these past few years, and I didn't just mean the tattoos now dotting her skin or the funky colors she dyed her hair that changed weekly.

There was something...darker about her now. Ella used to be the most free spirited of us all, content to dig in the dirt, planting flowers and daydreaming about the days when she'd be able to make a career out of her passion. And she'd sort of succeeded by working for Fanny at the flower shop, but it wasn't the same. Being surrounded by all that vitality should've made her happy as a clam. Instead, she seemed lost, like a shell of her former self.

The rest of our sisters and I agreed it was thanks to her piece of shit boyfriend, but if there was one thing the Delatou women were, it was stubborn. There was nothing we could say or do to make her see reason, not until she was ready to hear it.

On the flip side of Ella's dark coin was Brie, who bounded over to the table, basking all of us in her glow like a ray of sunlight. Her hands were full of platters of an array of her scones and danishes, and her employee followed behind her with a tray of various coffee products for each of us.

Amara and Chloe breezed in one after the other as Brie returned with another tray, this one piled high with breakfast sandwiches and croissants. The scent of fried meat greeted my nose, and I was sliding a bacon, egg, and cheese biscuit with tomato and avocado onto my plate before Brie had even set them down.

She reached out and playfully slapped my hand. "Greedy," she scolded as I took a massive bite.

"Starving," I corrected, grinning at her with a mouth full of food. God, my sister was so fucking talented. I would happily eat her food all day, every day.

Once we'd all settled around the table, Brie even taking a few minutes off from fussing over us, we tucked into our food. As plates were cleared and Brie's confections disappeared, my sisters and I chatted about nothing in particular. Updates on Chloe's writing, her and Amara's pregnancies, the winery, flower shop, and bakery floated around us in the kind of easy conversation only sisters could master.

The only one who didn't open their mouth was me, though I was practically vibrating with the news of my partnership with Owen, damn near bursting at the seams to share my excitement with my favorite people. But I knew we'd circle around to it. And when Amara wiped the corners of her mouth and dropped her napkin onto her plate, her gaze locked with mine, and my moment had arrived.

"So, you met with Owen last week," she said without preamble.

I nodded.

"And how'd that go?"

Next to her, Chloe's brow furrowed. "Wait, back up. We're talking about Owen Lawless here, right? Why did you meet with him?"

"Yes," I said, then quickly brought her, Ella, and Brie up to speed on the partnership opportunity Amara had passed off to me. I explained how I nailed the proposal presentation and how I knew I had it in the bag but Owen wanted to talk to Cal first.

Amara snorted at that. "You knew Cal wouldn't reject you," she said to me.

"Well...I hoped. I know I'm not exactly his favorite person after that shit I pulled Memorial Day weekend, but..."

My second oldest sister waved her hand dismissively. "He loves you, Lia. He's past all that, and he knows you're more than capable of taking this on."

I grinned widely. "Which is exactly what he told Owen. You're looking at the new half-owner of a distillery!"

My sisters erupted into cheers, Brie sliding an arm around my waist to squeeze me from the side, the other three reaching out to pat my hands—Ella—or ruffle my hair—Chloe and Amara. Then Amara raised her coffee to the center of the table and the rest of us followed suit.

"To Lia!" she cried, and we all clinked glasses. Her gaze locked with mine, one of those golden eyes winking as she said, "I have a good feeling this is going to be everything you've been searching for and more."

God, I hoped she was right.

⚶⚶⚶⚶⚶ ⚶⚶⚶⚶⚶

After breakfast disbanded, I was hyped up on caffeine and adrenaline. I made a quick pitstop at home for my laptop and other things I'd need for my and Owen's meeting with the architect today, then headed into the city to go over a few things with him beforehand.

I gave Owen no warning that I was coming in early, and his brows drew together when he opened the door, sparing a quick glance for his watch.

"You're early," he said.

"I'm aware," I responded, pushing past him and making a beeline for the couch cushion I'd come to think of as mine after only two visits to this place.

I had a feeling Owen and I would be spending a lot of time ensconced within these four walls, so I was grateful his furniture was comfortable—and that he kept a fully stocked bar cart nearby.

"There's something I want to talk to you about," I said when I was comfortable, my laptop open on the glass-topped table.

"Okay..." he said skeptically as he came to sit across from me.

"I'd like to document the process."

"What process?" Owen asked.

I rolled my eyes, irritated by him playing dumb despite the fact that I offered no context. "Don't be stupid, QB. It's not cute."

"I'm not a QB anymore," Owen grumbled, and it seemed as though I'd pressed a sore spot. *Interesting*.

"Don't care," I said. "What I'm saying is that I want to document, well...everything. The meeting with the architect. The day we break ground. The entire build, designing the interior, distilling the spirits. All of it from start to finish."

"Why?"

I answered his question with one of my own. "Have you looked into me at all? Like, checked out my social media?"

"A little..." he admitted, but I could tell from his tone that he was fibbing to some degree. The thought sent a little thrill through me.

"So you're aware that I've taken my followers through every single day and detail of upgrading my house."

"Yes..."

"I want to do that here. Build a following before we even open. With your pretty face and my marketing prowess and social media management skills, we'll have people busting down the doors the second we're open for business." I sighed heavily, resisting the urge to pinch the bridge of my nose in annoyance. "This was all in my proposal."

Owen raised a skeptical brow. "When you say 'everything,' what exactly do you mean?"

"I'm not going to be telling people where you live or giving away your social security number but...in my experience, people like thinking they have access to celebrities, or well-known influencers. Since you're one and I'm the other, I want to give anyone who follows us an inside look at the entire process. Behind the scenes, Q&A sessions, voting on finishes. That sort of thing. An unfiltered look into the whole process."

He scraped his fingers through his sandy hair, the tattoo of his last name shifting like a flag along with the muscles of his forearm. In his short-sleeved Carhartt pocket tee, half of the curve of his biceps was visible where the sleeves suctioned to his muscles, and I had to clench my mouth shut to avoid drooling. Owen's body was incredible, and he was exactly the kind of man I'd already have gotten into bed with if my livelihood didn't rest on an amicable—and decidedly *not* physical—partnership with him.

"I know that's your thing, Delia, but I'm not entirely on board with giving the public that much access to my life."

"It's not your personal life, though," I protested. "It's just the business side of things."

"I don't know..." he trailed off.

"Look, if it'll make you feel better and get you to agree, I promise I won't feature you in any content. I know how to draw people in either way."

"I've noticed."

"What's that supposed to mean?"

"You rarely show your face in your own content," he said, lifting a shoulder in a half shrug. "People are obsessed with you anyway."

Ha! I thought. He *had* spent more time on my accounts than he let on.

"So it's settled then," I said, reclining on the couch, a smirk dancing on my lips. "I'll get our profiles set up this afternoon, and I can start posting content right away."

Owen still appeared unconvinced.

"Owen," I said softly. "This is why you brought me on. Trust me to handle this."

He mumbled something that sounded suspiciously like "it wasn't my choice" but I decided to ignore him. I was saved from having to respond anyway when a knock came at the door. Owen stood and admitted the architect.

The man strolled in, dressed in a charcoal three-piece suit and caramel-colored wingtip shoes. His thin, pale hair was combed over in a poor attempt to cover the shiny scalp beneath. Shorter than me, the top of his nearly bald head reached somewhere around my nose. Horn-rimmed glasses framed watery, pale grey eyes that swept right over me, and my hand proffered for an introduction, and settled on Owen.

Already, I didn't like this guy.

"Mr. Lawless," he said, heartily shaking Owen's hand. "Pleasure to meet you. I've really been looking forward to this project."

Owen offered a smile that tensed slightly at the edges. It

seemed I wasn't the only one who wasn't a fan of the man.

"We have been too," he said. "And we appreciate you making the drive up from Chicago to meet with us."

"We?" the architect asked. "I was under the impression you were taking on this project yourself."

"I was when we initially spoke," Owen said, then gestured to me. "But I've since brought on a partner. This is Delia Delatou."

"A woman?" the architect asked, surprised. Owen hadn't yet given me his name and, at this point, I didn't want to learn it. I'd be content to call him "the weasel" in my mind from now until the end of time.

"My family owns a winery on Old Mission," I said, my tone so saccharine I gave myself a toothache. "And we're building on a portion of a forty acre parcel I own."

The weasel's furry grey brows drew together and, as though I hadn't spoken, he returned his attention to Owen.

"Where would you like me?"

Owen led him to where we'd just been seated. The weasel unceremoniously lifted my laptop and dumped it on the couch, sweeping loose papers out of the way to make room for the large rolls of schematics secured under his arm. As he spread them out, Owen grabbed a couple paperweights from his desk—which I quickly realized were actually football awards—to secure the edges so we could study them.

Yeah, the man used *football awards* as *paperweights*. My god, I was so far out of my league.

After allowing my gaze to sweep across the first one, which was a full-color rendering of the entire front facade of the exterior, I blinked in surprise.

This was what Owen wanted?

There wasn't anything wrong with the plans, per se. The entrance was a monolithic thing constructed of chrome and glass, rising to a peak at the front with the rest of the building a lower, sprawling rectangle behind it. I barely listened as the weasel shuffled through the plans for the inside, speaking about how people would walk into a grand foyer where we could set up our gift shop and rest rooms. The bar beyond was full of sharp lines, reflective textures, and so much proposed neon my eyes hurt simply staring at the page.

"No," I said, cutting the weasel off in the middle of a sentence, finally finding my voice.

The weasel glanced at me, heaving a world-weary sigh, and Owen's forehead scrunched.

"No, what?" Owen asked.

"This"—I gestured at the plans, at the materials, at the weasel's whole...person—"isn't going to work."

"Why not?" Owen seemed genuinely curious, which I supposed was a good sign. This was the first test of our partnership and, while I was certain he didn't particularly appreciate my protestations, he was at least humoring me.

"It's too pretentious for this far north," I told him honestly. "It'll stick out like a sore thumb."

"And that's...a bad thing?"

"I was under the impression that was the point," the weasel said with an eye roll, and I cut him a glare.

"This won't be in the city," I snapped. "This will be in the country, the wilderness. We're not building with the intention of welcoming in wealthy clientele who will spend gobs of money on our spirits. I'm sure we'll get guests like that on occasion, but they won't make up the bulk of our patronage. We'll be welcoming in moms and dads, students on vacation and friends celebrating weddings. It just won't work. I have some—"

I reached for my laptop, but the weasel cut me off. "I'm sure you've spent plenty of time with your little daydreams, but let the big boys handle this, little girl." He turned to Owen. "Does she need to be here?"

"*She* is half owner of this building and the land it will sit on," I reminded him. "How dare—"

"Owen, can you please get your girl on a leash so we can approve the plans and move on?"

My blood instantly boiled, my cheeks flushing red hot with the rage rising in my chest. Who the *fuck* did this guy think he was? And what was Owen doing, standing there watching this man insult me and not coming to my defense? If this was how things were going to be...

With jerky movements, I gathered my things and stalked for the door.

I glanced at Owen over my shoulder and said, "Call me when you realize I'm right."

I stormed out and, the moment I threw myself behind the wheel of my car, I dialed my sister.

"Hey, Lia," Amara said when she answered. "How'd your meeting go?"

"Fuck Owen, fuck the weasel, and fuck this partnership!" I shouted. "How dare you get me into this?"

"Woah," my sister said. "Slow down and tell me what's going on."

Quickly, I explained the disastrous meeting, and by the time I finished, shouting expletives about the weasel and his stupid rodent-like face, Amara and I had dissolved into a fit of giggles.

Our laughter lifted some of the weight that had settled on my chest, the anger coursing through my veins ebbing.

"Really, Mar!" I gasped. "He looked like Timothy Spall with less hair."

My sister cackled harder, and I had to pull over on the side of the road as tears blurred my vision.

When we'd both composed ourselves again, I pulled back onto the highway that would take me home, wiping the stray moisture from my face.

"I needed that laugh," I said. "It's only day one and we're already fighting! I can't believe he didn't even come to my defense. He's supposed to be my *partner*. Remind me why I thought this was a good idea?"

"Because you were made for this, Lia," Amara said, her tone instantly soothing more of my frayed nerves. She was barely a year older than me, but there was nothing like having your big sister remind you of what was important.

And what was important here was that I was strong, intelligent, and capable. I knew the plans the weasel had brought us were garbage.

We didn't need endless chrome, glass, and shiny surfaces. This was a distillery on the north end of Old Mission, not a night club on Michigan Avenue in Chicago. We wanted to embrace nature, not fight it. My vision for the place was simple: a warm, cabin-in-the-woods vibe. From the outside, it would be unassuming. The exterior would be constructed to look like a log cabin, the inside walls the same wood, though planed and stained. Poured concrete floors. A corrugated steel bar with a bird's eye maple top and tables around the main room to match. The interior would be divided in three: the gift shop and bathrooms near the front, the bar area itself, and the stills at the back, viewable through a wall of plexiglass. I'd include a lot of natural elements, like more wood and stone, in the overall decor. Lots of warm, earthy tones. We'd include a patio off one side for outdoor seating in the summer sunshine that could easily be winterized with vinyl sheeting and a small, wood-burning fireplace in the corner. Plush, faux-leather seating that was easy to clean. A gravel parking lot.

It would be romantic and sexy, but rustic and cozy. Everyone who walked through the doors would feel like family, exactly as our patrons to the winery did. Obviously, I wasn't an architect or an interior designer, but I *knew* I was right.

Now I only had to wait until Owen realized it too.

chapter 5
Delia

CONTENT CREATION FOR BRANDS was fun and all, but sometimes, I tended to get a little exhausted by being a cog in the machine. When I first started renovating my house, I took on any partnership opportunity that came my way, simply to grow my following. As I got bigger, I was able to start being more selective, and now I only took on projects with brands I truly believed in who had a solid mission statement and were primarily female led.

Still, there had been something missing. And it wasn't until I was at the bakery one day, chatting with Brie about how she should let me do some content creation for her, and Fanny from the flower shop overheard, that I realized what it was.

Over the last few years, what started as shooting a few videos of Fanny and Ella making floral arrangements for a wedding and posting them on Fanny's severely neglected Instagram page had morphed into me helping all local businesses increase their online presence.

So now, I was the unofficial Apple Blossom Bay Chamber of

Commerce social media manager. It was a title I wore proud-ly—and free of charge. I loved being able to help my community in this small way, and I happily took my payment in the form of the occasional fresh floral arrangement, complimentary cup of coffee, or sandwich from the diner when I stopped by for lunch. It wasn't like I needed the money anyway, and accepting any sort of wage from the people of Apple Blossom Bay wouldn't have sat right with me.

While I waited for Owen to pull his head out of his ass, I decided it would be the perfect time to walk around town and prepare some posts. I lived only a few blocks off Main Street and, though the season was definitely shifting toward cooler and cozier months, it was still warm out, the sun shining brightly through the trees lining my yard. I dropped my bags off in my office, then turned right around and headed downtown.

Despite the fact that Labor Day had come and gone, the sidewalks of the main drag were still filled with people, mainly young couples without children or older ones whose children had moved on with their own families. As I weaved through them, intent on my destination of Blossom's, the flower shop where my youngest sister worked, I inhaled deeply and released it in a happy sigh, a smile blooming on my face.

The smile grew into an outright grin as I opened the faded, sunshine yellow door to Blossom's, the oxidized copper bell over the door tinkling joyously to greet me.

"I'll be right out!" my sister shouted from the back, so I took a minute to weave through the aisles while I waited, taking in the new plants and trinkets they'd added since the last time I'd been here.

My sister appeared, wearing a sage-green apron over black shorts and a white tank, her tattoos stark against her skin. Though still flushed with that Greek glow, she was paler than the rest of us, owing to the fact that she preferred to spend her time indoors reading or with her douchebag boyfriend.

Oops, did I say douchebag?

I meant complete asshole.

But you wouldn't catch any of us telling her that.

Not that she'd listen anyway.

"Hey, kiddo," I said brightly when she stopped in the middle of the store to stare at me, arms crossed over her chest.

"I'm barely a year younger than you," she sniped, exactly as I knew she would.

With Chloe at twenty-nine and Brie at twenty-five, only four and a half years separated my oldest and youngest sisters. At twenty-seven, I fell smack dab in the middle of that chaos. Honestly, I didn't know what my parents were thinking, having us all so close together, and I definitely didn't want to think about the fact that they spent the entire latter half of the nineties procreating.

I shook off a shiver and offered Ella my most winning smile.

"What're you up to today?" I asked her.

"Getting some arrangements ready for Mr. and Mrs. Tuggle's anniversary party this weekend."

"Oh!" I exclaimed. "I forgot that was this weekend. God, my street is going to be undriveable."

"You can come hang out here if you want," Ella said with a shrug.

I smiled at my sister. "I just might take you up on that. We could have a movie night!"

Ella's face broke into a grin and, given her typically sullen expression, it was like the sun coming out after endless days of grey.

"We can invite everyone and binge popcorn and candy!"

"Sounds perfect, El," I said warmly. "I'll let you drop the idea in the group chat."

Before we could make further plans, an elderly voice floated to us from the back.

"Is that Delia Delatou I hear?"

"Hi, Fanny!" I shouted, and a moment later, the woman appeared.

As usual, her shock of white hair was coiled in a bun atop her head, though I knew if she let it down, it would hang to her waist. She wore one of her standard floor-length cotton dresses in a floral pattern, the short sleeves exposing her deeply tanned and freckled arms from years spent in the sun among the blooms. When the weather got colder, she'd switch it out for a long sleeve one, but to this day—and I've known the woman for probably twenty years—I've never seen her wear pants.

Fanny approached me, smacking a kiss on my cheek when I bent to greet her. She was sort of the community grandmother, always fussing over everyone, being the first one to offer a helping hand when someone was down on their luck, and her gorgeous floral arrangements had cured more than a few broken hearts—my own included.

"What're you doing here?" she asked.

I waved my phone around. "Thought I'd get some content for the next few weeks."

"Perfect timing!" Fanny said, clapping her hands together excitedly. "Once we finish with the Tuggle arrangements, Ella and I planned to switch out the window display. I'd love for you to do one of those"—she snapped her fingers—"transition type things."

I giggled, knowing exactly what she meant. Fanny wasn't tech savvy, but I'd been working with her long enough for her to know at least a few of my tricks.

"Sounds good to me," I said. "Let's do a Timelapse of you guys finishing up for the Tuggles, and then we'll move to the window." I shifted slightly on my feet, eyes sweeping around the room. Nearby, my sister was bent over an orchid. Gently, her fingers traced the petals, her eyes closing as she inhaled deeply. Without thinking, I snapped a picture. Not for social media—no, this was for me. To remind myself that buried beneath Ella's seemingly cold and apathetic exterior still lived the little girl who loved to stop and smell the flowers.

When I was satisfied I'd shot enough footage at Blossom's for a few weeks' worth of Instagram, TikTok, and Facebook posts, I bid my sister and Fanny goodbye before trotting across the street to Sydney's. Sidney, the owner and granddaughter of the diner's namesake, greeted me warmly as I pushed through the door. Instantly, I was enveloped in the scent of pancake batter and freshly brewed coffee, and my stomach growled.

I bellied up to my usual spot at the long counter that ran along one wall, all chrome edges and Formica exactly like what you'd expect to find in a place that had been open since the 1930s. Sidney's great-grandparents had opened it shortly after *my* great-grandfather, Andreas, relaxed his iron fist on land in this town enough to start selling to people who wanted to settle here. They'd named the diner after their newborn baby girl, who would later inherit her legacy. Since, the diner had been handed down to the women in Sidney's family, finally ending up with her.

And you might be wondering why they were all okay with taking the legacy they'd been given instead of running with it. Didn't these people have dreams? Want a life outside Apple Blossom Bay?

The truth was—they'd been given the choice, exactly like my sisters and I had. But, like me, Sidney had left and came back. The people of Apple Blossom Bay were relatively simple people with one thing in common: we *wanted* to be here. We were proud to call this place our home. To us, the ability to keep the family businesses alive wasn't a noose around our neck, holding us back but a rock-solid foundation upon which to build our lives.

"What brings you in?" Sidney asked as she slid a steaming cup of caramel chai tea and glass of water in front of me.

"Well, I'm starving," I said, rubbing my stomach, which let out a well-timed grumble. "But I'm also making the rounds. Thought I should check in and see what you've got up your sleeve for the season."

"This is perfect timing!" Sidney said, tapping away at the tablet in her hand. I'd been here enough times over the years that I never ordered. I simply ate whatever Sidney decided she wanted to feed me that day—and loved every bite of it. "Pumpkin pancakes and apple cinnamon waffles are going back on the menu this weekend, so guess what you're getting for lunch?" Her eyes glinted as she smiled at me.

"Hmm," I said, tapping my finger to my chin. "A Reuben and sweet potato fries?"

Sidney tipped her head back and barked out a laugh. Even at nearly forty, she was still gorgeous, her naturally blonde hair long and silken. I always wondered why she wasn't married with a few kids running around, but anytime I asked, she said it was because she was married to the diner.

Secretly, I—and most of the town—thought she was in love with Mags who owned the ATV rental business up the block, and they were both too afraid to make a move.

But that wasn't any of my business.

Twenty minutes later, the counter in front of me was crowded with plates, including the promised pancakes and waffles, as well as a few samples of new sandwiches and salads Sidney was considering adding to the menu. As I ate, I took notes and shot content, including a behind-the-scenes interview with Sidney as she whipped up a fresh batch of pancakes for Mr. Richards. He wandered in as I took my first bite and demanded a stack of his own.

As she moved around her kitchen, both me and Mr. Richards shadowing her, I sighed contentedly. I loved my work for big, highly recognizable brands, and for the winery, don't get me wrong.

But absolutely nothing beat these days, when I spent hours immersing myself in the town, rubbing elbows with the locals and helping them promote their businesses.

Here, I was home.

My heart was completely full by the time I trudged up the front steps of my house. After leaving the diner, I'd gone to the grocery store to get the weekly update from Mr. Rinaldi, who provided me with the following week's price promotions. Then I'd bopped around between the three gift shops, each of them specializing in something different so as to not step on each other's toes, photographing new items and making note of upcoming sales and events.

I ended the afternoon at Granny's. Tanya greeted me warmly, settling a pint of Traverse City-brewed seltzer in front of me and asking if I wanted anything to eat. Ever the glutton, I ordered an appetizer platter, taking some aesthetic shots of it and my drink before I dove in. Then she sat across from me, and I took notes while she got me up to speed on upcoming specials. After that, we gossiped, the drama in other people's lives doing a sufficient job of distracting me from my own.

All day, I'd successfully managed to block out the dumpster fire of a meeting with Owen and the weasel that morning by surrounding myself with people who genuinely enjoyed my company and wanted my help. But now that I was at the end of my rounds, that fire that had banked as I wandered through town rekindled in my chest. Rage laced with shame and a sense of failure. Like I'd had my shot and opening my big mouth had bricked it off the rim.

Then again, standing up for myself was never a bad idea, whether small men vilified me for it or not. So at least I could be proud of that. That I didn't shrink myself to make that asshole weasel feel bigger and badder.

I was so full from all the carbs I'd consumed today that I could have passed out the second I stepped through the door, but I didn't even let myself sit down before hanging my purse on the hook in the foyer and turning around to head into my garage.

It had undergone many changes and been used for many things before I bought this property, but it was obvious from the architecture that my garage used to be a carriage house for the farm. When I moved in, it had been a cavernous space, the concrete floor cracked and grease-stained, the ceiling vaulted, trusses exposed. It had been cold and dingy, good for nothing save parking a car. And even that was dicey given the precarious and neglected condition of the building when I'd first taken possession, as though a strong wind would collapse it.

So it had been the first big project I'd taken on when I began renovations.

First, I'd split it into two spaces, the upstairs completely walled off and insulated from the parking area. I'd converted the upper level into a bright, open office space with a lounge area off to one side. I worked from home, yes, but I liked having somewhere to go in the mornings. Plus, I was more productive up there. Everything had been selected for both comfort and functionality, from my TikTok viral desk chair to the desk itself, which had the ability to be raised and lowered depending on whether I wanted to sit or stand. I had two free-standing monitors set up, in addition to my laptop station and iPad stand. One wall was dominated entirely by bookshelves, nearly overflowing with all the tomes I'd collected over the years.

With a sigh, I dropped onto my chair and slid up to my desk, shaking one of my monitors alive. A few clicks had me AirDropping the content I'd shot today, where I could upload it to my various editing software and prep for posting.

I was in the middle of editing the video of Fanny and Ella switching out the Blossom's window display when a light knock came at the door. I rose and padded over, expecting to find one of my sisters on the other side when I pulled it open. Instead, I gasped in surprise at the man standing there.

"What are you doing here?"

chapter 6
Owen

THE MINUTE DELIA WAS gone, and hopefully out of earshot, Clarke—yes, with an *e*; that really should've tipped me off that he was a pretentious, misogynistic asshole who only wanted to work with me because of my celebrity status—whirled on me.

"You need to get your bitch in line," he seethed.

My response was automatic, a gut instinct, a shot from the hip that required no additional thought or consideration for the consequences. Born from years of being the oldest, the protector, the leader, they were the easiest two words I'd ever spoken.

"You're fired." For good measure, in case it wasn't obvious to this prick, I tacked on, "Get the fuck out."

Clarke sputtered, his beady little eyes widening. "Yo-you can't fire me."

"I can," I assured him, "and I just did."

Clarke's mouth gaped for a moment until he said, "Fuck you."

"Hugo!" I shouted, and a moment later, my head of security appeared.

"Yeah, boss?"

"Get this prick out of my face."

"You can't! Who do you think you are? Do you know who I am? Who I've worked for? I designed houses for—"

Hugo dragged Clarke downstairs, his shouted words softening in volume until eventually quieting completely, leaving me in my silent office.

Well, that certainly hadn't gone as planned.

I should've known better. I only hired the idiot because he came highly recommended by my former offensive coordinator in Detroit. It would've been one thing had he been willing to work with us, been amenable to hearing Delia's ideas and implementing them.

Because I realized as soon as she'd gone that she *was* right. The glass and chrome and smoke and mirrors and neon? They weren't fit for northern Michigan. And, okay, I could take a lot of the blame here. When I'd hired Clarke and his firm to do the design for the distillery, I hadn't given him a lot of direction. I told him what I was doing and asked him to bring me an idea. I could admit, had Delia not been here, I probably would've been all in on the design. It was exactly the kind of place I would've frequented in the early days of my career, when I was young and horny all the time, looking to flaunt my wealth and status for anyone within my vicinity.

But this wasn't going to be that kind of place, and I should've done more research instead of being so blinded by my desperation to break ground and get this up and running as soon as humanly possible.

That was the problem with having money—the belief that, if

I simply threw enough zeros at someone, they'd get shit done quicker than they would for a normal person.

And, okay, a lot of the time it worked. But this project—there was something different here. It was new and exciting, yes, and I'll admit the addition of Delia changed the dynamic. In what way, I was still deciding. I didn't really believe in all that woo-woo, signs from the universe shit, but I'd be damned if there wasn't something magical sparking to life inside me as the pieces of this project slowly came together.

Maybe that was my dad's way of telling me I was on the right track.

So now, we needed to head back to the drawing board.

But first, I had to find Delia and apologize.

Knowing she wouldn't answer if I called her—and I certainly didn't blame her—I did the next best thing.

"Hey, Owen," Amara said when she picked up. "What's up?"

"Can you tell me where Delia lives? Or where she might be right now?"

"Why? Are you planning on groveling?"

"Yes," I said instantly. "I owe her an apology."

"You're damn right you do," Amara said, and I knew right then that Delia had already filled her sister in on what happened with Clarke. "How could you let this happen?"

"Hey now, I didn't know the guy was going to be an epic prick."

"Maybe not, Owen, but you also didn't defend her. You just stood there like a giant tool while that guy insulted her! I thought you were a better man than that."

"I know, I know," I said quietly, chastened by her tone. I *was* a better man than that. Throwing myself back into my desk chair, I removed my ball cap and carded my fingers through my hair. "Which is why I'm calling you. Tell me where she is. Tell me how to fix this. I don't think I have to explain to you how I'm not used to having people challenge me. It's not an excuse, but..."

"I get that," she said softly. "But you're not alone in this anymore."

"I know," I growled. "So tell me how to deal with her."

Amara barked out a laugh. "You don't 'deal' with Delia," she said. "This is supposed to be a collaborative effort, right? So *collaborate*. You agreed to the partnership, Owen, so act like it. Listen when she speaks, offer compromises. All she wants is to have a say in things, and by letting that guy run all over her the way he did, she's wondering why she got into business with you in the first place."

"Fuck," I breathed.

"Yeah," Amara agreed. "You really got yourself in some shit. But...she's at home. I'll text you the address."

"Thanks, Mar," I said, sagging with relief. "You're really saving my ass here."

"Your ass isn't saved just yet," she assured me, then hung up.

We'd barely disconnected when the text with Delia's address came through, and I was in my truck not a minute after, winding through the streets of Traverse City, heading north up Old Mission.

As I drove, another text from Amara came through, my truck reading it to me.

Amara: She's probably in her office,

which is above the garage. Just go in the side door off the driveway and the stairs are on the left. Good luck!

Good luck. Yeah, I had a feeling I was going to need it.

Twenty minutes later, I pulled up to Delia's house. Though I'd seen numerous photos of it on her socials—I'd been particularly intrigued by the comparison of when it was constructed to now—it was a whole other thing to be standing in front of the physical manifestation of all of her hard work. I had to admit, I was impressed. Though if there was anything I'd learned about her in the last week, it was that she was tenacious and had a head full of great ideas. Moving forward with the original architect and building plan without consulting her first was a mistake I wouldn't make again. Especially not with the reminder that she was responsible for *this* masterpiece, a house that belonged on the cover of a magazine but also felt lived in, like a real home.

I pushed out of the truck and inhaled deeply, my shoulders relaxing at the fresh, crisp scent of the nearby lake that wafted through the air. Then I steeled my spine and headed inside.

The stairs to the loft were right where Amara said they'd be. When I reached the little white door atop them, I knocked lightly. From beyond, footsteps padded nearer, the floor creaking softly under their weight.

When Delia swung the door open, her face fell from excitement to wariness in a heartbeat.

"What are you doing here?"

I winced, supposing I deserved her sharp, cold tone. "I came to apologize," I said, offering a sheepish grin. "Can I come in?"

I studied her face closely, watching as apprehension flitted across her features before she jerked her head in an approximation of a nod and stepped back to admit me.

I was surprised by how clean, bright, and open her office space felt, so at odds with the darker, grey garage downstairs. It was all creamy whites and earth tones with a few pops of soft pink in her desk chair, keyboard, and throw pillows on the sofa. I shoved my hands deep into my pockets as I stood in the center of the room and spun in a slow circle, taking in everything from her impressive desk setup to the wall of bookshelves stuffed full of paperbacks and hardcovers.

"What do you want, Owen?"

I met her gaze at last. "I told you: I'm here to apologize."

She pursed her lips, not saying anything as she waited for me to continue.

"Look...not having your back in that meeting, and letting Clarke talk to you like that? I fucked up."

Delia's forehead creased. "Clarke?"

"The architect?"

"Oh," she said, huffing out a little laugh. "I've been calling him 'the weasel' in my head."

I chuckled with her, my shoulders relaxing. If she was laughing, I was halfway to forgiveness.

"Well, he *is* a weasel, so that makes sense. And I fired him."

She gasped. "You did what?"

"I. Fired. Him," I said, enunciating every word.

"Why?"

"The way he spoke to you, for starters," I said, my jaw clenching, remembering the way I'd allowed him to do so. God, if I was her, I'd punch me in the face. Hell, if a man had spoken to my mother or sister like that in my presence, I wouldn't have hesitated to do so.

I really was an asshole.

"And because his vision wasn't working. He only wanted to work with *Owen Lawless*, the star quarterback. Not Owen Lawless, the businessman."

Delia's head dipped toward the ground as she said, "His vision sucked ass."

Unable to stand seeing her fold in on herself like that, I stepped closer, tucking my finger under her chin and lifting her face up. Touching her was dangerous, surely a gateway drug to deeper sensations, to lingering and intimacy, but I couldn't stop myself.

"It did," I agreed, staring straight into her eyes. "Your ideas are honestly incredible, Delia. I'm sorry for how he acted, and for not putting a stop to the whole thing before we got that far. This is your baby as much as it is mine, and it wasn't fair for me to make that decision without you."

Delia blinked slowly, her breath that smelled of cinnamon and sugar filling the air between us. Her tongue peeked out, the tip brushing along her lower lip. Everything in me tightened. My chest, my skin—my cock. I sucked in a breath and held it, not moving, waiting to see what she'd do next. And willing my cock to stand down.

After another beat wherein she moved almost imperceptibly closer, she heaved a lungful of air...and took a step back.

"Thank you," she said quietly, tucking her hair behind her ears, her eyes darting everywhere but in my direction. I didn't miss the way her hands shook, and I relaxed into the knowledge that our moment affected her exactly as it had me.

"How did you find me?"

"I called Amara," I said.

She groaned. "She needs to mind her own business."

"She cares about you," I said with a shrug. "And if it makes you feel better, she handed me my ass."

"Good," Delia said, but the word sounded anything but.

"What's wrong?" I asked.

Her eyes flicked to mine then. "I can't do this with you every time we need to make big decisions," she said in a rush. "All that shit Amara went through with Cal not believing in her and doing his level best to get her removed from her own company? Please, just...don't do that to me."

She seemed to choke down the rest of what she wanted to say, and I was desperate to hear it. This conversation was important for reasons I probably hadn't even realized yet.

"I won't," I promised.

"I know you weren't exactly...excited about working with me, but I promise I'm taking this seriously. Probably the most serious I've ever taken anything. This distillery and our partnership is something I am one hundred percent invested in, and I need you to believe that too. I'd never do anything to fuck it up." She paused for a moment, fists clenching and releasing, as though weighing what to say next. When she spoke, her words were softened. Quieter. More vulnerable. "You have your other businesses to fall back on, but for me..."

She trailed off, but I wasn't letting her off the hook that easily.

"For you, what?" I pressed.

"This kind of feels like my one shot to prove I can do more

than just take pretty pictures and make fun videos. That I can be a businesswoman like Mar and Brie, or creative like Ella and Chloe. If this fails…"

My heart softened, knowing that feeling of inadequacy all too well. On paper, I was wildly successful. But stacked up against my brothers? It was no contest. I'd only ever been good at throwing a football and getting smoked by guys twice my size. That was nothing compared to the actual heroics those guys performed.

One day—maybe—I'd share all of that with Delia. But this wasn't about me. This was about assuring her I trusted her, I believed in her, and we were going to make this work.

"This is an equal partnership," I said softly. "We make decisions together or not at all. Deal?"

Delia nodded, her lips curving upward slightly. "Deal."

"Now I know you haven't been sitting here stewing in your rage all day," I said, stalking across the room like I lived there and dropping down onto her small but surprisingly comfortable sofa. "So tell me what you've been planning."

Delia crossed to her desk and sat on the chair, crossing her legs under her and spinning to face me. "How do you know I've been planning?"

"Please," I said, pursing my lips at her. "I hardly know you, but I know you're always prepared for anything. You may have been too proud to approach me first after that disastrous meeting, which is fine because I really did owe you this apology. But I don't believe for a second you haven't spent some time coming up with a better idea."

As hard as I tried, knowing looking at her was a lesson in denying temptation I could only maintain for so long, I raised my gaze to hers. A pink flush decorated her cheeks, and I fought back a smile. Making her blush shouldn't satisfy me so much, but I secretly loved this softer, more vulnerable side.

Mentally, I shook my head. I couldn't get caught up in thoughts like that. Appreciating vulnerability in someone was a slippery slope. Friendship, we could do. Anything past that would be crossing a line I wasn't interested in. Well, my brain wasn't. My body would happily sink into hers at the first opportunity, but I was a thirty-seven-year-old man. I could keep those urges at bay and keep this partnership above board—and above the belt.

"Well, since you asked…" Delia said, turning her back on me in favor of clicking around on her computer. A moment later, a rudimentary rendering of a building appeared, and I audibly gasped like a damn school girl.

"You did this?" I said, rising to my feet to move behind her.

Delia shrugged a shoulder. "I'd already been working on it, which you would've known had you bothered to ask my opinion on anything."

I winced, knowing I deserved that shot.

"I'm sorry," I said again, but she merely waved me off.

"It's fine." Somehow, I believed her. "So here's what I'm thinking…"

I pulled a chair up beside her, ignoring how the few inches of air separating our bodies charged as I sat. God, what the fuck was wrong with me? It wasn't like I'd never been in the professional company of a beautiful woman before. I should've been able to control myself better.

But I'd be damned if there wasn't something about Delia that just...did it for me. It was a crying damn shame it was one of those look-but-don't-touch situations.

My eyes widened the more she spoke, my jaw unhinging further with each new facet of the design she revealed. It was perfect, all the little details carefully curated to create a unique but warm and inviting environment for our guests. She kept the building shape the same as what Clarke had proposed, but completely updated the facade and interior.

The longer I studied the exterior rendering, the more a sense of deja vu settled over me, like I'd seen it before.

And then I realized I *had*.

Somehow, Delia had designed a building that looked exactly like the home I'd grown up in.

My eyes flicked to the ceiling, to the sky beyond, offering a small smile and *thank you* to my dad...wherever he was.

As she threw things at me, I asked questions or offered suggestions on ways to improve. For the first time since we'd started this whole thing, it felt like a truly collaborative effort. Once we'd reviewed everything and crafted a plan to proceed, I rose from my chair, desperate for a breath of air not laced with the scent of her perfume.

As soon as I was on my feet, I withdrew my phone from my pocket, clicking through my contacts and tapping on my contractor's name.

"I'll get my contractor on this ASAP," I said. "I don't know why I didn't just use him in the first place."

"This is a big undertaking," Delia said. "Opening a new business."

"I've already opened *three* new businesses," I reminded her.

"Not from the ground up. There's a lot more riding on this than with the bar, club, or restaurant."

My shoulders tensed with the reminder. I did have a lot riding on this. My reputation as a business owner. My burgeoning empire and growing legacy.

Making my father proud.

But it wasn't only me I had to consider here.

Delia had just spilled to me her insecurity about what happened if this project went under, and if for no reason but that, I'd kill myself trying to make this a success.

For her sake, I'd accept nothing less.

chapter 7

Owen

I spent the rest of that week holed up in my office, practically glued to my phone and email as my contractor, Delia, and I corresponded back and forth about the new plans. I'd sent him Delia's drawings, and he'd managed to take her bare bones renderings and turn them into stunning digital 3D models. Thankfully, I'd worked with Jay frequently enough that turnaround was quick. The switch from Clarke and his firm to Jay's only set us back a week, but by the time the day finally came to start construction, my skin tingled almost uncomfortably with anticipation.

Monday morning, I pulled up to the job site early, inhaling a deep lungful of fresh air as I got out of my truck. I lived for this feeling, the high of the first day on a new project. It was almost like the start of a fresh football season, when the possibilities were endless. While I knew there were innumerable things that could—and would—go wrong between now and opening, it did nothing to quell the excitement bubbling up in my chest.

Truthfully, I wasn't even required to be here. Jay and his team had completed hundreds of projects like this over the years; they certainly didn't need a washed up football player overseeing things, pretending like I knew what I was doing when I didn't.

But...this was a big moment, and Delia and I agreed we wanted to be here. I wanted *her* here, to be present the moment our great adventure began.

At last, we were breaking ground.

The land, which was only a few miles away from the lot I originally wanted to purchase, was flat and free from trees, brush, and other natural debris, thanks to the maintenance crew I'd hired the second the ink on the deed was dry. While Delia and I had been dealing with the Clarke of it all, that crew had been hard at work out here. Jay's team could've done it, certainly, but as they were wrapping up another job, that would've only set us back further. I didn't have the patience for another delay.

I flipped my hat forward as I made my way toward the collection of men and women gathered near the heavy machinery, shielding my eyes from the early morning sunlight. The days were getting shorter, reminding me of the obscene amount of money I was paying to complete everything before Thanksgiving so we could open in early December.

As I got closer, I was pleasantly surprised to find Delia had beat me here, and was striking up conversation with one of the construction guys. I didn't miss the appreciative glances the others standing around shot her way. All of them carried on their own conversations while sneaking covert looks at her long legs in her slim grey pants. I had half a mind to call them out, to come to her rescue. But something told me Delia was fully aware of the way their gazes rolled over her, and I knew she could handle them herself.

So instead of doing something stupid in her honor, I stalked toward her. When she saw me coming, she offered me a wide grin. At her reaction, the guy she was speaking with turned, and I realized he was my contractor.

Brows drawn together, I picked up the pace. Jay turned fully to me and extended a hand when I reached them.

"Good to see you again, Owen," he said. "Been a while."

"Yeah, not since we opened Overtime last spring," I said, surprised by the span of time. "Did you guys have a good summer?"

He nodded. "We did. Been busy, so I can't complain. Good to be back on one of your projects too. This should carry us right up until winter, when I'll give the guys a few months off. I won't be surprised if most of them spend a lot of that time right here," he said, turning to survey the property. When he faced me again, he had a wide grin on his face. Something about it was so familiar, something outside of the fact that he'd been my go-to contractor since I opened Lawless five years ago.

"I'm really excited to get started," I said, shaking off that sense of deja vu and clapping my hands together. "And this, of course, is my business partner, Delia Delatou. Delia, meet Jay—"

"Daniels," she finished for me. "I'm aware."

That feeling I was missing something important snuck back up, and my eyes darted between the two of them. "You've met before?"

Jay and Delia shared a look before breaking into laughter. "You could say that," Jay said.

My ire rose the longer they kept me out of the loop, and I

blurted, "Will someone please tell me what the fuck is going on?"

Delia composed herself and said, "*Daniels*, QB. As in *Logan Daniels*, my brother-in-law? Jay is his dad."

My eyes widened, and I mentally punched myself in the face. I'd only met Logan for the first time a few months ago, but how in the hell had I never made that connection? Jay's company was literally called *Daniels* Contracting and Real Estate, owned and operated by him and his wife, Michelle.

"And look," Jay started. "I didn't want to say anything when you first hired us all those years ago because I wanted our talent and professionalism to speak for itself, but...you were referred to us by Brent Jean, weren't you?"

"Yes..."

"He's married to my older daughter."

"Jesus," I said. "That explains...so much."

And it did. I only really knew Brent in passing, in the way that athletes from different sports from the same city knew each other. My teammates and I would go to Warriors' games when they played at home on days we had off from practice, and they'd come to our games on Sundays if they didn't also have one. But when I'd made the decision to retire, a lot of guys from all over reached out, and Brent had been one of them. He'd also been one of the few who asked me, "what's next?"

I'd left college early, choosing to declare for the draft after my junior season—after my dad died—simply for the rookie signing bonus that kept the family ranch afloat while the entire Lawless family figured out how to move on and operate without our patriarch.

But despite foregoing my senior season and putting Oregon—and Idaho—in the rearview in favor of Detroit, it was important to me to finish my degree. Like most athletes, I'd majored in business, and completed my program remotely during my rookie season.

That had been...a lot, and not something I'd advise personally. But after losing my dad, then moving clear across the country from everyone and everything I'd ever known, I'd needed the distractions both school and football had offered.

All that to say I did in fact graduate, and my diploma hung proudly in the office at my house.

So when Brent had asked what my plans were with football over, I already had the answer—an answer I'd been armed with for years, for a distant day when my career ended. Unfortunately, that day came a lot sooner than I'd anticipated. Still, I'd been ready. I'd always planned on opening my own business, and when I found the listing for the building that now housed the night club, I felt a tug, an inexplicable pull toward it. Some higher power nudging me onto my next path.

I told Brent this, even going so far as to share the listing with him, one (future) business owner to another. He'd started a successful activewear company with his younger sister, so I trusted his opinion and guidance. What began as a text conversation turned to extended phone conversations wherein Brent bounced ideas around with me.

Then he gave me Jay's contact information, not sharing who the man was to him, only that he was the best and I could trust him to take care of me.

That's how I ended up here, looking like an idiot in front of said man and my business partner. God, I felt so stupid for not having made the connection before. Now that I knew, though, there was no denying Logan was related to Jay. The son was the spitting image of the father, from their hair color and blue eyes to the way they were built and how they smiled.

"Well," Jay said, "now that we got that out of the way, what do you guys say we get this show going?"

"Yes!" Delia cheered. "Which reminds me, I have a question for you."

Jay nodded and inclined his head toward an area he and his crew must've staked off in the last few days, which we moved toward. The scope of building, even the simple outline of stakes and strings, was impressive. It was hard—damn near impossible, actually—to gauge these things when they were scaled down on a computer screen. But seeing it like this? It was fully sinking in that this little dream of mine was finally becoming a reality.

"What's your question?" I asked Delia.

"I was hoping Jay would let you and I do a ceremonial first dig of sorts."

"Why would you want to do that?"

"Because," she said, shooting me a sidelong glare that was no doubt prompted by my irritated tone, "shooting some video and photos of this moment would be a great way to kick off our social channels."

Somehow, I managed to keep forgetting this was a big part of why Delia was here, was what she was good at. I supposed I was of an age where I had difficulty imagining how a few photos and some videos would draw people to our business, but I'd also participated in enough various ad campaigns over the years to recognize the benefit.

"Okay," I agreed at last. Then I turned to Jay. "Is that okay with you?"

"Perfectly fine," he said.

"Actually," Delia broke in. "I was hoping Jay would join us. We can do a couple shots with just us, but I want one of us shaking his hands or something. We can hang it up in the distillery when it's finished."

"Do you want me to get one of my guys to do this for us?"

"Sure," Delia said. "That'd be a lot easier than getting my tripod set up."

Jay turned and hollered a name at the group gathered nearby. One of the men broke free, ambling toward us. He spared no glances for me or his boss, his gaze focused solely on Delia. Appraising. Clearly wondering how he could find his way into her pants.

I didn't like it at all. After the shit with Clarke, I was feeling protective of the girl, and I didn't appreciate the way men tended to leer in her presence. She wasn't decorative, something sent here to dress up the job site. She was here because she owned this land, and because she was half responsible for paying them.

Before she could speak, her phone already brandished in her hand, I took it from her and passed it over to the construction worker. "We need you to take a video and some pictures of us breaking ground," I told him gruffly.

Jay disappeared briefly and reappeared with two spades, passing one to Delia and one to me.

"Where do we want to start?" I asked him, and he pointed to a spot on the edge of the staked outline of our building.

"Here is good."

As Delia directed the worker on what exactly she wanted him to do, I took a deep breath, anticipation dancing along my limbs. It was finally happening, the day I'd dreamed about for years. Lawless, Birdie's, and Overtime were successful, and businesses I was proud to have my name on. But I'd never built something from the ground up, and I couldn't wait to watch the distillery take shape over the next few months.

Once Delia finished her instructions, we took our places in the spot Jay had indicated. Delia counted us down, and we dug in. The gusto with which she approached the task surprised me. I'd half expected her to tease out a little clump from the surface, but she really slammed the shovel into the ground, going so far as to slam her foot down on the edge of the blade to drive it deeper into the dirt. The mound of earth she moved was bigger than mine, and when we paused with them on our shovels to pose for pictures, I couldn't help but grin at her.

"What?" she asked when she met my eyes. "Do I have something on my face?"

"Your face is fine, Whiskey," I said softly around my smile. "You just continue to surprise me."

She scoffed. "'Your face is fine.' What a compliment."

I opened my mouth, ready to tell her what I really thought of those beautifully arranged features, but snapped it shut. Now was not the time or place.

Hell, *never* was not the time or place.

"Is that it then?" I asked instead, gesturing between us.

She called to the construction worker, "Did you get what I asked?"

"Yes, ma'am," he said.

"Then yes, that's it."

After setting our shovels down, we paused for a few photos with Jay, and then left him to his work. He began barking orders, and the team moved in a perfectly synchronized dance, breaking apart to attend to their various tasks. Soon, the job site was a flurry of activity, the rumble of Diesel engines and shouted directions filling the fall air.

"Well, that was fun," I said to Delia, wiping my palms on my jeans. "I'm going to head back into the city. Worry about my other businesses for a while."

"Actually," Delia said, halting me with a hand on my arm. "There's something I wanted to talk to you about first."

"Okay…"

Delia laughed at my skeptical tone. "It's nothing bad," she said. "I promise. Just something I want to run by you about all this." She gestured behind us at the backhoe now excavating a bucketful of dirt from the ground.

"Want to go grab a bite to eat and discuss it?" I blurted. My stomach let out a loud grumble, and I grimaced. "Clearly, I'm starving."

"Growing boy and all," Delia said knowingly, reaching out to pat my stomach with a familiarity that somehow didn't bother me as much as it should have. "We can go to the diner. They have the best breakfast spread."

"Perfect," I agreed. "I'll follow you down."

The drive from the job site near the tip of the peninsula—not far from Delia's parents' house, she informed me—to Apple Blossom Bay took about ten minutes, mostly owing to the fact that the road was winding, the posted speed limit below fifty miles an hour. It gave me time—too much, in fact—to consider what Delia might want to talk about, to worry if it would instigate another argument between us. But I had told her we make decisions together or not at all, and I meant it.

As I followed Delia onto Main Street and parked beside her. In front of us stood an old-timey box car with a sign out front indicating it was Sydney's Diner. I took a moment to study my surroundings. I hadn't spent much time in the area, mostly only passing through on my way up to the winery or that one day last week when I'd gone to Delia's house. Unsurprisingly, it was the epitome of a picturesque coastal lake town. Striped awnings covered the entrances to businesses up and down both sides of the street, the brick facades painted bright, inviting colors. In the distance, down a gently sloping hill, lay the marina and the bay beyond, the water sparkling in the early morning sunlight.

Things here were quiet—slower. The slice of life I'd been chasing when I left Detroit with my tail between my legs after announcing my retirement. Living in Traverse City made sense because of its proximity to the businesses, and the Torch Lake house was my escape when I needed it but...I could see the allure of settling in a place like this.

When we walked inside the diner, greetings rang out in Delia's direction, and she returned each welcome in kind, knowing the name of every person seated at every table. I had to remind myself that the Delatous were basically the first family of this place. I wasn't overly familiar with their history, but I knew that Delia's great-grandfather settled here in the early 1900s.

This woman—she was beloved by everyone here. It reminded me of home, of Dusk Valley and the community exactly like this one that I'd left behind all those years ago.

"Well well well," a woman said as she pushed through the swinging door from the kitchen, eyes landing on Delia. "Two days in a row? To what do I owe the honor?"

"It's not you," Delia said flippantly, sliding onto one of the chrome and leather stools bolted to the floor at the long Formica counter. "It's the pancakes."

"Pumpkin spice makes gluttons of us all," the woman agreed, then turned her attention to me. "I know you."

She didn't, not in any way that counted, but I nodded. "Owen Lawless," I said, extending a hand. "Pleasure to meet you."

"Sidney," she said. "Before you ask, not *that* Sidney. *That* Sydney was my grandmother. My name is spelled S-i-d-n-e-y."

"Noted," I said with a smile, dropping onto the seat next to Delia. "Now what's this I hear about pumpkin spice pancakes?"

Delia turned to me, animatedly explaining the seasonal offerings, and how she recommended pretty much everything on the menu. Ten years ago, I wouldn't have come within ten feet of anything so fatty or sugary, but after years and years of a highly regimented diet, I now ate what I wanted, when I wanted. It took some getting used to, the knowledge that I didn't have to watch my weight anymore. I still worked out regularly and ate fairly healthy, but I didn't beat myself up when cravings got the better of me.

And the scents of cinnamon and sugar and butter twining in the air were making my mouth water.

After we placed our orders, Delia folded her hands together atop the counter, her entire countenance shifting from playful to serious in a second.

"Am I...in trouble?"

Her brow furrowed. "No? Why would you be?"

"You just look..." I waved at her face and posture in explanation.

"I'm in business mode now."

I snorted. "Okay then," I said, crooking my fingers for her to continue.

"Before I go ahead and make our social profiles and start posting stuff, I wanted to talk to you about the distillery name."

"What's wrong with the name?" I asked. "It's literally mine."

"And it's a great name, QB. It's just..."

I sighed heavily, hating that this normally blunt woman was beating around the bush now. "Spit it out, Whiskey. You're not going to hurt my feelings."

"Well, you already have a club named 'Lawless,'" she said slowly. "And I don't want people getting confused. I love the whole vibe you've got going with the names of the spirits, and I don't want to change any of that. But I had an idea..."

"Lay it on me, then."

"Unlawful Spirits," she said quickly. "It's still keeping with the whole theme, but it's different so people won't get confused by Lawless the night club and Lawless the distillery. They're two separate entities right? For branding and marketing purposes, we want to keep them as such."

Unlawful.

I turned the word over and over in my mind, mouthing it silently, testing it from every angle. Trying to come up with some way to refuse Delia, to tell her it just didn't work.

But—why? Honestly, it was perfect, and I was pissed I hadn't thought of it myself.

"That's a kick ass name," I said at least.

Delia's nose crinkled despite the wide grin on her mouth. "Don't say 'kick ass.'"

"Why not?"

"Because it makes you sound like an old man."

"I *am* an old man," I joked. Though, my career as an athlete often had my joints feeling far older than their thirty-seven years, so maybe it wasn't so funny after all.

Delia turned away from me, her lips forming words, low enough that I knew she hadn't intended for me to hear.

"Not from where I'm sitting."

I opened my mouth to press her, to beg her to repeat herself. But our food arriving saved me from poking that hornet's nest.

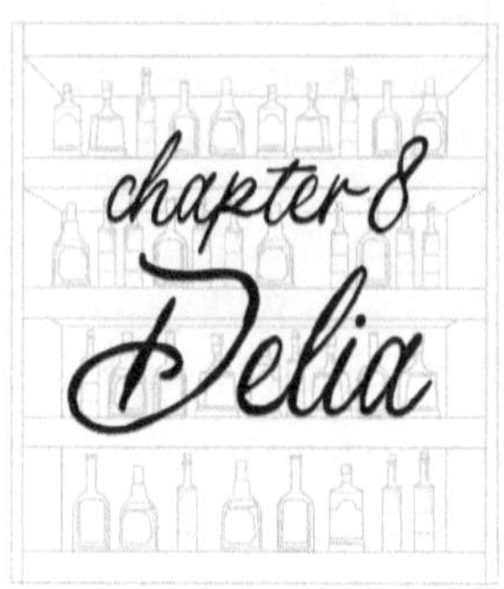

chapter 8
Delia

Maybe it made me basic, but fall was my favorite season.

With my birthday on Halloween, I felt a deep kinship with the autumn. My usual restless energy was somewhat soothed when the leaves began to change and the air smelled of decaying foliage. When temperatures dropped and Brie started serving up pumpkin spice lattes and hot apple cider at the bakery.

But that connection had its drawbacks, like how I somehow wound up on the planning committee for every damn fall festival event Apple Blossom Bay had.

From October first through Halloween, Apple Blossom Bay Fall Festival, or ABBFF for short, celebrated the harvest. The maple trees that dotted Main Street showed out, turning varying shades of vermillion, saffron, and burnt orange. With the water in the distance, the town was picturesque in a way that rivaled Salem this time of year.

Admittedly, it wasn't a hardship to give back to my community, not when its citizens had unknowingly given me so much—namely, my sense of purpose in the world. Before I'd moved home after college, started work on my house, and began running social accounts for business owners, I'd been listless. But the encouragement of my neighbors and family had sent me down a path that proved to be the best thing to ever happen to me.

On a particularly sunny afternoon during the second week of September, I found myself on the patio at the winery with Amara, Brie, and Ezra as we figured out logistics for the part the winery would play in that year's festival.

Being that Delatou, Inc. owned half of Old Mission Peninsula, a lot of which was forest or undeveloped plains, we opened our lands this time of year for the larger scale events. The fields near the old barn were planted with corn each year—which we then harvested, sold at the farmer's market, and donated the money back into the community in one way or another—and turned into a maze. Next to that was a pumpkin patch, which Dad or someone else would take guests out to on a wagon hooked up to a tractor, allowing people to pick their own gourds to take home. The barn was set up with a photo station, a small gift shop, and a few food stands that Brie and Ezra kept filled every day.

In addition, the community center and town advisory board put on a myriad of activities, including a haunted house and vendor bazaar.

Two hours—and several of Brie's hand-squeezed lemonades later—we had a solid plan in place for execution of this year's events. I had just returned to the table after using the restroom, intent on packing up my things to head into town for yet another meeting. Across from me, Brie had been gearing up to leave as well. Ezra held up a hand, stilling us both.

"Can I run something by you guys?" he asked.

That pulled me up short. Ezra Wendt rarely asked for anything.

"What's up, Ez?" Brie asked, slowly sinking back into her chair.

I offered my sister a reassuring smile. I didn't know if anyone else in the family was privy to this information, but Brie and Ezra had had a *moment* a few years back. When Ezra had first come to work for the Chateau, Brie had been twenty-two, freshly minted culinary arts degree in hand, and recently apprenticed with a pastry chef in Chicago. She'd been home for a brief winter break at Christmas, had taken one look at Ezra and fallen ass over tea kettle for him.

I didn't know the specifics of what had happened between them, only that it left Brie a little fucked up, always timid and wary around him, though she maintained professionality and cordiality when forced to interact with the man.

I felt for my littlest sister, deeply understanding wanting something you couldn't have. My only hope was that she found a way to move on one day—or that Ezra pulled his head out of his ass long enough to see that my sister was the most incredible woman, and he'd be the luckiest man alive to be with her.

With me and Brie staring at him expectantly, Ezra said, "I want to get more involved with the community, beyond all of this." He gestured to the winery, encompassing his work here. "So I was thinking about ways I could give back, and I thought perhaps hosting a fall dinner of sorts at the community center would be fun. I'm thinking a ticketed event with five to seven courses, each cooked by me and paired with a Chateau Delatou wine. I could do fall-inspired dishes with a Swedish flair."

I cocked my head to the side, studying Ezra. Something about him was...different. Gone were the shadows in his eyes, and the bags beneath them. He seemed brighter, peppier, like he wasn't simply moving through his life anymore in the wake of the tragedy that sent him running from NYC to ABB, but *living* it. I had to admit, it looked good on him. He was even more handsome with light in the chocolate depths of his eyes and a smile on his face.

Shifting my gaze, I looked at my sister, who sat still as a statue, mouth popped open slightly.

"And Brie," he said, turning to her fully. In response, my sister snapped her mouth closed, adopting that air of nonchalance she'd mastered in Ezra's presence. "I was hoping you'd contribute to the dessert course. Maybe you could come up with something to pair with the CD ice wine?"

"I—" Brie choked on the single letter, then cleared her throat loudly. "That sounds wonderful, Ez. Count me in."

"What do you need from me?" I asked.

"Marketing help," he said with a sheepish grin. "Even just word of mouth would be a major boost since you know everyone around here."

"I'll put out a blast on my social accounts," I said. "There will be a lot of tourists coming in for this, so I'll make sure people are aware it's happening. We can do flyers around town and post on the Chamber of Commerce's Facebook page too."

Ezra's shoulders relaxed a fraction. "Thanks, Delia. That

would all be amazing." He scrubbed a hand through his hair and said, "Now I just need to figure out logistics. I suppose I could cook it all at home..."

He trailed off, mumbling to himself and scribbling notes on the paper in front of him, seeming to have forgotten for the moment that Brie and I were still there. And though it had been blessedly quiet the last few weeks since I'd found a worthy project to throw my efforts into, that tiny little voice belonging to my inner chaos demon piped up with an idea. One I couldn't resist suggesting.

"You should use the bakery's kitchen!" I said brightly, and Brie's head shot up so fast her neck cracked. The look she gave me was positively lethal. "It's only a few storefronts up from the community center, and there's plenty of work space and storage."

"Storage I use for my shop," Brie said through gritted teeth.

I shrugged, unperturbed. "You can use that industrial sized fridge that takes up ninety percent of your kitchen upstairs," I said. "After the hell you put Dad and Logan through to get it up there, it's really the least you could do. Unless you want Ezra using that one instead."

My sister's emerald green eyes were laser beams designed to flay my skin from my body. Truly unfortunate for her that no magical powers ran through her veins.

"I really wouldn't want to impose..."

Both of us stared at Brie, waiting for her to make up her mind either way. Ezra clearly expected her to turn him down, and had sort of curled his shoulders in as if bracing for that rejection.

But I knew my sister better than that.

"No, no," Brie said, waving her hand. "It's fine. You're more than welcome to use the bakery."

Ezra's eyes widened, a smile halfway unfurling on his face before he bit down on it, offering a closed-lipped one instead. "Thank you, Brie. I'll...text you to sort out the details."

"Me too, please," I said. "When you've had a chance to nail down the date and time. Then maybe we can sit down and come up with a marketing plan."

"Sure," Ezra said, Adam's apple bobbing as he swallowed. "I'll be in touch with both of you."

"Great!" I said, clapping my hands. "Well, I have to get back into town for some more meetings, so I'll see you guys later!"

I knew there was no way I was getting out of the winery without Brie chewing me a new ass, but even so, I power-walked back inside and down the hall, toward the entrance and the parking lot beyond.

"Delia!"

Called it.

I stopped on a dime and turned to Brie, folding my arms across my chest, feigning boredom. The truth was, I'd acted completely out of pocket back there, but...if it got the two of them to figure their shit out instead of walking around each other on eggshells, then my work was done.

"Yes, baby sister?" I asked, tone saccharine.

"What the fuck is wrong with you?"

"Do you want the short answer or..."

Brie huffed, the sound a cross between a laugh and something of disgust. "What were you playing at back there?"

I answered her question with one of my own. "Remember last

Memorial Day, when I forced Amara and Cal into making out in front of all of us with that dare?"

"Yes..."

I shrugged. "This is your dare."

While she was momentarily struck dumb and silent, I left her standing in the lobby of the winery, making my escape before she could regain her bearings. She might not like me very much right now, but I had a feeling she'd thank me for meddling one day.

⁂

"Hey, Delia!"

I paused my exit from my final festival meeting of the day, spinning to face the man hurrying after me.

"Hey, TJ."

TJ smiled warmly, stuffing his hands into his pockets as he came to a stop in front of me. "You ready for another year of madness?" he asked, inclining his head to the group exiting the community center behind us.

I nodded. "This is always my favorite time of year around here," I said. "Fall is so...romantic."

"I never thought of it like that," he said. "I've always been a summer guy, so the weather changing always makes me a little mournful."

"Oh, I love summer too, don't get me wrong. Hard not to when you live in a place like this."

TJ chuckled lightly, then locked his eyes on mine. "So look, romance is kind of why I wanted to talk to you just now."

I narrowed my eyes, equal parts concerned and intrigued.

"Yes?"

"I was curious if you'd be interested in going on a date with me some time," he said, his gaze locked on mine and voice never wavering. "Even if it's just coffee or something."

Slowly, I blinked, allowing my eyes to sweep TJ's figure. He was probably only an inch or two taller than me with floppy brown hair the same color as his dark eyes. Physically, he was a little more wiry than I typically preferred my men. A few years older than me in school, he'd left for college and come back. Now he owned and operated one of the gift shops in town. In the slow season, he supplemented his income by picking up shifts at Granny's or doing odd jobs around town for other locals. I'd never heard anyone utter a bad word about him. He was nice. Probably too nice for me. And while my blood didn't heat at the sight of him, my proverbial dance card was doing nothing but gathering dust these days. What was wrong with one date?

Lately, I'd definitely been thinking about how nice it would be to share my life with someone. Owen was obviously not in the running, but spending so much time with a man had ideas of filling my house with a husband and children running through my mind. Seeing my two older sisters finding their soulmates and starting their families gave me a bit of FOMO. I'd never begrudge either of them their happiness—god knew they both deserved to have men like Logan and Cal worshiping them—but I wanted that life for myself. I wanted to be the one to tell my parents they were getting a grandchild, to have a ring on my finger, to change my last name.

I loved being a Delatou, obviously. But I wanted to be more than that—wanted what Mom and Dad had, a lifetime of ups and downs with my one perfect person at my side. I wanted to be a wife and a mother as well as a badass business woman.

Now here I was, being presented with the opportunity to potentially make that dream a reality.

"Sure," I said at last. "When are you thinking?"

"How about tomorrow? What's your schedule look like? Maybe we can do dinner at Granny's?"

"Tomorrow is perfect."

And so, the following evening, I found myself walking down the leaf littered streets in the direction of Granny's. TJ had offered to pick me up when he called—not texted, an action I wasn't sure I liked—earlier to confirm details. It wasn't that I didn't like talking on the phone so much as phone calls were far harder to ignore than texts, and I was a busy woman. Anyway, I'd brushed him off, telling him it was silly for either of us to drive when we both lived within walking distance of the restaurant.

The whole of Apple Blossom Bay lived within walking distance of Main Street.

When I pushed through the heavy wooden door, I squinted, giving myself a moment to adjust to the dim interior. I scanned the space for TJ and found him quickly, as he'd risen from his seat to wave at me.

As I reached the table, TJ leaned in and pressed a chaste kiss to my cheek, surprising me.

"Sorry," he said sheepishly, gesturing to the booth bench across from him. "Couldn't help myself."

"It's fine," I said, hoping my smile was placating and not belying my discomfort at having my personal space breached without my consent.

A second after we'd settled in, Tanya appeared at our side, smiling brightly. "Hey, Delia. TJ. What brings you in tonight?"

"We're on a date!" TJ said excitedly.

Jesus.

Tanya's gaze flicked between us, assessing. The woman had been my neighbor for years, having bought her house on our quiet street not long after she'd taken over Granny's from my family. She'd become like a second mother to me, looking after me, making sure I was safe and taken care of when my own mom was several miles away on the other end of the peninsula. Outside of my family, she knew me best, and I could practically see the wheels in her mind spinning. Questioning. Wondering why I was on a date with a guy I'd never once expressed any interest in during all the years we'd known each other.

Truthfully, I'd asked myself that same series of questions several times over the last twenty-four hours.

But TJ was a nice guy, and nice guys were few and far between. I was willing to give him a shot. If it worked out, lucky me. If it didn't, at least I could say I tried.

"That's great!" Tanya said, though her eyes lingered on me as though asking if it were, in fact, great. I gave her a tight, close-lipped smile. With a near imperceptible incline of her head, indicating she understood, she moved on. "What can I get you guys to drink?"

"I'll just have water," TJ said. "What about you, Delia?"

I studied him. "You're not going to have a beer or something?"

"Oh, I don't drink," TJ said. "Never really saw the point."

"I—" I let whatever I had planned to say die in my throat. I didn't have anything against people who didn't drink. That wasn't my choice to make for them. But...a large part of my life revolved around alcohol and the consumption of it. Having grown up in the area, that was something TJ knew. Five minutes into this date, and the contrasts in our lifestyles were glaringly obvious.

It had me wondering why he'd asked me out in the first place—and why I'd agreed.

chapter 9
Owen

IT WAS FINALLY TIME to admit it: despite my apprehension to work with her, Delia Delatou was damn good at her job.

Truthfully, it didn't shock me, not in any way that mattered, at least. It was only surprising in the way that, for someone like me who was too old school to really lean into the social media craze and use it to expand my reach—something I'd never needed to do anyway; my name, face, and status did that for me—the numbers from that first month were staggering.

Since curiosity killed the cat and all, I couldn't help checking our accounts daily. Delia had given me our login info with specific instructions not to touch anything. I didn't open any DMs, respond to any comments, follow or unfollow anyone. I simply...looked. Hovered in the digital background. Watched the videos she posted, read the carefully typed out captions and perfectly staged and filtered photos. It was...impressive.

Somehow, she'd found a way to make it all feel personal, like a conversation between friends, without ever giving our followers anything beyond the most surface level details. Our own faces never appeared in anything after those initial shots taken the day we broke ground. Delia focused a lot on the crew, having one guy explain the process of pouring the foundation, or another walk viewers through raising the walls and installing the trusses. She'd also conducted a few interviews with Jay, who provided progress reports and shared his confidence that we'd be open for business before Christmas.

Those words were music to my ears.

Secretly, I loved watching her work, took pleasure in the way she flitted around the job site, phone and camera permanently attached to her hands. She was so confident in everything she did, from the way she lined up a shot to the way she interacted with the construction guys.

Things were running smoothly, and I'd even pitched in to help the guys on a few occasions.

One day, at seeing me getting my hands dirty, Delia decided she also wanted to contribute.

"I want to try!" she shouted when I descended the ladder after pounding a few nails in. I could've done it with the nail gun, but there was nothing quite so cathartic as each strike of the hammer against the nail head.

I knew better than to judge a book by its cover, but Delia looked like she could barely lift the hammer, much less swing it and drive a nail into an oak board.

Still, the construction guys had been all for it, whistling and cheering her on. I wasn't at all on board, terrified she'd hurt herself somehow, so I hovered nearby as she climbed up the ladder. I stood slightly off to the side, chuckling softly when her tongue slipped out from between her lips as she concentrated. Her eyes narrowed on the nail she'd pinched between the thumb and pointer of her left hand. Then she lifted the hammer and swung.

The nail tacked into the board, and Delia grinned down at me. "I did it!"

"You sure did, Whiskey," I said. "Now finish it."

She did as I told her, careful swings slowly driving the nail deeper.

Having gotten bored with the whole production, like watching paint dry, I couldn't help my gaze straying to something far more interesting—her ass.

She wore a pair of obscene faux-leather pants that molded to every fucking sinful curve of her lower body, from the perfect swell of her backside to the lines of her quads, tapering to trim calves and delicate ankles.

Everything about this woman was a goddamn wet dream, and my eyes glazed over as I imagined what it'd be like to peel her clothes away, to have her naked and willing beneath me, to make her come apart over and over again.

Which is how I almost missed it when she accidentally pounded the hammer into her fingers, let go of the ladder in favor of cradling her hand, and slipped backward.

Only muscle memory from years of football had my feet moving, my arms reaching out to cradle her body against mine before she hit the ground. She landed with a soft sigh, eyes wide as she stared up at me.

"Nice catch, QB."

"Best of my life."

Those last four words slipped out easily, but I couldn't find it within myself to wish they hadn't.

Call it...wishful thinking.

If the blush rising to her cheeks and the smile she worked so hard to hold back was any indication, Delia was more than a little pleased by my words. I preened with the knowledge.

Thankfully, she had no idea I'd been checking her out, but as I hustled her off the job site so I could take her somewhere to ice her hand, I didn't miss the way Jay smirked at me.

Clearly, he'd seen the whole damn thing.

But as long as Delia remained blissfully unaware, I didn't give a fuck who caught onto the fact that I was down bad for this girl—the situation growing more dire by the day.

Besides, while I'd been busy ogling her that day, she'd been sitting on a particularly, for lack of a better word, *sexy* photo of me. As it turned out, I hadn't been the only one checking out my partner's goods.

As soon as I'd seen the picture pop up on our Instagram, I called Delia.

"What the hell is that?" I asked unceremoniously when she answered.

"What the hell is what?" she replied sweetly, feigning innocence.

"Don't play dumb, Whiskey. It's not cute."

"I'm assuming you've been lurking on our social profiles," she said with a laugh.

I ground my teeth together. "Yes."

"So what's the problem?"

"The problem, Delia," I said, her name akin to a curse word, "is that you're objectifying me!"

She scoffed. "Please, QB. No one has a body like that unless they want people to see it. Not to mention you're literally fully clothed!"

"I maintain my physique because I don't know any other way to live," I said because it was the truth

"Suuuuuuuure," she replied sarcastically.

"What happened to not including me in any content? You promised."

"I'm sorry," she said sincerely, sobering instantly. "If you want me to take it down, I will. Just say the word."

Was that what I wanted? Admittedly, our follower count had grown drastically, and I'd be an idiot to think it had nothing to do with me. After all, I'd seen the notifications, and the comments kind of made my skin crawl. This must be how women felt all the time, when men objectified them simply because they couldn't control themselves.

"I don't like the way the women are talking about me. Like I'm an...object."

"I really am sorry," she said. "I didn't think..."

I sighed heavily. To be fair, my face wasn't even in the shot, and as Delia had pointed out, I *was* fully clothed. Taken from the back, my arms were raised overhead, back muscles flexed and pulling my white tee taut. My Levi's hung low on my hips and molded to my backside. Above the waist, the black band of my boxer briefs and the dimples at the base of my spine were visible where my shirt had ridden up. My forearms were corded from the strain, my biceps bulging, truly testing the limits of that cotton. My Lawless Ranch ball cap was flipped backward on my head, the white logo highlighted on the faded maroon fabric in the midday sun.

The caption read, "QB's still got it."

So even though my face wasn't visible, thanks to Delia, everyone knew it was me anyway.

If I were a woman, I could see my allure—and they certainly did. The comments were full of drooling faces and fire emojis, and our DMs were clogged with more of the same.

It was…a lot.

At least none of my tattoos were showing. I had a feeling that the sight of my ink would bring out a whole different level of feral from our female followers.

I had four tattoos, each of them representing some special moment, person, or place in my lifetime. The first, of course, was my last name on my left forearm. It was the first tattoo I'd ever gotten, freshly eighteen and cocky in a way that meant I thought it'd be cool to get my last name permanently marked on my skin in a tough-looking font. It spanned the full length of my ulna from wrist to elbow. There was also the barbed wire that wrapped high around my right biceps, the ends meeting to form "L for L." Each of my brothers had the same, which stood for "Lawless for Life." I had a compass on my left pec, right over my heart, the coordinates for my family's ranch etched above due north, and a dream catcher running along my right ribs.

I loved all of them equally, had worked with an artist in Detroit for hours, painstakingly planning out the details of the compass and dream catcher to get them exactly right, but the latter was easily the most special.

My dad had always wanted his children to dream big. Though

the Lawless Ranch had been in his family for generations, he'd never lorded it over us, never pushed us to want to run it, never forced us into thinking we had no other option but to stick around Dusk Valley for the rest of our lives. He encouraged each of us to go out and experience life, to chart our own paths, let the stars guide us wherever they may. If that journey led us home, then so be it.

My dad had been my fiercest supporter, my loudest cheerleader, and never told me I couldn't do something. Only asked what he could do to help me achieve my goals.

Which was why his death had dealt all of us such a massive blow, the kind of soul wound that would never fully heal. At least not for me, no matter how much time and distance I put between me and the day I'd gotten that call.

Reflexively, I thumbed his wedding ring on my pinky as my eyes scanned the photos decorating the walls of my office, snagging on the one taken nearly seventeen years ago. We were all huddled at center field, the Pac-12 logo scuffed and faded from the game beneath our feet. Aria was five, all crooked teeth and pigtails, swimming in one of my jerseys as I held her in my arms. My parents stood at my sides. My brothers, ranging in age from nineteen down to ten, were a mix of gangly limbs, Ducks tees, and braces, fanned out around and behind us. All nine of us grinned widely for the camera, both because the Ducks had just won the conference championship thanks to my five—four passing and one rushing—touchdowns, and because we were simply happy to be together. It was the final time the entire Lawless clan had been photographed together.

Dad died two weeks later.

And two weeks after that, two days before I was set to play in the Pac-12 championship game, I got the dream catcher tattoo in memory of him. It became a talisman and a reminder. Everything I did from then on wasn't for myself anymore. It was for him and the seven other people in that photo with us.

"I just..." I started, coming back to myself and the conversation with Delia. I removed my hat and drove my fingers through my hair. "Next time, ask me before you use me as a thirst trap. We make decisions together or not at all, remember?"

"Aye aye, Captain," she said, then hung up.

God, this woman was going to be the death of me.

By the end of the week, both our TikTok and Instagram accounts had over ten thousand followers each, and buzz surrounding the distillery was reaching a fever pitch. We'd received countless messages and emails from influencers wanting to collaborate with us, everyone from travel bloggers to food and beverage reviewers. When a popular Food Network host reached out to do a segment with us after we opened, I could grudgingly admit my backside—and everything else Delia was doing—was good for business.

And the longer I watched Delia work her magic on our business, the more I realized my other ones could use the same touch.

❧❧❧ ❧❧❧

The second week of October, when our weekly status meeting disbanded, Jay and a few of his men headed back to the site, but I asked Delia to hang back.

"What's going on?" she asked.

Her tone was laced with apprehension, and I quickly placated her. "Nothing serious," I said. "I just have a proposition for you."

Delia quirked a brow but didn't say anything, giving me room to proceed.

"I want you to take over social media management for Lawless, Birdie's, and Overtime."

Her eyes widened comically, her mouth popping open slightly. "Are you serious?" she asked.

"Dead," I confirmed.

"But...why?"

"I've seen how hard you work, Whiskey. I've been paying close attention the last month, and while I was skeptical at first, the things you've done with the Unlawful social accounts are insanely impressive. I'd like your help driving traffic to my other businesses."

"Really?" she asked, gaze pinging around my face, as if gauging my seriousness. Despite her clear reservation, her eyes were bright, alive with excitement and hope. In that moment, I realized that this may be the first time—or at least one of very few instances—when someone recognized Delia's eye for detail, talent, and passion, and rewarded her for it instead of writing her off as a silly girl who spent too much time on her phone.

"Yeah," I said with a reassuring smile. "You're clearly talented, and I could really use your help."

Delia leapt from her stool, arms outstretched, but held herself back at the last second. As if she was going to throw herself into my arms and barely kept herself in check. Honestly, I would've welcomed that hug. Instead, we settled for a handshake that felt far too impersonal.

"Oh, and as far as salary goes," I began when she once again settled into her seat. I rattled off a number, one I'd reached after careful research of what she could be making working for some big time firm and a conversation with Cal about what I could reasonably afford.

In reality, I could *reasonably* afford to buy the entirety of Traverse City, but that was beside the point. I had a financial manager for a reason, and he informed me I couldn't blow my entire wad on Delia.

No seriously, those were his exact words, and they conjured up images of blowing something far naughtier on Delia. Of her tan skin marred by my cu—

"Absolutely not," Delia said, pulling me from my deviant thoughts.

"It's only fair," I told her. "I checked, and I talked with Cal."

"I can't accept it."

"You can," I assured her, brooking no room for argument, using the same tone I'd perfected over a lifetime of corralling younger siblings and two decades of leading football teams. "And you will."

Her cheeks pinked, and she opened her mouth, presumably to refute me again.

I cut her off before she could.

"Seriously, Whiskey. You deserve this."

"Okay," she said quietly. "I'll do it."

The hue of her face deepened, and she dropped her eyes to the table in front of her, her hair falling around her, hiding her from me.

My fingers itched to tuck under her chin and force her to meet my gaze, to reassure her she was worth every good thing she got and then some.

But that wasn't my job. My job was to be her partner—maybe even her friend, eventually. No more and no less.

Thinking of Delia Delatou in any capacity outside of anything strictly platonic was a recipe for disaster.

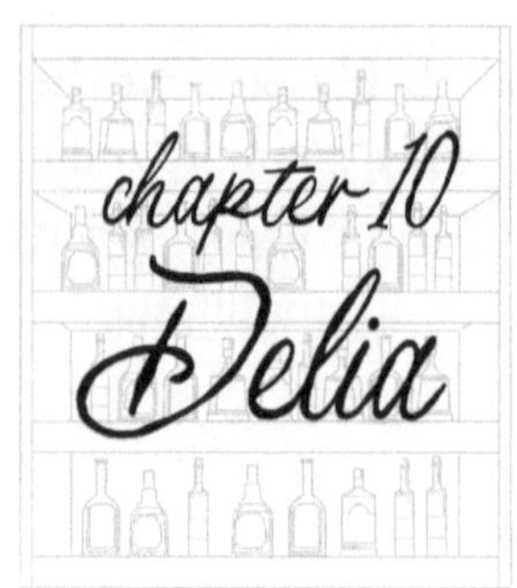

chapter 10
Delia

THE ENTIRE DELATOU GANG descended on Owen's restaurant Friday evening for our weekly family dinner. By the entire gang, I meant *everyone*. Me, of course, Mom and Dad, Chloe and Logan, Amara and Calvin, Ella and her dumbass boyfriend, Alfie, Brie, and even Ezra, his son, Hansen, and his father, Fredrik, who insisted we call him Rik. Ezra had invited himself because, and I quote, "I refuse to miss a meal at a place like Birdie's, especially if you're paying." While he wasn't technically family, he'd been working for us long enough to feel like part of it.

Tonight, we were celebrating my new title as social media manager for Birdie's, Lawless, and Overtime.

"Well," my dad said, clapping his hands together. "What kind of wine do we want?"

"Josh!" Alfie quipped, and every one of us Delatou girls glared daggers at him, save Ella, who rolled her eyes and huffed out a little sigh that sent her bangs floating.

My father leveled a finger at him from the head of the table.

"Utter that name again in my presence and they'll never find your body."

"Easy, big guy," Alfie joked, raising his palms placatingly. "It was just a joke."

"A really fucking bad one," I mumbled.

Alfie's sharp features narrowed on me. "Fuck off."

My hackles rose, and I looked to my sister for backup. Ella only turned her face away, pretending to examine the wine menu though we all knew Ezra would be selecting for the table.

So I returned my gaze to her boyfriend, the little pissant, and said, "You are aware I'm paying for your meal tonight, right?"

"And?" Alfie sneered.

"And if you speak to me like that again, I'll hang you out to dry."

Alfie's eyes flared, challenge accepted, but my sister settled a hand on his forearm. "Back off, Alf," she said quietly.

After a beat, Alfie did as he was told, mumbling, "whatever" as he turned to Ella and whispered something in her ear that had her face going pale.

Before I could address the situation, could find some way to rid us of this leech sucking the life out of my sister, Owen appeared at my father's side, settling a hand on his shoulder.

"Welcome, Delatou family," he said, grinning broadly. "What brings you in?"

"Celebrating my new position," I said, smirking knowingly at Owen.

"New position?" my mom asked. "What new position? You're not leaving the winery, are you?"

"Of course not," I said, waving a hand. "The Chateau is stuck with me forever."

"It's your legacy," my father said, "so I would hope so."

Actually, it's Amara's legacy, I thought wryly, but figured it was best not to speak that aloud. Instead, I simply said, "Owen offered me a job."

"Doing what?" Chloe asked.

"Managing social media for Lawless, Overtime, and...Birdie's!" I said, flinging my arms out wide to gesture at the restaurant around us. "Hence why I wanted to treat us all to family dinner here this week. I'm technically on the clock."

I met Owen's gaze and couldn't help shooting him a wink.

His eyes held mine as he said, "If you think you're paying, you're sadly mistaken, Whiskey."

"Ha!" Alfie said, an expression of triumph surely gracing his stupid face, but I couldn't tear my eyes away from Owen.

Something was happening here, something I couldn't quite put my finger on. Almost as if he was making it his personal mission to...take care of me? But why would he want to do that?

God, I didn't know anything anymore.

"Thank you," I said quietly, knowing the words were soft enough that they wouldn't reach his ears but he could read them plainly on my lips.

"In that case," my father boomed, "get me your most expensive bottle of CD!"

The table broke out in laughter, and the corner of Owen's mouth ticked up.

"I'll let the waitstaff know," he said, eyes still not leaving mine.

"Why don't you join us?" my mother offered. "We'd love to hear how the distillery is coming, and Delia doesn't tell us anything."

My face heated. "I would if I ever saw you."

"Exactly," my dad said, leveling me with that intense, pine green stare. "Have you forgotten where we live?"

"Of course not," I said. "I've just been busy."

My dad faced Owen again. "Stop monopolizing my daughter, Lawless."

Owen chuckled. "Apologies, sir."

Then, seeming to accept my mother's invitation, Owen moved around the table and pulled a chair from one nearby, stopping between me and Alfie. It took a moment for the little shit to recognize the hulking male form bearing down on him, but when he did, he looked up at Owen, eyes wide.

Still, he apparently couldn't leave well enough alone, because he said, "Can I help you?"

"Move." That single word in Owen's deep timbre left no room for argument, and Alfie wisely scooted his chair without another word, nearly scrambling in Ella's lap, who moved over further to make room for Owen.

I expected him to create some separation between us once he was seated, but he remained where he was, his thick, rock hard thigh pressed against mine. He seemed oblivious to the way my skin heated with his proximity. He could've easily intimidated Alfie into moving further down but chose to stay at my side.

What the fuck did that mean? Was it normal to lose my mind over a simple, completely innocent touch from a man?

I knew the answer, I just wasn't ready to confront it quite yet.

"You're mean," I said quietly, ignoring the way my body reacted to him.

"Hardly," Owen whispered back. "Someone needs to teach that kid a lesson."

I snorted, delighted that Owen had picked up on Alfie's horribleness so quickly.

"We've been trying to for three years," I said.

Before I could further enumerate Alfie's flaws, a group of waiters appeared brandishing several bottles of Chateau Delatou wine, and they moved around the table in a well-choreographed dance, filling glasses quickly.

Owen growled, a low sound of warning, when Alfie attempted to refuse, saying he hated wine and would rather drink tequila.

"You'll drink it, and you'll like it," he said, his voice vibrating through my entire body thanks to his proximity. "Or you can leave."

"You can't make me."

"I own this building, you little shit," Owen snarled. "That's the least of the things I can make you do."

Fuck, this was going to be a long meal.

"Blech," Brie said from down the table as she sipped her glass of cab. "Too dry."

"Excuse you, young lady," my father said. "I worked very hard to perfect that blend."

"Should've tried harder," she said under her breath, but Dad still heard her.

"Watch it, Brie," he said. "Take one more shot at my prized possession and I'll take your bakery away."

Brie gasped theatrically, knowing both that the Cabernet recipe was far from his most prized possession and that he didn't have the power to take away the bakery—that resided with Amara.

"You can't do that, Daddy," she said cheekily, sticking her tongue out, "and you know it."

"I can damn sure try."

"You do, old man," Brie started, "and you'll never taste my baklava again."

My dad slammed his fist into his chest as though he'd been fatally wounded. "You wouldn't dare."

Brie tipped her nose in the air. "Fuck around and find out."

"Brie!" Mom scolded as the rest of the table broke into a fit of laughter.

God, I loved these people—except Alfie. Even on the bad days when I wasn't entirely sure where I fit in the grand scheme of things, I knew I belonged *here*. Knew how much they all loved and rooted for me. Understood in a bone-deep way how much our parents had given us with this life and this family. In my sisters, they'd given me everything.

My laughter cut off abruptly as Owen's hand closed around my knee, and my gaze flew to his. The look on his face—joy edged with pain. My nerves were alight, practically singing under his touch, but I only cared about him.

"Are you okay?" I asked.

"Fine," he said, clearing his throat. "Just...missing my own family."

My heart melted into my stomach, and I placed my hand atop his, squeezing. "You can have mine whenever you want."

His face softened, the tightness around his eyes smoothing away. "I'll be taking you up on that."

"I hope you do."

I said a lot more in those four words than I'd ever intended, and I waited for fear to paralyze my body.

Only, it never came. A sense of rightness settled on my bones at the thought of sharing these people with him, of welcoming him into the family.

"Just one condition, Whiskey," he said, lips twisting into the hint of a smirk, his ocean eyes twinkling.

"What's that?"

"Get rid of Alfie."

I tipped my head back and laughed.

Dinner was delicious, as I expected, though I seemed to spend more time on my phone than I did enjoying each new course. Truly, though, none of it felt like work. I loved content creation, and I was damn good at it. It was immensely satisfying to have someone like Owen, who didn't owe me anything outside of our partnership and didn't really take anything regarding social media marketing seriously, to recognize that about me. At first, it felt like he was only throwing me a bone, and I wanted to argue with him that he was doing fine on his own. But after he'd given me access to the social accounts—he'd been the one managing them himself for years, with sporadic help from random employees—I understood there was definitely room for improvement. So I was making it my mission to take things to the next level. Owen and I could become a dynamic duo, taking the Traverse City nightlife and restaurant scene by storm. Him, with the face and the name, and me with the marketing chops.

In the month since we'd started working together, I'd come

to enjoy my time with him. More than I cared to admit, which was dangerous. Something buzzed in the air between us whenever he was within my orbit—or maybe that was simply wishful thinking. Maybe I was assigning more meaning to his general friendliness and bone deep desire to take care of those around him.

But I couldn't wish for Owen to be anything but my partner and now, I supposed, my boss. That had turned out horribly for Amara and Calvin. Still, I could admit, if only in my own mind...the man was a smoke. Sex on a stick in scuffed Ariat boots and denim that hugged his perfect ass. Owen was exactly the kind of man I was drawn to—a little rugged on the outside with a heart of gold. I practically drooled every time I looked at him, my core clenching around some appendage of his I'd never feel inside me. Privately, I mourned the loss of all the things those big hands would never do to me.

When dinner disbanded at last, I was close to coming out of my skin from his nearness.

Owen disappeared to the back of the Birdie's, and the rest of my family headed in their separate directions. After exchanging tense words with Ella, Alfie stormed off.

In the end, only Ella, Brie, and I remained, gathered on the sidewalk in the rapidly descending nighttime.

"Can we go out tonight?" Ella said without preamble.

"You don't have to ask me twice," I assured her with a smile, then turned to Brie. "You in?"

Brie shrugged. "I don't have anything better to do."

I shared a look with Ella, and both of us broke into giggles. "We appreciate the enthusiasm," Ella said.

"You guys want to come over and get ready at my place?" I asked. "I need to upload the content from tonight to my computer and change. Where do you want to go?"

"Lawless?" Ella asked quietly. "I haven't been in forever, and it's…"

She trailed off, so I prompted, "It's what, El?"

"Alfie won't go there," she said, refusing to meet my eyes. "Not before, but definitely not now that he feels like Owen slighted him."

I scoffed. "Owen can't slight someone in his own damn restaurant."

"*I* know that," Ella said defensively, crossing her arms and giving me a stare down she'd perfected years ago. "But you know how Alfie is."

"Don't I ever."

"What's that supposed to mean?" Ella asked coldly.

"How about we don't do this?" Brie said, stepping between us. "Let's head back up to ABB and rendezvous at Delia's to pregame. Deal?"

"Deal," Ella grumbled, and I only nodded.

❧❦

On the drive back down the peninsula to Traverse City later that night, I finally cracked. I'd played nice with Ella while we got ready at my place, schooling my temper to something far more manageable by the time she'd arrived at my place, Brie following shortly behind. But the silence in the car was eating me alive, the tension between us suffocating.

"What's going on with you, El?" I asked softly.

In my periphery, I saw my sister stiffen in the passenger seat. She was silent long enough that I thought she'd blow me off, brush whatever was going on under the rug like she'd been doing often these days—for years, actually.

Instead, she said, "Alfie and I got in a fight as we were leaving Birdie's. Actually, we've been fighting a lot lately."

"About what?" Brie asked from the back.

"The list of things we don't fight about would actually be shorter," Ella said with a soft, bitter chuckle.

Neither Brie nor I laughed with her.

"So what was today's about?"

"Owen," she said. "And Dad. And the way the men we surround ourselves with treat him."

"Maybe if he wasn't such an asshat..." Brie said quietly.

I expected Ella to protest, to whirl on our youngest sister and dig into her.

So I was surprised when, in place of harsh words, Ella's sniffles and choked back sobs filled the otherwise silent car.

"Fuck," I said, pulling over onto the side of the road abruptly, the car behind me honking and swerving around me.

In a moment, I was parked and turned toward Ella, Brie and I both waiting her out as she composed herself, all of our hands linked together.

"It's not even worth talking about," Ella said at last. "He just doesn't like anyone, you know? He hates all of you. He can't stand Mom and Dad, and he's so rude to Logan and Cal anytime we're around them. I just...I'm so exhausted."

"I don't understand why you don't just leave then," Brie said.

Ella sniffed, lifting her free hand to swipe at the tears rolling down her cheeks. Her eyes met mine, their vibrant green depths near glowing in the dashboard lights.

"I love him," she said simply.

I squeezed her hand tighter. "You can love someone and recognize they aren't meant to be part of your life."

Clearly, that wasn't what she wanted to hear. She withdrew her hand from ours and faced forward, dropping the visor and flipping open the mirror to check her makeup. Conversation clearly over, I shared a weary look with Brie in the rearview before pulling back onto the highway and resuming our trek into the city.

I decided to act as our designated driver that night. For one, I wanted to get both of my sisters back up to Apple Blossom Bay in one piece, and two, it seemed like a bad idea to be drinking when I was also working for Owen, planning on giving his social media followers a "night in the life at Lawless" look at the club. It had been so long since I'd gone out that, despite the fact that I was here on Owen's dime, I couldn't help myself from slinking to the center of the dance floor and giving myself to the music for an hour.

Plenty of guys came up to me, grinding behind me, slipping their hands up and down my body. I entertained those bold enough to approach; their wonton touches didn't bother me. That was what places like this were for—losing yourself to sensation. Indulging in a fantasy before returning to the real world. The club was a bubble, an alternate reality. With the lights low and the music loud, it was easy to forget all of my hang-ups.

Well, mostly all of them.

No handsome man swaying behind me to the music could distract me from the fact that they weren't the hands I wanted on me.

Damn, that was a dangerous thought. Then again, it wasn't like it would ever happen, right? So really, what was the harm in daydreaming?

Still, Owen was somewhere in the building, and my body knew it.

When I couldn't stand it anymore, when I found myself spending more time scanning the crowd, searching for a particular backward ball cap and set of broad shoulders, I gave up, deciding to seek him out.

After all, we were partners. I was allowed to check in on him, wasn't I?

Hugo stood sentinel at the end of the hall to Owen's office, and he returned the broad smile I shot him as I breezed past. When I reached Owen's door, hand poised to knock, to announce my presence, I paused instead. Taking a moment to study him. He was bent over his desk, one elbow braced against it, chin propped up in his hand as he wrote something with the other.

As it turned out, Owen was a lefty, and I was mesmerized by the angle of his hand as it swept across the paper on which he wrote. His biceps flexed slightly as it moved back and forth across the page, the skin between his brows creased, pinched in concentration.

God, he was a beautiful man. It was truly a shame I'd never have him.

"Working hard or hardly working?" I asked, finally announcing myself.

Owen's head shot up, mouth half open as though to shout for security. When his eyes landed on me, though, his gaze softened.

"Hi," he said quietly.

"Hey."

"What're you doing up here?"

I briefly considered crafting some lame ass excuse, pulling an idea for the distillery or his socials from thin air, but really...I didn't want to lie about wanting to be near him.

"Wanted to see you," I said with a shrug, playing it off like it wasn't a huge deal.

"Well, here I am."

chapter 11
Owen

WELL HERE I AM?

God, what the fuck was I saying? What was wrong with me?

I didn't know, because my brain had short circuited, and it was all thanks to that dress.

That goddamn dress.

The way the sage green fabric clung to Delia's lithe form honestly should've been a crime. The top suctioned to her breasts and torso before the skirt flared and swished around her toned thighs, showing off her long legs, her feet slipped into a pair of gold, open-toed stilettos. If I was a weaker man, the skirt would already be shoved up around her waist as I bent her over my desk.

God, I wanted to punch myself in the face. This woman was my *partner*, and my sort of employee. I'd seen the bullshit she dealt with from men online, and witnessed firsthand the way that jackass Clarke treated her. The last thing she needed was another man thirsting after her—least of all *me*.

I rose from my chair, intent on gesturing her inside, offering her a seat and a drink, but my arm got away from me and knocked over the two fingers of whiskey I'd poured myself when the noise from downstairs reached a fever pitch.

Yeah, I'd taken to drinking instead of simply closing the door.

First, I needed the cacophony of my guests to drown out my errant thoughts. Second, I needed the liquor to loosen my limbs after spending nearly two hours earlier inhaling Delia's scent and letting her warmth seep into my body. Only, I hadn't even managed a sip before my sexy as fuck business partner appeared like a gorgeous mirage in my doorway.

I'd been a certified dumbass not to have moved away from her at dinner, and I was paying for it now in the form of tension in my shoulders and a half-hard cock.

The dress wasn't helping.

The liquid spread slowly, instantly soaking all the papers I had on my desk, including the to-do list I'd been working on when Delia appeared.

Seriously, what the fuck was this woman doing to me? We'd been in this office alone together countless times since getting into business together, and I'd never acted like this before. I'd been fully in control of my body, like I always had been. In that moment, though, I'd felt an awful lot like I'd magically reverted to my gangly preteen, brace-faced self. That awkward kid who'd stumbled over his feet on the way to ask the pretty girl in class to be his date to the upcoming homecoming dance.

I supposed there was something different about the circumstances. Beyond the windows, instead of the midday sunlight, there was nothing but blackness broken only by streetlights. The music from downstairs provided a steady, thumping background rhythm, matching my heartbeat. My skin felt too tight for my body, my breath loud and rapid.

Suffice it to say, my mind was giving me all kinds of ideas, the kind I needed to stay far away from. As though it had all played out on my face, when I looked at her again, Delia's expression was bemused.

"Want a drink?" I croaked, leaving the mess on my desk to move around to my drink cart.

Delia shook her head, those dark chocolate locks brushing against the exposed swells of her breasts over the collar of her dress. It was so long that I could wrap it around my fist a few times before tugging her head back and zeroing my attention in on her throat. Settle my lips over her pulse and lightly scrape the spot with my teeth...

I shook my head. Fuck, I had to get it together. If I popped a boner in front of her, it'd be obvious what I was thinking about, and I refused to put her in that sort of uncomfortable position.

"At least come in and sit down then."

A moment later, the door clicked shut behind me, cutting off the worst of the noise from downstairs. For the first time since she'd arrived, though she'd further secluded us in here, I could breathe, could hear myself think. For all my anxiety over being near her earlier, her presence suffused the air with a warmth and safety I wanted to bask in forever.

"Why did you offer me your land?" I blurted. I needed to regain control, to steer the conversation toward business. The situation in my pants was seconds away from growing dire, and I'd do anything to prevent that.

Thankfully, Delia had taken a seat on the couch—the one I'd

come to think of as *hers*—those perfect, tanned stems of hers crossed in a way that had the dress riding precariously high. I sat simply to give myself a worse vantage point. I settled my own arm awkwardly on my thigh, using my hands clasped in front of me to hide my crotch. It took every fucking ounce of willpower I had to meet her eyes instead of look my fill at her beautiful body.

She shrugged again, and I found myself growing irritated with her nonchalance. First shrugging when she said she wanted to see me, as though that knowledge didn't have my heart swelling in my chest, sending satisfaction zipping through me. And I understood not wanting to appear too eager, but...we were becoming friends, weren't we? She was allowed to come see me, whenever she wanted.

But I didn't understand how she could remain so calm and collected when I was fucking losing my mind over her.

"You didn't want to build your forever home for your future family?" I asked, hopefully prompting a verbal response.

Those whiskey eyes met mine, something I couldn't read flashing across them. "I guess I never imagined that for myself. I want a family, but..." she trailed off, that goddamn shoulder hitching up again. "Plus, I love my farmhouse, and I put a lot of work into updating it. *That* is my forever home."

"That still doesn't answer my question."

"I guess I was waiting for the right project to come along."

"And that project was me?"

"That project ended up being *our* distillery," she corrected.

"Fair enough."

Delia glanced around the room, doing everything she could to not look at me. When she noticed the photos I'd hung around the room, she got up, offering me a view of her posterior, of the groove of her spine and the smooth skin of her upper back.

Of her ass, which was round and perfect under the hem of that dress.

That ass would haunt my dreams, would drive me insane with how badly I wanted to sink my teeth—and maybe something else—into it.

Jesus, I was in a bad way.

The frames featured a collection of my families, both blood and sports, displayed there to remind me who I was and where I came from, to ground me every time I stepped foot in this office.

Her hair swishing against her bare skin was the only sound in the room as she studied them, and as I studied her.

At last, she lifted her arm and tapped one with a long, manicured fingernail. It was the candid shot of the Lawless clan from homecoming. Our final family photo.

"Who are they?" she asked.

"My parents and siblings."

"All of them?" She glanced over her shoulder at me, her eyes wide.

"All of them," I confirmed. "You act like you've never seen a big family, Miss Middle-Of-Five.

"Okay, true," she said with a giggle, continuing along the walls, pausing every so often. Her silence as she studied the pictures made my skin crawl. As if, by looking at them, she could see right into the darkest depths of my soul.

I breathed a massive sigh of relief when she turned and asked, "How many of you are there?"

"Seven. Me, five brothers, and a baby sister."

"Baby?" Delia asked, brow raised, like she'd never used the same term to describe Brie, who was only two years her junior.

I knew she had, because I'd heard it.

"She's fifteen years younger than me, so...yeah. *Baby*."

Delia's eyes widened and she said, "What about your brothers?"

"Trey is 35, Lane is 33, the twins, Finn and West, are 30, and Crew is 28."

"Twins?" Delia asked, whirling on me fully. "And do they all look like you?"

I willed away the jealousy that spiked in my chest, resisting the urge to rub a palm against my sternum at the intrigue in her tone. "We've all got varying shades of sandy blond hair and blue-green eyes," I said vaguely, taking a page out of her book and shrugging.

In truth, all of my brothers were handsome bastards, but I wasn't about to tell Delia that.

"Where do they all live? Where are you even from?"

"They're all back home in Idaho. Including my sister, Aria."

"Let me guess," she said with a smile. "She's a singer. Or she wants to be."

"Naturally," I said. "How could she be anything else?"

"Self-fulfilling prophecy and all that," Delia said, nodding sagely. "And your brothers?"

I quickly explained what each of them did, and Delia whistled low.

"What about your parents?"

"Ahh..." I started, swallowing around the lump that had taken up residence in my throat. "My mom is in Idaho too. She's sort of the den mother for all the hands at our family ranch, and she helps my brothers out where they need it. My dad is...gone."

I choked on the final word. It had been nearly seventeen years, and it was still difficult to talk about.

My tone must've conveyed enough because Delia didn't press for more. She simply said, "I'm sorry."

"Thanks," I croaked.

"Your family, though...all of you are impressive. Like my sisters."

"Like *you*," I emphasized. "And I wouldn't call being a washed up, retired pro-athlete all that impressive."

Delia met my eyes again, her whiskey depths swimming with something I couldn't name. "So you know what it's like then," she said, so softly I barely heard.

"What what's like?"

"To grow up in a family where your talents can get swallowed and overshadowed by those of your siblings. Then again"—she cocked her head to the side, that heavy, dark curtain of her hair fanning down one of her arms, her intoxicating eyes doing a full sweep of me from head to toe—"you became an NFL quarterback who won two Super Bowls in ten seasons, was named MVP in one of them, and are now a highly successful business owner. So maybe I should be asking your siblings that question."

"I'm not—" I scrambled for a way to phrase this in a way that made sense to her. On paper, yeah, I was successful. And while I'd loved playing football—had always been destined to do so—I recognized that it wasn't an essential profession like cops, teachers, and medical services. I finally settled on, "I'm a quick thinker and good at throwing a football. My brothers are literal heroes. They're certainly mine."

She stepped toward me, tentatively at first, testing whether I'd back away before taking her next. But I couldn't move even if I wanted to, completely entranced by that whiskey gaze and the way it seemed to see right through me. Like she could see the soft underbelly beneath my muscles.

"You're someone's hero too," she said, settling a warm palm on my arm.

I sucked in a breath at the contact, and the moment lengthened between us. Time seemed to warp and stretch, cocooning us in a bubble where I forgot about everything that existed outside of it.

I could think of nothing but the blood pumping through my veins, her pulse fluttering against the smooth skin of her pretty neck, and how badly I wanted to press my lips, my tongue, my teeth to that spot—and everywhere else she'd let me.

Delia inhaled and leaned toward me.

Fuck, we were really doing it, weren't we? There'd be no going back, and I didn't give a fuck. Despite being someone who made a life and career out of being cautious, I welcomed the recklessness of this moment with open arms.

With her, I wanted to be wild.

I wanted her so badly I was afraid I'd die if I didn't shoot my shot. I tilted my head to the side, lifting a hand to delve my fingers into her hair—

And then my office door flew open.

We jumped apart like we were on fire.

"Boss," Hugo said, unperturbed by what he'd interrupted. "We've got a problem."

I didn't look at him, stare still locked on Delia. "So handle it."

"Ahh…" Hugo started. "As much as I'd like to—and I tried, as did the other guys—unfortunately this one requires your…special touch."

Fuck.

That could only mean one thing: some belligerent asshole was demanding to see the boss, and he wouldn't take no for an answer. We'd had a few instances like this since I'd opened the place, and there was only one thing that would quell this brand of drama—me making an appearance. But I knew from experience that me dragging my ass downstairs would have one of two receptions. Either everyone would settle as I slid behind the bar, or a dangerous riot of excitement would ensue as people pushed and shoved their way to the front and center of my attention.

Delia cleared her throat and retreated further, sucking in a deep breath. "I should get back to my sisters anyway," she said, not looking at me.

"Hugo and I will walk you down," I said. "I don't want you getting caught in the crossfire."

She quirked a brow dubiously. "How bad could it be?"

Those proved to be famous last words, which we discovered quickly as we descended onto the main floor.

The second I stepped off the final stair, I was mobbed, Delia pressed close to my side, jostled between me and Hugo.

Cheers had gone up when I appeared on the landing, and the moment I reached the floor, the crowd surged, my patrons desperately seeking my attention. Shouts of my name rang out, and random objects waved in the air over our heads—everything from napkins and receipts to, inexplicably, a pair of panties and a white tank top. I didn't want to know who they belonged to, wasn't interested in learning if tonight was yet another night in which naked women traipsed around my club. My only focus was Delia, who had reached for me before the mass of people closed around us and glued herself to my side.

I'd never forgive myself if something happened to her because of me.

"I want you to leave!" I yelled at her over the melee, curling my arm around her waist to keep her from getting swept away. "Grab your sisters and get the fuck out of here."

Delia shook her head. "I'm not leaving you to deal with this by yourself! We're partners, remember?"

"Not in this business we're not!"

"I don't care."

I laced my fingers through hers, shifting her slightly in front of me, trying my best to shield her from the worst of the sharp elbows finding their way into my own back and sides. Hugo and other members of my staff ran interference around us. "I'm not by myself," I said, my lips pressed to the shell of her ear so I didn't have to shout. "I have my security team."

"Yeah, and they're doing a great job," she said, her sarcasm punctuated by glass shattering nearby.

And, okay, she wasn't wrong. The crowd pushed and shoved against me and the four hulking men, two of whom were former offensive linemen who had protected my ass for much of my ten years in Detroit.

I'd found myself in a few of these situations since opening the club, but tonight felt different. There was a malice in the air I hadn't experienced before, and the hair at the nape of my neck stood on end. I'd spent so many years allowing grown men to throw their bodies at me, had suffered enough scrapes and bruises—in addition to a few concussions and broken bones, saying nothing of my career-ending injury—that nothing really phased me anymore.

But tonight? I was scared.

Not for myself. I was big, heavy, and strong. I could take care of myself.

No, I was worried for Delia.

"Will you please just go?" I wasn't above begging, and if I could've got down on my knees amidst the crush of bodies, I would have.

Delia vigorously shook her head, slamming into my body as someone pushed her from behind. Her eyes were steely, defiant, as she said, "No. I'm staying here with you."

Why was she so goddamn stubborn? Why wouldn't she just leave and let me handle this myself?

A trainwreck was approaching, and it seemed no matter what I said, we'd both be here to greet it.

I saw the collision a breath before it happened.

A man lifted a bottle, clearly intent on breaking it over Hugo's head with the man's back turned to him like a goddamn coward. I wasn't close enough, not without shoving Delia out of the way, and I refused to throw her to the wolves like that. But she must've seen my gaze widen, because she turned to find what I stared at. Quick as lightning, her hand snatched out, her fingers circling the man's wrist. The strength in those slender arms surprised me as she held him off, even as the caveman in my chest roared at me to come to her rescue.

The man with the bottle whirled on her, other arm raised, fist clenched as though preparing to drive it into the center of her face. Before I could move, though, one look at her beauty had him grinning, slowly and slyly, both arms lowering. Two seconds flat and she had him fully entranced.

I knew the feeling.

"Helloooooooo, gorgeous," the man slurred.

I groaned. Whoever was bartending tonight was getting a severe reprimand for not cutting him off before this shit started.

"Put the bottle down," Delia said firmly.

"Or what?"

Seemingly out of nowhere, the younger Delatous sisters appeared at her back, and Ella held Delia's phone out to her.

After a few taps of the screen, Delia began recording, holding the camera right in the man's face.

"Or I'll blast this video of your face all over social media and get you blacklisted from every club and bar in this entire fucking country."

The man sneered. "You don't have that kind of pull."

Delia stepped closer, a feline grin on her face. "Try me."

"I'd listen to her if I was you," I said, and the man's eyes widened as he took me in.

"Owen!" the man yelped like we were old friends. "I just wanted to say hi and get an autograph."

"Hi," I deadpanned in response. "What's your name?"

The man grinned, digging into his shirt pocket and withdrawing a dirty napkin. "Ned," he said, extending it to me. "Ned Fleck."

"Well, *Ned*, you're not getting an autograph," I said, barely restraining myself from swatting his hand away. "In fact, you're never setting foot in one of *my* establishments again." I inclined my head toward Delia. "Wanna go for broke?"

After a beat in which the man's gaze darted back and forth between me and Delia, he settled for spitting, "Fuck you, you stupid bitch," at her.

That was a mistake.

Rage boiled my blood, a killing calm settling over me. Like it was fourth and goal with the game on the line, and the linebacker across from me had me in his crosshairs. Like he'd just insulted my mother, and I was going to make him live to regret it.

With a gentle palm against her stomach, I pushed Delia out of the way, behind me and into the embrace of her sisters...

And drove my fist into the bastard's face.

One hit was all it took before he was on the ground, blood spurting from his nose. From his back, the man hissed like a snake, threatening to call the cops, to sue me, to take all my money and businesses away from him.

He continued to spew vitriol at me as my team lifted him up and carried him out the door.

chapter 12
Owen

IN THE WAKE OF the physical altercation, the chaos in the club died in an instant, the building becoming so quiet I could probably easily hear a whisper from the other side of the dance floor. Once the douchebag was gone, I saw no reason for me to stay open any longer.

"Everybody out!" I shouted. "Lawless is officially closed for the night!"

Groans rose from the crowd, but I simply met Hugo's eyes over the heads of my guests. With a knowing nod, he began ushering people out onto the street, and I breathed a heavy sigh of relief that this nightmare was finally ending.

"Where the fuck is she?" a voice yelled from the entrance.

Or maybe not.

"I'm sorry, sir. You can't come in here," the bouncer at the door told whoever it was, though he was short enough that I could only see the top of his head.

"My girlfriend is in there, you dumbass. Get out of my way!"

"Alfie?" Ella whispered from behind me, and I turned to her as she pushed past Delia and Brie, weaving through the crowd to greet her guy.

"What is he doing here?" Brie asked quietly.

"Who the fuck knows," Delia replied, then grabbed her sister's hand. "C'mon. We better go see what the fuss is about."

Silently, I followed behind the Delatou women as they made their way toward the door.

I didn't know much about Ella's boyfriend beyond the fact that I hated him. He was the opposite of everything I stood for, especially where women were concerned: misogynistic, prideful, overly invested in archaic gender roles. Even a few hours in his presence made me realize how much he belittled Ella. And if I knew anything about the Delatou women, first from that summer with and subsequent years knowing Amara, and now working side by side with Delia, it was that they didn't take kindly to men telling them what to do. This guy must've had a really magical dick to make Ella act this way—or he was gaslighting the shit out of her. Either way, I didn't like it one bit, and I could tell her sisters didn't either.

All through dinner, I hadn't missed how the corners of Delia's eyes pinched with worry as she silently observed their interactions. Alfie managed to put Ella down at every opportunity, even over things as inconsequential as her asking for a second glass of wine or wanting the last little piece of bread.

The guy needed to be taught a lesson, but unfortunately, it wasn't my place to do so.

"What the fuck are you doing *here*?" Alfie spat at Ella, and instantly my hackles rose. I inhaled deeply, schooling my temper.

The last thing I needed was to drop another guy with a fist to the face tonight.

"My sisters wanted to go out," Ella said simply.

"You didn't need to go with them," he said. "In fact, I'm fairly certain I told you not to."

"She doesn't answer to you," Delia said coolly, and though I couldn't see her face, I knew that whiskey gaze was burning a hole through Alfie.

"She does, actually," he said. "Mind your own fucking business."

"Excuse you—" I started, fully preparing to—well, I didn't know what yet, but I knew it didn't involve sitting here while this little twit insulted Delia and Ella.

But Delia's warm palm settled on my chest, somehow instantly soothing me as she said, "He's not worth it." Then she angled her head to look at her sister. "Remember what I said in the car."

Ella's face pinched, her eyes lining with silver, but she dipped her head. Her shoulders rose and fell as she inhaled and exhaled sharply, then once again faced her boyfriend.

"I'm sorry," she said to Alfie. "Let's just go."

"Good girl," he said, as though praising a dog. "I don't know why you wanted to come here anyway. I told you these guys your sisters hang out with are a bunch of tools anyway."

The leash on my rage frayed, near snapping, and only Delia's hand still resting on my pec kept me in check.

As Alfie led Ella away, gripping her upper arm too tightly for my liking, she glanced over her shoulder and mouthed, "I'm sorry," to her sisters.

"God, I fucking hate that guy," Delia grumbled.

"Me too," Brie said, looking at her sister. "You ready to go home?"

"I'm going to stay and help Owen clean up this mess, actually," Delia said, looking at me. "If that's okay with you."

"Of course. I'll drive you home," I said. I wasn't going to turn down the chance for more time with her. "But you don't have to."

"I want to," she assured me. Then to Brie: "Are you okay to drive?"

Brie nodded. "I only nursed a single drink, wanting to keep an eye on Ella when you disappeared."

Satisfied her sister would be safe, Delia passed her keys off to Brie. "I'll come get the car tomorrow. Or you can crash in the guest room. Whichever you want."

"I'm not going to say no to sleeping in the world's comfiest bed," Brie said, shooting her sister a wink and disappearing into the night.

"The world's comfiest bed?" I asked, quirking a brow at Delia.

"It's nothing fancy," she said with a shrug. "Just one of those Purple mattresses, but it's a king. She can only fit a full in her apartment above the bakery, and she's a bit of a starfish when she's sleeping. Personally, I don't understand why she doesn't just buy a house with a bigger bedroom. It's not like she can't afford it."

I knew each of the Delatou girls had sizable trust funds, though all of them were content to work for their money, a trait I'd always appreciated both in them, and in their parents for instilling it.

"So why doesn't she?"

"She likes being close to the shop," Delia said, and I instantly understood. After all, I spent ninety percent of my time in my office upstairs, the control freak in me needing to be as near to my business empire as I could be.

Before I could say anything else to Delia, Hugo approached.

"Security footage from tonight has been combed and...edited. Our guy has been added to the blacklist."

Delia gasped and looked at me. "That's a real thing?"

I nodded. "I've got a document in my computer with the people who have pissed me off enough to never be allowed back through the doors."

Delia's eyes widened. "How many names are on it?"

"Enough," I said, winking.

"Fuck!" Delia cursed suddenly. "I'd forgotten about the video I took." She unlocked her phone and tapped around, holding it up to show me as she deleted the video of me punching that guy in the face.

"No one will ever see it. Though we should probably take care of that," she added, gesturing to my knuckles.

I'd experienced injuries far worse, but as soon as she mentioned it, I couldn't ignore the stinging of my split skin. She moved behind the bar and scrounged up a clean, dry towel, filling it with ice. Then she strode back out onto the floor and dropped down into a booth, scooting over and patting the seat next to her.

"I'm sorry your first night on the job didn't exactly go as planned," I said when I settled at her side, wincing as she set the towel on my knuckles. "And I really wish you wouldn't have confronted that guy."

Delia scoffed. "You don't have to worry about me, QB. You think that's the first time I've been caught in the middle of a bar fight?"

I raised a brow. The thought of her being involved in something like that had that basic instinct to *protect, protect, protect* once again rising within me. I lifted my uninjured hand and rubbed my fist against my sternum, trying to soothe the sensation.

I realized in that instant that Delia Delatou didn't need saving.

She needed a partner, an equal, someone who always had her back and believed in her ability to handle her own shit. She was a woman fully capable of making her own choices, and the beast in my chest needed to stand the fuck down.

"What happened?"

"It was blazing hot in the dead of summer, and there was a band that night at Granny's, so the whole place was packed. I was sweating worse than usual thanks to line dancing song after song."

Line dancing? God, why did the thought of her two-stepping have desire tightening my skin? I could easily picture her in a pair of boots, jeans clinging to her long legs, and a little red bandana as a shirt, moving around the dance floor in my arms.

What the fuck, Lawless? I mentally slapped myself. *Get your shit together.*

Delia continued, oblivious to my internal strife. "I stepped outside for some fresh air, and I heard shouting coming from around the side of the building. When I went to investigate, I found a guy with his palm wrapped around a girl's throat—and not in the sexy, hand necklace kind of way—pushing her up against the side of a vehicle. *My* vehicle."

My lizard brain latched onto the words "hand necklace," wondering what my own would look like around Delia's pretty neck.

Fucking hell, I needed to cool off.

Clearing my throat, I said, "So what'd you do?"

"Told him to back the hell off. Instead of slithering away after being caught, he came at me. I had a bottle of beer in my hand, and when he lifted his fist to do god knows what to me, I beat him to the punch...literally."

"You didn't."

Delia smirked, shifting the ice around on my hand. "I did," she said proudly. "Hit him squared on the jaw."

I winced at the thought of a sturdy, glass bottle slamming into my cheek. God, she continued to surprise me. Tough as nails with a backbone of steel. My brother Lane would have a field day with her. "What happened after that?"

"The guy I'd been with at the time came outside looking for me and caught the asshole just as he was about to lunge for me. It pissed the guy off enough that he swung at my date...and got arrested for assaulting an off-duty police officer."

A cop? Of course she'd dated a cop. Hadn't I just been thinking about her and Lane too? *That* was the kind of guy she should be with. Not me, the washed up quarterback who's never once saved a life. Who hasn't carried burn victims out of flaming buildings, or thrown himself in front of a bullet to save another human. I definitely hadn't protected the goddamn President of the United States.

Throwing a football and getting people to drink was all I'd ever been good for. I went from providing daytime entertainment on Sundays to nighttime entertainment every other day of the week while Delia was dating fucking *cops*.

The self-loathing I experienced in that moment damn near choked me. For being unable—or maybe unwilling?—to do anything worthwhile with my life. I'd simply made it possible for my brothers to do those things instead. Not to mention, there wasn't any reason for me to be jealous about who Delia was or wasn't dating. That was none of my business. *Our* business was as far as I should take any concern for her.

Though Delia had stayed behind to help me clean up, we found ourselves spending the next half hour in that booth, chatting about nothing and everything. She left my side only once to dispose of the towel and ice when my fingers were so numb I could barely move them. And while my body certainly had notions of grandeur where she was concerned, I managed to keep myself in check, and found myself enjoying that quiet, easy time with her. Where we weren't arguing over some distillery related thing or flitting from one task to the next. It was like we'd been friends forever.

It should've embarrassed me how badly I wanted to be her friend, knowing that's all we'd ever be. The almost kiss earlier had been a moment of weakness brought on by the dim lighting and her sexy little dress. It was a line we couldn't cross for so many goddamn reasons—and I hated every single one.

"Everyone is gone and everything is cleaned up, boss," Hugo said when he approached the table and popped our little bubble. "Me and the guys are going to head out. You leaving too, or are you going to be here for a bit?"

I spared Delia a brief glance, then checked my watch, noting it was well after one in the morning. "We'll follow you out."

After locking the doors and setting the alarms, I walked Delia to my truck, internally giddy when she didn't protest my insistence I open her door and help her into the cab.

Tonight had been...exhausting, to say the least. Being a business owner—particularly of establishments that sold alcohol—often wasn't easy, but it should've been easier than this.

I'd never understand why people thought they deserved some sort of exclusive access to me because they were coming to my business. Even when I was actively playing football and representing the city of Detroit, I never enjoyed that part of it. The fame, this god status normal people assigned to us simply because we played a sport on an international stage. We weren't the kind of people who deserved that level of praise and hero worship.

Hero worship should be reserved for *actual heroes*, people saving lives every day by running into burning buildings or working in emergency rooms or serving in our armed forces.

I'd done what I could while in the NFL, using my celebrity status to contribute to numerous charitable and nonprofit organizations over the course of my career, but it never felt like enough.

"You okay over there?" Delia asked, pulling me from my internal raging. "I can literally hear your wheels turning."

"I'm fine. Just...thinking about tonight," I said. "People are fucking crazy."

Delia huffed out a laugh. "Understatement of the century." She shifted slightly in her seat, angling her body toward me.

"Does that happen a lot?"

"That's probably the"—I drummed my fingers on the steering wheel as I counted—"sixth major incident since I opened the club. Though tonight, at least no one but me and that asshole ended up bloodied."

Delia folded a leg under her butt, and that fucking dress rode up, barely covering the apex of her thighs. My gaze darted down to that darkened alcove between her legs, but I quickly tore it away, focusing on the road.

"I've gotta hear *that* story," she said.

So I told her, how this guy—who I'd actually had a few issues with back in Detroit; the man really took the whole hero worship thing to a level I had never experienced before and I hoped I wouldn't again—came into the bar, somehow made it past security, and showed up in my office. A shiver passed through me at the memory of that crazed look in his eyes, how I'd narrowly talked him out of my office and back downstairs. How I'd slid behind the bar to serve him a drink and, when I made another one for a customer standing next to him who, by the way, *did not* make me fear for my life, he turned to that girl, hauled her back against his chest, and held a fucking knife to her neck.

"And *then*," I continued when Delia sucked in a shocked breath, "when Hugo tried to intervene, in his haste to scramble away, the guy cut the girl he'd been holding hostage—nothing major—and fell backward, winding up with the knife lodged in his own leg. His fall caused a chain reaction. You know one of those comical things you see in movies? He bumped into another guy, who accidentally dumped his drink on a girl nearby, whose boyfriend took offense and punched him in the face, and then a whole brawl ensued. The cops were called, multiple ambulances arrived to deal with all the wounded, and the fire department showed up for crowd control. It was…not a highlight of my entrepreneurial career."

"So what you're telling me is there's never a dull moment when you're around," Delia said, and I glanced over in time to see her eyes shining with glee, a small smirk tipping up the corners of her full mouth. "Maybe we're more alike than you thought, QB."

I held that stare longer than was probably safe while behind the wheel, but I couldn't look away. I hadn't consumed a drop of alcohol that night, but I was drunk all the same.

Delia had that effect.

I swear something shifted between us then. I was transported right back to that moment in my office when I'd nearly thrown caution to the wind and kissed her.

But the moment broke when I was forced to return my attention to the road, and like a balloon being deflated, that shimmering in the air dissipated.

When I pulled up in front of her house, Delia slowly unbuckled and stared at me expectantly, as though waiting for me to make a move.

But I wasn't going to. Wasn't going there with her.

I couldn't.

"Good night, Whiskey," I said softly, avoiding her gaze like a fucking coward.

After a beat, Delia said with a resigned sigh, "Good night, QB," and got out of the truck.

I waited until she stepped inside, offering me a small wave then flipping off the porch light, before I drove away. As I wound my way through the sleepy streets of Apple Blossom Bay, I breathed the first lungful of air I'd managed in hours. Hugo interrupting us in my office before anything could happen had been a blessing, and only my barely-there self-control had stopped me from rectifying that wrong before she got out of my truck.

Working and sleeping together, while ultimately working out in their favor in the end, had made things so messy and complicated for Amara and Calvin. I was going to learn from their mistakes. I didn't need *messy* or *complicated*. I'd had enough of that bullshit with my ex, and the other women I'd screwed around with during my playing days. What I needed was to get the distillery open and keep my dick out of Delia Delatou.

chapter 13
Delia

MY FAVORITE PART OF those first two weeks of October was seeing everyone enjoy the fruits of my labors. And that's not me saying the whole festival wouldn't have been possible without my help, because each member of this community equally contributed. But...I did a lot, and the corn maze in particular was my pride and joy. That year, I'd instructed the planters to create a maze shaped like a giant Jack-O-Lantern, complete with a crooked-toothed smile. I'd stopped by one day on my way up to the distillery site to check in on things, and was greeted by the happy sounds of children's laughter and screams carrying on the wind. The barn was full of people milling in and out, each and every one of them munching on one of Brie's creations and singing its praises.

TJ was there too, driving the tractor, grinning and waving wildly at me from behind the wheel. My responding greeting was, admittedly, lackluster in the face of all that enthusiasm.

"You going to be around for a bit?" he shouted at me as he

puttered past.

I shook my head, thankful I had plans. "No! I have to run to the winery and then up to the distillery job site."

"Okay," he said, unperturbed by my brush off. "I'll call you later!"

Please don't, I thought as I offered a final wave and headed toward my car.

We'd only seen each other twice since our date at Granny's. Thankfully, he hadn't tried to kiss me or press our relationship into physical territory beyond hand holding. I wasn't sure what I'd do when that day inevitably came.

Honestly, it was a wonder I hadn't cut him loose. I felt bad stringing him along, but I also wasn't ready to snip that cord quite yet, wasn't ready to give up on something that could morph beyond the superficial friendship I felt for him.

God, I was the worst.

But I didn't have time to worry about it.

Preparations for Ezra's Wine & Dine event were in full swing, and he'd sent me a text the night before, stressing about getting the food and wine pairings just right. Not one to turn down a free Ezra Wendt meal, I told him I'd come by the winery today and we'd figure it out together.

But I hadn't been prepared to find Owen bellied up to the island in the center of the kitchen when I walked in.

I couldn't help the grin that spread across my face. "What are you doing here?" I asked as I slid onto the stool next to him.

Owen shrugged. "Ez needed help. I'm happy to offer my palate."

I looked at Ezra, who smiled blandly. "Then why am I here?"

"I needed both of you," he said.

I held back a snort. The guy was good, I'd give him that. There was no way this wasn't payback for forcing him and Brie to work together on this event. Truthfully, if anyone should be here helping him make these decisions, it would be her, not me.

But I digress. With Owen's warmth seeping into my side despite the few feet between us, his heavenly male scent combining with the various dishes Ezra had in the works, wrapping me in a warm, comfortable blanket, I wasn't going to complain.

"So what's first?" I asked.

"The first course is appetizers, and I'm planning on offering three of them so there's a bit of a selection. I was thinking pumpkin deviled eggs, stuffed mushrooms, and bacon wrapped Brussels sprouts."

Owen groaned next to me, low and long. The sound shot straight between my thighs, settling there like a pulse. Hell, if I was going to have to put up with that the entire time we were here? I wasn't sure I'd survive.

"And what were you thinking for the wine?"

Ezra moved around to the side of the island, where several bottles of CD wines were grouped together, shuffling things around until he came away with a bottle of bubbly.

"Prosecco," he said, holding it out to me. I accepted it and poured Owen and myself each a small glass.

A moment later, Ezra settled a long, narrow plate in front of each of us, each topped with an egg, mushroom, and Brussels sprout.

"So, before you take a bite and are like, 'what the fuck, Ez,' the deviled eggs aren't actually made with any pumpkin. They're just made to *look* like a pumpkin in the way I piped the yolk mixture, darkened it with a few drops of food coloring, and added that little piece of chive to look like a stem."

With a flourish of his hand, he instructed us to proceed, and I didn't need to be told twice. Deviled eggs were one of my favorite appetizers. Normally I'd stuff the entire thing in my mouth in one go, but I wanted to savor this. As I bit off about a third, flavors exploded on my tongue. The bright, tangy yolk, mayonnaise, and Dijon mixture. The slight bite of the paprika. The smooth texture of the egg white with the creaminess of the yolk—it was divine.

Owen once again made that noise in the back of his throat, and I glanced over to find his entire egg gone, his cheeks bulging. Once he'd chewed and swallowed, he said, "Fucking hell, Ez. Are you sure I can't convince you to come work for me?"

Ezra cut me an apologetic glance, as though it mattered to me whether he stayed at CD or went to work at Birdie's. "I'm happy here," he said.

"Job is yours whenever you want it," Owen said, turning his attention to me. "No offense."

"None taken," I said, chuckling softly at the glob of egg yolk mixture that had settled on the corner of his mouth. Before I could stop myself, I reached up and brushed it away, my thumb snagging his soft, plump lower lip to the side. And without thinking, I popped my thumb into my mouth, sucking it clean.

"You missed some."

Owen didn't react, only stared at me for several long heartbeats before dropping his eyes back to his plate, suddenly engrossed in the next appetizer offering.

Naturally, the mushroom and Brussels sprout were equally as delicious as the egg, and I told Ezra so, agreeing the Prosecco was the perfect pairing for all three—something light and effervescent to complement the heavier foods.

Even as we continued to eat, panic coursed through me over what I'd done. I'd crossed so many lines, touching Owen like that, and the way he refused to look at me indicated I'd made him uncomfortable—something I'd never forgive myself for. Why hadn't I kept my hands to myself? What was it about this man that had me ignoring all the red flags begging me to turn back?

Owen himself wasn't a red flag. In fact, as far as men went, he was the biggest *green* flag I'd ever seen. Everything about him urged me to pass GO, to collect that two hundred dollars.

But that wasn't our relationship, and Owen wasn't a prize I could take for myself. Eventually, he would belong to someone else. I had to content myself with being nothing more than his business partner and friend.

"Next," Ezra said, returning my attention to the task at hand, "we have butternut squash soup. The squashes are sourced locally, which is something that's very important to me, as you know," he added to me. "I'm trying to use local ingredients wherever possible, but I'm also trying to keep recipes relatively simple. I want to show the great citizens of Apple Blossom Bay that creating beautiful, delicious, restaurant-quality food doesn't have to be difficult or expensive."

I nodded, completely on board with that plan.

My family was an outlier on the peninsula. The people of this area were firmly middle class. They worked hard for their money and lived comfortably if modestly. The fact that Ezra—a relative newcomer to the area and someone I knew was well-off thanks to the behemoth salary he'd received at his previous job—recognized this and wanted to make these dishes accessible warmed my heart.

"How much are you selling tickets for?" Owen asked.

"Fifty bucks," Ezra said. I already knew this, but the amount was still staggeringly low—the wine alone would eat up a sizable chunk of any budget had the winery not been donating all of it.

"I'd like to match however much you make," Owen said.

"Me too," I piped up.

Ezra looked at me. "You don't have to do that, Delia," he said. "You already give so much to this place."

"Please," I said, waving him off. "It's the *least* I can do. Which reminds me...have you decided where you're donating proceeds yet?"

"Well now that the event is bringing in three times as much as I'd anticipated"—he shot each of us a glare—"I can help more people. I was thinking Farms for Folks, the volunteer fire department, and..."

"And what?" Owen prompted.

"The last one was kind of a pipe dream but now that I can make it a reality, I'd really like to set up a scholarship fund at the high school in Traverse City for a kid who wants to study culinary arts. I wouldn't be where I am today if someone hadn't offered me a helping hand when I needed it, and now it's time for me to pay it forward."

I breathed deeply, willing the threat of tears stinging my nose away, and gave Ezra a smile.

"You should ask for Brie's help with that last one," I said

quietly.

"I'll think about it," Ezra said, equally as soft. Then with a harsh clap that had me jolting on my chair, he brusquely moved onto serving the soup.

The next hour passed in a flurry of great food, delicious wine, and good company. After my earlier faux pas, the tension between me and Owen was still thick enough to cut with a butter knife. He seemed inclined to ignore it, though, so I followed his lead.

When we wrapped up, Brie having strode in toward the end to present us with the dessert course options, which were being paired with our world-famous ice wine at Ezra's request, Owen disappeared with barely a goodbye to me.

Maybe everything I thought I'd felt between us over the weekend at the club had been in my head, a fever dream brought on by the strobe lights and chaos. If that was how he reacted to me simply wiping food off his face, I'd clearly misread everything.

"What's his problem?" Brie asked when Owen was gone.

"Delia touched his mouth," Ezra said unhelpfully.

Brie's face scrunched in confusion, her green eyes narrowing on me. "Explain, please."

Quickly, I recounted the few, innocuous seconds that seemed to throw off our entire dynamic. When I finished, my sister said to Ezra, "Remember that day Amara and Cal came in here for the summer menu tasting?"

Ezra's answering grin was positively feline. "Why do you think I invited these two here today?"

Brie barked out a laugh. "You're wicked."

Ezra shrugged. "It worked so well last time."

"And that wasn't even on purpose," Brie added with a chuckle.

"Will someone tell me what the fuck you guys are talking about?"

They shared the kind of look that told me a thousand words passed unspoken between them in those few seconds of eye contact. Then Brie said, "Nah."

"You little shit."

"You'll figure it out soon enough."

"Whatever," I huffed out as I rose from my seat.

"Hey, before you leave," Brie said, stalling me, "I wanted to ask what your plans for Halloween are."

"Well, it's my birthday, so same as every year."

"Halloween is your birthday?" Ezra asked, surprised.

I smirked. "Explains a lot, doesn't it?"

He responded with a laugh before saying, "So what's the same-as-every-year plan?"

"I'm hosting a party!"

"Party" was a woefully inadequate way to describe the extravaganza I threw every year. I tended to be extra in pretty much everything I did, but I took my birthday seriously, and the fact that it fell on a holiday only added to the madness. I'd deck out my garage, have Brie help me whip up an impressive array of snacks and treats, and force all my friends and family into dressing up.

It was also a given that I'd have the best costume. I had a list in my phone of costumes I'd used in previous years and ones I hadn't yet. This year's might be my favorite yet—an old-fashioned madam. I'd found my dress from a company that specialized in historical dress recreations—and paid a pretty penny to have it custom made and shipped from California. I'd only tried it on once when it arrived to be sure it fit correctly, but I couldn't wait to spend an entire night in it. The details of the dress were so painstakingly crafted that I felt like I was wearing a piece of history. I'd never worn so much clothing—the heavy skirts and full bodice covering me from chest down—yet felt so...sexy. Maybe it was the act of sliding into a different skin, of imagining myself as the type of woman who would've worn such an outfit, who made her living overseeing a brothel.

With a start, I realized we were less than two weeks away from the big event. My instantaneous shock and worry must've been evident on my face, because my sister smiled and said, "I'll be over after I help Ez clean up for a planning session."

I moved to her side and pressed a smacking kiss to her cheek.

"You're the best sister ever."

"I know." I shot her a wink as I strode for the door. "And as your best sister ever," she called after me, "I should tell you that if you don't invite Owen, I will."

That little shit.

Still, her words stuck with me as I drove home, and by the time I'd pulled into my garage, I'd worked myself into a bit of a state, knowing if I didn't call Owen then and invite him, I never would.

Blessedly, the phone rang through to voicemail—and I refused to consider he was blowing me off—and I left a long, rambling message before hanging up in horror and studiously ignoring my phone the rest of the day.

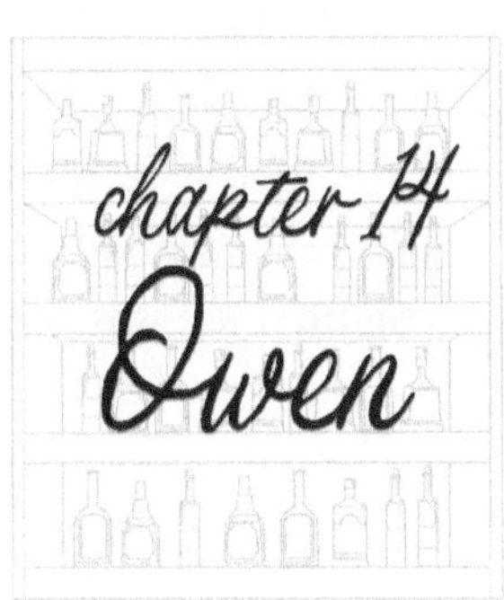

"Hey, QB. It's me. Listen, I'm not sure what you're up to next weekend, and you're probably going to be holed up at the club like you are every Saturday but if you're miraculously free or whatever, I'm having a birthday slash Halloween party at my house and it'd be really cool if you stopped by. I mean, everyone would love to see you. But also totally fine if you can't make it. Okay I'm going to go now. See you at our meeting on Wednesday. Bye!"

I listened to Delia's rambling voicemail no fewer than ten times, my grin growing wider with each one. Despite my horrible overreaction to her touching my mouth, she *wanted* me at her party. Truthfully, it wasn't even the touch that sent me over the edge. It was the way she'd shoved that thumb in her mouth and sucked it clean, heat flaring in eyes that never left mine. That was dangerous territory, to allow ourselves to remember we were a man and a woman with urges and not strictly business partners who needed to keep our southern regions far away from each other.

But the fact that she was pushing past the awkwardness from earlier—and my rude and abrupt departure—to invite me meant something to me. It meant she really wanted me there, and if she wanted me there, I'd be there. No questions asked. The club could handle itself for a night. That was, after all, why I paid my men so handsomely.

My first order of business was to pull together a costume. I wanted to make this special for Delia, to really put an effort into dressing up and not half-ass it like normal.

So I called my inside source for ideas.

"What's your sister wearing to her party next week?" I asked unceremoniously when Amara answered.

"Hello to you too, Owen," she said. "How are you? Business good? How's that big ass family of yours?"

"Sorry," I said sheepishly. "I'm good. Business is great. Family is happy and healthy."

"That's good," Amara said. "Now what can I do for you?"

"You can help me figure out what to wear to Delia's party next weekend. What are you and Cal dressing up as?"

"Bella and Edward," Amara said, the names proudly leaving her lips like I was supposed to know what they meant.

"I have no idea what that means."

"I didn't either!" Cal shouted from the background, and I laughed.

"They're fictional characters. Ever heard of *Twilight*?"

"Only in passing," I said. Aria had been obsessed with it when she was in high school and talked my ear off about it every time I'd called home for three months straight.

"Okay well in the final book, Edward, the vampire, gets Bella, the human, pregnant. So that's what we're going as. Edward and pregnant Bella."

I chuckled again. Leave it to Amara to base an entire costume around the baby growing in her womb.

"That's great, Mar," I said sarcastically, and I heard Cal snort in the back. "Can we get back to the matter at hand?"

"Which is?"

"What is your sister dressing up as?"

"Why do you want to know?"

"Why can't you just tell me?"

"Because you're sketching me out," she said. "Tell me why you want to know."

"Because I want to wear something to complement her!" I shouted.

Only deafening silence greeted me.

"I mean—" I started as I scrambled to backtrack.

"Oh, no, Owen," Amara said. "I don't think so. You're not getting out of explaining that."

"I just..." I trailed off, then whispered, "I don't know what I'm doing."

"Well, as long as you're not going to fuck her over or fuck her up, I'll tell you."

"Never," I promised.

I didn't know what exactly I was agreeing to, but I knew I meant it. Amara seemed satisfied because she said, "She's dressing up as an old Western brothel madame."

Immediately, an idea came to mind. It wouldn't even require me to go shopping because I already owned everything I needed.

"Thanks, Mar," I said, intent on hanging up and going about my day, but she stopped me.

"I feel like I should warn you."

"Warn me about what?"

"TJ."

Unbidden, my blood pressure rose, and I gritted out, "Who is TJ?"

"This guy she's been seeing."

Wait, what? She'd been seeing someone and didn't tell me? Then again...why would she? I was no one to her. Except, I thought our moment at the club had shifted something between us—hence this ridiculous phone call.

"And you're telling me this, why?"

"Because he'll be there. As her...date, I guess."

"Don't worry, Lawless," Cal piped in. "You're much better looking. That guy is a dweeb."

"Ryder!" Amara protested, and I distantly heard the sound of a smack over the roaring in my ears.

"Just saying," Cal added.

"Well, you're not helping. TJ is...nice."

"Nice," I spat. "Delia doesn't need a nice guy."

"It's not up to you to decide what Delia does or doesn't need," Amara scolded.

Inhaling deeply, I held the air in my lungs for five counts, then let it go slowly, allowing the action to ground me. "You're right. Either way, I don't care about...TJ." I spat his name.

"You may not care about him, but you definitely care about *her*," Cal said with a chuckle. "The longer you deny it, the worse it'll be on both of you."

I hung up before either could say anything else to piss me off, though Cal's parting words echoed in my head.

Clearly, things were changing, and my irritation over mention of Delia dating some lame ass guy only proved that. Even armed with that knowledge, I didn't give a fuck if I'd look like a fool showing up in a costume that coordinated with hers.

I was doing it anyway.

The moment I pushed into Delia's garage the following Saturday, my eyes locked on her, like she was a lodestone pulling me in.

Nearly every inch of her was covered by her dress, save her face, the smooth column of her neck, the gentle slopes of her shoulders, and the high swells of her breasts. The sharp ends of her collarbones dragged my gaze to a sunburst-shaped pendant hanging from the wide piece of black velvet wrapped around her throat. The sleeves of the dress draped off her shoulders and stopped right above her elbows, the black lace running the whole way around, before it turned to a burnt orange fabric that swept to the ground. Velvet slippers peaked out beneath the hem as she moved about the room, conversing with her guests.

She was stunning, looking like she'd stepped off the silver screen from one of those Old Western movies, a starlet greeting her adoring fans.

Even though I was having all kinds of them, I didn't want to give Delia any ideas about where we might end up, and I had half a mind to turn tail and race out of here before she could spot me.

But I was too late, and I silently cursed as she turned that megawatt smile on me—and at the satisfaction that surged in my chest.

"Howdy, partner," she said in a terrible Southern accent when she reached me. "You clean up nice."

I scoffed. "My street clothes are nicer than this, Whiskey."

"I like it," she said, still grinning toothily. "We kind of match."

I shrugged, attempting to play it cool despite the fact that we *kind of matched* on purpose. "I didn't know what to wear, and I just had all this lying around." Not a lie, but so far from the whole truth it may as well have been on a different planet.

She quirked a brow. "Even the buckle?"

"Even the buckle," I confirmed. "My dad rode bulls for a few years in his early twenties and won a couple championships. This is the buckle from one of those belts. Plus, you forget I was born and raised in western Idaho. This is basically everyday attire on my family's ranch."

"You're telling me you wore a bolo tie and that hideous cowhide vest every day?"

"Faux cowhide," I corrected. The Lawless ranch had long since stopped slaughtering animals, but that was a story for a different time. "And they were both also my dad's."

"Shit, QB," she said, eyes widening as her hand flew to her mouth. "I'm so sorry. I didn't mean—"

I waved her off. "It's okay. You didn't know."

I still hadn't worked up the strength to share the full story with her, to tell her how and when I'd found out. It wasn't because I didn't want to. It was more because I wasn't ready to pry the lid open on that can of worms and spill my grief at her feet. I'd spent a lot of time over the last seventeen years carefully locking it away.

Plus, those weren't the kinds of things you shared with business partners.

Then again, I showed up wearing what, from the outside, looked an awful lot like the other half to her couple costume. So *maybe*, it was time I stopped lying to myself.

"Delia!" someone shouted from behind me, bounding up to us so quickly they knocked me into her. My hands on her upper arms steadied her, narrowly saving her from spilling her drink down her dress.

I whirled on the person, who turned out to be a twenty-something man several inches shorter than me, his floppy hair and long face giving him the countenance of a puppy.

"Watch where you're going!" I growled at him.

"Sorry," he said, though the grin never left his face. "Just coming to get my girl for pictures."

"Your girl?" I choked out, glancing at Delia.

Her eyes were wide, face panic stricken. "He's not...it's not..." she started quietly, but the guy cut her off.

"TJ," he said happily. "And you are?"

"Owen Lawless," I grumbled. It took everything in me not to puff my chest out and stare down my nose at him.

"Wow," TJ breathed. "It's a pleasure to meet you, sir."

I hummed noncommittally.

I needed to make something clear: I tried to see the allure. I really did.

But I couldn't find a single thing about this guy that should've snagged a woman like Delia. His eyes and hair were the same color, a nondescript brown that was easily forgettable. He was narrow, especially compared to my broad frame, and probably only five-ten, though I would've bet good money he told people he was six-feet. His entire air was...eager. The brightness in his eyes, the grin, the fucking *dalmatian costume.*

I didn't like the guy on principle, mostly because I thought he had delusions of grandeur where his relationship with Delia was concerned.

A man like this could never satisfy her, not the way I could.

TJ turned to Delia. "Ready for some pictures, milady?" He proffered his arm like some Victorian gentleman. Delia only stared at me. Waiting.

But for what?

"Go."

A simple command. Two letters. One syllable. But the way her face fell, the way she reared away from me, you'd think I shot her.

It was better this way. Her with him, me...alone.

After they walked away, Amara and Cal appeared at my side.

"I see you've met TJ."

"Yes."

"Oooooh," Cal said. "Someone is testy."

"How long has that been going on?" I asked, not bothering to look at either of them, unable to take my eyes off Delia and the dweeb.

"Since about mid-September, I think," Amara said. "He asked her out after one of the festival planning meetings."

I winced as he gestured widely and half his glass of something I couldn't name on sight sloshed all over, spilling on the hem of Delia's dress and the concrete at their feet.

"And she...likes him?"

Out of the corner of my eye, I saw Amara shrug. "It's not that deep, Owen. I think she's just...lonely, if I'm being honest."

"But...why?"

"We've all always talked about having families of our own one day," Amara said, linking one hand through Cal's and settling the other on her stomach. "And now that Chloe and I are actually doing it, I think she feels left out."

God, how badly did I also want a family of *my* own? A love and life to fill the void left in my dad's absence?

When I didn't say anything else, Amara and Cal moved away in favor of conversation with Brie, Ella, Ezra, and Liam Danvers, the winery's agricultural engineer—though most people referred to him simply as "the grower." It seemed the entire Chateau Delatou staff was here.

Instead of joining the fray, I remained sentinel against the wall, pounding whiskey like water and covertly watching Delia entertain her guests, TJ following her around like the animal he'd dressed as. Every time he touched her, I flinched, hating the familiarity between them. How the fuck had I not known she was seeing someone? And after the almosts between us at Lawless and again outside this very house that night, what was going through her head? Was she sleeping with him?

My teeth clenched painfully at the idea.

Needing to clear my head, I stepped outside and stalked across the lawn then down the block to my truck. Stuffing myself behind the wheel, I closed my eyes, slamming my skull back into the headrest a few times, trying to jar myself out of my bad mood.

I had no right to Delia, no claim over her time, and no say in who she spent it with.

But I wanted her. I wanted that claim, to monopolize her time, exactly as her dad had accused me of at dinner that night. I wanted *more* nights like that, molding our families and lives together.

She'd snuck up on me, and since visions of a future with her had entered my mind, I couldn't shake them loose.

A tap against my window had my eyes flying open, and I found Delia pressing her face against the glass, gesturing for me to roll it down.

"What're you doing out here?"

"Where'd your boyfriend go?" I retorted, not bothering to hide the iciness of my tone.

"I sent him home."

That pulled me up short, taking the edges off some of my irritation. "Why?"

"It wasn't working out," she said simply.

I dared a quick look at her, and though she didn't meet my eyes, a small smile bloomed on her lips despite her arms crossed defensively over her chest.

"I'm sorry to hear that."

"Get out of the truck, QB."

With a sigh, I rolled the window back up and did as she asked.

"What's your problem?"

"I don't have one."

"Then why were you hiding out in your truck like a loser?"

I exhaled sharply through my nose, schooling my temper. "Just needed a moment."

"You done?"

I grinned and nodded. Knowing that TJ had been kicked to the curb had significantly lightened my mood. I playfully bumped her shoulder with mine and followed her back into the garage.

"So, I know your birthday party is the last place you want to talk about work, but maybe Monday we could sit down and figure out a plan for setting up some stills and get some batches of spirits going? If Jay and the team stay on task, they'll be done in less than a month. I want to get everything perfected so we have plenty on hand for the opening."

Delia grinned at me. "It's a date, QB."

It's a date. It's a date. It's a date.

I hated the way my heart soared at those words.

Later, after the party had wound down and the bulk of her guests were gone, only Delia, Amara, Calvin, and I remained.

"Are you sure you don't want help cleaning up?" Amara asked as Delia politely but insistently shoved her sister toward the door, Cal not far behind.

"I'll help her."

Both sisters stopped dead.

"Oh, that's not necessary," Delia told me. "Really."

"Please."

Delia studied me for a long beat, then shared an unreadable look with her sister. Cal merely quirked a brow at me in question, but I ignored it.

"Fine," Delia said at last, realizing this was a battle she wouldn't win.

Then she gave her sister and Cal kisses on the cheek goodbye, and they left us alone.

"Where do we start?"

"Just help me get the perishables into the fridge," she said, indicating the small white appliance in the corner. "The rest I'll deal with tomorrow."

In silence, we covered the snack trays and put caps on any half-full bottles of mixers, carefully stacking it all in the refrigerator. It took far less time than I would've liked, and Delia didn't utter a single word save directing me to do one thing or another.

When we were done, I scrubbed a hand over the back of my neck, shuffling on my feet. "Well, I guess I better head back."

"Do you want to stay?" Delia blurted.

My brows rose. "Stay...here?"

She nodded. "I don't want you driving back into the city after you've been drinking, and I have a guest room."

"The world's comfiest bed," I said, remembering Brie's comment from that night at Lawless.

"The same one," she confirmed. "Please. I would feel better if you didn't drive."

She was worried about me, and the knowledge pleased me deeply.

"Of course," I answered, because how the fuck was I supposed to say no?

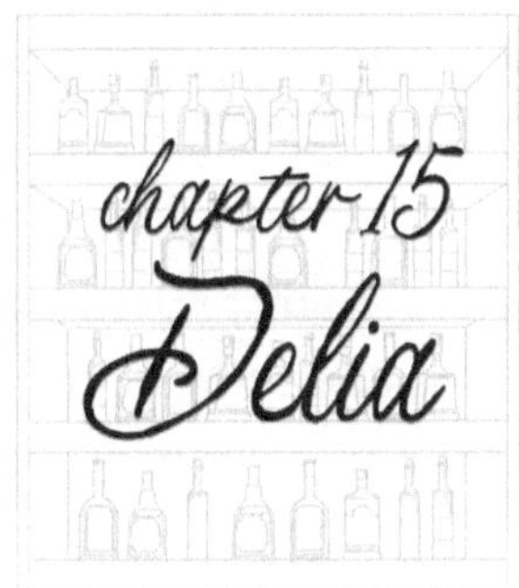

chapter 15
Delia

I WOKE UP THE morning after my party feeling surprisingly perky given all the tequila I'd consumed. After Owen showed up wearing a costume that matched mine perfectly, I lost my head a bit. TJ had dressed as a fucking puppy—a little too on the nose if you asked me—and he hadn't held a candle to Owen in his Levi's. The way the denim molded to his ass, the massive belt buckle drawing the gaze right to his crotch, and the well-worn cowboy hat shading his baby blues...damn, he was stunning. An echo, albeit a more rugged, grown up version, of the teenager he'd been running around his family's ranch in Idaho twenty years ago.

And my stupid heart had practically sung at the sight of him, even if his discomfort was obvious in his hands shoved deep in his pockets, his head bent, completely hiding his face from view. The way he'd walked into my party had been a far cry from the Owen Lawless I'd come to know.

TJ certainly hadn't helped matters, and seeing them standing side by side was a formative moment for me. TJ was a head shorter than Owen and eight years his junior. Skinny next to Owen's bulk. Pale where Owen was tan. Fresh and smooth faced where Owen's was rugged stubble and scars. Boyish where Owen was all man.

I couldn't have Owen, and that was fine. But I realized in that moment that TJ also wasn't the guy for me. When he'd brazenly asked me if I wanted to spend the night together, I'd politely but firmly sent him on his way.

We hadn't even kissed, for crying out loud.

His...enthusiasm for dating me was palpable, and he'd been a lot more invested than I had been. Thankfully, he'd handled my rejection admirably, and I found I didn't feel an ounce of sadness over the end of our relationship.

I stretched myself awake, taking a moment to work out the kinks and stiffness from sleep, then got up, relieved myself, and headed down to the kitchen. Outside my windows, the day was bright and clear, fall still holding us in her grip, winning this last battle before winter ultimately won the war.

As I did every morning when I entered my kitchen, I lifted the little remote off the counter and clicked on the power for the Bluetooth surround-sound system. Morgan Wallen's gritty, beautiful voice filtered through the room. I wiggled my hips, humming the words as I prepared my cup of coffee.

While that was percolating, I moved to the fridge, taking out my pre-cut frozen fruit, almond milk, Greek yogurt, and spinach—the ingredients for my favorite pre-run smoothie.

I'd been blessed with a metabolism that kept my body fairly thin regardless of what I ate or how often I worked out. And

I used to take my gym time very seriously, actively engaging in strength training as a way to stay toned and fit. But once I moved home from college, driving into the city every day for a workout wasn't a commitment I'd been willing to make, and while I had the room, I also hadn't wanted to designate any of my home's square footage to gym space. So I'd taken up running, and quite frankly, it was one of the better ideas I'd ever had. Going out for a jog had become an integral part of my morning routine—when I could stomach the weather. Winters here could be brutal, and on the days when it was snowing or below freezing, I'd do yoga in my living room instead.

Ten minutes and three songs later, freshly blended smoothie raised to my lips for that first delicious sip, I spun from the counter—and let out a scream.

"Nice dance moves."

Hand to my chest, I sucked in gulps of air, my heart racing a thousand miles a minute. "What the fuck," I breathed.

"You forget I was here?" Owen asked.

I sure as hell had, and he knew it. I guessed I'd consumed more tequila than I thought, if I'd forgotten about offering my guest room to the hottest man I'd ever laid eyes on so he wouldn't have to drive back into the city so late.

"I did," I said, offering him a sheepish smile. "Sorry."

"It's fine," he said with a wide grin. Then tilted his head toward the ceiling and added, "I didn't peg you as a country girl."

"What kind of girl did you peg me as then?" I asked, more brazen than I had any right to be considering I wasn't wearing pants.

"EDM," Owen said immediately. "You look like a rave girl."

I arched my brow. "I don't know what a 'rave girl' looks like, but I feel like I should be offended."

"No, of course not. It's just…" Owen opened and shut his mouth a few times, panic flitting briefly across his face before he said, in a rush and voice low, "I bet you look good in fishnets and pasties."

The comment had me choking on my smoothie, and I hurried to the sink so I could spit out the mouthful I'd inhaled before I made matters worse. When I turned back, I was so dumbstruck, all I could do was stare at him. I was surprised, both by his words and by the color blooming high on his chiseled cheekbones. If there was anything I'd learned in the short time since we'd started working together, it was that Owen Lawless had walls as tall as the Eiffel Tower. I wasn't delusional enough to think I'd be the one to break them down. But this moment of weakness from him? This rare admission that he'd noticed me in the same way I couldn't help but notice him? That maybe this attraction I felt for him wasn't all in my head, nor entirely one sided?

It knocked the fucking wind out of me.

When I awoke this morning, I hadn't wanted to examine last night too closely, which was partly the reason I'd forgotten I'd invited him to stay. I hadn't wanted to admit that I liked people asking me if he was my boyfriend thanks to the unintentionally coordinating costumes, and how much I hated the lead weight sinking in my chest when I had to choke out that he was "only my business partner." I couldn't allow myself to bask in the glow of his obvious jealousy that I'd invited a date.

But now…was everything changing?

Owen cleared his throat, rubbing the back of his neck and

shifting awkwardly on his feet. I still hadn't said anything, but I needed to. I needed to save him—to save *us*, to salvage this thing before the moment expanded and morphed into something we couldn't get past.

So I did the first thing that came to mind.

"Would you want to come to this family thing with me today?" I blurted.

Owen's nervous fidgeting stilled, his gaze slowly raising to meet mine. God, I could drown in those eyes, the exact color of the turquoise waters off the shores of Macedonia where my dad's ancestors hailed from. It would be as easy to drown in their depths as it would the ocean.

"Family thing?" he asked, and I didn't blame him for his skepticism.

"It's an old Delatou tradition," I said quickly. "On the first of November every year, we crush grapes the old-fashioned way."

His eyes widened. "Old fashioned as in…"

"Yep," I said, grinning. "With our feet."

My skin from the soles of my feet to my ankles would be stained purplish-red for weeks after, but it had always been one of my favorite days of the year. These days, we had machines to do the heavy lifting, but I loved that we still kept the old-school grape crushing tradition alive. The liquid yielded from our efforts would end up dumped behind the barn, but it was a fun throwback to the days when wine had been made that way. Plus, it served as a reminder of the difficult work the Delatou men and women before us put into making the winery and our entire business enterprise a lasting success.

As little girls, my sisters and I had treated it as a national holiday. We'd wake before the sun, begging Mom and Dad to take us to the barn to get started. Vividly, I remembered the first time I'd sunk into a bucket of red grapes, could easily recall the soft give of them underfoot as I worked my toes into them. The sliminess as the skins split open, the stems poking the delicate skin of my arches. How my thighs and calves would burn after hours of standing and stomping and squishing.

As we got older, the occasion had grown into a day-long celebration. We'd crack open the first case of ice wine from the season before, grill on the ancient charcoal fire pit Dad built outside the barn when he was a teen, and celebrate with one of Brie's latest confections from Granny Smith's recipe book.

Owen opened his mouth, and by the way the skin between his brows puckered, I thought for sure he'd reject me.

But the man continued to surprise me.

"I'd love to," he said softly.

I couldn't hold back the wide grin that unfurled on my face.

"Great!" I said, unable to curb my enthusiasm. "Do you want—"

"I need to go home," he said quickly. "You know, to shower and change. Can I meet you there? Just tell me where to go."

I explained how to get to the barn, though given that we'd only closed down the corn maze for the season the day before, there were still signs out on the dirt two-track indicating the way. Owen nodded, agreeing to be there by noon, then took off without another word.

Maybe things weren't changing between us after all.

Now, more than ever, I needed my run, needed to let the steady cadence of my footfalls on asphalt drown out my roaring thoughts.

So I laced up my Hokas and set off.

* * *

The run proved to be completely useless, and I'd managed to work myself into quite the state by the time I arrived at the barn later. When I pulled into the little gravel lot off to the side, I counted cars, realizing I was the last to arrive.

Even Owen had beat me.

At least the man was punctual, though it did nothing for the nerves writhing in my gut.

With a heavy sigh, I pushed out of my Jeep, dragging my feet the whole way to the barn. Facing the firing squad wasn't high on my list of priorities today—or ever. Still, I squared my shoulders the moment before I rounded the corner to the giant opening created by the doors swung wide, my chin lifted high as I stepped onto the concrete floor.

My dad spotted me first, brow furrowing at my silent entrance. Normally, I'd make a scene, make everyone aware that I had arrived. Today, I wanted to be as small as possible, and he quickly recognized something was off with me.

When he approached, he folded me in a tight hug, and I allowed his Old Spice scent and fatherly warmth to wash over and soothe me.

"You okay, kiddo?" he asked softly against my hair.

"I don't know," I answered honestly.

My sisters and I didn't typically keep secrets from our parents. Sure, when something happened, we always told each other before we told them, but our parents were normally apprised of whatever the situation not long after. In fact, in recent memory, the only time I could think of where we did withhold information was when Amara and Calvin started their...*mutually beneficial* situation. And, of course, they were unaware of my college...escapades. Mostly because I was terrified Daddy would go scorched earth if he found out. So in that moment, I gave him the truthful response. I didn't know if I was okay. My emotions were a swirling, confusing maelstrom. I couldn't make sense of anything—and Owen wasn't helping matters.

As though my thoughts had conjured him, when my father released me, holding me at arm's length to study my face, my gaze collided with Owen's over his shoulder.

At least he looked as nervous as I felt, with his hands stuffed deep into his pockets as he awkwardly lingered in the doorway.

In reality, *I* shouldn't be nervous at all. This was *my* family. My event. My home turf. He should be the one feeling like they're walking into the lion's den.

He must have been hiding out until I arrived, because at his appearance, an uproar from my family ensued. After my sisters passed me around for hugs and kisses on cheeks, Owen shuffled to my side.

"Hey, Whiskey," he said softly.

"Hi," I said, not bothering to hide the edge to my tone.

Before either of us could speak further, an arm looped through mine, and the blend of my mother's signature perfume enveloped me.

"I wasn't aware you were bringing a date, Delia," she said as she leaned in to press a kiss to my cheek. "It's good to see you,

Owen."

"You as well, Mrs. Delatou," the man responded.

My mother giggled. Yes, actually *giggled* like a goddamn school girl. It seemed even happily married, middle-aged women weren't immune to the Owen Lawless charm.

"Please," she said. "Call me Lena."

Several beats too late, I grumbled, "He's not my date."

"Then why did you invite him?" my mom asked, a twinkle in her eye as she winked before striding away.

Because I desperately want it to be, I thought in the direction of her retreating form. Even knowing it was the worst idea for a multitude of reasons, I wanted Owen in bone-deep ways.

I just wasn't sure I was allowed to have him.

On the far side of the barn, the rest of our group had gathered around an array of wooden buckets, the kind made to look like the bottom half of a wine or whiskey barrel. I knew without looking that each was layered with about a foot of red and white grapes. Soon, the barn would be filled with squeals and laughter as we sank our feet into them.

Before I could take a step to join them, Owen's hand wrapped around my upper arm, holding me back.

I turned to face him. "What?"

Owen frowned. "I'm sorry," he said quietly. "For this morning. I made things weird with my fishnets comment and running away after. I just...I don't know what I'm doing here."

"With what exactly?" I asked, though I could already guess the answer.

"You."

"Join the club."

"This wasn't supposed to happen."

"Technically," I corrected, "nothing *has* happened." I didn't tack on *yet*, but I wanted to. The word hung in the air between us anyway.

Owen gave me a pleading look. "You know what I mean."

"We can ignore it if that's what you want," I said, though the words were barbed wire scraping my throat as they left my mouth.

"And what do *you* want?" he asked.

"I don't know," I said. God, I was getting sick of those three words. When would I ever figure my shit out? I was twenty-seven, for fuck's sake. Shouldn't I have moved past the indecisiveness of youth and inexperience?

"Well, you let me know when you figure it out."

And with that, he was gone, gobbling up the distance between us and my family like he couldn't get away from me fast enough.

When did things between us get so complicated? It was supposed to be a business partnership and nothing more. So why was I having all kinds of thoughts of a future—a family—that involved him?

Somehow, despite the obvious tension between me and Owen, he fit himself into my family dynamic with ease. Maybe it was the former athlete mentality still running through his veins, or the fact that he came from a large family as well. Whatever it was, everyone obviously loved him. The easy way in which he spoke with my sisters and parents. How quickly he got used to Logan's particular brand of Golden Retriever energy. How he'd managed to even charm my dad who, as a rule, hated any guy we brought home. It wasn't difficult to imagine him there all the time. To picture him coming to family events and attending holidays at my side. He slotted in perfectly, just another one of the guys, another significant other for my sisters to rib endlessly like they did Calvin and Logan and for my mother to fawn over.

He quickly became one of us, and I realized that was what I had been searching for with TJ—with all of the guys I'd dated in my lifetime. Having someone at my side, and *on* my side, was a high unlike any other. That hole in my heart rapidly filled with his easy smiles and carefree laughter. I wanted to keep him here forever, but I wasn't sure that was a dream I should be chasing. While a friendship had easily bloomed between us in all the time we'd spent together the past few months, I wasn't sure it should go beyond that.

For both our sakes, it was probably best if I got my wild, rampant dreams and desires under control before I fucked everything up.

chapter 16
Owen

THE MOMENT MY FOOT first sank into the bucket of grapes, I let out a yelp that Cal mercilessly teased me about for the rest of the day.

What could I say? Have *you* ever crushed grapes with your feet? Unless you've done it, it was a difficult sensation to explain. The squishy texture, the way they popped open under pressure, spilling their guts out all over my toes. The coolness from being housed in the shade of the barn for god knew how long. And the liquid that collected the further the grapes broke down.

All of it was weird.

And I was having the time of my life.

Needing a bit of space from Delia, mostly to give her a chance to sort herself out, I found myself in a bucket between Ella and Brie. The two could not be more different, both from each other and from Delia. As the youngest, Brie was quiet—presumably from a lifetime of yielding her voice to her older and more extroverted siblings. She reminded me a lot of my brother Finn, the soft, careful foil to his loud and proud twin, West. From an outsider's perspective, she seemed more intentional, both with her words and her actions. When I'd first met her, she'd still been in college—about the same age as my sister was now—and it was pretty impressive to see the growth she'd undergone in the five years since.

Ella, on the other hand, wasn't quiet so much as she was sullen. Where her sisters' skin was unmarred by ink, Ella's arms were lined with tattoos. Her hair was chopped to her shoulders and bright pink streaks framed her face. With her denim shorts—that had to be men's, based on the length and the fact that they were cinched like a paper bag with a brown, braided belt at her waist, and not in the fashionable way—and oversized band tee tucked into one side, she gave off a starving artist vibe.

I'd spent enough time around people, studying them and learning their ticks, to recognize the clothes, the hair, the heavy eyeliner and ink, were only masking some deep-seated insecurities.

But that was none of my business.

After grape crushing concluded, we hosed off and headed over to the winery, where Ezra had been slaving away all day to prepare an epic buffet-style feast for the family. As plates were loaded and we settled at the long table, a pang of jealousy echoed through my chest.

Being around the Delatous, I couldn't help but miss my own family. I hadn't been home in ages, coming up on two years if my quick mental calculation was correct. And it wasn't that I didn't want to see my mom and siblings, because I did. The easy rapport between the Delatou sisters reminded me of how easily my brothers and I conversed. Our ages old inside jokes weaving into every conversation, years and years of it being the Lawlesses against the world, every formative moment of my life until I left for college involving them. All of it made me feel safe and *seen* in a way no other people or place ever had.

No, the reason I didn't like going home was because every corner of that town, of Dusk Valley and our ranch, held a memory of my dad. And most days, it was simply too much for me to face. For a man who'd make a career of staring down two hundred and fifty pound guys, knowing any one of them could break through my offensive line and drive my ass into the ground, I was a coward where that was concerned.

Hell, he'd been gone nearly seventeen years and I still hadn't visited his grave.

At least, not since the day we buried him.

❧ ❧

"Lawless!" my roommate Bucky shouted from the living room. "Get your ass out here and entertain our guests!"

"They're your *guests! And I'm busy!" I hollered back.*

Not technically a lie, though Bucky wouldn't appreciate why I wasn't joining the party. The end of the semester neared, and I had a lot of studying to do. Could I have saved it for our daily, team sanctioned tutoring sessions? Absolutely. But I didn't get to be the starting quarterback for the University of Oregon Ducks by only working out and doing drills when my coaches told me to. I applied that same drive to earning my degree.

It was Thanksgiving weekend, and we were on bye until we

played in the Pac-12 championship the following Saturday. Still, we had to practice, which meant I wasn't able to go home for the holiday. I wasn't overly heartbroken by that fact. As the eldest of seven kids—including five boisterous younger brothers—I relished the separation from my family more often than not. Maybe that sounded bad. Truthfully, I loved my family, but growing up in that farmhouse damn near bursting at the seams to contain us all, sharing a room with my next oldest brother, Trey...well, having a room to myself for the first time since the twins had been born thirteen years ago was a luxury I wasn't eager to be rid of.

The pregame going on in the living room didn't bother me, though. Since I'd moved off campus at the start of my sophomore season last year, Bucky and I had roomed together, and I'd gotten used to his noise. It was early enough yet that things were chill, just a few guys from the team and random jersey chasers hanging out on our couches, watching the few college games on and shooting the shit. By midnight, they'd all clear out, leaving our apartment for greener pastures—namely the football house, where four of our teammates lived and routinely held parties.

I avoided those like I always did. I wasn't much for drinking to begin with, never having gotten the taste for it like other teenagers from back home and my college classmates had. Maybe that was the natural born leader in me. Or the fact that my only goal in life since I'd first picked up a football at age ten had been to play professionally. I wouldn't stop until I got there, and things like underage drinking—I was only twenty, after all—or blowing off my homework, while innocuous enough decisions in the moment, could be a slippery slope that led to dangerous consequences.

Okay, maybe I was a bit of a tight ass, but I liked to think of it as simply knowing what I wanted and going after it.

I was halfway through the end-of-semester bookkeeping project that counted for half my GPA in my accounting class when my stomach let out a loud grumble. I briefly lifted my eyes to my alarm clock on my nightstand, noting it had indeed been longer than I'd thought since I'd last eaten. After inputting one final formula on the spreadsheet I had opened on my desktop, and tapping the save button to make sure I didn't lose my work, I rose from my chair.

Since I'd started college roughly two and a half years ago, I'd filled out a lot. The twig I'd been in high school had nothing on the muscular man I was now. Working out harder than ever meant I had to eat a lot more to maintain my weight and bulk, and it seemed like every day my diet changed, necessitating the addition of higher protein and more calories to counteract the loss I sustained while lifting or running drills.

When I swung open my bedroom door, Bucky let out a low whistle.

"The troll emerges," he said in a low, theatrical voice.

"I'm not a troll," I grumbled.

"My bad," Bucky said with a chuckle. "A hobbit? A...goblin? No." He looked at his friends, as if searching for the correct term in their faces. "What are those things that burrow?"

"Gophers?" one of the girls supplied.

"Gophers!" Bucky said happily, snapping his fingers. "That's what you are, Zero."

"Zero?" another girl asked.

"His jersey number," Bucky said.

The first girl who had spoken widened her eyes. "Wait, you're Owen Lawless?"

Ugh, I hated Bucky in that moment. Why couldn't he have kept his big mouth shut?

"I am," I said, not impolitely but definitely indicating I wasn't interested in further conversation. I turned my back on them and headed for the kitchen.

"You know you're, like, leading the fan vote for the Heisman, right?"

Narrowly, I leashed my surprise. I hadn't known that, but the news had pride swelling in my chest. Next to a victory in the Rose Bowl, which I had every intention of leading my team to in January, winning the Heisman Trophy—awarded to college football's best player—was something I wanted desperately. I had another season to play after this, but to earn the Heisman as a junior, while not unheard of, would be an impressive feat because it happened less frequently than senior players winning. I'd have to call my dad and tell him.

Pulling open the fridge, I selected a few Tupperware containers, the team nutritionist and chef having drilled into me the importance of meal prepping so I didn't have to waste any of my precious free time during the week cooking. All I had to do was mix my protein—which happened to be chicken—rice, and vegetables in another container and nuke it. While I waited for it to heat, I went to my room and grabbed my water bottle, then returned to fill it.

The girl was still talking about me, as though I wasn't standing there, as though the other two men in the apartment didn't also play football.

I was blessed to have gotten a full ride to college to play the sport I loved so much. But I'd be damned if being a quarterback wasn't the loneliest thing in the world sometimes. Despite performing in front of tens of thousands of people every weekend, I didn't particularly enjoy the spotlight.

"He's unreal," she continued. "The best quarterback the Ducks have had in two decades."

"He *is* standing right here," I growled.

"Bro," Bucky said, cutting me with a glare.

I shrugged. "If she wants to fangirl, she can go somewhere else."

"Wow," she said, huffing out an incredulous laugh. "No one told me you were an asshole."

"I'm not an asshole," I said. And really, I wasn't. This girl was just grating on my last nerve. "I just don't fuck with jersey chasers."

"*An asshole* and *a virgin*," she sneered. "It all makes sense now."

Before I said anything further, I turned my back on her, hoping I faced away in time to prevent her from seeing the way my cheeks heated with her comment.

She'd struck a little too close to home.

For the record, there was nothing wrong with being a virgin at twenty. My priorities were elsewhere. Between school and football, I didn't have the time for—nor did I care about—relationships with girls.

I supposed I was a bit of an enigma in that regard. I'd fooled around in high school, and a bit my freshman year, but I'd never...what's the baseball euphemism? Crossed home plate? Hit a home run? Either way, I'd never done it, and that was fine.

When the microwave beeped, I heaved a sigh of relief, removed my food, and retreated to my bedroom.

My phone rang before I could take a bite.

Call it intuition, my sixth sense perking up and taking notice, but the moment I saw my brother West's name on the caller ID, I *knew something was wrong. My heart sank like a lead weight into my stomach.*

West never called me. Normally it was everyone else calling me about West, even five-year-old Aria who didn't even have a phone of her own.

With shaking fingers, I answered.

"Hello?"

"O," West said, his voice hoarse. Flat. Stunned.

My heart dropped into my ass.

"What's going on, little brother?"

"I..."

I heard it then, and it had the hair on my arms rising. In the background, someone let out a keening wail, the sound so full of pain and despair it shot me right in the chest. My blood ran cold.

"West," I said sternly, my tone edged in panic. "What happened?"

"It's Dad," he said, voice cracking on the last word. "He's g-g-g-gone!"

And then my heart stopped.

I tried, unsuccessfully, to get him to explain further, but he'd started crying so hard I couldn't understand anything beyond his blubbering. After interminable minutes of freaking out but unable to get any answers, Trey came on the line.

"You gotta come home, big bro."

That was it. Six words had me throwing random shit in my backpack, homework and dinner long forgotten.

My limbs were shaking so bad I could barely stand as I once again emerged into the living room, my teammates and their guests glancing up at me with wide eyes. My anguish must have been written all over my face.

"What happened?" Bucky asked, setting his beer on our shitty coffee table and rising to his feet.

And so, for the first time, I uttered the words that would become the most painful new reality I'd ever have to endure.

"My dad died."

I made the normally-nine hour drive from Eugene to Dusk Valley in just over seven, breaking more than a few traffic laws, ignoring every speed limit in my desperation to reach my family.

My dad died. My dad died. My dad died.

Those three words were an irritatingly persistent companion, a metronome marking the passage of time.

But I didn't cry.

No, I saved that for the moment I pulled up in front of the main house on the ranch. When my mother walked out, right down the porch steps, and collapsed in my arms.

Together, we clung to each other, her hoarse sobs mixing with the fresh sounds of mine, my tears dampening the top of her head as hers soaked the front of my shirt. Suddenly, I was seven again and had just fallen off my horse, snapping my left tibia and fibula clean in half. That was the last time I'd cried so hard, and the last time my mother held me as I did.

I finally collected myself enough to inhale more than the shallowest of breaths, and I pulled back from my mom. Her face was pale beneath the pink splotches, eyes red-rimmed and puffy. She offered me a smile that wobbled at the edges, and I returned it.

"It's good to see you, baby," she said, reaching up to pat my cheek.

"I don't understand," I said. "What happened?"

"We don't know the details yet," she said. "He was out in pasture Y with the ranch hands installing a new fence and, according to them, he just dropped. There one second, gone the next. Oh, Owen," she wailed, burrowing her face into my chest. "What are we going to do?"

Something clicked into place for me then, all of my tears magically drying up like I'd turned off a faucet. I couldn't afford to fall apart, not when my entire family was busy doing the same thing. Not when Mom had just lost the love of her life, her soulmate, the man she should've grown old with. Someone had to hold it together, to handle funeral arrangements and all the other details that needed sorting now that he was gone.

Someone had to keep this family—and ranch—afloat.

At that moment, I decided that someone *was me.*

As it turned out once the medical examiner in Boise had done an autopsy, my father had an intracranial aneurysm that ruptured, killing him instantly. It was of little comfort that he hadn't felt any pain, but more so that he'd gone doing something he loved—working his ranch.

In the days and weeks and months that followed, while I was physically in Eugene, on flights and football fields with my team, my mind was a million miles away, back in Dusk Valley, Idaho with my family.

Despite my obvious grief, I powered through, leading us first to a Pac-12 championship, and then a Rose Bowl victory.

And the moment my season wrapped up, I hired an agent and declared for the draft, forgoing my final year of college eligibility. A lot of people thought it was because my dad would've wanted that, and that was part of it. But the truth of the matter was I had to take care of my family, and my rookie signing bonus and an NFL contract set us all up for life.

The rest was history.

"Owen?" someone asked softly from beside me.

Coming back to myself, I blinked to clear the cobwebs of my memories and turned to meet Delia's eyes. My food, half eaten, had grown cold in front of me. No one else at the table seemed aware of the mental journey I'd just taken.

"Hi," I said, giving her a small smile.

"Hi," she said back, concern obvious in the single syllable. "Where did you just go?"

I swallowed hard, not wanting to dive into all my trauma but wanting to be truthful with her.

"I miss my family," I told her quietly. "But this is...wonderful. Thank you for inviting me."

Her gaze softened, some of the tension that had lingered between us all day lightening. "Anytime, QB."

God, how desperately I hoped she meant that.

I'd meant what I said earlier. The second she figured out what she wanted, I wanted to know.

We hadn't even done anything beyond the most innocent touches and shared a few *almost* moments. But it didn't matter. Every moment I spent with her simply solidified the fact that we were friends—*good* friends. Being around her was as easy as breathing. And I've always thought friendship was a solid foundation for the best, more intimate types of relationships. Look at my parents. They had been best friends, and I got that same vibe from Delia's as well. So when she got her head on straight and decided what she wanted, I hoped that thing was *me*, because I was done for. Completely and utterly gone for this woman.

chapter 17
Owen

THE FOLLOWING WEEKEND, I found myself back in Delia's garage. This time, it was just the two of us, and still, nothing was resolved. She hadn't been steering clear of me exactly, but the easy rapport we'd developed over the past few months was strained. As though she was trying to maintain that professional boundary.

And that was fine. I could wait her out. I wasn't sure when my perception of Delia switched from simple business partner to someone I was interested in romantically. Maybe it was the way she'd stuck up for me that night at the club, or watching the way she interacted with her family.

Probably, it was seeing her pants-less and dancing around her kitchen last weekend. It was impossible to ignore that previously slumbering part of me that opened its eyes, lifted its head, and said, "*Mine.*"

Clearly, my entire opinion of her had been wrong from the beginning, and I was doing my damnedest to make up for it.

All I wanted was a chance. And I'd give her however long she needed to come to terms with that fact—to recognize that she wanted me too.

That evening, Delia invited me over for a little tasting session, our first batch of spirits at last ready to sample. We knew in order to get really good liquor, they'd have to sit longer than six days, but we wanted to see if we were on the right track. Surprisingly, Liam had offered to set up some at home stills in his garage and keep an eye on them for us. In the wake of that combined with the success of his and Amara's canned wine cocktails, Delia and I had agreed to bring him on as a consultant, and we were paying him nicely for his help.

He should've been here too, but he'd had to bail at the last second. I wasn't too mad about it, excited about being alone with Delia.

It was barely five p.m., the sun clinging to the horizon before sinking below it when I pulled into her driveway. The first time I'd shown up here, the night of the party, it was pitch black. And when I'd left the next morning, I had been in such a rush to get away from the new and unexpected feeling swirling in my chest that I hadn't given my surroundings much thought. Now, though, in the pre-dusk light, I looked my fill.

Delia and the previous owners of the home had clearly gone through a lot of trouble to maintain the structures' original facade and integrity. With its wide wrap-around porch and gambrel roof, it was easy to imagine the home sitting alone surrounded by fields, with chickens pecking at errant seed spread on the ground and cows mooing softly in the distance.

The garage had clearly been a carriage house once upon a time, with a gabled roof, the points of which someone—presumably Delia—had accented with decorative corbels. It was painted a sage green that beautifully offset the bright white of the house, and vice versa.

It wasn't difficult to imagine the days when this entire neighborhood had been nothing but fields of crops and dirt roads.

I rapped lightly on the garage door with my knuckles, mainly to alert her of my arrival, and Delia's voice rang out a moment later, inviting me in.

The space looked vastly different than it had last weekend, what with two vehicles parked in the bays. Half of one was occupied by a drop cloth that had two sawhorses with a half-painted hollow core door balanced between them—presumably Delia's latest DIY project. To the left of the space, Delia waited at the top of the stairs, a soft smile on her lips.

My mouth dried out. How was it possible the woman made a simple pair of loose-fitting jeans and an oversized Apple Blossom Bay Fall Festival tee look like couture?

"Come on up," she said.

We moved into her office space, Delia's steps confident and unhurried, completely oblivious to the turmoil roiling in my gut. When she turned to me again, the cool air from her brief trip beyond the cozy warmth of the room had tightened her nipples into peaks against her shirt.

She wasn't wearing a bra, and I nearly went to my knees before her, begging her to let me taste her.

Fucking hell, I had to get my shit together.

Five bottles were lined up on a side table, one for each of our spirits: Outlaw Vodka, Bootlegger Rum, Highwayman Whiskey,

Bandit Gin, and Hustler Bourbon.

The first time I'd shared the names with her, Delia had been gleeful over each of them, and I'd preened under her praise. Having a last name like mine made it easy to lean into those Wild West vibes, when criminals run rampant across the dusty trails.

Delia poured us each a finger of the whiskey into two highball glasses, handing me one before lifting hers. Her fingers brushed against mine, sending an electric current up my arm. While I was giving her time to come to terms with what she wanted, whether she wanted to pursue something further with me or not, it didn't stop me from wanting her in a bone deep way.

And as her skin came into contact with mine, her breath hitched in a way that told me she wanted me too, that she wasn't as unaffected by the connection between us as she pretended.

So what the fuck were we waiting for?

I cleared my throat and lifted my glass between us. When Delia mirrored me, I said, "To Unlawful."

Her echo of my words was barely more than a murmur, and then she was lifting the liquor to her lips, opening her mouth only slightly to let the liquid trickle in. I couldn't tear my attention away as she savored the sip, letting it linger before swallowing it down. The muscles in her slender neck contracted, and it suddenly became the most fascinating thing I'd ever seen.

"Damn, that's smooth," she said, her voice husky, eyes sparking when they met mine.

Like your skin, I thought, resisting the urge to stroke a finger down her cheek and prove it to myself.

Being around her was difficult, especially alone like this, with nothing but these four walls to bear witness if I were to grip the delicate point of her chin in my hand and tip her head back. If I ran my free hand down a thigh, hitching it high around my waist.

If I were to seal my lips over that plush mouth.

Fuck, I needed to get it together.

"Owen?" Delia said, and I shook my head, returning to the present. While I'd been lost in thoughts of her, she'd moved across the room to one of the oversized rolled arm chairs. And like a dumbass, I was still standing in the middle of the room, my eyes probably glazed over from my thousand-yard stare.

"Can I ask you something?" I blurted, moving to sit in the chair beside hers.

Her brows drew together, but a smirk played on her lips as she said, "Technically, you just did."

"Okay, smart ass. Let me rephrase." I batted my eyelashes and gave her a beatific smile. "Delia, I have a question for you."

Tucking her feet up under her, she giggled and said, "Proceed."

"Why did you dare Amara to make out with me at the lake that night?"

Delia blinked, clearly surprised, like she hadn't been expecting that question. Truthfully, I hadn't planned on asking it. But the way I felt about her was changing rapidly, and this was one thing that had continued to nag me. I couldn't quell my curiosity any longer.

With a sigh, she said, "I wanted Cal and Amara to admit there was something there. That things were happening between them. I'm not saying I'm proud of the way I acted, but...I don't like watching people needlessly suffer when the issue could be solved with a simple conversation or one moment of bravery."

Then where's your *moment of bravery?* I wanted to ask but wisely bit my tongue.

I pushed that thought away and said, "And Amara kissing Cal in front of us was that moment for her?"

Delia nodded. "Mar is a rule follower. She always has been, and she's always done exactly what was asked of her when it comes to the family business. Her relationship with Cal is the first time I've ever seen her rebel and do something for herself. Call it a woman's intuition or maybe just the fact that I know my sister that well, but...I had a good feeling about them. That they were endgame. As it turned out, I was right." I opened my mouth to say something, though I wasn't entirely sure what, but she continued. "I am sorry, though. For dragging you into it. That was shitty of me."

"I accept your apology," I said, sealing my forgiveness with a clink of my glass against hers.

She was silent for a beat before she leapt from her chair, some invisible tether snapping. "I just have all this...energy!" she said, pacing the length of floor from the chair to her desk and back. "And it often manifests in chaos." Stilling, she turned to me, hands on hips and added, "Like, you know how everyone talks about having an angel on one shoulder and a devil on the other?"

I nodded.

"I don't know if I have the angel," she admitted, gaze dropping to the floor. "But I definitely have a devil, which I affectionately refer to as my inner chaos demon. And if I don't pull the prover-bial fire alarm from time to time to take the edge off, bad things happen."

"Like what?" I asked, intrigued. I'd seen the energy she described flashing in her eyes now and then. She radiated the same spiritedness as my brother, West.

God, those two would get on like a forest fire.

Her eyes met mine again, a heavy sigh raising and lowering her shoulders dramatically. Then she said the last thing I ever expected.

"You're not the first older guy I've ever had a crush on."

I smirked, wiggling my brows. "You have a crush on me?"

"Not the point, QB."

She was right, of course. The more time I'd spent with her, the less the ten years between us mattered to me. I'd come to realize that, once you reached a certain stage in your life, age really was just a number. I'd only been using the gap as an excuse not to work with her before because I'd thought she was a wildcard.

And she was, only...not in the ways I expected.

"How old are we talking here?"

"He was forty to my twenty-two."

I whistled low, mostly to hide my shock. Nearly twenty years between them? Who had this guy been? Why was I compelled to rip his head from his body?

I could do it too. And with a goddamn smile on my face.

"What happened?" I asked softly, tone completely at odds with the rage and jealousy coursing through me.

For long, seemingly interminable moments, Delia didn't respond. She moved to the little side table where the five bottles sat. This time, she poured herself two fingers of the vodka, draining it quickly before refilling it. Then she moved back to the chair opposite me and sat, spine and shoulders curved inward.

"He was one of my professors at Northwestern."

My blood chilled.

"You don't owe me anything, Whiskey," I said, reaching out my arm to circle my fingers around her right wrist. "But I'm here if you want to talk about it. I'm always here."

I didn't want to force her to talk about anything she didn't want to, but the ice in my veins demanded answers.

She looked at me then, her eyes lined with silver and pain, cheeks pink with...embarrassment?

What the fuck did she have to be embarrassed about?

Get yourself in check, Lawless, I coaxed myself. *Flying off the handle right now does no one any good.*

"Accounting has never really been my strong suit," she started, eyes darting around but always coming back to meet mine. "So I started taking advantage of his office hours early in the semester. I wanted to get a jump start on understanding the material so I wasn't floundering when exam time came. At first, everything was normal. He was attentive, but not overtly so. He never touched me, his gaze never lingered, he never made any suggestive comments.

"Until the week before I turned twenty-two. I was gearing up for my birthday and Halloween, so that day, I'd tested out my costume makeup. Nothing crazy, but more than I typically wore. I was dressing up as a vampire, and I wanted to make sure I really nailed the smoky eye, you know?"

Being the man I was, I obviously had no idea, but I didn't dare speak and interrupt her.

"Something in his entire demeanor shifted when I walked into his office that day. I still remember exactly what I was wearing. A red plaid skirt, one I'd worn probably ten times already that semester, and this gauzy white blouse with black tights, a red headband, and black flats. The whole thing was very Blair Waldorf."

Okay, that reference I understood. I was in my teens when *Gossip Girl* first aired.

"And I just didn't stop him when he leaned in to kiss me," Delia continued, voice barely above a whisper. "He was...handsome. Not in the way you are, but softer. Prettier, in a way. And the fact that he was older and showing *me*, this lowly college junior, attention? I couldn't help myself. It was so frowned upon, but so...hot. The stuff people write forbidden romances about. But we were never destined for a happy ending."

"So how did it end?"

"The more time we spent together, the less like myself I felt," she admitted. "Instead of doing normal college girl things, I was spending all my free time with him. And because he was my professor, that meant we holed up in his house, or took weekend trips to B&Bs in small towns where no one would recognize us. At first, it was so romantic. But...well, you know what they say about rose-colored glasses. I had mine practically glued to my face. Pretty much right around the time I told him I loved him, and he responded with, 'Of course you do, my pet,' I realized how stupid I'd been. All he wanted from me was sex and the thrill of fucking one of his students. So I broke it off. Thankfully, by then, the semester had ended so I never had to see him again unless we randomly bumped into each other on campus.

"It fucked me up, Owen," she continued quietly. "And I'm still not sure I deserve to be happy because of it."

"What? No," I said quickly, shaking my head. "That's not

how it works, Whiskey. You were young. You didn't do anything wrong. *He* is the one who doesn't deserve to be happy."

"Logically, I know you're right. But nothing about the way I feel is logical."

"Does he still teach there?" I asked through clenched teeth, mentally calculating how long it would take to drive from here to Evanston. I hated the man for taking something so precious from her.

Delia shook her head, slipping her wrist from my grasp to lace her fingers with mine, as though anchoring herself to the present, lest the past sweep her away. "He got fired after it came to light that he'd been sleeping with a student."

I sucked in a gasp. "You got caught?"

Another head shake. "Someone else came forward."

"Jesus Christ," I swore, squeezing her hand. "I'm so sorry, Delia."

After swiping at her eyes with her free hand, she said, "So to answer your earlier question, of course I have a crush on you. But I don't know if I'm ready, Owen. That relationship broke me for a long time, and is solely responsible for the chaos demon that lives in my brain. I haven't been in a relationship that wasn't purely physical since then, and you deserve better than that. Especially at your advanced age," she added with a chuckle, and I gripped her hand tighter in warning. With a sigh, she added, "It's hard for me to trust, and I know you've never done anything to show me I *can't* trust you, but I need time."

"Then time is what you'll get."

"Thank you," she whispered, offering me a watery smile.

"Now I have a question for you."

"Shoot," I said.

"Were things ever serious with my sister?"

"No," I answered immediately. "It was just sex, Whiskey. A summer fling. We're just friends now."

Delia nodded. "That's what she's always said too, but I needed to hear it from you."

"Turns out, she wasn't the Delatou sister for me."

Delia blinked slowly at me. "Are you saying I am?"

I shrugged. "I'm saying you could be if you give us a chance."

"I'm trying," she whispered. "But…"

"You need time. I know."

Delia grinned, her shoulders relaxing, and my entire chest lit up at the sight of it.

I pulled my hand away to take a fortifying sip of my whiskey, then steered the conversation to safer ground.

"You should try exercising," I said. "It'll take the edge off."

Delia's forehead scrunched in confusion. "Off what?"

"All that pent up energy."

It was something I was all too familiar with, thanks to the million younger siblings and pushing myself for years with football.

Delia was once again on her feet, lifting my empty glass out of my hand to refill it. As she poured liquid—it looked like the bourbon this time—she glanced at me over her shoulder.

"You talking about sex?" she asked. "You offering?"

I nearly choked on my own spit. Once I'd composed myself by hacking up a lung, I sighed, scrubbing a hand over my face. Leave it to her to make light of sex right after telling me the story of a man preying on her naïveté and the power he held over her.

"No, like weight lifting. Cardio. Yoga. Normal shit."

"Sex is normal."

"Delia," I sighed, exasperated.

"What? It is! And I prefer it. If I'm going to work out, it should at least feel good."

"Well clearly, that's not working for you," I bit out.

"How do you know?"

"You're practically vibrating. Every time I see you, you're a rapidly fraying rope about to snap. And I don't think that has anything to do with your work-life balance, because you love your job, and you love your life outside of it. Whoever you've been fucking"—I thought of TJ's dweeb ass, though I'd bet all my money they never got that far—"wasn't doing it right."

I was playing with fire here, but this conversation was suddenly like a train wreck I couldn't look away from. I wanted—*needed*—to see it through.

Delia frowned, propping her fists on the gentle swells of her hips. "I'll have you know, QB, that I have fabulous sex."

I smirked, understanding the words for what they were: lies.

And that bothered me. This woman was loud and riotous and way too sexy for her own good. But she was also insightful, loyal, a hell of a business partner, and one of the hardest workers I'd ever known. Beneath her seemingly tough-girl exterior was a soft underbelly of trauma and pain that needed to be handled with care.

If she was mine, she'd never have to lie about being satisfied. It would simply be a reality. But I'd take care of her in other ways too. In all the ways she'd let me.

That was dangerous territory to consider for so many reasons, the least of which being the story she'd just shared with me. This situation itself was too precarious—me and her cozied up in her garage, sampling our spirits. Already, the alcohol buzzed in my veins, setting my nerve endings alight exactly like her eyes did every time they met mine. They were a dangerous combination, the liquor and those caramel depths. I couldn't afford the inhibitions either would provide if I imbibed too long. Not right now, anyway.

When I took Delia for the first time, it would be because she was clear-headed. Not because alcohol got the best of us.

When I claimed her, we'd both be of sound mind and body.

"Come workout with me one day," I said.

"Why?"

"Just give it a chance," I implored. "Who knows, you might like it."

"I run nearly every day," she grumbled.

"You run because it keeps you fit and nothing more," I shot back.

Delia gaped like a fish, and I grinned in satisfaction of having pegged her motivation so easily.

"You checking out the goods, QB?" Delia quipped, turning her hips side to side. But something in her eyes clued me into the fact that how I handled her question mattered in a big way.

"All women's bodies are beautiful, Whiskey. Yours is no exception. Only a fool would say otherwise."

Her cheeks heated, and a small, pleased smile danced on her lips. But she recovered quickly, schooling her expression to neutrality. "So what's wrong with running to stay fit, then? Clearly it's working."

"Nothing," I said, shrugging. "And I'm not saying running

isn't hard. It takes a level of mental fortitude few possess. But clearly it's not enough to dispel all your excess energy. What I am saying is...don't you want to be strong too?"

"I am strong."

I snorted. "Your arms are string beans." To demonstrate, I looped a palm around her biceps, my thumb easily meeting my fingers.

"I renovated this entire house myself, QB. That takes some level of strength, don't you think?"

"So prove it," I dared. "Come workout with me. Just once. See how much better you feel after."

"And if I don't?"

"Then you don't do it again," I said. "What's the harm in trying?"

What was the harm, indeed?

chapter 18
Delia

Agreeing to workout with Owen was the worst idea I'd ever had for so many reasons, mostly because I hadn't mentally prepared myself for what seeing him shirtless and sweaty would do to me.

No, that's a lie—well, not the entire truth anyway.

While Owen's glistening bronze skin was surely distracting, I hated to admit he'd been right. I wasn't particularly strong, and the workout he'd created for us put me through the ringer, working muscles I didn't even know I had.

Oh, but Owen knew, and he tortured me for an hour.

I should've known better than to think he'd take it easy on me.

Then again, I didn't want someone to take it easy on me, had prided myself on doing the exact opposite whenever possible. Take the night before for example. It would've been much easier to keep my mouth shut and not share with Owen the darkest, most embarrassingly painful story of my entire life. But I *wanted* him to know, wanted him to understand where I was coming from where this thing between us was concerned. And he'd taken it all in stride, simply being a calming, stolid presence next to me while I dumped the whole thing in his lap.

My crush for him deepened in that moment. Actually, it was well past a simple *crush*.

When I walked into the gym, Owen stood in the center of an empty expanse of rubber floor mats, rapidly jumping rope. I had to snap my mouth shut to avoid drooling. He was dressed head to toe in Detroit Mustangs gear, a black ball cap flipped backward. The ends of his hair were already damp and clinging to his neck. Vibrant orange shorts hung low on his hips, displaying the band of his boxer briefs. His tee was black, the Mustangs logo so faded from wear it was practically nonexistent. The sleeves were ripped off, presumably by him, the bottom half missing to reveal the peaks and valleys of his lower abdominals.

God, I wanted to press my tongue into those grooves, to taste the salty perspiration off his skin.

There was this guy on TikTok who posted thirst traps of himself sweaty and lifting weights, and like...if Owen spontaneously grew a mustache? I'd be taking him for a ride without a second thought.

"What are you doing?" I asked, forcefully shaking myself from my trance. "Is this your idea of a workout?"

"I'm warming up," he said, his breath relatively even despite how quickly he was moving. "Grab one and join me."

"Okay..." I trailed off, moving over to the collection of hooks on the far wall and selecting a rope that seemed about right for my height.

I rejoined him and said, "Now what?"

"Now jump."

So I did, thinking it couldn't be all that difficult if kids routinely participated in the activity.

I was humbled quickly.

It had been a long damn time since I'd used both the muscles and coordination skills necessary to perform such a task, and after the third time of catching the rope around my ankle and nearly eating shit, Owen—who, mind you, could barely stop laughing long enough to get the words out—took pity on me and told me to do jumping jacks instead.

Now that he was no longer playing, Owen told me he liked to participate in what he called "functional" strength training versus the traditional kind that required lots of barbell and pulley machine usage.

Instead, he asked me to grab a couple dumbbells from the racks at a weight I felt confident I could repeatedly lift over my head, then once again met me in the center of the gym.

"So first," he said, hefting his own dumbbells—more than twice as heavy as my measly ten pounders—up to his shoulders, "we're going to do squat to overhead presses, or squat thrusts."

He demonstrated the movement, his thighs straining against his shorts as he dropped into the squat, straightened back up, simultaneously pushing the dumbbells over his head, then returned them to the neutral position at his shoulders.

His biceps bulged deliciously, and I struggled to concentrate around mental images of him manhandling me in bed.

"When you reach the top of the movement"—he held the dumbbells overhead again—"I want you to squeeze your glutes together. Keep your belly button pulled in, core engaged, and avoid rounding your back."

"Okay," I said, bobbing my head, my ponytail swishing, attempting to get myself in the game. "I can do this."

"That's the spirit," Owen said, grinning. "We'll start with three sets of ten reps. I'll do them with you."

Though I used my leg muscles regularly to run, it was nothing compared to the hell squats unleashed. By the end of the first set, my quads, glutes, and shoulders were on fire. I wasn't sure how I'd make it through two more rounds, nor how I'd survive an entire workout with this man.

As though sensing my struggle, Owen said, "You can switch those out for lighter weights if you want."

And give him the satisfaction? Absolutely fucking not.

So I powered through, grateful when he gave me a thirty second break between sets, though it was barely long enough for me to gulp down some water and attempt to marshal my breathing.

We alternated upper and lower body movements, or combined the two for a whole body exercise, though always targeting the same muscle groups. Owen made everything look easy. It wasn't that he wasn't breaking a sweat doing everything he instructed me to do, it was more that everything appeared so effortless for him. I had to actively remind myself he was an athlete, had played professional football for a decade. He was used to this.

The bastard even made burpees look easy.

At one point, while I struggled to lift myself off the floor in the middle of one, Owen paused briefly to whip his shirt off, claiming it was getting in the way.

Personally, I thought he only wanted to torture me further. To show me what I was missing.

His body was a work of art, every muscle beautifully defined, as though a sculptor had carefully drawn his modeling tool across a mass of clay, deftly shaping every hill and hollow of his shoulders, arms, chest, and abs.

The man even had a goddamn gold chain around his neck, an oblong circle hanging from it. He was sex on a stick, a goddamn snack I wanted to consume.

Jumping to my feet at last, I paused and smirked at him, inclining my head toward the chain and pendant. "Is that so you won't forget your name?"

Owen glanced down at his chest, where the circle hung in the valley of his pecs. "Nah," he said with a chuckle. "It's my number. When I started playing football, I chose the number zero because it looked like an O, but then I carried it with me through each level I played in after that. My college and pro teammates all called me Zero."

"That's sweet," I said, giving him a smile. Briefly, he returned it before barking at me to finish my burpees.

I only survived them by imagining that chain dangling in my face as Owen rocked in and out of my body.

It went on like that, Owen showing me moves that he made look as easy as lifting a twig off the ground while I huffed and puffed my way through them. Still, I couldn't help but enjoy the jelly sensation that overtook my limbs the longer I worked, and the way my mind went blissfully quiet of everything save executing the movements properly to avoid injuring myself.

And I definitely enjoyed every time Owen corrected my form.

I nearly gave into the attraction between us in one such instance. He had me doing bent over rows, here I hinged at the hip, arms extended, then brought my elbows to my hips and back down again. Apparently, I wasn't hinging correctly—okay, I knew I wasn't; the twinge in my lower back before he put me straight proved that—so he set down his own weights to assist.

Every nerve ending in my body lit up when he put his hands on me, and there was no way he missed the way I shivered at the contact.

One hand he placed on the small of my back, right over my tailbone, his pinky one brazen flex away from my ass, and the other he spread over my stomach.

God, his palms were massive, spanning nearly the entire width of my torso.

I was a goner the moment he pressed lightly, shifting me, and said, "Tilt your hips, Whiskey."

It was impossible not to imagine him speaking those same words in bed, my ass in the air, him positioning me right where he wanted before he took me from behind.

I had to guess Owen had the same idea, because as soon as he said it, he stilled a beat before pulling his hands from my body like I'd burned him.

Things were awkward after that, which annoyed me to no end. We were physically attracted to each other, and I didn't understand why we couldn't explore that without feelings getting involved.

I had to admit, though, exercising had done the trick. I was more settled than I'd been before we started, like that typical buzz of energy coursing through my veins was quieter. Not gone entirely but...still.

Workout done, Owen and I found ourselves seated on the floor, doing some stretches to cool down, when I decided to throw caution to the wind.

"Owen, I have a question."

"Shoot," he said, his voice muffled by the floor where he had his forehead pressed in child's pose.

"You're physically attracted to me."

"Not a question," he said, raising slightly to look me in the eye. "But yes."

"And I'm physically attracted to you."

"I thought you had a question."

"I'm just wondering...why can't we explore that? Why *aren't* we exploring that?"

Owen rose fully from his forward fold and rocked onto his butt, extending his legs in front of him, resting back on his palms. The portrait of calm, cool, and collected while my insides squirmed. All that work we'd done to quiet my inner chaos was undone in a heartbeat with the way he looked at me. Like I was a gift he wanted to unwrap.

"I'm too old for games," he said at last. "I'm playing for keeps now. I want you, badly, in ways I can't quite explain. But those ways include more than just your body, and until you decide you're ready to give me everything...we're at an impasse."

My heart rate ratcheted up, skin tingling with the promise in those words.

"So you're saying you won't take my body unless I give you my heart too?"

"Yes. I'm a greedy and possessive man, Delia. It's all or nothing for me."

My relationship, if you even wanted to call it that, with TJ had been doomed from the start. I'd wanted to start dating, and he was the first man who'd asked. But I wasn't entirely sure "man" was an appropriate term for him, because compared to Owen? This chiseled, perfect male specimen sitting before me?

TJ was a mediocre appetizer.

Owen was a five course meal at a Michelin starred restaurant.

To consider them the same species was laughable.

Owen saw who I was, who'd I'd been, and who I could be, and hadn't balked at any of it. Even in the beginning, after our first little bump in the road, he'd quickly altered course, becoming a collaborative business partner and good friend—and I'd done the same in return. He put up with my constant photography and videography for our socials, my endless questions from the comment sections that I only asked to annoy him. He was hard working and had his shit together. Not to mention, he got along great with my family.

Hell, even my dad loved him.

And then there was last night, when I'd laid my bleeding heart bear and he took it all in stride. I didn't miss the anger flashing in his eyes as I'd shared my trauma, and I could only imagine the scenarios of murder that had filtered through his head, but he never let that emotion bubble out.

He was cool in the face of pressure, attentive, kind, loyal. A natural leader and caretaker.

In short, I could do a lot worse than Owen Lawless.

But...I thought maybe Owen Lawless could do a lot better than me.

"Maybe—" I started, but my words were cut off by the door

from the men's locker room flying open.

I leapt off the floor quickly, feeling like I'd been caught in a compromising position and wanting to distance myself from Owen.

And a good thing too, because none other than Calvin Ryder walked through the door, fully dressed in business attire.

"What do we have here?" he asked, a shit-eating grin on his face.

"Helping Delia blow off some steam," Owen said, rising to his feet next to me.

"I'll bet," Cal said with a wink in my direction.

"What're you doing here?" Owen asked. "You stalking me?"

"Yeah, actually," Cal said. "I wanted to see if you wanted to get lunch."

Ignoring Cal for the moment, Owen stared at me, exasperation clear on his face. It was obvious he wanted me to finish what I'd been about to say, but I couldn't. Not in front of Cal, and not when I still wasn't sure myself.

About any of it.

So we agreed to have lunch with Cal—on the condition that he invited my sister—at Birdie's, which was right down the road from the gym. It was closed, but knowing the owner had its perks. Together, we constructed a meal out of leftovers Owen's chef had in the fridge, including the creamiest mac and cheese I'd ever had, thick slices of beefsteak tomatoes we sprinkled with flaky salt, pepper, and drizzled with balsamic, and bell peppers stuffed with a turkey burger concoction.

I tried hard to ignore the fact that the whole thing felt like a double date. We sat at a booth in the dining room, laughing and talking. Amara and Cal were on one side, their fingers laced, her hand absently resting on the swollen belly carrying their child. Owen and I were side by side on the other, and though we didn't touch each other, something still sizzled in the air between us. It was getting harder and harder to deny myself, and I wondered how far I could bend before I broke.

When Cal and Owen rose from the table to bring our empty plates back to the kitchen, my sister's gaze narrowed on me.

"You like him," she said, those shrewd golden eyes, brighter than my own, practically boring a hole in my skull.

It wasn't a question, and I didn't treat it as such.

"I do," I whispered.

"Why do I sense a 'but' coming?"

"I don't know if I can let myself go there. For a number of reasons, the least of which is that we're partners. I'd never forgive myself if our business went up in flames because I couldn't keep my proverbial dick in my pants."

"That's actually Owen's job," my sister said with a snort, and I swatted at her.

"You know what I mean, Mar. I just...the whole working together and fucking thing didn't exactly work out for you and Cal. So who am I to think it would for me?"

"Working together *and* being together may not have worked out for me and Cal," she said, nodding in agreement. "But being together *did*. And you and Owen aren't us. There's a level of respect and collaboration between you two that Cal and I sorely lacked in the beginning, which was the root of all our problems." She settled a hand on the small swell over her abdomen. "Even so, what I got in return is everything to me."

"There's also the fact that you've fucked him," I blurted.

My sister pursed her lips, clearly unimpressed with my deflection. "Don't use me as an excuse, Lia. If you want him, and he wants you, there's nothing insurmountable stopping you from taking and running with the happiness you could find."

❧ ❧

The next day, I found myself at the job site, wanting to shoot some progress content and start measuring for furniture and artwork. Jay and his team had made impressive progress, with the entirety of the building framed in, trusses up and roof on, and walls insulated and ready for drywall. It was starting to look like a real business, and the thought of decorating had me giddy.

I was inside, after Jay instructed me to put on a hardhat and watch my step, standing in the middle of the cavernous space, spinning in a slow circle. Plans whirled in my head, thoughts of fabrics and textures, fixtures and paint, art and other tchotchkes. The door creaked open behind me just as I withdrew my tape measure, and I turned to find Owen striding toward me.

I couldn't help the wide grin that spread across my face. "What're you doing here?" I asked.

"Same as you," he said, shrugging. "Checking on progress." As if noticing it for the first time, he frowned at the tape measure in my hand. "What're you up to?"

"Measuring for furniture," I said. "I know there's a lot of work to be done before we get to the staging part of the process, but I wanted to get a jumpstart on ordering. Think it would be okay if I just stored everything up here? I could pile it all up in the center of the room and throw drop cloths over it or something."

"Why not just use the barn? Wouldn't it all be safer there?"

"Well, that's family property."

"And you don't think your family would be okay with you storing stuff there?"

"I guess I never thought to ask."

"They love you, Delia. I think they'll be fine with it."

I waved him off, not liking the way his words twisted up my insides. It was too early in the day for feelings talk.

"That reminds me," I said. "I want to travel somewhere and do research. Check out different bars and get inspiration, you know? I was thinking Chicago, maybe."

"Actually," Owen said, "there's something I wanted to run by you."

"Okay..."

"I got asked to shoot a Super Bowl commercial and a print ad for a company I've worked with in the past, and I'll have to go to New York for a few days. Why don't you come with me?"

chapter 19
Owen

WHEN I WAS FIRST drafted, though my rookie contract and signing bonus amounted to more money than I'd ever seen in my lifetime, I'd taken on every opportunity I could to make extra. A lot of what I'd earned I sent home to my mom, helping her take care of my siblings as well as making sure the bills for the ranch were paid. My dad may have been gone, but I'd be damned if we lost the ranch too.

The first time I sent a payment home, in the form of a fat ass check, my mom called me and threw an absolute fit.

"You know I can't accept this, Owen! This is your money!"

"Exactly," I said, smiling at her over Skype. *"It's my money to do whatever I want with, and I want to make sure the ranch doesn't go under."*

"But five hundred thousand dollars!?" she protested.

"You do realize I signed a contract for over sixty-five million, right, Mom? Including an additional seven million dollar signing bonus?"

"Over six years," she quipped back. "You should save that. Invest. Buy a house."

"I could buy fifty houses and it still wouldn't put a dent in that money, and you know it."

"I just...I can't accept this, honey."

"You can," I assured her. "And you will."

"Why are you doing this?" she asked with a sniffle.

"Because Dad is gone," I said bluntly. "That means I'm the head of this family now. And as the head of this family, it's my job to take care of y'all."

"I'm the parent," she said. "It should be me doing the caretaking."

"Just let me have this!" I burst out. "Please, Mama."

My mom sighed heavily before giving me a terse nod. "Okay," she said. "But I'm setting some ground rules."

"Here we go," I muttered.

There was commotion in the background as the twins stumbled inside and appeared on the screen, West covered damn near head to toe in what looked like mud, Finn wearing a sheepish grin next to him. They were fourteen and absolute hellions.

Mama was on them in a flash, grabbing them both by an ear and towing them back out the door. "What have I told you two about staying away from that crick?!" Her shouted words floated back to me, muffled my distance, and I couldn't help chuckling.

When she finally came back, she found six-year-old Aria seated in her place, showing me how she was teaching herself to braid on the hair of a creepy-looking, dark-skinned bust she called Sasha.

"You're doing great, kiddo," I told her warmly. "But Mama and I need to have a grown up conversation now. Go play in your room."

"Okay, Owen!" she said brightly, hopping up and scuttling off to her room—the only one of the Lawless siblings to have their own.

"A young girl needs her own space," my dad had said once.

Aria had always been his favorite, probably because she was the only one who hadn't given him ulcers. Though, had he lived, I had no doubt she would've followed in our footsteps.

"Now about these rules," I drawled as my mom retook her seat.

"You only send enough for ranch expenses," she said. "I'll send you invoices as we get them, and you pay them. Just until I can hire someone to take over and handle all of that in house."

"Not necessary."

"What isn't?"

"Hiring someone to take over. You've got Cyrus there. He was Dad's right hand for twenty years. I think he knows how to run the place."

"Well sure he does, but don't you think he's ready to retire? The man's nearing sixty!"

"Has he said he wants to retire?"

"No..." she said, rolling her lips together. "Actually, he said I've got his help for as long as he needs me."

"Perfect," I said. "One less thing you have to worry about. What's next?"

"I can't let you give me money to take care of the boys and Aria," she said. "We'll make due."

"With what, exactly? Mama," I said, exasperated. "The twins are fourteen and growing like weeds. Trey needs to be focusing on college, and Lane needs to worry about finishing high school. And what are you going to do with Aria? Dress her in the boys' *hand-me-downs forever? Give her even more of a complex about being the only girl in a family of men?"*

"Who are you and what have you done with my son?" she asked, squinting at me in the screen.

I shrugged. "I had to grow up sometime."

The conversation had gone on like that for another hour, my mom fighting me at every turn about every little bit of help I wanted to offer. In the end, we agreed I'd provide them with a modest allowance for groceries, clothes, and other day-to-day necessities. I set up a bank account with my and Mama's names on it that she could draw from in case of emergency, and I'd pay all the ranch-related expenses only so far as operational or unforeseen costs went.

I'd told my mom I had to grow up sometime, and sometimes, I thought I'd grown up a little too fast. Even now, I was driven by the need to do everything myself and also to care for those around me. I paid my employees well, with benefits packages they wouldn't find anywhere else. I took care of everyone and everything around me without blinking, without balking.

I'd spent nearly as long without my dad as I'd had him, and all I wanted was for him to be proud of me. Part of that was making sure my family didn't have to worry about anything after he'd died, especially not my mother, who was grieving deeply but still had to keep six other humans alive.

All that to say, I'd pretty much said yes to every opportunity my agent sent my way: modeling underwear, jeans, socks, tees, boots—all of which I still received promotional packages of, all of which I still wore routinely—doing commercials for sports drinks and supplements, participating in State Farm insurance commercials for five years straight, and a slew of other things I'd rather not discuss because I was still too embarrassed to even recall them.

I'd racked up a lot of time in front of the camera in my day, had gotten quite good at playing a part, which led to brands still reaching out all these years later, wanting to work with me.

It'd been a long time since I said yes, but when my manager had passed along both of those opportunities—first, a Super Bowl commercial for NFL PLAY 60 and an ad campaign for a name brand clothing company—I knew what I had to do.

It just happened to work out that Delia wanted to go on a research trip for the bar, giving me the perfect opening to ask her to join me.

Though, when I invited her, I hadn't expected shock as a reaction.

"You want me to come with you to New York?" she asked.

"That's what I said, isn't it?"

"But why?"

"New York is an epicenter of nightlife," I said. "What better place for us to check out some bars and lounges to see what kind of vibe we're going for at the distillery."

She gnawed on her bottom lip, considering. "What kind of commercial are you shooting?" she asked. "Am I allowed to be on set?"

"It's for the NFL's national youth health and wellness program," I said, "and we're shooting in Central Park."

"But you're retired."

I placed a palm over my heart in mock pain. "Ouch, Whiskey. You wound me."

She giggled and rolled her eyes. "You know what I mean."

"I won't be the only retired athlete participating, if that makes you feel better. There's a decent mix of retired guys and current players. Should be a good time."

"And what about the photoshoot?"

I named the brand, resisting the urge to nervously rub the back of my neck. "I'm not sure what exactly I'll be modeling," I added.

Her eyes widened. "Forget the commercial. I want to be on set for *that*."

"You can have whatever you want if you come with me."

"Deal," she said quickly, and I couldn't help but laugh.

"Perfect. I know it's short notice, but I have to leave tomorrow."

"How am I supposed to get a flight that fast?"

"Don't worry about anything, Delia," I assured her. "Just show up at the TC airport at ten tomorrow morning, and I'll have everything taken care of."

"What's that supposed to mean?"

I winked. "Wouldn't you like to know?"

"Yes!" she shouted at my back as I left. "That's exactly why I asked!"

My only response was to tip my head back and laugh.

⁂

Keeping her in the dark on our travel plans was made worth it when she pulled up the next morning and stepped out of her Jeep, jaw dropping comically.

"We are not going in that," she said as she approached, a man rushing past her to get her luggage from her car.

"Sure are," I told her, moving closer and settling a hand on her lower back, lightly guiding her toward the plane's stairs. "You've never flown private before?"

"Nope," she said, dramatically popping the *p* as she rounded the corner into the aisle bisecting the opulent cabin.

The entire thing was creamy, high-end fabrics and faux-wood accents. On a small table between two of the cushy armchair style seats rested a bottle of bubbly and two flutes on a shiny silver tray. The carpeted floor muffled Delia's steps as she moved further into the space, spinning in a slow circle to take it all in.

"This is ridiculous," she said.

I shrugged. "I'm not above flying commercial," I said. "But with such a short turn around between getting the call from my manager and needing to be in NYC, this made more sense. Plus"—I moved to the bubbly and poured us each a glass, handing her one—"this is much more fun."

"It's definitely something," she said, sipping the sparkling wine. Her eyes flew to mine. "This is CD."

I scoffed. "Did you really think I'd make you drink anything else? I picked up a bottle from Birdie's this morning."

"You are..."

"Amazing? Wonderful? Incredibly sexy and handsome?"

"Those last two are kind of the same thing."

"All of the above then," I said, shooting her a wink.

Our flight attendant appeared then. "We're about ready to taxi," she said. "You should take your seats."

Twenty minutes later, we were in the air, and an hour after that, Delia slumped back in her seat with a happy groan, her napkin landing on her empty plate.

"I'm never flying commercial again."

I had to agree. It had been a last minute decision to have my chef at Birdie's prepare me and Delia breakfast of eggs Benedict, home potatoes, and Greek yogurt parfaits loaded with strawberries and blueberries.

Simple, but delicious. Not to mention, I knew it was her favorite.

Delia and I had spent plenty of alone time together, but never like this. We were encased in a metal tube hurtling through the air somewhere over Canada. No prying eyes, no nosy sisters or financial managers here to barge in on us.

Something about it was almost romantic. And I was doing everything I could to avoid thinking about the fact that there was a bedroom not twenty feet away from where we sat.

I swore this woman could read my mind sometimes because, with a furrowed brow, attention zeroed in on the mimosa in her hand, she said, "Are you a member of the Mile High Club?"

In the middle of a sip of my own drink, I practically choked, coughing roughly to expel the liquid from my windpipe. When I collected myself and looked up again, Delia met my eyes with a Cheshire smile on her lips.

"I'll take that as a yes."

"I—" Fuck. The last thing I wanted was to be talking about sex with this woman when I *thought* of nothing else. Actually, no. The last thing I wanted was to be talking about the fact that I'd had sex with women who weren't Delia. But, she'd asked, and I wasn't going to keep it a secret from her.

"I am, yes," I rasped at last.

"What was that like? Who was it with?"

"I'm not talking to you about this," I grumbled.

"Why not?"

"Because it's not important."

"Why? You embarrassed?"

I looked her dead in the eye and said, "Because if I have my way, the next woman I fuck *anywhere* will be *you*."

The last one too, I wanted to add, but I didn't want to freak her out, and we still had two hours left of this flight.

Delia snapped her mouth shut around whatever she'd been about to say next and, apparently intent on ignoring me, withdrew a small, rectangular device from her purse. I watched as she clicked it on and, almost immediately, her eyes began darting across the screen.

"What're you doing?"

She spared me the briefest of glances. "Reading."

Okay then.

※

Though I knew Delia had been to the city before, I couldn't resist pointing out all my favorite places as the hired car drove us to our hotel. I'd taken the liberty of booking us at the Ritz-Carlton Central Park, though it physically pained me to book us separate rooms. Not because of the price tag, but because I desperately wanted Delia to give into this pull between us, to stop fighting me. I was hoping the trip would finally do the trick.

Delia said little as we checked in and headed to our rooms to freshen up before we had to leave again, first to the Park for the commercial shoot, and then to meet one of my buddies for dinner.

"You know, you don't have to come with me," I said as the elevator deposited us on our floor. "You can stay here, or go shopping or something."

"It's fine," she said. "I want to see you at work."

"And you don't mind going to dinner with my buddy after?"

"Not necessarily," she says, her previous quietness suddenly yielding to perkiness and a mischievous glint in her eyes. "But I have a better idea."

My eyes narrow. "And what exactly is that?"

"You'll see," she sing-songed as she moved down the hall toward her room. "I have to make some calls first, but maybe cancel with your buddy."

"Done."

Delia laughed. "Send my regards, but I promise this will be more fun."

"Okay..." I said slowly, not entirely trusting her to keep us out of trouble. That expression—if I was a betting man, I'd say it was the physical manifestation of her inner chaos demon. "Meet back here in an hour?"

"You got it, QB." With a mock salute, she disappeared into her room.

That woman was going to be the death of me.

An hour later, we were striding through Central Park in the direction of a group gathered in the middle of a flat expanse of lawn. A perimeter was staked out by numerous cameras and other various videography equipment. The day was slightly overcast, a chill in the air. I couldn't wait to get moving, to let adrenaline warm my limbs.

As we approached, a tall Black man broke free from the group, his loud whistle cutting across the distance between us.

"Well, well, well!" he shouted, a wide grin displaying his straight, pearly white smile. "The Zero has returned."

I groaned, though I couldn't help mirror his smile. "You do know it's just 'Zero' right?"

"You sure?"

"I think my stats speak for themselves," I shot back, lightly slugging him on the shoulder before wrapping that arm around his neck and hauling him in for a hug.

"It's good to see you, old man," he said when we pulled apart.

"You too, kid. Saw that Hail Mary you threw last weekend. Your form is *almost* there."

Jalen threw back his head and let out a deep laugh. "That pass was fucking perfect, and you know it."

I did know it, but this was how our relationship worked. If we weren't giving each other shit, something was seriously wrong.

That final season before I'd retired, the Mustangs had drafted Jalen Jackson. It wasn't because they'd expected me to be on my way out before the next season started, but because we'd gone through a string of god awful backups. Guys picked up from other teams in an attempt to find someone who could fit into our offensive scheme well enough to pick up the slack if I went down with an injury.

Not that my shoes were particularly easy to fill. With a football in my hand, I felt more at home than anywhere else, save the ranch house in Dusk Valley with my chaotic family around me. Becoming an NFL quarterback was really an inevitability given my talent, though I still worked my ass off for every iota of success I achieved. I'd broken a long standing passing record in my first season, and threw for an astonishing thirty-five touchdowns in my rookie year. I was awarded the Rookie of the Year. By the time I turned twenty-five, having been in the league for four full seasons, I had broken several more records, and all of my stats pointed to me continuing to get better with age. When I tore my rotator cuff, I'd been at my peak, and I easily could've played another ten years.

But Jalen had stepped up when I'd gone down, slipping easily into that QB1 role. His rookie season had been nothing short of incredible—though not as impressive as my own, a fact I loved to remind him of every time we saw one another.

Jalen's eyes connected with something over my shoulder, and I turned, having momentarily forgotten about Delia in the excitement of seeing an old friend. Her gaze was...assessing, as though dissecting the interaction between me and Jalen, then filtering the information she gleaned through the things she already knew about me.

It wasn't that hard to figure out, honestly. Jalen was simply another younger brother, another kid I'd taken under my wing and made myself personally responsible for.

"And who do we have here?" Jalen asked, that grin now edged with something like appreciation.

"This is Delia Delatou," I said, settling a hand possessively on her lower back, ushering her into our little powwow. "Delia, this is Jalen Jackson, starting quarterback for the Detroit Mustangs."

"Pleasure to meet you, Jalen," Delia practically purred, extending her hand for him to shake.

Jalen took it in both of his, lifting it to his mouth and pressing a lingering kiss to the back.

"The pleasure is all mine, Ms. Delatou," he said, and their gazes lingered.

With a jolt, I realized they were the same age, and I had to admit, they'd make a gorgeous couple.

But Delia Delatou was *mine*. She wasn't going to be something else Jalen took from me.

Fuck, it was going to be a long afternoon.

chapter 20
Delia

WATCHING OWEN IN THIS sort of setting was...jarring, to say the least. I'd seen the man sweating through his tee at the job site, shirtless at the gym, in business casual at the office, and up to his shins in wine grapes.

This new one was disconcerting for the simple fact that it never ceased to amaze me how easily he slid into each role. Owen Lawless was a man of many talents, and it appeared that being a chameleon, shifting himself into whoever he needed to be for whatever he was doing at the moment, was one of them.

I wondered who he truly was beneath all that people-pleasing.

I wondered if *he* even knew.

Still, despite that smile he plastered on his face for Jalen and the other players he was shooting with, I didn't miss the jealousy that flared in his eyes every time Jalen and I conversed.

I loved the thrill it sent through me.

While he filmed, I took the opportunity to get plans in place for that night. When he was done, we were running short on time if we wanted to head back to the hotel and freshen up before heading to Midtown.

As he approached me, lips flattened, brow furrowed, I said brightly, "You ready?"

"For what?" he asked, still scowling.

"The surprise I planned!"

"Delia..." he sighed, shoulders drooping. "I'm not really in the mood."

"Please?" I begged. "It would mean a lot to me."

That turquoise gaze collided with mine then, and I knew he'd say yes if only because he didn't want to let me down. I hated that he felt that way, and I hated myself a little for using it to my advantage.

"Fine," he said at last.

"Great!" I clapped, then grabbed his arm and pulled him away, throwing hasty goodbyes over our shoulders.

Ten minutes later, I deposited him outside his room.

"What am I supposed to wear?" he called after me as I retreated to my own.

"Whatever you want."

"Birthday suit," he said with a nod. "Got it."

"Owen!" I hollered back with a giggle. "Jeans. T-shirt. Your boots. Pretty much exactly what you've got on."

With a mock salute, he disappeared behind his door.

I hadn't packed much that would work for tonight, but I figured I couldn't go wrong with jeans, a white baby tee, an oversized denim jacket, and my white Nikes. I quickly touched up my makeup and pulled half of my hair up into a twist atop my head, leaving the rest straight down my back. With my fingers and lobes decorated with gold jewelry, I was as ready as I'd ever be.

After a final twirl in the mirror, a knock came at my door.

"Coming!" I yelled, rushing across the room to let Owen in.

"I'm disappointed you yelled that fully clothed with a door between us, Whiskey," he said when he pushed inside. "I'd rather you be screaming it for different reasons."

I blushed, dipping my head, my hair curtaining me momentarily from his view while I collected myself. He only chuckled and said, "You ready?"

"Yep!" I said, turning from him to grab my purse and phone.

"You going to tell me where we're going yet?"

"Nope." We moved down the hall and stepped into the elevator just as my phone dinged with an incoming message that our Uber had arrived.

As we approached our destination, I directed our driver to pull around toward the back of the building.

"Whiskey…" Owen breathed when we pulled up.

I grinned wider. "You ready for this?"

"How did you pull this off?" he asked as we got out of the car, craning his neck to marvel at the historic venue before us. "Aren't Original Six matchups always sold out?"

"They sure are. Lucky for you, I know people," I said with a wink, then grabbed his hand and towed him to the back security entrance of Madison Square Garden.

I happened to be scrolling through Instagram earlier when I discovered the Detroit Warriors were in town taking on the New York Lakers. Immediately, I texted Berkley Jean, formerly Daniels, asking if she was in the city. Her husband, Brent Jean, was the star of the Warriors' team. As it turned out, she was, and she left me and Owen suite-level access passes at the door we were about to step through.

After making it through security, we were directed toward an elevator that shot us up to suite level. I'd been to Warriors' games in Detroit before, so this sort of treatment was nothing new to me. Owen, however, Mr. Former Pro QB, had his eyes comically wide, drinking in every new sight as we stepped off the elevator and headed down the hall toward the suite.

When we pushed through the door, there was barely a heartbeat of time for me to get my bearings before someone tackled me in a hug, knocking me backward into Owen.

"Lia!" the voice squealed. A voice I knew well.

I pulled away, eyes darting across the face of my eldest sister, Chloe.

"Coco!" I squeaked in return. "What are you doing here?"

"Berkley asked if Logan and I wanted to take a weekend trip!" she said. "What are *you* doing here? Did I know you were traveling?"

I snorted. "Since *I* didn't know *you* were traveling, do you really need to ask that?"

"Fair enough," my sister said with a wide grin. "God, it's so good to see you! I feel like we haven't talked in months."

I rolled my eyes. Chloe, the novelist, was the queen of over-exaggerating. "We literally talk every day."

"But not in person," she protested. "I miss you."

I pulled her in for another hug, squeezing her tighter. "I miss you more," I whispered against her hair.

Behind me, a throat cleared, and I pulled away from Chloe to turn and give Owen a sheepish grin.

"Sorry, QB," I said, moving deeper into the suite so he wasn't standing awkwardly in the doorway. "I wasn't expecting her to be here."

"It's okay, Whiskey," he said, tone low but a wide smile on his face. He looked over my shoulder and added, "Nice to see you again, Chloe."

"You as well, Owen. Come in, meet everyone!"

"Everyone?" I asked, dubiously. "You mean Berkley and Brent's family?"

"There are a few other people here too," Chloe said, gripping my hand and pulling me toward the wall of glass looking out over the arena.

Below, the teams were on the ice for warmups, circling endlessly around their own zones, taking shots on net. Some were stretching along the boards, feet kicked up on the half wall at the benches, or down on all fours, rolling their hips to warm up their hamstrings and quads.

Crowded along the exterior wall of the suite was an impressive group of people. It wasn't difficult to determine which two were Brent's parents, both dark-haired and blue-eyed, his dad tall and broad-shouldered like his son. Nearby, beneath the heads and shoulders of people gathered around her, I could see the top of Berkley's blonde head. Nearby stood a tall brunette woman, a baby in her arms, a hulking blond man standing at her side. Then there was my brother-in-law, a Warriors cap settled on his head, bright blue eyes and wide grin trained on me.

"Little sis!" Logan said, pushing through the crowd to scoop me into a hug. "Good to see you!"

"Hey!" someone—I assumed Berkley—yelled from behind him.

"You're my little sis too, Berk," he said back.

"Obviously," she replied, eye roll evident in her tone.

I couldn't help but laugh, loving this extended family like it was my own. They were equally as crazy as mine, and loved each other as fiercely.

When the crowd parted to reveal our arrival, Berkley let out a yelp of excitement, unceremoniously shoving her nearly two-year-old son, Brooks, into her father-in-law's arms before rushing over to wrap me in a hug.

Owing to the fact that she was only a few inches over five feet, Berkley's face wound up smooshed against my chest, but I didn't mind. The girl had always given the best hugs, and now that her brother was my brother-in-law, she was even more like family than she and the rest of the Daniels clan had been growing up. Only a year older than me, she had graduated high school with Amara.

"How are you?" I asked when we broke apart. "I see Brooks, but where's Bentley?"

Berkley turned and pointed at the brunette with the baby I'd clocked earlier. "With his auntie. Lexie!" The woman lifted her head, hazel eyes locking on mine, cool and assessing.

Damn, she was stunning. Tall and thin, similar in stature and complexion to me and Chloe. Honestly, she could have passed for a sixth Delatou sister.

I didn't know what it was, but I liked her instantly.

With confident, unhurried steps, Lexie approached us, the blond man trailing after her. When she reached us, she handed the sleeping baby Bentley to his mother.

"Delia, this is my best friend, Lexie," Berkley said, tucking her youngest son against her shoulder and absently rubbing circles along his back. His little cheeks were squished against a set of noise-cancelling ear muffs, long, dark eyelashes fanned across them. Then she gestured to the man. "And this is her husband, Mitch."

"You used to play for the Warriors," Owen said. "Didn't you?"

Mitch nodded, and Owen stuck his hand out. "Owen Lawless," he said when Mitch grasped it. "I played for the—"

"Mustangs," Mitch finished. "I remember."

"Shame about your back," Owen told him.

"And your shoulder," Mitch replied, offering him a commiserative smile.

Berkley and Lexie simply nodded, and it seemed everyone knew what they were talking about but me. I made a mental note to ask Owen about it later.

"It all worked out in the end."

Mitch hooked his arm around his wife's waist, pulling her back against him. "It sure did."

Owen glanced at me then, and while I couldn't decipher the emotion swimming in his eyes, I knew it had everything to do with the couple in front of us, and how obviously in love they were. In fact, we were surrounded by happy couples—Berkley's babies the evidence of hers while her husband was on the ice—and I couldn't ignore the desire that surged within me.

Desire for that same happiness. Desire for a family of my own.

Desire for Owen.

The only problem was finding a way to make myself believe I deserved it all with him.

⚜ ⚜

The Warriors beat the Lakers by a score of two to one, Brent having scored the game-winning goal. Afterward, Brent, Berkley, Lexie, Mitch, Chloe, Logan, Owen, and I went out to a swanky bar uptown, a place Brent and Berkley assured us would be perfect inspiration for the distillery, while Brent's parents took their boys back to the hotel. It was strange to be going out on what was essentially a quadruple date without actually being in a relationship, but I didn't protest. I liked the way Owen tucked me into his side in the giant SUV that delivered us to the bar, and how he grabbed my hand after helping me out, lacing our fingers together as we followed my friends inside. His touches came more freely these days, as though he was doing everything in his power to convince me taking a chance on us was a good idea.

And it wasn't that I thought it wasn't. It was more…that twenty-two year old girl inside me who'd had her heart shredded by an older man, one who only wanted me for one thing, was having difficulty now, at twenty-seven, putting myself in that position again.

Owen wasn't that douchebag professor; I knew that. But that was the first and last time I'd truly been in an "adult" relationship, and I struggled to give anyone the power to hurt me. I'd barricaded myself behind steel reinforced walls for the last five years, and it was going to take some time to tear them down.

But all thoughts of Owen flew out of my mind the moment we walked into the bar. An audible gasp left me as I took in the space around us, pausing right inside the door to spin in a slow circle, soaking everything in.

The walls were paneled to look like logs, the bar top and tables all smoothly sanded and sealed light wooden slabs—birch, if I had to guess—the floor a bronzy poured concrete. The more earthy touches were balanced by multiple crystal chandeliers hanging at regular intervals, plush, burgundy velvet couches, and mahogany leather chairs with brass studding details. Soft jazz music played in the background as patrons conversed quietly.

It was exactly the vibe I was going for with Unlawful: rustic elegance.

As I withdrew my phone to start taking pictures and videos, not wanting to forget a single thing about the space, a hand settled on my lower back and a low voice met my ear, sending goosebumps skittering across my skin.

"Do you want me to buy this entire building, pick it up, and move it to Michigan?"

I scoffed, tipping my head back into Owen's shoulder to glare up at him. "Absolutely not."

"I could, you know."

"I know you *could*," I told him. "But Unlawful is going to be much better than this."

"And how is that?"

"Because it's ours."

Owen grinned, his palm sliding around to my hip as I turned into him.

My god, he was beautiful. Staring into his eyes right then,

I couldn't think of a single damn reason why I was fighting this. My tongue dipped out to trace my bottom lip, and Owen followed the movement, his eyes turning stormy in an instant. His nostrils flared, head tilting slightly, angling toward me—

"Get a room!" someone yelled, and I jumped away from him like I'd been burned, my cheeks heating as my sister's cackle floated past us.

"That was close," I breathed as I moved away from him, hoping it was too low for him to hear.

His hand shot out and locked on my wrist, and though I didn't want to, knew any prolonged eye contact would destroy my resolve, I met his gaze anyway.

"This isn't over," he growled.

"Of course not," I grumbled as he led us to the table where the rest of our party waited.

"About time you join us," Logan smirked when we sat in the two remaining seats; I wound up sandwiched between Owen and Berkley.

"I was taking pictures for inspiration," I protested weakly.

"Right, little sister," Chloe said from across the table, winking. "That's exactly what it looked like. The last time a man looked at *me* like that"—she shot her husband a sly smile then settled a hand on the swell of her abdomen—"I wound up pregnant."

Hoots and hollers rose from the rest of our group, but Owen and I weren't laughing. Yet again, my face flamed. I wasn't embarrassed about the prospect of being with Owen, or of him in general. I'd be stupid to be ashamed of a man like him, who had nothing but light and goodness at his core. I was embarrassed that these people were making assumptions about something that Owen and I had yet to figure out ourselves. I didn't like having my private business publicly examined, and I knew Owen's experience as an athlete had turned him into even more of a recluse than myself where his personal life was concerned.

Thankfully, before I could argue further, a waiter appeared at our table, taking drink—virgin for Chloe—and appetizer orders. When he left, the conversation moved on to something else, and I turned my attention inward, unable to stop marveling at this space.

Once the initial discomfort over Logan and Chloe calling me and Owen out wore off, our evening passed smoothly, full of stories and laughter, good food, and excellent drinks. When we'd finished eating, Brent suggested we head to the rooftop bar for a nightcap, assuring us that, despite the November chill, it would be toasty thanks to numerous outdoor space heaters.

Even if it had been freezing, I would've wanted to see it simply for the view it offered. Manhattan spread out beneath us, a sea of glittering lights like the sky above us was reflected in the city. I remained at the railing alone, and a moment later, my sister, Berkley, and Lexie approached. Chloe handed me a margarita and inclined her head to a nearby conversational grouping, where four rolled arm chairs were angled toward a small glass table.

My sister wasted no time interrogating me once we'd taken our seats.

"What is going on with you and Owen, Lia?"

"Nothing," I said quickly, which wasn't entirely a lie but also not the whole truth.

"Doesn't look like nothing," Lexie said. "And that's coming

from someone who knows nothing about either of you beyond what I've learned in the last few hours."

Ignoring both her and my sister, I looked at Berkley.

"How did you do it?" I asked quietly.

I knew about Berkley's past. We were from a small town, after all. Had gone to high school together. I knew about her ex, and the way he'd manipulated, cheated on, then ultimately broke up with her when she questioned his loyalty. I felt a kinship with her in that regard, to have our first serious relationships betray us so deeply. But she was beyond happy now, and I wanted that for myself.

"It's easy to be brave with the right one," she said softly, giving me a little shrug and a smile, though the latter was directed across the rooftop at her husband, who stood with the three other guys, conversing.

"But what if he's not?"

"You won't know unless you try," Chloe said, reaching out to settle her hand atop mine, her touch instantly grounding me.

"I know I don't know you, Delia, but speaking from experience"—Lexie glanced over at her own husband, who looked up at the same moment and shot her a wink—"I fought it for a long time with him—"

"Too long," Berkley interrupted on a fake cough into her fist.

"—and in the end all I did was waste that time. I knew from the moment I met him he was the one. It just took a long time for my mind to catch up, for it to recognize that the person meant for me would take care of my heart if I gave it to him. Do you think Owen is that guy for you?"

"I don't know."

"I think you do," Lexie said, smiling faintly and inclining her head toward the guys. "I think you've known it all along."

And when I glanced up at them again, Owen was already looking at me.

chapter 21
Owen

"WHAT DO YOU THINK they're talking about over there?" Brent asked, inclining his head toward the women.

"Knowing our wives," Mitch said to his best friend, "probably us."

I quirked a brow. "They have a habit of that?"

Logan snorted. "Those two are thick as thieves," he said, pointing at his sister and Lexie. "And with Chloe added to the mix...well, you've seen how Delia is with her sisters, right? It's like that."

"What's going on with you two?"

Though I kept my eyes trained on my whiskey glass, I knew Brent was asking me. "I don't know."

Mitch snorted. "Been there, brother."

I looked up at him then. "Seems we have a lot in common."

Mitch nodded sagely. "It really was a shame about your shoulder," he said quietly. "Speaking from experience, I know how hard it is to go down like that."

I shrugged, not wanting to get into it here and now. I knew he understood, and that Brent likely did too, having been on the frontlines when his best friend lost his career. Not to mention getting onto that ice every night with the knowledge that the same thing could happen to him.

"It worked out okay," I said, though my shoulder twitched slightly, as though itching to pick up a football and give it a toss. There were days when missing the game was the phantom pain of a long lost limb, but I powered through.

In the grand scheme, I had a lot to be thankful for.

"How's the distillery construction coming?" Logan asked. "My dad has been MIA for months now."

I grinned sheepishly. "It's good. We're just about ready to start painting and decorating, which is why I asked Delia to come with me this weekend."

Logan snorted. "Yeah, *that's* why you brought her."

I gave him a good natured slug on the arm as the four of us devolved into laughter.

"I like her," I said quietly. "A lot more than I ever thought I could or planned on."

"They sneak up on you like that sometimes," Mitch said, staring across the rooftop at his wife. "You never really see it coming."

"Psh," Logan scoffed. "I saw Chloe coming from a mile away."

"Yeah well you've literally known her your entire life," Brent reminded him. "Personally, I never saw Berk coming. But once she showed up...I was done for."

"We know," Logan and Mitch said simultaneously, and I choked on a laugh as Brent crossed his arms petulantly over his chest.

"So what exactly are you waiting for?" Mitch asked me.

"Her," I said. "She's been through some shit, and I'm not trying to rush her. She's also so much younger than me, you know?"

Logan rolled his eyes. "She's twenty-seven, man. Not exactly *young*."

"I know, it's just..." I trailed off, unsure how I wanted to finish that statement. They seemed to get what I was saying, though—Mitch especially.

"I waited a long time for that girl," Mitch said. "I would've waited forever if that's what she needed from me. She's it for me, and even when it killed me to give her that space, she was worth it."

I scrubbed a hand over my face then tossed back the rest of my whiskey, the burn down my throat doing nothing to soothe the fire Delia ignited in my blood. Still, I couldn't look away from her. I was mesmerized by the way the firelight danced on her dark hair, turning it more milk than dark chocolate, by the way those same flames set her eyes aglow.

And when she glanced up to find me staring, I held those whiskey depths with my ocean ones, wondering if she could read all over my face what I was thinking. That I wanted to be part of more nights like this in more than just a physical sense. That I wanted to bullshit with my married guy friends while our wives sat across the room gossiping about us, about our kids, about the fucking PTA or whatever other bullshit they wanted. That I wanted to mold our two massive families together, to make her sisters mine and my brothers and Aria hers.

That maybe, if she'd have me, I wanted forever with her.

⁂

"What was the comment you made to Mitch earlier about his back?" Delia asked in the car on the way home from the bar.

I shifted to face her, her profile illuminated by the passing street lights. "About five years ago, only a few seasons after my shoulder injury, he took a bad hit in a game that aggravated an old lower back injury. He was forced into early retirement or he risked paralysis in his lower extremities."

Delia gasped. "God, that's awful."

I nodded, though she wasn't looking at me, and swallowed around the lump that had lodged in my throat. Talking about this stuff was always difficult for me, dredging up memories I'd rather stayed buried. "It is," I agreed. "It's...hard. Giving it up. Losing it. This intrinsic piece of you is just gone suddenly, and you have to figure out how to fill the hole."

"Which is why you started your little business empire," she said, shooting me a grin, teeth flashing in the dark, and slapping a palm down on my thigh.

Her warmth spread through me instantly, and it took every ounce of willpower I had to keep my cock from hardening. I only covered my hand with hers and growled, "There's nothing little about it, Whiskey."

Our car pulled up to the hotel then, and as she exited, she tossed over her shoulder, "We'll see."

Fuck, she was going to be the death of me.

As we strode into the lobby, I extended my stride to catch up with her, unable to resist the urge to hold her hand. When we touched, she only looked up at me briefly, giving my fingers a squeeze as we made our way to the elevator.

Safely ensconced inside, without looking at me, Delia said quietly, "You can talk to me about it, you know. Any of it. Losing football. Your dad."

"I know, Whiskey," I whispered. "But I don't want you to have to carry that on top of all your shit."

"I don't mind," she said, turning to face me. "In fact, I'm *asking* you to let me. Let me bear some of the burden for you. I trusted you with my so-called 'shit,' so why can't you do the same?"

"It's not that easy."

"It could be," she said. "You're just being a man about the whole thing."

The elevator doors opened then, and she ripped her hand free from mine and stomped off down the hall. I chased after her, catching her around the waist before she could unlock her door.

"Owen!" she squealed as I hauled her backward, in the direction of my room. "Put me down right now!"

"No," I grumbled.

Even as I keyed open my door, I wasn't sure what I'd say to her, what words I'd be able to force out of that locked cage inside me where everything I didn't want to face lived.

But maybe...this moment with this girl was the perfect time to face them.

"What is wrong with you?" Delia shouted as I set her on her feet in the center of my massive suite.

"You wanted to talk," I said.

"Yeah, *talk*. Not be manhandled by a broody quarterback."

"Retired," I reflexively reminded her.

She rolled her eyes. "God, you're infuriating. If you don't want to tell me, I'm not going to force you, Owen. I'll just go back to my room and go to sleep. We can forget this ever happened."

Before she even moved, I took a step to the left, anticipating her intention to shove past me and blocking her path.

"I do want to tell you," I said quietly, though I held her gaze. "In fact, I think you're the only person I *can* tell. But that doesn't mean I'm not terrified you'll look at me differently afterward."

"You think I didn't feel that way dumping all my shit on you?" Those whiskey eyes were fierce, boring into mine, cutting straight to my soul. "But I did it anyway. Berkley said something to me tonight that I think you can benefit from right now."

"And what is that?"

"That it's easy to be brave with the right one. So I'm asking you to be brave right now, QB. For me. For...us."

The last word was spoken barely above a whisper, but she might as well have shouted it for how loudly it echoed in my mind, in my chest, in my heart.

"Us?"

She nodded. "Can you do that?"

"Can I at least change first?" I asked, gesturing to my jeans.

"Duh," she said. "I'll run over to my room and be right back."

"Absolutely not," I said, catching her wrist before she could leave. "I'm afraid if I let you go, by the time you come back, I'll have lost my nerve. Or that you won't come back at all. I'll give you a shirt to wear."

One of Delia's brows arched. "Just a shirt?"

"You got a problem with that?"

"Of course not," she said, though the thickness of her tone said differently. "Just...keep your hands to yourself."

I raised said hands in the air and backed up a step. "Whatever you want."

I moved into my bedroom and withdrew two tees from my suitcase, turning to toss one at Delia, who stood at the threshold.

"You can come in, you know," I said.

Delia vehemently shook her head. "I'm good here."

I chuckled. "You can use the bathroom," I said, nodding at the door adjoining it to my room.

Delia nodded and rushed past me, ripping the tee from my hand as she did. I quickly stripped, shoving my legs into athletic shorts and donning one of my endless, well-worn Carhartt shirts.

The bathroom door creeped open, and my mouth dried out when I took in Delia. My shirt hung to mid-thigh, more than covering all the important bits, but I didn't stop my mind from wandering. Even with the knowledge that nothing was happening between us tonight, I couldn't help the way my imagination ran rampant with ideas about the positions I could contort those long legs into when I finally got her naked.

Yes, *finally*. At this point, we were an inevitability, even if something still held her back. Maybe she wanted all our cards on the table, and it was my turn to fold.

Whatever she needed, I'd happily give it to her.

We settled on the plush, deep-cushioned couch in the sitting room, pressed close together.

There wasn't really an easy or wise place to begin my story, so I unceremoniously dove in at the most logical: the night I found out my dad died.

"I'd been studying when I got the call," I started. "It was Thanksgiving weekend, but with finals coming up and mandatory practices, I just couldn't swing the few days off to head home. I had just made dinner, and my roommate and a couple other teammates were at our place pregaming, all of them giving me shit for not going out to the party with them."

And all of it poured out: getting the call from West, listening to my mother wailing in the background, Trey finally telling me I needed to come home. Getting there and allowing myself one moment to break down before I took over, holding my family together in the wake of losing our glue.

"Although, as it turned out," I mused, "Mama was really the glue."

Delia squeezed my fingers tightly. Grounding me. Making it easier to get this next part out.

"Internally, I sort of fell apart, though from the outside it probably looked like I used his death as a motivator, a reason to throw myself even harder into football and school. And I kept my head on straight for the game, for my teammates, but away from that...I was a mess. Drinking more than I ever had, hardly sleeping or eating. It was honestly a wonder I didn't faint any time I stepped onto the field. And who knows how long I would've continued like that if Trey hadn't stepped in."

"What happened?"

"My mom and siblings hadn't been able to make it to the Pac-12 championship game, and they barely scrounged up enough money to make it to the Rose Bowl game. Afterward, after photos and interviews and all of my other obligations were over, Trey locked me in a hotel room with him and basically forced it all out of me."

I told her about my fit of rage, how I'd never acted like that before or since. How Trey understood that I needed someone there for me while I fell apart, since I'd been the one doing so for everyone else for over a month at that point.

"It was brutal," I said softly, wincing. "The things I said. About myself, about my dad. I cursed anyone and anything I could think of. But it was cathartic in a way, you know? Finally letting someone else carry that weight."

"That always helps," Delia snarked, a callback to how this conversation started in the first place, and I shot her a glare that quickly morphed into a smile that matched hers.

"*Anyway*," I continued, pinching her thigh. "Trey scheduled me an appointment with a therapist back in Eugene, and I saw her twice a week until I left for the draft and everything that came after.

"And things were almost...*good* after that. The weight of losing my dad, of taking on so much responsibility crushed me less and less every day. I moved out to Detroit and settled into my new life. The next ten or so years were...smooth."

"Until they weren't," Delia said.

"Until they weren't," I agreed. "Losing the game hadn't been like losing my dad. It was, after all, only a game. But when that game had provided for me and my family for a decade while my brothers and Aria grew up, while *I* grew up, when it gave me something to look forward to when the black clouds of grief shrouded me...it wasn't easy to let it go."

"Your whole identity had been wrapped up in it," Delia said.

"It's normal to mourn that."

I nodded, my throat thickening with emotion. "I started going to therapy again after that, and I still speak with her once a month or so. Just to keep myself on track."

When I realized I'd never take a meaningful NFL snap again, I'd be damned if it hadn't felt like getting the call that Dad died all over again.

"That's how Jalen and I know each other," I said, absently stroking my thumb across the smooth skin of her thigh. "They drafted him the same season I got hurt. Backing me up wasn't easy for him, I'm sure. He'd been a hotshot in college. And I knew stepping into my shoes when I went down was probably the hardest job in the league that season. But he continued to impress all of us with his poise and hard work that year. When I ultimately decided to retire, I knew I was leaving the team in good hands. He still calls me for advice, and I watch every one of their games just so I can give him shit about some nonexistent error he made. Having a good guy like that, and a hell of a talent, taking my place made things...easier somehow. It would've been harder giving up my spot to an asshole."

"And how does it all feel now?" Delia asked. "To have this separation from it all? From both of those losses?"

I shifted so I could drape her legs across my lap, reaching up to tuck a lock of her hair behind her ear.

Staring deep into her eyes, I said, "A lot better with you around. I think I was just coasting before you showed up. And then you came in with your chaos and your demands and all that goddamn energy and...it was impossible not to bask in your light, Whiskey. To look at you, to be near you, and not want to be more than just a shell of a man.

"This thing between us...I think it brought me back to life."

The weight on my shoulders lessened significantly with the admission, and I heaved a long, steady breath, smiling at her as I softly exhaled.

Delia's eyes shone brightly in the dim light of the room, and when she spoke, her voice was a hoarse, breathy whisper.

"I told you it was easy to be brave."

OWEN AND I TALKED late into the night, both of us falling asleep without ever deciding to do so. An undercurrent of sexual tension pulsed through the entire interaction, every touch heightened, every glance setting my skin on fire. It scared me, how much I wanted him, how badly I wanted to shove him back into the couch cushions, straddle his lap, and have my way with him. But in the same way I wouldn't want anyone to touch me after an emotional purging like the one he'd endured, I refused to let us go there. For his sake and mine, I wanted us both clear-headed when we took that final step.

Still, when I woke the next morning wrapped in the cocoon of his body, I felt safe. Cherished. Like a woman worthy of this man who had absolutely no idea how good he was. I was officially making it my job to remind him of that, to make him see himself the way I did. Even if another part of me practically begged on her knees in my mind to let him fuck me.

Shifting slightly, I pulled back enough to look at him. His

brow was smoothed in sleep, his hair sticking up in a thousand different directions, his full mouth slightly parted, each exhale blowing light puffs of air against my forehead. I grinned as I buried my face against his chest again, not wanting to get up quite yet.

Only, Owen's alarm had other ideas.

"Nooooo," he groaned sleepily, his arms wrapping tighter around me. "Do we have to?"

"I'm afraid so, QB," I said. "Or did you forget you have to get all pretty and have your picture taken today? And then we've got the charity gala tonight!"

The trip to New York had been fortuitous on that front, allowing Owen to accept an invitation to a charity function supporting at-risk youth across the country. I'd never known that particular struggle myself, and I knew Owen hadn't either, but with platforms as large as ours, we couldn't in good conscience not support something so underfunded and vital to the survival of our society.

Owen's hand swept down my spine, his fingers sinking into my ass hard enough that I yelped as he growled, "Don't call me pretty."

"Don't grab my ass."

His eyes flew open, and apparently I'd faked discomfort better than I thought, because his hand was gone in an instant.

"I'm sorry," he said quickly, trying to snake his other arm out from beneath my body. "I wasn't thinking."

I locked my fingers into the front of his shirt to hold him still, to keep him near, a laugh bursting free. "I was joking, QB. I kinda like it when you get all possessive and squeeze my ass like that."

Owen made a deep, low sound in the back of his throat that rumbled over my entire body. Once again, his palm settled over one of my cheeks, the tips of those long, thick fingers lightly digging into the bare flesh around my underwear. "Don't start something you can't finish, Whiskey."

"Why not?" I asked, my voice going breathy as my heart rate sped.

He responded by sliding his hand down to the back of my thigh and hooking it over his hip, slipping his own between my legs. A breath away from my core, the insistent throbbing of my pulse in my clit begged for friction. The hard length of his cock pressed between us, and my mouth went dry. Even through his boxer briefs, his size was evident.

Fuck, how badly I wanted to shed my panties, pull his shorts down, and shift until he could slide inside me. It was obvious he wanted me equally as bad.

"We don't have time for all the things I plan to do to you."

His words sent a shiver through me, goosebumps raising on my skin, and his answering chuckle was nothing short of wicked.

Before I did something rash like make him prove it, I shoved hard on his chest, his hold on me breaking and sending me tumbling off the couch to the floor. I was back on my feet in an instant, collecting my clothes and rushing to the door and out into the hall, Owen's dark laugh following me the whole way.

∾∾∾∾∾ ∾∾∾∾∾

I thought distance from Owen during the photoshoot would quell the desire coursing through my veins.

That was before I realized said photoshoot would vastly consist of him being shirtless and posing in underwear that hugged his ass and...other things.

It all started out innocent enough. They had him pose in an array of tops and pants, tugging up the hem of a tee up here and there to display the iconic waistband of the brand's underwear, offering me tantalizing glimpses of his abdomen.

At one point, he'd donned a cowboy hat, jean jacket, and those favored pair of scuffed boots he wore everywhere, and I swore I got pregnant in that moment. It was so easy to imagine him exactly like that on the Lawless Ranch instead of the set, his skin golden brown and glistening with sweat under the sun instead of the bright artificial lighting.

This was yet another place where Owen slipped into a new persona seamlessly, but it didn't bother me as much as it would have before. After last night, I had a clearer picture of who he was beneath the many hats he wore, and I had to admit—*that* man, the one with demons and scars he tried so hard to keep from everyone, was just about the sexiest thing I'd ever laid eyes on.

I was falling harder for him every day.

Especially when he disappeared behind a curtain and emerged moments later clad in nothing but black boxer briefs, exactly like the ones he always wore. I wondered if he received a lifetime supply or if he loved them so much he bought them in bulk.

Either way, the man was a goddamn specimen, with every muscle on his large body perfectly defined, honed from years of hard work and showing no signs of softening. I must've made an audible sound at all that skin on display, unable to tear my eyes away from his pecs and the sandy hair that dusted them and the valley between, because one of the assistants standing nearby nudged me with an elbow.

"He's gorgeous, isn't he?"

"Easily the hottest man I've ever laid eyes on," I agreed.

"Are you his girlfriend?" she asked, and I didn't miss the annoyance that tinged her words.

"No," I said, which wasn't technically a lie. Although, I wouldn't mind that label. I wouldn't mind a lot of things where he was concerned. "His business partner."

"What kind of business?"

"We're opening a distillery back in Michigan," I said. "He invited me out here with him to do some market research and get some inspiration for our design scheme. I'm just tagging along to this," I added, swinging my arms around at the space, which was actually a mostly empty apartment on the third floor of an industrial building.

"That's cool," she said, though her tone implied she felt the opposite.

From my peripheral, I studied her as best as I could. She was a few inches shorter than me, with wispy blonde hair, high cheekbones, and porcelain skin.

My best guess was that she'd rather be the one in front of the camera, but something prevented her from doing so. As an assistant to the photographer, I assumed she felt some sort of ownership over the models and other celebrities that came across her path. I could easily imagine her getting off work, going out for drinks with her girlfriends, and spilling all the tea—maybe even making up little scenarios of things that never happened to make herself look and feel more important while those friends gushed over her.

All that to say, I didn't appreciate the way she'd been glued to my hip since Owen and I arrived, like I was an interloper here.

And okay, maybe I was. But that man? The one currently sprawled out on crisp white bed sheets while the photographer hovered over him, the shutter on his camera going wild?

He. Was. Mine.

When shooting paused for a moment so Owen could change into different underwear, these ones bright orange with the logo printed in black on the band, I stepped away from the assistant to move closer to the action.

Owen must've clocked me, because he glanced up as I approached, shooting me a smirk as my eyes once again strayed to his chest.

"Like what you see, Whiskey?"

I shrugged, the portrait of nonchalance. "Not bad for an old man."

"He has aged like fine wine," the photographer, an obvious Frenchman by his accent, said as he fiddled with his camera, switching out one lens for another. He looked up at me then, eyes widening. "Who are you?"

I pointed a finger into the center of my chest. "Me?"

"Yes, darling," he said, stepping closer, his gazing sweeping me from head to toe. It wasn't lecherous or uncomfortable. It was simply an artist examining a subject. "Who are *you*?" He pointed at Owen, who watched us curiously. In fact, everyone in the room had their attention on us. It was so quiet, you could hear a pin drop. "Do you know him?"

"He's my business partner," I said, anxiety flaring in my chest. What was with the third degree?

"Partners? Ah, but that is perfect!" He clapped his hands together excitedly, like a child being presented with his favorite treat. "Sonya, we brought women's wear, yes?"

"Yes, sir," the woman who'd been speaking to me earlier said, rushing up to join our little powwow. "But surely you can't..." She trailed off, cutting me a glare, as though she didn't want to finish what was surely about to be a rude comment right in front of me.

Because doing it behind my back was so much better.

"I can," the photographer said vehemently. "And I will." He turned to me again. "What is your name?"

"Delia," I said. "Delia Delatou."

"Delia Delatou and Owen Lawless," he sing-songed. "A match made in heaven. I am Felix Alain, and I am quite pleased to meet you."

"You as well," I said, a bit dumbstruck as I shook his proffered hand. "But...what exactly is happening?"

"Oh, my dear, you are too cute," he said, tapping my nose with his pointer finger. "You're going to feature in this ad campaign with Owen!"

"I'm going to *what*?" I asked, incredulous. "But I'm not a model!"

"Neither am I," Owen reminded me. "C'mon. It'll be fun."

"*Fun*? I've never done this before, QB! I have no idea what I'm doing!"

Owen prowled toward me, his steps tentative, as though he expected me to bolt at any second. Truthfully, I considered it, but then he was in front of me, settling those big hands on my shoulders. The man had no right to be so commanding dressed in only underwear.

"You can do this," he assured me. "You take photos all day long. So pretend you're one of your subjects. Felix Alain here is going to make this as painless as possible for us." He stared deep into my eyes, imploring. "Do you trust me?"

"Of course," I said without hesitation.

"Good," Owen grinned. "I promise it'll be okay. Plus, I've always thought you were too hot to be hiding behind the camera. This is your moment to shine."

I couldn't help but choke out a laugh, the knot of nerves in my chest unraveling and melting away instantly. Heaving a deep sigh, I nodded. I could do this.

With Owen at my side, I could do anything.

On shaky legs, I followed a petulant Sonya to a bedroom in the back corner of the apartment. Unceremoniously, she threw a bra and panty set onto the bed and chirped at me to get dressed before leaving the room again.

I quickly stripped out of my clothing, goosebumps raising on every inch of my exposed skin as I stepped into the intimates. The bra was lightweight cotton with a scoop neck that matched the same orange of Owen's shorts. There was a wide, white band across the bottom with the brand logo stitched in black, and the panties matched. Before leaving the room, I took a moment to twist and turn in the full body mirror resting on the floor in the corner, deciding I looked amazing. The bright fabric popped against my olive skin, the cut of the panties making my legs look miles long, my modest chest perked up in the sports bra. I felt sexy, and excited anticipation mixed with nerves pricked at my skin. I sent a silent prayer up to whatever unseen force nudged me to get an emergency wax and take an everything shower before this trip. As it was, everything below my waist was smooth as silk.

With a deep breath, I opened the door and stepped out into the bright living space.

Immediately, the hair and makeup team descended on me, running a brush through my mane and dabbing powder along my t-zone. Thankfully, I'd been blessed with dark, thick brows and lashes, and per Felix Alain's instruction, I wasn't allowed to wear any makeup but a little highlighter on my cheek and collarbones.

When I'd gone into the room to change, Felix Alain had been directing Owen toward a white leather chair, but when I stepped onto the set, the heat from the lights instantly warming my skin, Owen was once again positioned on the bed. He was in the center of it, upright on his knees, hands on his hips while he waited for me.

God, give the man a cape and he'd be a fucking superhero.

"You are breathtaking, my dear," Felix Alain said, settling a hand on my lower back and ushering me deeper onto the set. "Now I want you to get up there next to Owen. With two of you, we are going less for sexy and more for sensual. Romantic. A couple waking up and lazing the morning away in bed. In fact..."

He trailed off, spinning and snapping his fingers at another assistant. "You. Get me one of the denim classic button downs for Miss Delatou."

"I've got it!" Sonya shouted, rushing across the room and

hurrying over with the shirt, unceremoniously throwing it at my head despite obviously wanting to get in Felix Alain's good graces.

God, I wanted this to be over if only so I could get the hell away from her negative energy. I was already nervous enough, both at the thought of being on camera, posing for photos that would appear in an *international ad campaign*, and also over doing this with Owen. I'd barely kept my hands to myself this morning, and now I was being given permission to put them all over his chiseled body?

Lord help me.

I stuffed my arms into the denim shirt, grateful for the small amount of modesty it provided me. I wasn't ashamed of my body in the slightest, but I'd never put it on display like that before. Where everyone in the room was watching me, analyzing me. Surely Sonya's little brain was spinning, critiquing every inch of my skin.

My pulse reached cardiac event levels as I knelt on the bed and shuffled over to Owen, though the nerves instantly receded when I looked into his eyes. Their ocean depths were calming in a way that nothing else in my life was. As if it was the most natural thing in the world, Owen reached out, resting one hand on my hip, the other dragging the collar of the shirt back to reveal one strap of the bra, my bare shoulder, and my chest down to the barest hint of my ribs along my side. Distantly, I heard the shutter of the camera going off as Owen danced his fingertips across my exposed flesh.

Goosebumps raised in their wake, and I sucked in a breath.

"It's just us, Whiskey," he whispered. "Remember how you

felt about me this morning? Just imagine we're back there."

Pretend? I could do that.

"I wanted you so badly."

"Yeah?" he asked, voice rough. "What did you want from me exactly?"

My core turned molten, heat pooling between my legs. "I wanted you to move my panties to the side and slide your fingers through my pussy."

Owen groaned, barely loud enough for me to hear. "Would you have been wet for me?"

"Soaked," I breathed. "And I wanted you to kiss me."

"I've been waiting for you to let me."

Then he moved until his lips were centimeters away, until my exhales became his inhales, until a simple, slight shift forward from me would have us locked together.

But not here. I didn't want that first time to be in front of a crowd of people, all of whom were being paid to watch our every move.

Still, the world had melted away so completely as we cocooned ourselves inside that bubble that I practically jumped three feet in the air when Felix Alain's voice rang out.

"Are you sure you two are not more than business partners?" he crowed. "My camera is on fire! This is going to be a wildly successful campaign, I can feel it. These photos are..." He pinched his fingers together and brought them to his mouth, pulling them away with a "muah!" "*C'est magnifique!*"

"I'm sure," I croaked, and Owen only smirked.

"Well, you should be," Felix Alain said. "The way you two look at each other? The chemistry? It is explosive."

"One day," Owen said, loud enough for everyone to hear, though his gaze never left mine. "One day she'll be mine."

I only smiled mildly. I wasn't about to correct him—to tell him I already was.

chapter 23
Delia

THE TIME BETWEEN THE photoshoot and leaving for the charity gala was a much needed reprieve from Owen and his whole...everything.

My social battery was seriously depleted, but I couldn't exactly beg off from attending a charity function. The last thing I felt like doing was getting all fancied up and schmoozing with rich people, but it was important to Owen, so it was important to me.

I was nervous about being near him all night, about the comments and questions people would throw our way about our relationship. But when I let him into my room when the car arrived, I couldn't help but chuckle, some of that anxiety melting away at the way his eyes comically widened as he took me in.

"Whiskey," he groaned, scrubbing a hand over his face, his mouth hanging open, lower lip catching on his palm.

"What?" I asked innocently.

"That fucking dress."

"This old thing?" I said, shimmying my hips side to side, the little gems decorating the bodice sparkling in the hotel room lamps.

"Old," Owen choked out on a laugh. "If that dress is old, then I'm the Pope."

I crossed my arms over my chest and narrowed my eyes at him. "What're you saying right now, QB?"

Owen stepped closer and slid his arms around my waist, pressing a chaste kiss to my forehead before quickly backing away. It was as if he couldn't stand not touching me, but also couldn't handle prolonged contact.

"You are...resplendent, Whiskey."

"Resplendent," I repeated, preening. "Awfully big word for a jock."

He laced his fingers through mine to tug me from the room, his tone low and promising as he said, "That's not the only big thing I've got."

Fuck me, I was in so much trouble.

***

Leave it to rich people to turn the fight against poverty into such a goddamn spectacle.

The event was being held at some swanky event space in Midtown. Honestly, I didn't pay much attention to where we were. My entire world had narrowed to every point of contact between me and Owen. My hands and arms and thighs tingled every time he brushed up against me. We'd only just arrived, and I was damn near ready to combust.

For his part, Owen was cool as a cucumber, seemingly unaffected by my nearness. In fact, it would've given me a complex had he not gripped my hand tighter, anchoring me to his side every time I attempted to pull away.

"You stay here," he growled. "All night."

I only nodded, sipping my sparkling wine and fighting off a shiver at the possessiveness of his words.

God, I was in a bad way.

It got worse when we moved deeper into the party and I stood idly by while he chatted with every single person who stopped him. He always made sure to introduce me, never offering up who I was to him, instead allowing people to make their own assumptions about us. It was a nebulous explanation I appreciated, not knowing myself what we were. Business partners? Obviously. But...more too. Even if we hadn't acted on it yet, those thoughts and feelings were there, and I knew it was only a matter of time.

The event—unsurprisingly given the ticket price—had a fancy, sit down dinner. Though the food was good, it honestly didn't hold a candle to Ezra's cooking.

A sharp stab of homesickness hit me square in the chest, practically knocking the wind out of me. These last few days with Owen had been a lot, and I was genuinely excited to head back to Michigan in the morning. To get myself back on solid ground and figure out where the hell we went from here.

As soon as the wait staff cleared away our dessert plates—a crème brulée that didn't come close to my sister's—I excused myself to use the bathroom, needing a moment to breathe, to settle myself enough to make it through the rest of the evening.

I'd never really suffered from anxiety, but I think I understood people who did in that moment. My throat was thick with emotion, my chest tight. When I pushed into the restroom, I approached the long marble counter inlaid with a trio of sinks and grabbed a handful of paper towels from the basket nearby. Dampening them with cool water, I pressed them to my neck and chest, letting the moisture soothe me, taking deep, calming breaths.

My heart rate slowed at last, and I tossed the towel, then relieved myself.

When I returned to the ballroom and found Owen in the crowd, what serenity I'd found evaporated, replaced by annoyance and a fierce wave of possessiveness. A lithe blonde woman in an ice blue evening gown hung on his arm, her head tipped back in laughter over something he'd presumably said.

Red clouded my vision.

Though I tried to school my expression into indifference as I approached them, Owen must've seen the tightness around my eyes and correctly interpreted the flat line of my mouth, because he politely extricated himself from the woman and moved toward me. His hands were slightly raised in a placating gesture that pissed me off even more.

"Who is this?" I asked sweetly, plastering the fakest smile I'd ever given on my mouth.

The woman's brown eyes scanned me from head to toe, and her lip curled slightly. "Temperance Schaefer," she said, making no move to shake my hand. "And you are?"

"Delia Delatou," I said, slipping my hand through Owen's arm. "Owen's business partner."

I wanted to say more, to tell this woman that I was *his* in every sense of the word, but I'd be damned if I stooped to that level. She wouldn't get those admissions from me before Owen himself did.

Temperance raised a brow, glancing pointedly at where we touched, then up at Owen. "Business partner?"

"Yep," Owen said. "Delia partnered with me on the distillery. We're even building on her family land."

"That's...cute," Temperance said, and I wanted to rip her hair out.

I grew up with four sisters. I wasn't a stranger to jealousy, especially not since my sisters and I were so close in age and best friends on top of being family. But growing up around that many women, after a while, had anesthetized me to the effects of that particular emotion. We'd fought over boys and clothes and literally everything else so often in our teen years that few things phased me these days. I genuinely believed there was room at the table for everyone in whatever industry you happened to be in. Men were already making it their personal mission to pigeonhole us into being homemakers and solely responsible for child rearing, so we shouldn't be treating other women the same.

But this woman? And women like her? They were responsible for sending feminism back to the suffragette movement.

"We're not even open yet and already have over fifty thousand combined Instagram and TikTok followers," Owen said proudly, covering my hand comfortingly with his. "And it's all thanks to Delia. Did you know she has her own wildly successful social platforms?"

"Oh really?" Temperance purred. "I'm not sure I've heard of

you."

I shrugged. "You can find me at DeliaDIY if you ever want to see what I do."

I bit back a grin of satisfaction when her eyes widened.

She'd clearly heard of me, had probably scrolled my TikTok for costume and party favor ideas. Though, I doubted she got her hands dirty with any real DIY. To me, she seemed the type to pay someone to do that for her. But I could guess fashion and lifestyle were a different story. I'd made a killing from brand deals by doing try-on hauls, get-ready-with-me videos, and decor reveals. I'd bet good money she religiously watched my videos.

"I'll have to check it out," she said noncommittally, waving a hand dismissively.

"I think you could really benefit."

I gaped up at Owen. Those exact words had been floating in my own mind, but I'd had zero intention of ever speaking them. For him to come to my defense like that in such a small way? We'd come so far from the early days of our partnership.

I wanted to hug him then, to wrap my limbs around his body like a monkey in a tree. To press my lips to his and imbue the kiss with every swirling emotion inside me.

I was absolutely crazy for this man, and it was time I started acting like it.

Thanks to the seemingly endless glasses of bubbly after dinner, I was a little unsteady on my feet by the time we dipped out of the gala and returned to our hotel. I couldn't help the slight sway of my body with the elevator as we rode up to our floor.

When we stepped out, I made my way down the hall, knowing Owen would follow, and grateful a moment later that he had. As we neared the door to his room, the spike of my heel caught on the carpet and I stumbled, throwing my hands out to hopefully break my fall before my face did.

Only, the impact never came. Instead, strong arms wrapped around my waist and hauled me back into a warm, solid wall.

"Be careful, Whiskey," Owen breathed against my ear. "Can't have you breaking that pretty face of yours."

I spun in his arms, heart rate kicking up at our proximity, though I was emboldened by the alcohol coursing through my veins. "You think I'm pretty?"

Owen chuckled, a disbelieving sound, but he sobered his expression quickly. "You're the most stunning woman I've ever laid eyes on, Delia. Inside and out."

"Prettier than Temperance?" I practically spat her name.

"Ahh," Owen said knowingly. "So that's what this is about."

"Is not," I protested weakly, dropping my gaze to the space—or lack thereof—between us.

A finger tucked under my chin, slight pressure tipping my head back until I met Owen's eyes.

"It's okay if you're jealous, you know," he said softly. "Means you care. Means you want me. But I also need you to know there's nothing to be jealous of."

"You sure?" I asked petulantly, breaking our stare to fix on a random point over his shoulder. "She sure looked cozy and perfect hanging off your arm when I came back from the bathroom."

"Look at me." The demand in his tone brooked no room for

argument, and my eyes snapped back to his in an instant. "When you're in the room, no one else exists. And when you're not around, I'm wishing you were." He leaned his forehead against mine. "God, Whiskey. When are you going to put us out of our misery?"

I swallowed hard, pulse thrumming rapidly, heat sparking in my veins. That's what Owen was: an inferno, scorching everything in his path. Sucking all the oxygen from my lungs and burning my resolve to the ground. Any protestations I may have had went up in smoke in an instant.

He wanted me. He'd said as much more than once, and continued to show me he wasn't going anywhere. That he was willing to wait for me to figure my shit out. And somehow, I knew, even without him saying, that if the thing I wanted turned out *not* to be him, our working relationship would be okay. Would it be painful to move on from this attraction without ever giving in? Of course. But we'd be alright, because Owen wouldn't accept anything else.

If that's what it came down to, he'd faced enough hard truths in his life to take my rejection in stride.

Lucky for him—for both of us, really—I did want him. More than just physically, though that pull was stronger than any I'd ever felt before. I wanted him more than I'd ever wanted anything or anyone in my life.

And god, I was sick to death of this holding pattern I'd put us in.

Decision made, in answer to Owen's question, I simply shifted impossibly closer and pressed my mouth to his.

chapter 24
Owen

Delia was kissing me.

Ho-ly fucking shit, *Delia Delatou was kissing me*.

I was so shocked I'd barely pursed my lips to meet hers, ready-ing to fucking *consume* her, when she pulled away, hand flying to her mouth.

"Oh my god," she said through her fingers, cheeks going pink. "I'm so sorry. Forget I did that."

She pressed her palm against my chest, pushing away, but I caught her by the wrist before she could get too far, dragging her back into an embrace. My fingers dove into her hair, grabbing a fistful at the nape of her neck, the other hand sliding down her side and around her back to grip a handful of her ass.

That glorious ass that continued to haunt my dreams, ever since the day she'd fallen off that ladder.

"Where do you think you're going?"

"I—" she started, voice low. "You didn't kiss me back."

"You surprised me," I said. "It won't happen again."

The promise in my tone had her eyes turning molten in a second, and as soon as a smile began to tip the corners of that plush mouth up, I captured it with my own.

God, she was sweeter than I ever could've dreamed, and the chaste press of my lips against hers turned explicit and insistent in a second. Delia's fingers curled into the front of my dress shirt, dragging me closer still, until not even a grain of sand could fit between us. Her tongue slid along the seam of my mouth, teasing, and I opened for her, our tongues tangling in a sloppy, desperate dance. In that way you kissed when you couldn't get enough of someone and all finesse went out the window. Maintaining sense gave way to chasing sensation. My world narrowed to those points: the sharp sting of her nails digging into my pecs; the bite of her teeth against my bottom lip; the heavy curtain of her hair like silk against my forearm; her perfect backside in my palm.

This kiss was the culmination of our mutual longing. It was the dam finally breaking, the chains unlocked, the vault door on our desire opened wide at last.

My cock thickened between us, and Delia shifted her hips slightly, tilting toward me, as though desperately seeking the friction I couldn't give her with so many layers between us.

Regrettably, I removed a hand from her glorious body to dive into my pants' pocket and withdraw my room key. I reached around her, blindly holding the card out toward the door. A moment later, the faint beep and click of the lock permeated my senses, and I pressed down on the handle, walking us backward into the room. Finally claiming Delia had me wanting to shout from rooftops and mountain peaks that this woman was *mine*.

I couldn't be bothered to tear my mouth from hers for even a second, but I needed to get us out of that hallway. To get her alone where I could strip her down and worship her.

Once inside my room, I spun us so her back was against the door. When she reached for my belt, I gripped her wrists in my hand and pinned them above her head. Delia whimpered into my mouth, and the sound was nearly my undoing. I needed her skin under my lips, couldn't resist dipping to her neck. I sucked on the skin at her pulse, soothing the sting of my teasing bite with my tongue. Licking a path up the slender column of her throat and nipping at her jaw, her earlobe.

I buried my face in the crook of her neck and inhaled, branding every minute detail and sensation of this moment onto my memory. The surreality that I finally had this woman in my arms wasn't lost on me.

"Fuck, Whiskey," I breathed. "You've been driving me crazy for months. Do you have any idea how badly I want you?"

"Probably about as badly as I want you," she said, her statement punctuated by a gasp when I palmed her chest, cupping those gorgeous tits in my hands and thumbing her nipples, peaked against the fabric.

My fingertips trailed lower, dancing down her sides. Gripping a handful of her dress, I yanked it up, intent on exploring all the uncharted territory beneath. God, I couldn't wait to delve into her pu—

"Wait," Delia gasped, hands coming to rest on my pecs. She didn't push me away, but I stalled like a deer caught in headlights.

"What's wrong?" I asked. "Am I groping you? Shit, I'm sorry."

"No, nothing like that," she said, laughing lightly. I had difficulty focusing on her words, too distracted by her lips, bee stung by my kisses. "I just...don't get mad at me, but I don't want to do this here."

"Do what? Kiss me?"

"I love kissing you," she whispered. "I mean...what comes next." She gritted her teeth, and I yielded a step, using the distance to study her expression. "I don't want to, for lack of a better term, *consummate* this thing between us here."

"But *why*?" I asked, genuinely incredulous.

Delia gave me a sad smile, and I mentally reeled myself in. I wanted her so badly I could barely think straight. I needed to hear her making those breathy, gasping sounds into my mouth. To have her digging her nails into my hair with my face between her thighs. But if she was saying no, then that wasn't happening.

At least, not tonight.

Now that I'd had a taste, I needed the whole fucking meal. I'd do anything she wanted to get it, including pumping the brakes.

"We're drunk, Owen," she reminded me, tilting her head to press a kiss to the underside of my jaw. "And when we fuck for the first time, it's not going to be a rushed, one-night-in-a-hotel hookup. When we fuck for the first time, Owen Lawless"—she tiptoed her fingers down my chest and abdomen promisingly, though she stopped well short of my waistband—"we will be spending *days* in bed."

I bent to nuzzle her neck, inhaling a deep breath of the perfume that lingered on her skin. I wanted to get lost right here, in her, but I made myself pull away after stamping her scent on my memory. Instead of hiking her dress up around her waist, hauling her into my arms, and sliding my fingers deep in her pussy, I linked my hand with hers. Lifting it to my mouth, I pressed a kiss to the back, then wordlessly opened the door and escorted her out.

When we reached her door, I faced her. "Sure you don't want to at least spend the night with me? *Sleep only*, scout's honor," I said, raising three fingers.

Delia shook her head with a giggle. "You're too tempting."

I dropped a kiss on her forehead. "The feeling is mutual, Whiskey," I said with a wink when I pulled back. I gave her hand a squeeze, then let go. "Good night."

"Good night, QB."

In the week that followed our trip to New York, I quickly realized I should've tried harder to get Delia to spend the night with me there. Upon touching back down on Michigan soil, we were both so busy with other shit that we barely saw each other in passing, much less had time to spend *days* in bed, as Delia had promised.

By the end of that week, I'd had enough. I was edgy and irritable, and the people around me were starting to take notice.

Namely, my best friend.

"What the fuck is wrong with you?" Cal asked that Friday morning.

We were seated in my office, going over financial projections for the holiday season. Or, rather, Cal was *trying* to do that. My mind was a thousand miles away, or however far away Delia was from me at that moment.

"I kissed Delia," I blurted. "In New York. Well, she kissed me first, and then we started making out right there in the hallway."

"What hallway?"

"At the hotel, dipshit," I said. "I drop all of that on you, and that's the part you latch onto?"

"Sorry," Cal said. "I'm just...surprised? But also not? You guys have been dancing around each other for months. Honestly, it's about time."

Somehow needing that reassurance from a man who was already inextricably linked to the Delatou family, I found myself relaxing with Cal's words. "How do you think Amara is going to feel about it?"

Cal scoffed. "Why would she care? Whatever you guys had was over ages ago. We're happy, and now it's your turn."

I grinned. "Thanks, man."

"So what's the problem, then?" he asked. "Obviously something is bugging you."

"Major case of blue balls," I admitted. "We didn't take things further than kissing in New York because...well, the *why* isn't important. But we've been back for a week and I've hardly seen her, much less had the chance to get her alone."

"So call her. Ask her on a date. It's Friday afternoon, you're the boss, and she works for herself. Make the time right now."

I considered that only briefly before realizing Cal was right, and that it truly was that simple. Before I'd even made a move to reach for my phone, Cal was collecting his things and shooting me a hasty "goodbye" over his shoulder as he disappeared.

Delia answered on the first ring.

"Hey, stranger."

I smiled, her voice a balm to my frayed nerves. "Hey yourself. What're you up to?"

"I was actually just about to call you," she said. "I've got some mood boards for the distillery decor made up, and I wanted to run my ideas by you."

"That's perfect," I said. "Because I've been dying to see you all week."

"You have, huh?" she asked, tone suggestive.

"Yes. Don't think I've forgotten what you started in New York, missy," I said playfully. "So I was calling to beg you to let me take you on a proper date."

"Why?"

"I figured I should feed you before I break your back."

Delia barked out a surprised laugh. "Let's get business out of the way first," she said. "Where do you want to meet?"

"How about The Locker Room?"

"Why not your office?"

"Because too many people interrupt me here. The Overtime building is closed right now, so I can have you all to myself."

"I like the sound of that," Delia said. "See you in like twenty?"

"Perfect. Drive safe."

"Will do," she said, then the line went dead.

She showed up with a massive black bag dangling from her arm, weighed down with I didn't even want to know what.

Women and their purses, I thought with an eye roll.

Still, I welcomed her with a chaste but lingering kiss to her cheek, then directed her to one of the booths at the side of the room, scooting in next to her.

She withdrew her laptop, fired it up, and navigated to some

software that held a slideshow of her work on the so-called mood boards.

"You've been busy," I mused, impressed.

"Lots of excess energy," she said, smirking at me.

"I would've happily taken care of that for you, you know."

"You offering sex this time, QB? Or are you going to put me through another hellish work out?"

I scoffed. "It wasn't *hellish*. Admit it, you loved it."

"I *loved* seeing you shirtless and sweaty."

"Just say the word, Whiskey."

She shoved me playfully then settled her fingers on the keys of her laptop. "Work first."

"Play later?" I quipped.

She ignored me, instead launching into her presentation.

"What happened to all of this stuff being too pretentious this far north?" I asked when she finished speaking, gesturing to the higher end finishes and luxury fabrics. Honestly, it reminded me of that place we went to in New York. I loved it, but I was confused.

"I meant the plans for the exterior," she said with a sigh. "Inside, luxury is fine. Encouraged, even. We want warm and cozy and inviting, but also masculine and sexy. We want rustic but we don't want people to feel like they're in some shoddy cabin in the woods."

"And why do we want all of that?" I was genuinely curious, especially given the stink she'd put up about the facade in that meeting with Clarke.

"To give people an experience. Your name is synonymous with wealth and fame, right? The club and Birdie's are part of that brand, and this will be too. We want people to feel rich and celebrated when they come through those doors, even if they're in the middle of nowhere, Michigan."

"I'm not sure…" I said, eyes sweeping over her collages.

I mean, honestly—velvet? In a distillery? She couldn't be serious.

"I need you to trust me on this, QB," she said, bracing her hands on her hips. "I know what I'm doing."

"I do trust you," I assured her, and I meant it. Despite my protestations, I could admit I didn't know shit about interior design. If this was what she wanted, this was what she'd get. "And if this is the direction you want to go, then we're in agreement."

She narrowed her eyes on me. "Just like that?"

I shrugged. "Just like that. We're partners, and I can admit my expertise doesn't exactly apply to design concepts."

Delia grinned, delighted. "Thank you."

"Now…is it time to play yet?"

She giggled and smacked my chest. "You're insatiable."

"Only for you. When are you going to let me kiss you again?"

I couldn't fight it anymore. These months of dancing around this attraction between us, the sample of her sweet mouth I'd gotten in New York—it'd all driven me mad.

I wanted her, and while I had every intention of wining and dining her first, the caveman in my chest was screaming at me to claim her *now*.

Delia raised a brow. "What happened to feeding me first?"

"It's only a kiss," I said.

"'Only a kiss,'" she scoffed. "You know kisses are gateway drugs."

"Yours certainly are." Delia's cheeks pinked, and I grinned. "Tell you what, Whiskey. You beat me in a game of pool, and we'll postpone the kiss until later. But if I win, I'm taking it here and now."

"That's it? Win a game of pool and we kiss at a time and place of my choosing?"

"That's it."

She extended her hand, and I took it in mine, shaking on our deal.

Unsurprisingly, I wiped the table with her, finishing her off in only three turns. Both times I'd lost my turn only because she distracted me by running her hands up and down her thighs, toying with the hem of her skirt and lifting it higher and higher. My mind had blanked, muscle memory deserting me.

I almost felt bad. Not for winning—I was, at my core, a fierce competitor—but because Delia was so bad. Later, I'd teach her how to play.

As she put our cues back, I headed for the doors, first the one to the street, where I also hung a "closed for private party" sign, then the one to the bar upstairs, flipping the locks on both of them.

"What're you doing?" Delia asked as I was turning the dead-bolt on the door to upstairs.

"Taking my reward," I said as I faced her again.

"And we need the door locked for that?"

Anticipation thickened the air around us as I stalked toward her and backed her against the rail of the pool table, my hands resting by her hips, bracketing her in.

"Did you notice I didn't specify *where* I was going to kiss you?"

Delia's breath hitched. "I just assumed you meant my mouth."

I slowly licked my lips.

"I didn't."

"Then what's the sign for?" she asked, breathless.

I splayed my palm over the front of her throat, my thumb notching under her jaw and tipping her head back. "We both know we're not stopping at a kiss. And no one but me is going to hear you screaming my name as I pleasure you, Whiskey. No one gets to watch me fuck you until you come so hard you see stars, and I'm not risking being interrupted."

"Promises, promises," she said, though her shaky tone belied the attempt at bravado.

"This is your chance to back out. If you don't want this, we can leave now and pretend it never happened, but…"

"But what?" she prompted.

I could feel it in the air then. Some big, momentous shift was coming. My next words would change everything. We'd dabbled before, flirted with the idea of giving *us* a go. But this? This was uncharted territory, a life-altering leap off a cliff.

"I've wanted you for weeks. *Months*. If I kiss you right now, there's no going back. There's no stopping, no waiting until later. If I kiss you right now, you're mine. And I promise," I said, dropping my voice low and bending until my lips brushed her ear, "if you let me have you, I will make it so fucking good for you."

I felt more than saw the shiver pass through her, as though the air between us had suddenly electrified and zapped her skin. I felt like that too, like a live wire ready to spark.

Delia pulled away, staring into my eyes. "What if I don't want you?"

My heart stopped dead in my chest, though my mind kicked into overdrive. Had things changed for her in the last week? Was that why I'd hardly seen her? A thousand insecurities ran through my brain, memories surfacing of women who only wanted me until they had me. Who preferred the chase to everything that happened after. Had I only been projecting my feelings on her, hoping she'd reciprocate? Had last weekend been an anomaly brought on by endless sparkling wine and forced proximity?

"You don't?" I asked tentatively.

Her expression remained serious a beat longer before a slow smile unfurled, her eyes glinting with mischief. "Please, QB. Have you seen yourself? Of course I want you."

I exhaled in a whoosh and bent to nip at her neck. "You're going to be the death of me."

"I'm good for you," she said, placing a hand over my racing heart. "Gotta keep you young."

I grinned and cupped her cheeks. "You are good for me. And now I'm going to be so fucking good to you."

"Do your worst."

My mouth was on hers before the words were fully out.

Against her lips I said, "Nah, Whiskey. You'll get my best. You'll get everything."

"Everything?" she asked.

"All of it," I confirmed, peeling away to stare into her eyes, hoping I conveyed everything I meant with those three words. For good measure, though, I added four more. "Mind, body, and soul."

chapter 25
Delia

MY BODY QUIVERED IN anticipation with that proclamation, of him giving himself fully to me before he'd ever even had me, and something deep inside my heart seemed to settle.

This man was endgame for me. I knew it as surely as I knew my own name.

In response, I arched into him, feeling his hard length press against my stomach, his hands anchoring at my waist. His words never failed to turn me into a pile of mush, and I wanted to see what else he could do with that mouth.

"Then give me all you've got, QB."

His lips captured mine in an instant, his tongue sweeping in, exploring. I met him with equal fervor, driving my fingers into his hair and knocking his hat from his head. He pulled away, only far enough to press kisses to my cheeks, to nibble at my jaw and lick a path down my throat. His stubble deliciously scraped my skin.

And then, he was on his knee before me—only one, like dropping down after receiving the snap in victory formation at the end of a football game.

"This little fucking skirt," Owen said, rubbing the hem between his fingers. "Every time you wear it, I go insane."

I stilled at the sense of deja vu that washed over me, and though I tried to recover quickly, Owen was too perceptive to have missed it.

"What's wrong?"

"He—" I croaked, then swallowed and tried again. "He said something similar to me once...about this exact skirt."

Why hadn't I gotten rid of it? Burned the damn thing to ash? The skirt belonged to college Delia and all the shit she'd dealt with. I'd ruined a good thing by wearing it again.

Owen was on his feet in a flash, palms pressed to my cheeks gently, his ocean depths boring straight into my soul when our gazes collided. "I'm not him, Whiskey. I want you for so much more than sex. We'll set this fucking skirt on fire together if that's what you want. Do you understand me?"

I nodded. The way he looked at me, with such hope, respect, and admiration, did wonders to replace those old, painful memories with these fresh, happier ones.

"Use your words."

"Yes, I understand. I know this is different. That this is more."

Owen grinned. "It's *everything*, Whiskey. Now sit back and relax. I'm going to take care of you. Make you forget every other man but me."

Anticipation built along my skin as he once again knelt and immediately flipped my skirt up around my waist.

And groaned.

"No panties?"

"Easier access," I smirked.

"You are..." Owen's soft exhale fanned across my pussy, sparking heat in my core. "...my fucking dream girl come to life."

"And you're the man I always wanted for myself but never thought I could have."

Owen only stared at me in wonder for long moments, as if stunned he was here with me. I grinned at him, one of those big, dopey things, silently telling him the feeling was mutual.

"I've thought about this pussy far too much," he said at last, clearing his throat and returning his attention between my thighs. "About tasting it, fucking it with my fingers, about how good it would feel wrapped around my cock. I've gotten myself off with images of you in mind, groaning your name to my empty house, wishing you were there. I want to destroy this pretty little cunt, Delia. Until you're begging me to stop."

"You filthy man."

At last, he touched me, swiping a finger through my slit, collecting my desire on the tip of his finger. "And you're a dirty girl," he said. "Already fucking dripping for me. But don't worry, Whiskey"—he stared up at me, those bright blue eyes now stormy, pupils blown wide—"I clean up my messes."

And then he stuffed his finger into his mouth, moaning around it as he licked the digit clean. Like I was the best thing he'd ever tasted.

I reached out and cupped his face, the stubble on his cheeks like sandpaper against my palms. God, I wanted to feel that on the delicate skin of my inner thighs, rubbing them and my smooth pussy raw as he feasted on me.

"Owen, you have to touch me now."

"Yes, ma'am," he said, and dove in.

He started with one long drag of his flattened tongue from the smooth skin below my entrance all the way to my clit, and I bucked against his face. It had been so long since I'd let a man touch me like this, and the fact that it was *Owen*? My brain chemistry was forever altered from that one lick.

He toyed with me, pressing kisses to my lips, running his tongue along the creases of my thighs, but never quite putting his mouth where I needed him. My hands dove into his hair, attempting to direct him, but the man was a brick wall and easily resisted.

"Patience, baby."

Baby. Fuck, I shouldn't love that so much. "Say it again."

"You like that, huh, *baby*?" he asked against the skin of my thigh, and his words zinged through my entire body.

Such a small word. Four letters. Two syllables. But it felt like so much more. Like a claiming.

Without warning, Owen dove in, giving me another long drag of his tongue that ended with him sealing his mouth around my clit. I moaned loudly, falling back onto my elbows on the felt of the pool table, and he chuckled into my flesh, the rumble delivering a delicious friction to that bundle of nerves. While his lips and little scrapes of his teeth worked me over, he raised his hand and dipped a finger into my entrance, only up to the first knuckle. I squirmed closer, needing to be filled by him. Wanting him to make good on his promises to fuck me with his hand. To ruin me.

"More."

"Touch yourself," he said, pulling away. "Show me how you make yourself feel good."

"Why?"

"So I know what to do."

I sat up and stared him down. "Aren't quarterbacks supposed to be good with their hands?"

"I'm *amazing* with my hands, Whiskey. Don't get it twisted. But there's nothing more important to me than your pleasure, and I don't want to do anything you don't like."

I couldn't argue with that.

Tentatively, I slid my hand down my body, lightly brushing my fingers over my pussy. If such a thing were possible, his eyes darkened further, like the ocean in the throes of a hurricane. That muscle in his jaw twitched as he ground his teeth together.

I spread myself open with two fingers, then used those same digits to slowly circle my clit.

"Tell me how it feels."

"Incredible," I answered honestly. I was so keyed up it wouldn't take much to set me off. "I like to start slow. To toy and tease myself. It makes me come that much harder when I finally let go."

"My girl likes edging," Owen said. "Noted."

I increased the pressure a touch, and a moan fell from my lips, my head dropping back and eyes closing.

"I don't think so," Owen said, and my head snapped up. "Eyes on me."

"Only if you touch me."

"Fuck yes," he said, not even taking a beat to think about it. "I'm gonna fuck you with my hand while you pleasure that pretty pink clit. How does that sound?"

"Yes please," I whimpered, bearing down harder.

Owen moved forward and once again slipped a single digit into my entrance. He exhaled softly as I involuntarily clenched around the intrusion, sending shivers skittering across my skin.

"How many fingers? Two? Three?"

"Three," I breathed, desperate for him to fill me.

Owen chuckled. "Needy, filthy little girl," he said. "We'll start with two and work our way up."

Making good on his promise, he slid two fingers inside me, and I underestimated exactly how big his hands were. I'd never felt more full in my life. The stretch stung briefly before soothing into pleasure that zinged up my spine. My own hand faltered as he slowly pumped in and out of me, his eyes locked on that spot where we connected.

"We had a deal," he growled, and I hastily started moving my fingers over my clit again. My arm jerked, barely able to focus as he fucked me.

There was no finesse left in my movements when Owen finally took pity on me and lifted his other hand, brushing mine out of the way to spread me open himself. As his fingers picked up speed, he sealed his mouth around my clit. I'd already been hovering on the edge, the pressure in my core a slow build.

But Owen was done fucking around.

That wave stacked higher and higher as his hand pumped faster, as his tongue flicked over me, fluttering in a cadence designed to wring maximum pleasure.

I broke apart seconds later, my pussy pulsing around his fingers, my arms shaking violently as I struggled to hold myself upright. The wave crashed and crashed, pulling me under repeatedly. When I was sure it would recede, Owen suckled me, twisting his fingers and sending me under again.

When I finally floated back to the surface, my chest was heaving, and Owen was grinning wickedly at me, all satisfied arrogance.

Then again, he had every right to be.

"Holy fuck," I breathed, all other words having completely deserted me, my mind wiped blank.

I felt the loss immediately when he withdrew his fingers, and I watched with rapt attention as he brought his hand to his mouth and individually licked them clean.

"My new favorite flavor," he said through a grin.

"Come here." I grabbed him by his collar and he let me pull him to his feet until he was bent over me. I craned my neck and he met me halfway, our mouths crashing together. My taste on his lips and tongue was intoxicating, and I wanted to make him feel even a fraction of the pleasure he'd given me.

I reached for the fly of his jeans, but he stopped me.

"What're you doing?"

"I want to make you feel good," I said against his mouth, making another grab for his waistband.

"No," he said, firmly but gently pulling my hands away.

I reared back at that. "No?" I said with a brow quirked. "Owen, you're hard as a statue." I palmed him through his pants for emphasis, and he hissed through his teeth. "Let me take care of you."

"Later," he breathed, though I could tell his control was barely leashed.

"Later?" I repeated dumbly.

"We have time, Whiskey," he said, tapping his watch. "Remember what you said in New York?"

Realization dawned, and I grinned. "*Days* in bed."

"*Days*," he confirmed. "So first, we're going to go somewhere more private, and then *maybe* I'll let you have your wicked way with me."

Anchoring a hand at the back of his neck, fingers filtering through the strands of his hair, I brought his mouth to mine again. "Lead the way, QB."

chapter 26
Owen

THE SEXUAL TENSION BETWEEN us was as thick as smoke in the cab of my truck as I drove us from the bar to my house. Delia was quiet in the passenger seat, and I followed her lead. It wasn't uncomfortable. I think we were both considering what we'd just done—and what we were about to spend the rest of the weekend doing.

I'd told her once that I was a greedy and possessive man, and every nerve ending in my body buzzed with the need to fully claim her, to drive my cock inside her and mark her as mine forever.

Some of that tension eased when we pulled up to the gate of my house and I rolled down the window to punch in the code.

"It's one-one-two-seven-zero-eight," I told her. "If you ever need it."

The day my dad died.

Unbidden, a wave of grief coursed through me, and terror gripped my chest. My dad had passed so suddenly, there one second, gone the next. I never got the chance to give him a proper goodbye. I couldn't even tell you what my last words to him were. Even all these years later, I wasn't sure if that was a blessing or curse. I was on solid ground mentally, but the problem with grief was that it wasn't linear, and the reminder that these moments on this plane are so fleeting snuck up on me at the worst possible times.

Delia reached out and grabbed my hand, giving it a quick squeeze, grounding me, then pulling away as I put the truck in park. Having her here, knowing we were set on a course to—hopefully—forever, reminded me how easily I could lose her. She was another person I cared about deeply who could be gone from my life in an instant, and panic gripped my chest.

The second the door into the mudroom off the garage closed behind us, the leash on my control snapped, and I was on her. Shoving her into the wall, slipping my hand beneath her skirt and cupping a handful of her ass.

"Bed," she growled as my mouth descended on hers, punctuating the word with a nip of my bottom lip.

"No." The beast in my chest needed her now, was unwilling to wait the seconds it would take to walk us there.

Normally, I could keep those demons at bay, could maintain my composure. But in the comfort of my own home, with Delia in my arms? I knew I was safe to fall apart if I needed.

As if sensing the shift in me, though she didn't know why, Delia reached up and cupped my face, leaning back to stare at me. "I know," she said quietly, and I didn't have to ask what she meant. Somehow, this woman could feel the chaos of swirling emotions inside me. Probably because she frequently experienced a similar phenomenon.

We were far more alike than I'd ever thought.

"I know you want to fuck me right here," she continued. "That the caveman in your chest is screaming at you to do so. But we have time, Owen. So much of it. A lifetime, really. There's no rush here."

But I knew better than anyone that lifetimes weren't guaranteed, that they could be cut short and ripped away in a flash. That knowledge was what drove me now.

I sighed deeply, the exhalation carrying the weight of the world. "The gate code is the day my dad died," I said, offering no further explanation. Delia didn't need it; she simply nodded in understanding. I tipped my forehead against hers. "I haven't even had you yet, but I don't know what I'd do if I lost you," I admitted.

"You've always had me," she said quietly, tilting her face to press a soft, featherlight kiss to my lips. "And I know the loss of your father still haunts you, but be here with me right now. Feel me, Owen." She pressed her hands to my chest, and I removed mine from under her skirt to skate them up her sides, along her arms, over her shoulders and into her hair. Touching every inch of her I could reach. Proving she was, in fact, very much alive and not a figment of my imagination. Cradling her head, I lightly massaged my fingertips into her scalp. "I'm real. I'm safe. I'm yours."

I nodded, then pushed back from her to kick my boots off. Delia slipped out of her own shoes, and I reached for her hand, pulling her through the house.

We passed from the mudroom to the laundry room, then the

kitchen, eventually entering the open space of the living room, where the staircase served as the centerpiece. I didn't pause to let her take in my home, only silently led her up the stairs and straight to my bedroom.

The moment we crossed the threshold, our hands were groping, mine pulling her tight sweater over her head, her reaching for the hem of my Henley. In seconds, we were naked, and I settled my hands on her hips, pushing her toward the bed. She folded when her knees met the edge, landing softly on her back on the mattress.

With her hair splayed out around her, all of her smooth, olive skin on display, her subtle curves and modest chest? She was every one of my wet dreams come to life.

I leaned in and slanted my mouth over hers. She tasted like her namesake. Like the smooth, smoky bite of whiskey. Like that first sip coating my taste buds at the end of a long day. Soothing warmth with the promise that everything would be right in the world once I got to the bottom of the glass, once the tension in my shoulders and jaws and temples had eased.

She tasted like mine and looked like forever.

I knelt on the mattress and settled between her thighs, simply staring at her.

"What're you doing?"

"Looking at you."

"Why?" The self-consciousness was evident in her tone, and she shifted slightly to band her arm over her breasts.

I traced a finger over her lips, marveling at their softness, and using my other hand to pull her arm away from her chest. "Don't hide from me, Whiskey. Every inch of you is perfect. You look…"

"Like what?" she prompted when I trailed off.

"You look like I'm done looking."

Delia's smile was brighter than the sun. "Guess you got more than you bargained for when you agreed to partner with me," she said.

"I've made some poor decisions in my life," I said, bending until I was a breath away from her lips. "But letting you into it was not one of them."

She smiled. "I did say you wouldn't find anyone better."

I pressed my mouth to hers, back up a bit and said, "And you were right."

"I usually am."

"I guess I better reward you for being the smartest woman alive then."

"About time."

I growled and captured her lips, devouring her, pushing her into the mattress. Her hands were everywhere: my hair, my chest tweaking my nipples, nails scraping down my back, settling on my ass, pulling me closer.

Like a key fitting to a lock, my cock notched at her entrance, her desire coating my tip. I reached between us to brush it across her slit, spreading that moisture down my entire length.

"I haven't been with anyone in a long time, Whiskey," I said. "And I get tested regularly. They've all come back clear."

"Is that your way of asking if it's okay to fuck me bare?"

"Yes."

"Well, I'm happy to report that I have also been celibate for a long time, and my last annual also came back clear. *And* I'm on birth control."

"You and TJ never...?"

She shook her head vigorously. "That wasn't...there wasn't anything there. I was only trying to forget how badly I wanted a certain quarterback."

"Retired," I growled, though joy bloomed in my chest with the knowledge that I hadn't been alone in the wanting her all these months like I'd thought.

Her fingertips trailed over the ridges of my abdomen. "Hottest *retired* quarterback I've ever seen." Her gaze flicked up to mine, her whiskey irises aflame. "Hottest *man* I've ever laid eyes on."

"Flattery will get you everywhere," I said, then slowly slid home.

With a moan, she took me perfectly, hips tilting to accept all of me in one steady thrust.

Fully seated, I groaned, dropping my forehead to hers. "Fuck, Whiskey. I knew you were made for me. Do you feel that? Do you feel how perfectly you fit around me?"

Delia whimpered in response, and I straightened to lock my attention between us, retreating slowly before slamming back in. I loved the way her tits bounced with the movement, how she slammed her eyes shut and tucked that full bottom lip between her teeth. As though she was stopping herself from making any noise.

I freed her lip with my thumb, then dipped the finger into her mouth. Her eyes flew open, and she bit down on it, swirling her tongue over the pad before I withdrew. "Don't hold back, baby," I said. "I want to hear you. Tell me how good you feel."

"I'm so full," she said. "It's so good, QB. But I need more."

"Fast and hard?"

"Mm," she moaned as I increased my pace.

"Touch yourself."

"Why?" she asked, almost as though she couldn't help being contrary, but she slinked those long, thin fingers, between her legs, the deep red tips obscene against her clit and next to my flushed and swollen cock as I pumped in and out.

"We're a team."

"In this?"

"In *everything*," I corrected. Already, my orgasm coiled at the base of my spine, tingling my skin, preparing to unleash. "I need you to come with me."

She didn't say anything in response, only flattened those three fingers and rubbed herself with quick circles. Her nails scraped my shaft with each of my thrusts. With her other hand, she reached up to grab hold of my chain.

"Been waiting for the day I had this swinging in my face."

It was too much. Too much sensation, too much pleasure, too much energy pushing against my skin, begging to be let out. Too many sinful words from my filthy girl.

I dropped forward, my hands on either side of her head, my hips slamming into her. All finesse lost to the desire to send us both over the edge. My balls drew up tighter at the same moment her walls clamped like a fist around me. We barreled toward that cliff, out of control and unable to stop. Delia met every pulse of my hips greedily, her grip on my chain anchoring me close.

As if I was going anywhere.

We went soaring off the ledge in unison, Delia's orgasm tearing a scream free from her throat as she pulsed forcefully around me. My arms collapsed, my entire body weight pressing Delia deeper into the mattress as I buried my face in her neck, groaning her name mixed with unintelligible words into her skin as I spilled long and hot inside her. The edges of my vision darkened, my muscles quaking. Her whole body spasmed beneath me, the aftershocks rolling like endless waves over her, her pussy still pulsing around me long after I'd emptied myself.

When she stilled at last, I lifted myself and brushed her hair off her face.

"Sorry for crushing you," I whispered, pressing a kiss to her forehead.

"There are worse ways to go," she laughed, offering her mouth to me.

I gave her a peck then pulled away and sat up, slowly pulling my cock from her warmth.

"Ah," she breathed as I slipped free.

"Sensitive?" I smirked.

"A bit."

Though it should've taken some time for me to be ready for round two, when my eyes caught sight of my cum leaking from her, my cock instantly perked back up.

I reached down and stuffed my finger into her entrance, and she twitched.

"Fuck," I cursed. "I'm going to fill you with my cum at least once every day just to watch it drip out of this pussy."

She heaved herself up to sitting, then scrambled onto all fours and turned her ass to me. "How about we go again right now?"

I swore again as she dropped to her forearms, raising that perfect ass into the air. Begging for me to take her like this.

"You're ruining me, Whiskey."

"That's funny," she said, angling her head to look over her shoulder at me. "I distinctly recall you saying you were going to *destroy my pretty little cunt.* So get to work."

And who the fuck was I to say no to an offer like that?

Before I'd really thought it through, my hand shot out and smacked her ass. Instantly, her skin reddened in the shape of my palm. I was about to apologize when she said, "Do that again."

"You liked that?"

"Find out for yourself."

I brought my other palm down on the other cheek, and she dropped her head, moaning loudly. I reached between her legs, delivering a light slap to her pussy, and the moan grew in volume.

"Fuck," I marveled. "You are...everything."

I gripped my cock at the base and pumped it roughly until it fully stiffened in my hand. I scooted forward until the head brushed her flesh. "Tilt your hips for me, love."

She obeyed, her pelvis angling to right where I needed her, and I roughly shoved inside. Delia's head rose, back arching on another moan.

"Rough, QB," she gasped. "Manhandle me."

My hands latched onto her hips hard enough that I knew she'd have bruises tomorrow. She whimpered in pleasure, throwing her ass back to greet each of my forward thrusts. I gave myself over to my carnal desires, the desperation to fuck her hard spurring me on.

I'd never had an equal in the bedroom before. Never been with someone who allowed me to bring my fantasies to life, but that's what Delia was doing for me. She met every punishing slap of my hips into her backside, her flesh rippling with each contact. I reached down and wrapped her hair around my fist, pulling her head back, holding her in place as I used her body for my most basic needs. Her moans of encouragement pushed me further, and I was a fucking goner when she cried out as her orgasm snuck up on us both and tore her apart. My free hand slapped her ass again, and I made her feel every second of that pleasure as I relentlessly pumped her through it. Her body quaked, my hand in her hair the only thing keeping her upright.

Despite her pleas, I didn't slow, and the climax rolled and rolled through her. My own once again gained steam, my cock almost painfully engorged as I pushed myself toward it.

This girl might very well kill me, but buried in her pussy was the best way I could think to go out.

"Come on my back, QB," Delia managed to gasp out.

My thrusts slowed a fraction. "But—"

"You can blow inside me again later," she said, breathing heavily as she turned her head to give me a saucy grin. Her hair was a wild mess from my hands. "Right now, I want you to paint my skin. Mark me."

"You are fucking sinful, my girl," I said through a groan, letting go of her hair to reach around and find her clit. She twitched against me, a breathy moan falling from her lips.

"Only for you."

Helpless to resist giving her anything she wanted, I pulled free. Dropping my hand from her clit to the bed, I curved over her back. My other hand flew up and down my length, twisting and squeezing, imagining her mouth and her pussy around me. She rose up onto all fours to watch me, shifting the curtain of her hair out of the way.

"That's it, baby," she said, eyes wide with wonder and desire. "Come for me, QB."

I let go with her words, coming in long spurts over the smooth, golden skin of her back. Fuck, this woman. I could do nothing but stare down at her in amazement, intensely satisfied by the sight of my desire decorating her naked flesh. I was struck by the urge to memorialize this moment, to brand it on my brain.

So I leaned over to get my phone off the nightstand, where I'd tossed it as I stripped earlier.

"What're you doing?"

"You're always taking photos of me," I said as I snapped several in quick succession. "Now it's my turn."

"Owen!" she yelped, rising onto her knees and spinning toward me. "You can't do that!"

"The hell I can't," I said, smirking at my phone, at the sexy photos now gracing my camera roll. "Damn, baby. That's one for the spank bank."

"You don't need a spank bank," she said, swiping for my phone, but I held it over my head and out of her reach. "You've got the real thing."

Curving my palm around the back of her neck, I dipped my head and hauled her in for a kiss.

"You're goddamn right."

chapter 27
Delia

As Owen's lips met mine, my stomach grumbled insistently, and I pulled away from him with a giggle.

"Feed me," I begged.

He pressed a kiss to my hair then got off the bed, padding first to the bathroom and returning with a washcloth. Gently, he mopped his release off my skin, both from my back and between my legs. Then he moved to the walk-in closet on the far side of the room. I took the opportunity to admire his backside, from the hard-as-a-rock glutes, the hills and valleys of his back, the groove of his spine, all decorated with red scrapes left by my fingernails. I loved that I'd done that to him. Though the marks would fade, I liked to think they cut deeper than the surface, that I'd claimed him on a soul-deep level.

He certainly had all of me.

When he emerged, he was dressed in a pair of Mustangs gym shorts and carrying a tee and a pair of his boxers, which he tossed to me—a foresight I appreciated, having forgotten I'd come here without panties.

I slipped it over my head and crawled off the bed, sliding my legs into the shorts before following him downstairs to the kitchen.

I was surprised to find his refrigerator fully stocked. He worked so much, I expected it to be empty or, at the very least, full of take-out cartons or leftover containers. Instead, it was packed, the food all carefully arranged. He began shifting things around, pulling open drawers and piling things on the counter. After a quick trip to the pantry, he constructed us each a sandwich on whole grain bread, piled high with thick slices of turkey, provolone cheese, lettuce, and tomatoes. On the side, he spooned healthy servings of some sort of pasta salad tossed with olives and peppers in an Italian dressing.

As soon as the paper plate was set in front of me, I dove in with gusto, my stomach practically eating itself at that point.

"Hungry?" Owen asked with a chuckle as he moved around to sit beside me at his massive kitchen island.

"Starving," I said after swallowing a mouthful of sandwich. "*Someone* worked me to the bone today."

"There's more where that came from too."

I grinned. "I look forward to it."

He nodded at my plate. "Food first. Then I want to give you a tour."

"Why?"

"Because you're going to be spending a lot of time here."

Deeply pleased by his answer, I inhaled my entire plate with a speed that surprised even Owen, who finished only moments before me. Once he'd tossed our trash, I slid off the stool and turned toward the cavernous living room.

The walls were bright white shiplap, one dominated by a massive river rock fireplace, live edge, floating oak shelves branching out on each side and decorated with an array of framed photos. Another consisted of windows that soared from the floor to the delicate peak of the roof, centered around a tall sliding glass door that led onto a deck. The lawn beyond gently sloped to Owen's private beach, the waves of Boardman Lake lapping against the shore.

"Why did you choose this place?" I asked. "I mean, instead of something on the bay or closer to the city?"

He shrugged. "Privacy."

He inclined his head and led me from the room, down a short hall where three more doors branched off. One opened into an office that offered the same view of the water.

"When I first moved to Traverse City, it was a bit of a culture shock. It was easy for me to get lost in Detroit after my injury. I barely left my house. I paid people to deliver me groceries and other necessities, only venturing out for physical therapy in those early days. One day, I got sick of moping and made a plan, deciding it was time to take a good hard look at my future. Even then, even before I'd gotten back on the field and tested myself, I somehow knew I wasn't going back. Call it that sixth sense that guided me my entire career but...yeah," he finished on a rough sigh, and I laced our fingers together.

"I actually lived on the third floor of Lawless when I first moved here," he told me, and I blinked up at him, surprised.

"I didn't know there was an apartment up there," I said.

Owen chuckled. "There wasn't back then. I slept on an air

mattress for two months while Jay and I gutted the club and I searched for a house. I found this place right as work finished, which was perfect timing because then we set our sights on converting the empty space up there into two apartments. I've had the same two couples renting them for the last seven years."

"Is there anything you can't do?"

"TikTok," he said instantly. "It makes no sense to me."

I giggled. "That's why you have me."

He bent and dropped a kiss on my mouth. "Lucky me."

"So anyway...buying a house out here?" I prompted.

"Right," he said. "Traverse City is a lot smaller than Detroit, you know? And when word got around that I'd moved here...I had a bit of a stalker situation. This girl kept sneaking upstairs at the club and leaving things at my door."

"What kinds of things?"

"Creepy collages she made of photos from my playing days, love letters...her undergarments."

"Oh my god," I said, bursting out laughing. "She took jersey chasing a little too far."

"She scared the shit out of me," he admitted. "So I had to install all kinds of security measures on the place, and immediately started looking for a house. I needed to control who had access to me, and I got really lucky when I found this place. It used to be a vacation home for an older couple who lived in Lansing, and they were looking to sell it quickly so they could move to Arizona to be closer to their kids and grandkids. I installed the gates and a top of the line security system. The only people who know the codes are me, Hugo, Cal, and my housekeeper."

"And now me."

"And now you," he confirmed. "Don't make me regret it."

I gave him a cheeky grin. "Give me a couple more orgasms and I won't."

"That's all it takes, huh?" he asked, smiling wickedly at me before lifting me up and tossing me over his shoulder. He practically sprinted through the house back to his room, both of us laughing the whole time.

Our next joining was soft and slow, a true moment of hearts and souls coming together as one. And after what seemed like eons, we finally drifted off to sleep.

I woke several hours later, the world beyond the windows dark, the light of the moon casting shadows across Owen's bedroom. The wind howled as rain pelted the glass, a storm having rolled in while we rested. But I was safe and warm in his embrace, skin on skin, my back to his chest.

Despite the four—or was it five?—rounds we'd gone earlier, even passed out, Owen was somehow hard against my ass.

As though sensing I was awake, his arms tightened around me, and he gripped my hand in one of his, lacing our fingers together. Something cool and metal met my skin, and I brushed my pinky over it.

"What's with the ring?" I whispered.

Behind me, Owen breathed in deeply, his exhale warm against my bare shoulder where he'd rested his chin. "It was my dad's wedding ring," he said softly, voice husky and thick with sleep.

God, every time he mentioned his dad, my throat clogged with emotion. I couldn't imagine the pain and grief he dealt with every day. Suddenly, I was gripped by the desire to make this man the happiest he'd ever been. To give him a reason to smile every day, if only to lessen the obviousness of the hole in his life where his dad should've been.

And since his cock still pressed insistently against my backside, I knew an easy way to bring him pleasure right then. I wriggled a little, bringing our lower halves closer together.

"What're you doing?" he asked, tone amused.

"You're hard."

"Your ass is pressed against my cock," he said. "Of course I'm hard."

"We should do something about that."

Owen didn't say anything, only moved the arm that had been banded around my waist, running his hand down my side until he reached my thigh. It was too easy to let him open me up, to hook my leg over his thick quad, the coarse hair there tickling my smooth skin. I shifted a bit to look at him, and he slipped his hand between my legs, fingers brushing across my slit.

"Don't toy with me," I whispered.

"I don't want to hurt you," he replied, sliding two fingers inside me, pumping them slowly. "Gotta get you ready."

My breath left me in a whoosh, and I spread my legs wider, giving him a better angle.

I reached for his cock, gripping him a little roughly. "I need you."

With a sigh, he withdrew his fingers, and he covered my hand with his own, guiding his cock to my entrance and slowly pushing inside.

"Fuck," I said on an exhale. He hadn't even started moving, but the way he filled me was a sensation I'd never get over. "Nothing has ever felt as good as you, QB."

"Or you, Whiskey."

Then he moved, a languid advance and retreat of his hips, his cock deeply branding me every time he was fully seated. Even in this half-awake haze, his hands were seemingly everywhere. Tweaking my nipples. Pressing against my clit, slow circles timed to the pump of his cock. His mouth moved along my shoulder and the back of my neck, pressing biting kisses and soothing them away with his tongue.

My orgasm built slowly, my nails digging into the hand he'd anchored on my thigh to hold me wide for him as he drove me higher and higher.

When I came, it was with a hoarse, near-silent cry as he shot me into the sky. I was floating in the cosmos, stars dancing along the backs of my closed eyelids, exactly as Owen had promised all those hours ago.

I returned to myself at last, limbs deliciously limp as Owen continued those languid strokes inside me, not having joined me on my trip to space. Not seeming in a rush to get there, either.

"Are you ever going to let me sleep tonight?" I asked, and he slipped free as I turned in his arms to face him.

He responded with a noise that rumbled through his chest and mine, his eyes remaining shut as he pressed a kiss to my forehead.

"You started that round," he said at last. "And I didn't even get to come."

I hummed, burying my face in his chest, burrowing deep into his scent and warmth. "I could take care of that."

He grumbled when I found his nipple in the dark and flicked my tongue over it, dipping my hand between us to palm his cock, the length coated in my release, smoothly slipping through my fingers.

I rolled into him and shifted him onto his back, rising up to straddle his lap, his cock nestled between us. A moan came from deep in his chest at the pressure of my body.

"I'm too wired to sleep," I said, digging my nails lightly into his chest, rocking my hips experimentally. He groaned in response, and I grinned. "I can't get enough of you."

His hands came to rest on my hips. "Are you trying to kill me?"

"Definitely not," I said.

"Sure feels like it."

But he didn't move me off him, though he easily could have. Despite his protestations, his cock twitched against my ass, telling me he wanted this as badly as I did.

I shifted, pressing his cock into his stomach as I moved along it, his girth spreading my pussy open, his thick head teasing my clit with every undulation of my hips.

"Fucking hell, woman," he gasped. "Fucking your pussy like this? It's almost as good as being buried inside you. Those smooth lips feel incredible."

I tapped my mouth, biting down on my bottom lip. "Maybe I'll let you fuck these ones next."

"You gonna choke on it?" he asked, his fingers sinking deeper into my flesh, holding me steady while I slid my slit across his length over and over. I couldn't wait to wake up covered in bruises tomorrow.

"Yes, baby," I said, moving faster. There wasn't enough friction to get me off, but I wanted to unravel him the way he'd been doing to me all day and night.

He rewarded me a moment later, his cock pulsing against my

slit as he came in spurts all over his stomach.

I slowed and stilled, reaching down to drag my finger through his cum, spreading it across his skin. Then I lifted my finger to my mouth and closed my lips around it, licking it clean. His musky, salty flavor burst on my tongue, and I moaned.

"Filthy little girl," he whispered, the words reverent. Praising.

"Filthy old man," I shot back.

Unable to stop touching him, I reached out and traced my fingers over the compass inked on his pec. "What do these numbers mean?" I asked.

"They're the coordinates for the ranch. So I always know which way is home."

"That's...ridiculously sweet," I said, smiling down at him. Every new thing I learned about him made me fall harder, and the sentiment behind that tattoo only added to it.

He removed one of his hands from my thigh and patted the dream catcher on his opposite side. "This one is for my dad," he said quietly. "He always encouraged me and my siblings to dream big, so now I'm reminded of that every time I see it. If you look closely, you can see his initials etched onto one of the beads."

Squinting in the dark, I leaned forward until I was inches away from the tattoo. Sure enough, on one of the little beads drawn to look like it was holding a feather in place on a piece of suede hanging off the hoop, three initials were sketched onto Owen's skin. I bent further until my lips brushed his warm flesh, pressing a kiss to that spot. Owen only hummed happily in response.

Then I shifted and pressed myself against the length of his body, not caring that his cum, which we hadn't cleaned up, now decorated my stomach as well.

"I don't know how we're ever going to go back to real life after this," he said, sweeping my hair off my face, tucking it behind my ear to meet my eyes.

I pressed a kiss to the tip of his nose. "This is real life now, QB."

chapter 28
Owen

"WHAT WAS IT LIKE growing up on a ranch?" Delia asked the next morning over breakfast.

Around four that morning, we'd finally managed to burn off enough of the desire driving us to pass out for a few hours. I'd woken Delia shortly after ten with my head between her thighs, then hauled her out of bed for a real breakfast.

It was Saturday, the sky outside gunmetal grey, rain lashing the windows. The lake was dark and choppy, dotted with white caps as far as the eye could see.

The perfect day to stay inside and make it my mission to fuck this woman in every goddamn room of this house. I wanted her memory everywhere, filling these rooms with her sounds, with reminders of the pleasure we'd found together.

And then I wanted to keep making more, both inside and outside these walls, forever.

"Loud," I said at last with a chuckle. "At least when my brothers came along. But chickens make constant noise, cows are always mooing, and if a horse gets spooked by something in the night, they wake the rest of them up with their neighing. The house isn't that far away from the main barn and pens, and my bedroom faced out that way, so I never really got to sleep in. I supposed that made it easier once I started playing competitively and training happened at all hours of the day. I learned to survive on very little sleep."

Delia rolled her eyes. "And you were complaining about me keeping you up all night."

"Don't get confused, Whiskey," I said, pausing my flipping of our French toast to point the spatula at her, "I'll never tire of that perfect pussy of yours. Getting no sleep to fuck you is hardly a hardship. But I feel like I ran a marathon. I'm not getting any younger, you know."

She popped a grape in her mouth and said, "Could've fooled me."

With a smirk, I turned from her and after a final flip, plated the French toast and slid a stack in front of her, along with butter, syrup, and powdered sugar.

"Eat," I said. "Then maybe I'll have you for dessert."

"Promises, promises."

I chuckled as I sat down next to her, diving into my own meal.

"To truthfully answer your question," I said around a mouthful, "growing up on a ranch was probably a lot like growing up on the peninsula. We were outside all the time, running through the fields, messing with the animals, getting into all sorts of trouble. But we weren't doing drugs or getting arrested, so Mom and Dad let us have our freedom."

A wave of nostalgia crashed over me, had me wishing for

simpler days. When it was just me and my brothers, raising hell, always discovering some new hidden gem on the ranch property. Like the swimming hole tucked away behind a tangled copse of trees a thirty minute walk from the house. Or the fast-rushing creek we'd taken to floating down on logs when we were feeling extra rebellious.

"The summer before I left for college, Trey and I got this idea to go rafting down this creek on the property," I started a bit wistfully. "We invited all our friends, had some older guys buy us cases of beer, tied like thirty tubes together and set off. It was a blast...until we were ready to get off the water and realized we had floated too far away to walk back. My dad was spittin' mad when he came to pick us up, a whole slew of other parents in tow to collect their own children. We'd ended up twenty miles from home and drunk off our asses. Trey and I were grounded and forced to stay within sight of the house for a month, which, I'm sure you know as a free range child yourself, was pure hell."

Delia laughed. "That does sound a lot like growing up on the peninsula. All of my favorite childhood memories involve my sisters and being outside."

"Mine too," I said. "Because we were so close in age, Trey and I had a habit of encouraging each other's recklessness. Dad tanned our hides more than once because of it."

God, I'd have given anything to talk to Dad now. To tell him about this woman that had stolen my heart.

"He would've loved you," I said quietly.

"I wish I could've met him. But I want to meet the rest of your family," she said, at last looking up at me. "I want to see where you grew up."

"Whenever you want, Whiskey," I said earnestly. "Say the word and we'll be on a flight. You'll fit right in with the chaos."

She smirked at me. "It's kinda nice having a sugar daddy."

On the heels of mentioning my own dead father, the word 'daddy' shouldn't have had my cock perking up, but I'd be damned if it didn't turn me on.

"Daddy?" I asked. "Our age gap isn't *that* big."

"You know," she said slowly. "In my romance novels, older men *love* being called 'daddy' in bed. It's a major turn on for some."

"Yeah?"

"*Yeah*," she emphasized, studying me, eyes darting across my face as she gauged my reaction.

"And how do you feel about it?" I asked tentatively.

"I mean...you're not old enough to be *my* father," she said, "but I'll admit you definitely give 'daddy' energy."

I huffed out a laugh. "What the fuck does that even mean?"

"You're an alpha male. A leader. I don't know how to explain it. It's an intangible vibe certain men give off, and you have it in spades." She studied me. "How do *you* feel about it?"

"Honestly? I'm hard as a statue." I reached for her nearly empty plate, shuffling it and mine to the side.

"I wasn't done with that!" she protested.

"I don't care," I said, turning her seat so I could grip her under the thighs and lift her onto the counter. "I'm ready for dessert." I reached beneath the hem of my tee Delia wore, a faded black Mustangs' one with my last name and number emblazoned on the back, gripping my boxers by the waistband. Delia lifted her hips and I slid the underwear off, tossing them unceremoniously behind me. Then I met her eyes as I added, "And daddy gets what daddy wants."

Delia shivered, goosebumps breaking out on her arms and legs. She gripped the tee as though to pull it off, but I stilled her.

"Keep it on," I said. "Lest you forget who you belong to."

"Never."

"That's right, baby. You're mine." I lifted a hand and brushed my fingers over her lips. "This mouth." Lower to her chest. "These tits." Further south to the apex of her thighs. "This pretty pink pussy. You might as well get my name tattooed on all of it."

Leaning back on her forearms, Delia opened her legs wide and anchored her heels on the edge of the counter, spreading herself wide for me.

"Eat up."

She didn't have to tell me twice, and with a growl, I dove in. I showed her no mercy as I licked her from back to front, then sealed my lips around her clit and sucked hard. She bucked against me, and I chuckled against her flesh, my tongue fluttering rapidly against that bundle of nerves. This was as much for me as it was for her; all of her pleasure was. I loved unraveling her, loved the way her thighs quaked and clamped around my head the closer she got. Lived for her noises, her murmured praises, her hoarse cries of my name.

The way she whimpered, "Daddy, please," right as she approached that precipice.

Fuck, I was already hard as steel, but that stiffened me further, almost painfully so.

"That's it, Whiskey," I said as I shoved my fingers inside her and curled them against her inner wall. "Come for me."

She blew apart, crying my name out as she shook, her pussy gripping me tightly and pulsing.

"O!" she screamed, and I didn't know if it was an exclamation or a shortened version of my name, but I didn't care.

"That's right, pretty girl," I murmured against her slick flesh. "O, as in *Owen*, the *only* man who can take care of you like this."

"The only one," she gasped out.

"My good girl," I whispered, pressing a final kiss to her clit as she came down, licking her sweetness from my lips.

Then I rose and leaned over her, capturing her mouth with mine, letting her taste herself on my tongue. She came to me greedily, clenching my shirt in her fists, pulling me closer. I had half a mind to climb on top of her and fuck her right there.

We spent the rest of the day like that, alternately talking and tangling ourselves together, seeking pleasure. I was a man starved, like I'd been in the desert for too long without hydration, and she was an endless pool of fresh water. I finished showing her around my house, and we curled up in my small home theater, putting on one of her favorite 90s rom-coms while we shared stories.

She gave me a hand job that made a mess of my clothes, so I stripped, dragged her upstairs, bent her over the railing on the balcony off my bedroom, and fucked her from behind as punishment.

"Being bad is pretty fucking good," she said afterward.

I gave zero fucks about anything outside of our bubble. I couldn't have told you where my phone ended up after I'd used it to take photos of her the night before, and for the first time in a long time, my mind was as far from work as it could be.

There was only Delia.

It wasn't just the sex, either, though that was all-consuming and mind blowing. Our connection was one I'd never experienced before and surely never would again—not that I wanted to. It was so easy to be with her, the way we moved around the house, making meals, conversing, discussing everything under the sun. It felt like we'd been doing it forever instead of only forty-eight hours.

I never wanted her to leave.

"Are we like...together now?" Delia asked on Sunday afternoon.

We were curled up in my bed, my front to her back, facing out toward the lake beyond my windows. Sweat from our recent joining was drying on our skin, and the sun had finally come out, sparkling on the waves, the sky a bright blue blanket overhead.

"Yes," I answered instantly. "What a silly question."

She turned in my arms, and I loosened my grip enough for her to pull back and stare into my eyes. "We haven't exactly discussed it."

"I thought it was obvious," I said. "We've spent the last two days in bed together, Whiskey."

"So," she said, a bit petulantly. "Sex is one thing. A relationship is a whole other."

"I want that with you," I told her, raising a hand to rest it on the curve of her cheek. "I want *everything* with you."

"Don't you think it's too soon to be discussing stuff like that?"

"Absolutely not," I assured her. "I'm thirty-seven-years-old. I know what I want, and I never thought I'd find it. The day you shoved your way into my office and my business was the best of my life."

Delia hummed happily as I pressed a kiss to her forehead. "We'll have a serious conversation about this when we're not naked and sex-addled," she said. "But know I want everything with you too."

chapter 29
Delia

MONDAY MORNING CAME WAY too quickly, and our bubble was about to pop.

We'd briefly come up for air the night before to assure the people who cared about us that we were alive and well.

Even knowing we had to leave the house that day didn't stop us from extending our sexual hiatus a little longer.

"Whiskey," Owen whispered that morning, and my eyes cracked open. The sky beyond his windows was barely lightening, and a quick glance at his alarm clock told me it was barely past seven.

"Nooooo," I moaned, not wanting to move from the cocoon of blankets and his warmth.

"I know, baby," he said, dropping a kiss to my hair. "But we've got work to do."

Work. I scoffed. "Fuck work."

Owen chuckled behind me, his hand moving, his fingers skating across my skin, dipping lower beneath the covers. "We have to finish the distillery. Get those doors open."

My eyes flew fully open, excitement blooming in my chest despite the ungodly hour and desire to stay here with him forever.

"The last of the furniture is being delivered today," I said, voice still sleepy.

"And the movers are packing everything up from the barn and hauling it over," he reminded me. "We're so close."

"But I don't want to leave you," I whined.

Owen made a dismissive sound in the back of his throat. "You think I'm letting you out of my sight ever again?"

"Just sew my skin directly to yours," I said, burrowing deeper into him.

"Creepy."

I giggled as I turned toward him, and he instantly captured my mouth with his. "Only way to ensure we're stuck together forever."

Owen pulled away a breath, his expression serious. "We already are."

"Good," I whispered.

"Now come on," he said, tossing the comforter back. "We need showers. You're a dirty girl."

"Oh, *I'm* dirty," I said, sitting up and swinging a pillow at him. "You've had your face buried in my pussy all weekend, QB. I'd say you're the dirty one."

He reached down and slipped his fingers through my slit. "And what a beautiful pussy it is. Now let me take care of it."

We rose and raced to the bathroom, the early morning chill raising goosebumps on my entire body. Owen reached into the glass enclosed shower and spun the knobs, steaming hot water pouring from the various heads a second later.

Then he unceremoniously shoved me under the spray, following me in and hauling me against his body. As water ran in rivulets down my face, I tipped it up to him, and he slanted his lips over mine, his tongue instantly diving in. It was so easy to lose myself in him, in his lips, soft but insistent, his tongue brushing against my own, swirling it in a way that reminded me exactly what he could do with it further south.

Skating his hands up my sides, he cupped my breasts, massaging them, his thumbs flicking over my nipples. I moaned into his mouth.

"I haven't given these perfect tits enough attention this weekend," he groaned, dropping his forehead to mine to stare between us.

"You've got time now," I said saucily.

Owen growled and backed up, jerking his head at the built-in bench off to one side.

"Sit down. Feet tucked under you."

Anticipation danced along my skin as I did what he asked.

Once in position, the discomfort as my ankle bones ground into the tile was forgotten as he approached. His thick cock jutted obscenely from his body, and I would forever marvel at his size. I still wasn't entirely sure how it fit inside me, but god I loved the way it did. The snugness, that burn as he first pushed inside giving way to pleasure that blanketed my limbs when I acclimated.

He was perfection, from the tips of his mid-length hair to the long toes on his giant feet.

Yeah, I didn't think I was into feet either, but I was into

everything when it came to Owen Lawless.

"Push them together, Whiskey," he said gruffly, his hand slowly sliding up and down his length.

It dawned on me then what he intended, and I cupped the outsides of my breasts, shoving them together as he neared. Right in front of me, he tapped his head against my lips and said, "Give it a kiss."

My tongue flicked out instantly, licking up the precum that had beaded in the slit, then swirling it around the crown for good measure.

"Gonna fuck that mouth one of these days," he said absently. "But right now, I want to fuck these tits."

I sat up straighter, arching my back to push my chest out, and Owen slapped each boob with his cock before we maneuvered to settle it in my cleavage. I pushed them tighter together, trapping him, and he groaned, his hand coming to my hair.

With jerky movements, Owen slid his cock up and down between my tits, his eyes closing and head dropping back as I let him use me. Heat pooled in my core, my clit throbbing, and I shifted, seeking friction I couldn't find.

His shaft was deeply flushed, veins popping and throbbing, and I knew he was close. I wanted him to come like this, to paint my neck and my chin.

But he pulled away.

"Not yet, baby," he said when I made a noise of protest. "Need to come inside you."

He roughly lifted me to standing, my feet tingling as blood rushed back to them. Then he bent and hooked his forearms behind my knees, easily hauling me up and backing me into the shower wall. I was spread wide, couldn't move my legs with his strong arms holding me open.

"Put it in," he said and shifted his pelvis away from mine enough for me to grab him and notch his head at my entrance.

He pushed inside in a quick pulse, and I cried out at the intrusion, my head falling back against the tile.

He'd barely begun moving and already my vision was hazy. Through heavily lidded eyes, I watched him, his head bent to study the way he slipped in and out of me, water pounding his back, his hair soaking and plastered to his cheeks.

The juxtaposition of the cool tile against my back and the heat of the water and Owen's body at my front had every nerve ending in my body lighting, my release gathering dangerously fast.

It didn't take much to get us there. Owen's pace was relentless as he slammed into me over and over, chasing the release he'd already denied himself once. I wanted to come with him, so I anchored one hand at the base of his neck, holding on for dear life as I slipped my fingers between us and rubbed my clit rapidly.

We came in unison, Owen's movements turning jerky as he pumped through it, my hand clinging to him, leaving gouges with my nails in his shoulder as I screamed his name, the tile echoing it back at us.

Breathing roughly through our noses, Owen and I collided in a sloppy kiss, all tongue and teeth, desperately clinging to the connection as long as we could.

When our hearts slowed, he shifted out and set me down.

And as if he hadn't just fucked my tits and destroyed my pussy, he grabbed a washcloth from the little stand outside the shower and lathered it with body wash, gently soaping up my entire body, caressing me. There was nothing sexual about it, simply a good man taking care of his girl.

I appreciated the sweetness more, somehow, than the sinful version of him that had taken me against the wall minutes before.

"You are a dream, Owen Lawless," I told him as he massaged my scalp, working the eucalyptus scented shampoo into my roots.

I angled my head, and he bent to kiss me, murmuring against my lips, "And you're better than any reality I could've imagined."

I knew he wasn't going anywhere, that we were still going to see each other and figure out everything that came next together, but it was still strange to be leaving his house that morning—even if we were leaving together. It was almost like leaving summer camp, returning to reality after spending a weekend in a magical bubble where only we existed.

Our drive from his house to Overtime where my car had sat all weekend was quiet, though he gripped my hand tightly, absently drawing circles on the back with his thumb.

When he parked, he angled himself in the seat to face me.

"Promise me something."

"Anything."

"Promise me this isn't over when this bubble pops. Promise me you're still mine once you open that door."

My heart melted to a puddle in my chest and sank to my toes. Without a word, I climbed over the center console and settled myself in his lap, clasping his face between my hands and pressing my mouth to his. Once. Twice. Three times. Mentally punctuating three words I wasn't ready to say but definitely felt all the same. His hands tangled in my hair, holding me close as he exhaled deeply.

"As long as you promise you're mine too," I whispered.

"I'm not going anywhere, Whiskey," he said. "I've said it before and I'll say it again. I'll remind you every day if that's what you need."

"And I you," I promised.

Before I could retreat to my seat and get out of the car, Owen's hands settled on my hips, keeping me rooted in place.

"Let me take you to dinner," he blurted.

"Was there a question in there?" I asked cheekily.

Owen chuckled then said, "Delia Delatou, would you do the honor of going on a dinner date with me?"

"I would love to," I said, tapping his nose. "Name the time and place, QB, and I'm yours."

"Friday," he said. "Birdie's at seven. I'll come pick you up."

"Absolutely not," I protested. "You don't have to drive all the way up there for that."

"I would drive a million miles for you, Delia. A quick trip up the peninsula to get my girl is nothing. Besides, it's the gentlemanly thing to do."

I gave him a soft smile, my heart surely in my eyes. "I'm not sure what I did to deserve you."

"I'm the one who should be saying that, actually," he said, kissing me quickly. "Now you know I adore you, but I'm going to need you to get out of this truck before I haul you into the backseat and make you come so hard you forget your name."

With a giggle and a mock salute, I scrambled off him and to the passenger seat, then gathered my bag off the floor before opening the door. The late-November wind assaulted my bare legs, my skirt back on my body after being lost to Owen's bedroom floor all weekend, one of his oversized sweatshirts draped over my torso tucked into the waistband, enveloping me in his scent.

I was never washing it, nor would I probably ever take it off.

With a little finger wave, I got in my car and reversed out of the space. The second I was speeding down the street, Owen drove off in the opposite direction.

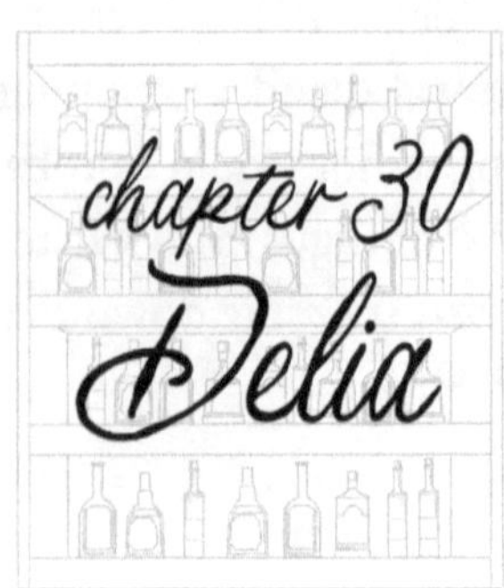

chapter 30
Delia

THE WEEK PASSED IN a flash, a blur of deliveries and staging, of stocking shelves and sampling spirits, of keeping my hands as much to myself as possible whenever Owen was within a twenty yard radius. We hadn't made it a secret that we were together now, but we were attempting to be professional at work.

Personally, *professional* could get fucked—and not in the good way.

I wanted his hands on me at every opportunity, and by the time Friday evening rolled around, I was damn near coming apart at the seams, desperate for some alone time with him.

Only, I frowned when we parked around the back of Birdie's instead of the main street.

"Why aren't we going in through the front?"

"You'll see," he said, hopping out and coming around to help me out.

Fingers laced together, he led me inside, guiding me down a hallway that bisected the kitchens from the restrooms and out onto the main dining floor.

The entire place was empty.

"What the fuck?"

Owen chuckled but didn't answer me, instead pulling me toward a circular table in the center of the room. At its side, a bottle of Chateau Delatou sparkling wine sat on ice in a bucket, and candles flickered on its surface, suffusing the area in a warm glow.

"Where is everyone?"

"I assume the chef and our waiter are in the kitchen," he said.

"I mean patrons, QB," I said, glaring at him.

"I closed Birdie's down tonight. I wanted you all to myself."

"You can't do that!"

"I can, actually," he said. "I own the place, remember?"

"You are…insane."

"Insane about you, yes," he agreed.

My heart lodged in my throat as my gaze swept the room. The lights were low, the space lit mostly by tealights and the dimmed wall sconces.

Owen's eyes sparkled as I caught his gaze, and inexplicably, my nose stung with unshed tears.

"This is the most romantic thing anyone has ever done for me," I told him, almost embarrassed by that fact.

"There's more where this came from, my girl," he said, winking at me.

Before I could respond, the waiter appeared from the back, carrying two goblets and a bottle of Chateau Delatou Merlot, which happened to be my favorite of ours.

"How did you know?" I asked, forehead creasing as I gestured at the wine.

"You mentioned it once in passing a long time ago," he said.

"And you remembered?" I asked, incredulous. "I don't even remember telling you!"

"I remember everything, Delia. Every word. Every like and dislike. Every outfit, every smile and glance and touch." He tapped his temple. "It's all right here."

I rose from my seat and moved to his side, plopping down on his lap and throwing my arms around his neck. Leaning in to kiss him, I whispered, "Thank you."

There was a world of things I wasn't saying encompassed in those two words, and Owen must've been able to read it all on my face. He simply said, "You're welcome."

I returned to my chair as our waiter brought out the appetizer course.

As usual, dinner was exquisite. We started with crunchy bruschetta topped with a diced tomato and onion mixture, then had a fall-inspired salad with butternut squash, avocado, more tomato, and roasted mushrooms on a bed of warm quinoa. The main course was surf and turf, though Owen ended up eating his entire steak and half of mine. We chatted the entire time, mainly surface level things that revolved around the distillery. We were nearing the finish line, and should be able to open the doors shortly before Christmas.

When the waiter cleared our main course plates and we waited for dessert to come out—though I wasn't sure where I'd put it; I was already damn near bursting—Owen met my eyes and said, "We need to have a serious conversation."

Icy dread rolled down my spine, but when Owen reached for

my hand, his warm fingers heating my chilled ones, I calmed instantly.

Jumping to conclusions wouldn't do anyone any good.

"Okay..." I said slowly, the word scraping my throat on the way out.

"I haven't had a serious girlfriend in a long time," he started.

"Temperance?" I asked, raising a brow.

"Yes, her," he said. "But...I'm falling for you, Delia. Hard and fast. Actually, I think I've been half in love with you for months. I realize we only just started this thing together, but I want to do it all with you. Business partners. Life partners. The whole fucking thing. I want to take you to Dusk Valley to meet my family. I want to wake up with you every morning and fall asleep with you in my arms every night. I know you're younger than me, so maybe that's not something you want right now, but...I'm old enough to know I want marriage and babies and the white picket fence. Fuck." Dropping his gaze, he punctuated the curse with a squeeze of my hand, and I couldn't help but giggle at his rambling. "I'm insane, aren't I? You're going to run screaming now, right?"

"No," I said quietly, and he looked up at me, the panic lining his face softening as he took in the tears lining my eyes. "I want all of that too, and I want it with you. I'm twenty-seven, Owen. I'm not some young adult just embarking on the rest of my life. I know who I am and what I want, and I want *you*. I want to take your last name and have your babies—one day."

He frowned. "One day?"

I reached out and prodded the corner of his mouth until it curved in the opposite direction. "We're endgame, QB. I just don't want to rush things. How about we start with 'boyfriend' and 'girlfriend' labels before we go slapping on any others?"

"I can do that," he said, grinning. "Though 'girlfriend' is a woefully inadequate way to describe what I feel for you."

I squeezed his hand tighter. "And you're not exactly a *boy*friend, either. Are you sure you're ready for this, though? For...me? I'm not exactly the easiest woman to love."

Owen lifted a hand to cup my chin in one of his palms. "I have waited my whole life to love you, Whiskey. And if I wanted easy, I wouldn't be here right now. I made a career of taking hits from guys twice your size and getting back up. Nothing you can say or do is going to break me. Throw whatever you need at me. Let me be your safe place."

My vision blurred as tears filled my eyes, and I sniffled. I'd forever marvel at whatever force brought this man into my life, and forever wonder what I did to deserve him. But I'd spend the rest of my life proving worthy of his love and the safety of his arms.

"As long as you remember that you can do the same, QB. I know you're all macho and hate talking about your feelings unless it's with your therapist, but if we're doing this, you need to know you can talk to me too. Let *me* be *your* safe place."

Owen swallowed hard and nodded. "Whatever you want, Whiskey. It's yours."

I nodded and gripped his hand tightly. "Now tell me something."

"Anything."

"Why do you really call me 'Whiskey'?"

Owen swallowed hard, his eyes darting away from me, and I

was surprised by the slight blush that crept into his cheeks. At last, our gazes collided again. "Your eyes."

"My eyes?"

"They're the exact shade of top shelf whiskey, and I swear I've gotten drunk staring into them more times than I can count. Everything about you intoxicates me, Delia, but those eyes? Fuck, I should've realized I was a goner that first time you came to my office and looked at me."

This man. Soft and sweet beneath that hard body of his, his gentle words the antithesis of his rough touches in the bedroom.

"I'm obsessed with you, you know," I said on a laugh, shaking my head. "It's not normal."

"The feeling is mutual," he replied, leaning forward to kiss me.

I was gripped by the sudden need to be connected to him right now, to seal our promises to each other with more than holding hands and kissing. To properly thank him for all he'd given me.

So I withdrew my hand from his and tossed my napkin onto my plate, then slipped out of my chair and ducked under the table.

"What're you doing?" he hissed.

"Showing my appreciation," I whispered back, settling between his legs and reaching for the fly on his dress pants.

"We can't do this here!"

"Somehow, I don't think the boss will mind," I quipped, pulling down his zipper and reaching through the opening in his briefs to extract his cock. Apparently, feelings talk turned my man on something fierce, because he was a steel rod in my hand. I circled him in my grip and squeezed. His hips jumped toward me, a strangled groan leaving his mouth.

"You wicked, filthy girl," he said, and it sounded like his teeth were gritted.

"You can punish me later, daddy," I said, then closed my lips around him.

"Fuuuuuuck," he moaned.

A moment later, I heard the waiter approach again, the china clinking as he set what I assumed was our dessert on the table.

"What happened to Miss Delatou?" he asked.

"Bathroom," Owen gritted out, and I chuckled around him. His length twitched against my tongue with the vibrations, and I flattened it, breathing deeply through my nose as I sank him deeper into my mouth.

"You can actually take off," Owen told him. "Tell Chef as well."

"Are you sure?"

"Positive!" Owen yelped when his head hit the back of my throat and I gagged around him. "I can clean up."

"Okay," the waiter said. "Thank you, Mr. Lawless. Enjoy the rest of your night."

"You too," Owen replied tersely, and I felt his entire body slacken the moment the man was gone.

"You are going to pay for this," he said, digging his fingers into my scalp and holding me to him as he pushed his chair back from the table, dragging me with him.

I only hummed, circling my palms at his base and pulling off with a *pop*, chasing my mouth with my hands. Saliva trailed from my mouth to his head, and he broke the connection by dragging his thumb along my bottom lip.

"Get up here," he said.

I shook my head, brushing his hand out of the way as I dove back in, my hands and mouth working in tandem as I drove him higher. Eventually I gave up keeping the pace, letting him loose to fuck my face, his fingers anchored in my hair as his cock branded my throat over and over.

"That's right, pretty girl," he said, as I looked up at him, eyes watering slightly, surely sending my mascara running in dark rivers down my cheeks. "You like choking on this big cock?"

Unable to verbally respond, I merely nodded, swirling my tongue along his length as he pumped in and out. I knew he was close when his hips began moving erratically, and at last he shoved deep inside and held me there. I breathed steadily through my nose, fighting off my gag reflex as he spilled in long, warm spurts down my throat.

I swallowed every drop.

"Fucking hell, Whiskey," Owen said when I pulled off him, sinking back into his chair, boneless. "That was..."

"I know," I smirked, licking my lips, his saltiness lingering on my tongue.

After tucking himself away, he stood and drew me to my feet, our dessert forgotten to desire as he pulled me from the restaurant.

"Your place or mine?" he asked once we were safely ensconced in his truck.

"For what?"

"For your punishment."

God, the promise in his words sent electricity sparking across my skin.

"Mine," I said. "Might as well be comfortable."

"Might as well," he agreed wickedly.

He made good on his promise to punish me, taking no mercy on me as he stripped me naked and repeatedly drove me right to the edge with his fingers and tongue before stopping just as I was about to blast apart. When he finally shoved his cock inside me, I swear to god I blacked out for a second, the pleasure emanating from our connection taking me the fuck out. It was too much.

And with one hand wrapped around my ankle, holding my leg straight against his torso, and the other thumb circling my clit, Owen pounded into me relentlessly. He set a punishing rhythm, and I could do nothing but hold on, waiting for that wave to crash and take us both out with it. It was like my orgasm was the goal line and the game was on the line. He wouldn't—couldn't—stop until he broke the plane and sealed his victory.

My release built rapidly thanks to Owen's previous torture, my nails digging into the hand he'd anchored on my thigh, holding me wide for him, as he drove me higher and higher.

At last, I shattered, my entire body shaking. My back bowed off the bed as my climax claimed me. Owen came with a roar a beat later, the clenching of my walls around him triggering his own release.

Every limb was deliciously wrung out and exhausted when I returned to my body, though my heart still beat wildly in my chest. When he withdrew and laid down next to me, pulling me against his chest, I could feel Owen's doing the same against my back.

Satiated, I hovered in that ephemeral place between awake and asleep, content and cozy in Owen's arms.

"I love your house," he said suddenly, pulling me back from the slumber I was about to drop into.

"I worked really hard on it," I told him, voice thick with fighting sleep.

"It feels like a home," he mused. "I think, maybe, when the time comes...I'd like to live here. If you'll have me, of course."

"And give up your place on the lake?" I asked, eyes still closed, though my heart thumped rapidly at the idea of building a home—*this* home—with him. "What about privacy and security?"

"Apple Blossom Bay is different from TC, Whiskey. And like you said, you worked hard on this place. There's plenty of room for us both, and I don't want you to have to give it up."

"I would for you," I said, rolling over to face him. "We could find a place that's ours."

Owen shook his head. "Not necessary, my girl. This is perfect."

I burrowed deeper into his chest, sighing contentedly as I once again drifted off.

There was something so soothing about him calling me "my girl," a sense of belonging I hadn't experienced in my life up to that point.

"I think I love you," he said quietly, his lips in my hair, dropping a kiss to the top of my head.

"I think I love you too," I whispered, then promptly fell asleep with a smile on my face.

chapter 31
Owen

THE FOLLOWING THURSDAY, AFTER spending yet another weekend with my cock buried deep inside Delia and a few days of work wherein I accomplished nothing of note, I approached Leon and Lena Delatou's front door.

"Are you shitting your pants?" Cal asked from beside me. "I'm shitting my pants."

"Yes!" I hissed on a laugh. "Why are we so nervous? It's not like we've never met these people before."

"I mean, I can't speak for you," Cal said, shifting uncomfortably on his feet, "but I'm pretty sure Leon still hates me for getting his daughter pregnant."

"But you love her, right?"

"Of course I do. More than anything."

"Then that's all that matters," I said with a shrug.

His eyes narrowed on me. "And do you love Delia?"

"I might," I said noncommittally. "But I'm not going to give you a straight answer before I tell her that."

Cal clapped me on the back. "Good man."

With a deep breath, I reached out and pressed the doorbell. The sound echoed through the house, followed by a shouted, "I'll get it!" from one of the girls.

A moment later, the massive oak door swung inward to reveal Brie, a bright smile and swipes of flour decorating her face.

"Hey guys!" she said, stepping aside and welcoming us in. "We're all in the kitchen. Mar! Lia! Your man friends are here!" she shouted as she took off back in that direction.

With a shared look of exasperation, Cal and I followed along.

The spacious kitchen was utter chaos, and I paused at the threshold to take in the scene.

The massive island was laden with numerous dishes, steam and scents of delicious food curling in the air around the heads of the six Delatou women.

Down the hall, I could hear the sounds of a football game blasting over the surround sound, and for once, that pang of longing didn't pierce my chest. The Mustangs always played in the Thanksgiving game, and though I watched—if only to give Jalen shit afterward—it always made me a bit melancholic. Now, though, I was just happy to be here, surrounded by this warm and inviting family.

When Cal and I entered, Amara unceremoniously dropped the hot dish she'd just pulled out of the oven on the stove to cool, then ditched the oven mitts and ran into Cal's arms. He caught her easily and swung her around in a circle, peppering her face with kisses.

"How are my babies?" he whispered.

"Good," she said as he deposited her on her feet, and she

stepped back to rub her bulging abdomen. "But little one is hungry."

"Food is almost ready," Lena said, and I genuinely had no idea which one of the women she was until she turned, their hair and body shapes so similar it was difficult to discern who was who.

But I didn't see mine.

A light tap came at my shoulder, and I turned.

"Looking for me?"

I grinned. "Hey, Whiskey."

"Hey, QB."

I shuffled toward her, feeling like a teenager hanging out with his crush for the first time, unsure what to do with my hands. Delia made the decision for me, reaching out and wrapping her arms around my waist. I fell into her, settling my hands on her hips and pressing my body against hers.

"Am I allowed to kiss you?" I whispered.

"I think you better," she told me. "Or my family will start asking questions."

I needed no further encouragement, and though it wasn't the consumption I wanted to perform, the light, chaste press of my lips to hers was enough to quell the bulk of my anxiety.

"You told them?"

"Of course I did."

"Does your dad want to kill me?"

"I think in the hierarchy of Daddy's favorite sons-in-law, you're firmly at number two." I raised a brow, and she added, "Logan, you, Cal."

I chuckled. "As long as I'm beating out Cal, I don't care. Also..." I trailed off, leaning closer to place a kiss on her neck right below her ear. "Sons-in-law?"

Delia giggled. "Call it a pre-empt."

God, how badly I wanted this woman to be mine in every possible way. I knew we were trying to take things slow, but I wanted her to take my last name, to be the mother of my children, to be the one I grew old with. And I wanted it all *now*.

Even though their time together had been cut short, what my parents had was a once-in-a-lifetime kind of love. The sort of relationship I'd looked up to and searched for my entire life. They were truly partners in everything, two halves of the same whole. Losing a loved one was difficult under any circumstances, but the loss of my dad cut my mom so deeply because she'd lost a part of herself. It was why she hadn't dated since nor had any plans to. My dad had been it for her, and giving even a piece of her heart to another would've dishonored his memory in her eyes.

I wanted that. And I felt confident saying I'd found it with Delia.

Still, I couldn't quite shake the melancholy that had me in its grip as we wandered deeper into the kitchen in the direction of the dining room and conversation swirled around us. In addition to Cal, Logan, and much to my dismay, Alfie, I was surprised to find Ezra, his son Hansen, father Rik, and Liam Danvers had all been invited to celebrate the holiday with the Delatou family. The house was bursting with love and laughter, but I couldn't fully let myself enjoy it.

It was the anniversary of Dad's death, and the knowledge that he was no longer here still hit just as hard as it had seventeen years ago.

I think Delia knew something was up with me, because she

tried her hardest to keep me occupied and entertained. Truthfully, all I needed was her. I would've been happy to curl up in one of our living rooms with a bottle of bourbon and the lights off. But I never strayed far from her, needing her within reach, grounding me.

At last, we sat for dinner, and several conversations started at once, each section of the table breaking into groups to discuss various happenings in the family, business, and Apple Blossom Bay. I sat quiet in the middle of it all, like I had those weeks ago when I'd first attended a Delatou family meal, simply letting the camaraderie wash over me. I silently ate my food and did my best to participate in conversation when a question was directed at me.

Particularly when Leon Delatou pinned me with those emerald green eyes.

"How're things at the distillery coming, son?" he asked.

I perked up, something tugging loose in my chest at his term of endearment. How long had it been since I'd had a man call me that? Probably not since the first time a coach had done it after my dad died and I lost my shit on him.

"Things are good, sir," I said, reaching under the table to grip Delia's hand. In an instant, all other conversations at the table died, attention wholly focused on us. "We should be able to open in three weeks?" I shot Delia a questioning look.

"Two, actually," she said happily.

"Hell yeah, man!" Cal said, slapping me on the shoulder. "Can't wait to try some of what you've been brewing up."

"Distilling, Ryder," Amara said. "What they've been *distilling*."

"Semantics," Calvin said, then glanced at her. "Bet you wish you weren't pregnant right now."

"You're the one who got me like this!" she shouted, tossing her napkin at his face.

Chloe, who was also pregnant, glanced up at Logan. "I, for one, don't mind being pregnant."

"Because you can't drink liquor anyway," Ella quipped from her other side.

"Remember your senior prom when you got so wasted on peppermint schnapps we had to sneak you in the backdoor of the school and into the gym just so you could attend?" Amara chuckled.

"God, don't remind me," Chloe said, gagging. "I still can't go near anything with mint."

"I've never heard this story," Leon said.

"That's because she puked it all up before we made Brie come pick us all up," Amara said with a snort.

Both Delatou parents whipped their heads to Brie. "You were thirteen!" Lena shrieked.

Brie shrugged. "Still knew how to drive."

Lena huffed a sigh out through her nose. "You girls are the reason I have grey hair."

The daughters exchanged glances and promptly burst out laughing, but it was Leon who spoke.

"You've never had a grey hair in your life, woman."

Lena cut him with a glare. "Don't even get me started on *you*."

"*Anyway*," Delia said. "Everything is up there, I just need to start staging."

"You want some help?" Chloe asked. "I've got some free time

now that I'm not on deadline."

"You're also pregnant," Logan reminded her.

"I know that!" Chloe shot back. "I'm not going to be doing any heavy lifting, but I can help with little stuff."

"I can help too!" Lena piped up. "I need to get out of this house and do something besides listen to your father drone on about fishing."

"I beg your pardon?" Leon said to his wife, hand coming to his chest like he'd been wounded.

"I love you, honey," she said absently, "but I don't care about trout or pike or tuna or whatever."

"There aren't any tuna in the Great Lakes," Leon grumbled, and I fought back a chuckle.

"I'll happily talk fishing with you anytime, Leon," Logan said brightly, and my laugh burst free at last, along with everyone else at the table.

Leon smiled widely, pointing his fork at Logan. "That's why Daniels is my favorite."

"Fishing aside," Delia said, once again pulling the conversation back to the distillery. "We're planning on hosting a little soft open in a few weeks. I'm thinking the thirteenth."

"We are?" I hissed at her.

"Oh, did I forget to tell you?" she asked with an overly sweet smile.

"Oh, that's wonderful!" Lena said, clapping her hands together. "We can make it a whole party."

Delia cursed softly next to me, and I looked down at her quizzically.

While Lena ran away with the party idea, looping Brie into

a conversation about pastries, Delia quietly said, "I should've known better than to bring that up in front of my mom. There's nothing that woman loves more than throwing a party, and I have a feeling our soft opening is about to become a lot grander."

"She could turn it into the Met Gala for all I care," I told her as I bent and pressed my lips to hers. "As long as you're at my side."

"Always," she promised.

"Get a room!" someone—Cal—yelled, and I pulled away from her, grinning sheepishly at her parents.

Lena had hearts in her eyes while Leon glared daggers at me.

Honestly, that felt pretty par for the course, and I didn't mind one bit.

After dinner, Ezra, Hansen, Rik, Liam, and Alfie all left, and the rest of us retired to the back deck. Though it was cold as hell out, an array of heaters and a massive fireplace, logs crackling and sparking with flames within, kept the chill away. Delia and I curled up on a loveseat together, a blanket tucked around us, my hands drawing idle circles on the skin of her lower back. Around us, her family was in various stages of winding down, though Ella and Brie were playing some sort of card game that involved a lot of slapping each other's hands. It was probably the most animated I'd ever seen the second youngest Delatou girl, and I had to admit, it was a good look on her. Even with the pink hair and fingers decorated with delicate tattoos, Ella more closely resembled her sisters with a smile on her face.

"What's the deal with Ella and her boyfriend?" I asked Delia quietly.

"You picked up on that?"

"Hard not to," I said. "The way he acted at Birdie's that night was appalling, and the way he treated all of you when he came to Lawless? He's lucky I didn't punch *him* in the face."

Delia snorted but said, "I'm glad you didn't. It only would've made things harder for her."

"Why is she even with him?"

Delia sighed heavily, her entire body rising and falling in my arms. "She's always been more free spirited than the rest of us. Alfie is a singer or rapper or something—albeit a terrible one—and I guess when she met him, she felt a kinship with that side of him, with the artist he apparently is. Now, I just think she's afraid to leave, afraid to give up on something she's given so many years to."

I hummed in understanding. "She reminds me a lot of my sister in that way. I know growing up with six older brothers who messed up more often than not wasn't easy. She had a habit of sticking with things even when she was miserable because she didn't want to be seen as a failure. My mom struggled a lot after Dad died, and Aria tried to make herself as small as possible, not wanting to add to Mom's stress."

I had always secretly hoped that she'd grow out of that one day, that she'd take chances on the things that made her happy instead of doing something because she thought she was supposed to.

"How come you didn't go home for Thanksgiving?" Delia asked suddenly, apparently jumping ahead on a train of thought inside that beautiful brain I'd clearly missed. "Why didn't you go see them?"

"Well...today is the anniversary of my dad's death," I said quietly. Delia gasped softly but didn't speak, so I pressed on. "It's just too hard sometimes. To go back there and feel his memory everywhere, like a ghost that won't let go. I miss him fiercely, and I'm happy to have those memories, but...I can't afford to spiral again, you know? I've been doing so much better since I moved up here. It's difficult to think about going back and potentially ruining all my progress.

"Plus, with the distillery—and you," I added with a poke to her ribs, "I haven't really had time."

"Did you talk to them about coming out here for the opening?"

"They don't really have the time either," I said. "They're all busy with their own lives and jobs." I pressed a kiss to the top of her head. "But it's okay. I'll see them soon, I'm sure."

Delia lifted her head and placed a kiss on my chest, right over my heart and the coordinates tattooed there.

"When you're ready, QB," she said, burrowing deeper into me, "we'll do it together."

"Do what?"

"Go to Dusk Valley."

"You'd do that for me?"

She tilted her face up to mine and said, "Haven't you figured out by now that I'd do anything for you?"

"Back at you," I said hoarsely.

"Plus, I'm part of your family now, just like you're part of mine."

"Am I really?" I asked.

She shrugged and nonchalantly said, "I sure hope so," though the tightness around her eyes told me my answer meant more than she was letting on.

The Delatou family was certifiably crazy, but they weren't so different from mine. A mass of children, the female counterparts to my nearly all-male one. Parents who loved fiercely. Significant others who would burn the world down if it would make their girl happy.

Yeah, I fit in perfectly around here.

I dipped my head and captured her mouth with mine. Against her lips I said, "I love you, Whiskey, and they're part of the package."

With a wide grin, she kissed me back, whispering, "Good answer. And I love you too."

THE TWO WEEKS FOLLOWING Thanksgiving came and went in a flash, though I knew exactly where all that time went. I spent every waking moment at the distillery, getting everything ready for the big day.

Suddenly, it was three days before our soft opening party, of which my mother had taken the reins and turned it into something far more upscale than the chips and dip I'd planned on.

Though Owen seemed at peace with the fact that no one from his family would be here to celebrate with us, I simply couldn't let it go.

Which is how I found myself on the phone Wednesday morning, waiting for the call to his mother to connect. It was a rare day when Owen and I hadn't lingered in bed. He'd run into the city to take care of his woefully neglected businesses there after a stern phone call from Hugo, and I needed to edit and upload some content for various businesses in town. I used it as my opportunity to hopefully pull together this surprise for him.

My hands were sweating so badly I could barely keep my grip on my phone, so I pulled it from my ear, tapped the speaker button, and set it on the counter.

"Hello?"

"H-hi," I said shakily. "Is this Mrs. Lawless?"

The woman chuckled. "Yes, this is Brigid. Who am I speaking with?"

"Oh, this is Delia Delatou, ma'am," I said quickly. "I'm Owen's..."

I trailed off, unsure how to label myself. I mean, he and I had settled on the standard boyfriend/girlfriend labels, but I had no idea if he'd told his mother about us.

"His girlfriend," she breathed, and I sighed in relief. "Oh my, it's so wonderful to hear from you, Delia. I've heard so much about you from Owen. And in that case, you can call me Birdie."

"All good things I hope," I said with a nervous laugh.

"The best," she assured me. "He's been talking about you nonstop for months."

I perked up at that, wanting his mom to spill all the tea. "Months, you say?"

"He's really enjoyed working with you," Birdie said. "Though it was easy enough to tell when things changed for him. The way he spoke about you shifted from the respect of a business partner to the romantic kind of admiration."

"When was that?" I asked, unable to help myself.

For me, that moment had happened that night in his office, when he first told me his father was gone, and I witnessed the absolute pain and devastation on his face. Though he'd tried so hard to keep it locked up and hidden from me, those kinds of raw emotional wounds weren't so easy to pack away, and it had been plainly written on every line of his body.

A fierce desire to protect him surged within me that night, and even though we hadn't gotten together for another month after that, I somehow knew we'd always end up here—even when I was fighting it, even when I'd thought it was the worst damn idea either of us had ever had.

"Oh, sometime in early October," Birdie said. "He called to tell me about that asshat that had caused a scene at the club, and told me how you were there. I guess being his mother, I just knew things were changing between you."

The same damn night.

"I know the one," I said. "I guess we both felt the shift that night."

I sniffled, tears burning my nose with this new knowledge, and she allowed me a moment of silence to collect myself.

"For what it's worth, I've never seen him like this. Sure, Owen has always been a caretaker, especially after his dad died. He took it upon himself to keep us from ruin that first year while we were all still figuring out life without him. But even before then, he'd spent his whole life acting as a third parent to his siblings. So it's nice that, with you, he's finally doing something for himself."

The tears fell freely now.

"He's the most amazing man I've ever met," I said, my words watery. "You raised him well."

"Thank you, honey," Birdie said. "He's lucky to have you."

"Nah," I told her. "I'm the lucky one."

Then again, I supposed we'd both lucked out to have found each other, to have this connection I'd never had with anyone else before. To feel like I'd finally found my other half, and to have Owen reassure me at every opportunity that he felt the same.

Owen had become a safe harbor, a soft place to land when I hadn't been looking for one or knew I needed it.

"So to what do I owe the pleasure of this call?" Birdie asked, drawing me out of my thoughts.

"Oh!" I said, remembering myself. "As you know, we're opening the distillery next week. He doesn't say it much, but he misses you guys, and I know it would mean a lot to him to have you here. He told me he asked and you all can't get away from work and whatnot, but I'm wondering if there's any way I can persuade you? I know it's short notice, so I understand if it's just not possible but—"

"Delia," Birdie cut me off. "He never asked us to come."

All the air in my lungs left in a whoosh.

"That little shit."

Birdie barked out a laugh, and in the background, I heard a deep male voice ask, "What's so funny, Mama?"

"Delia, do you mind if I put you on speaker?"

"Not at all."

A moment later, the line crackled with more sound, and Birdie said, "Say hello to Owen's girlfriend, Finn."

Finn. He had so many brothers it took me a moment to place which one he was. Quickly, I came to the realization that he was the tamer of the twins.

"Hey," he said.

"Hey," I replied a bit awkwardly. "I'm Delia."

"Nice to meet you, Delia. Now what exactly did you say to make my mom laugh like that?"

"I called your brother a little shit."

Finn snorted. "What'd he do this time?"

"Apparently, he told his girl that he invited us out to the opening of their distillery and we couldn't make it."

"What the fuck, I never got an invite!" Finn protested.

"Language," Birdie chastised, seemingly automatically. Knowing her eldest as well as I did, I had a feeling attempting to tame the filthy mouths of her boys was a losing battle.

"Sorry," Finn mumbled.

"We're going to need more details, Delia," Birdie told me.

So I quickly filled them in on the soft opening we were having on Saturday. How my entire family would be there, including my four sisters, a fact that greatly interested both Brigid and Finn, though for different reasons.

I didn't have the heart to tell Finn three of them were in deeply committed relationships, two of whom were pregnant.

"I'll pay for your flights and other transportation," I told them. "Whatever you need."

Birdie chuckled. "That won't be necessary, dear girl. We can get ourselves there just fine. You just tell us where to be and when."

I gave her the address of my parents' house, thinking it would be a good idea for them to convene there and come to the distillery together. If you were unfamiliar with the peninsula, it could be a little difficult to navigate, and the last thing I needed was Owen's family getting lost in the wilderness.

"Are you all going to be able to come then?" I asked hopefully.

"I'll make sure every one of my children gets on that plane, even if I have to physically carry them on it myself."

I smiled widely. "He's going to be so excited."

"After he gets mad at you for keeping this from him," Finn said with a laugh.

"You let me worry about your brother."

⁂

Up to that point, I'd given Owen strict instructions that he wasn't allowed to come see the inside of the distillery until I was fully finished staging and decorating, and I finally gave him the green light on Thursday evening. The next day, our bartenders would come in for a full day of training, led by none other than Liam Danvers. I always forgot he was a talented mixologist, and when he'd asked me in passing a few months ago if there was anything he could do to help, Owen and I jumped at the chance to get him involved.

First by managing the distilling operation, and now, in taking responsibility for each of the cocktail recipes we'd be offering.

So before we headed to have dinner at Granny's that night, we drove up to the distillery.

"You ready for this?" I asked, unbuckling my seatbelt and preparing to exit his truck.

"As I'll ever be," he said with a sigh as he followed me out, and I was chuckling as I met him around the front.

We threaded our fingers together, but before I could tug him to the doors, he stopped me, turning me to face him.

"There's something I haven't told you."

"Okay..." I said slowly.

"This whole exterior facade? It looks exactly like the house I grew up in."

"I...what?" I asked dumbly. "Why didn't you say anything before?"

He shrugged, bringing our linked hands to his chest. "I guess I was afraid of what it might mean. That you had unintentionally created something so precious to me."

"And now?"

"And now...I can't help thinking my dad sent you to me, that he's responsible for all of this." He swept his arm out at the distillery, then gestured between us. "He would've loved you so much," he said, his words so low they were nearly carried away by the wind before they reached my ears. "I know I've told you that before but...he loved Aria so much. He loved us boys too, but there's something different about that father-daughter relationship, you know?" I nodded, extremely familiar with the phenomenon. "And he would've loved having another daughter. He couldn't wait for the day me and my brothers started getting married. Always said once one of us found the one, the rest would fall like dominoes." He chuckled softly, shaking his head. "I guess we'll see, though I have trouble imagining West ever settling down."

"I wish I had the opportunity to meet him," I said, slipping my free hand around the back of his neck, lightly scraping my nails against the hair at his nape in the way I knew tended to ground him when stress or grief gripped him. I shifted our joined hands over his heart, feeling its steady, reassuring thump right down to my bones. "But he's right here. And I get to learn about him through you, and your brothers, sister, and mom when I eventually get to meet them. He's still with us, and when we visit his grave, I'm going to thank him."

"For what?"

"For you," I said, scoffing like he didn't already know that. "And for us."

His shoulders drooped several inches as he relaxed, exhaling on a slow breath. I rose onto my tiptoes and captured his lips with mine. He fisted his free hand in my coat and hauled me into his body as his tongue slipped along the seam of my mouth.

I'd never tire of kissing the man, of being wrapped in his arms as he devoured me. As he poured every bit of love and longing into the places where we connected. I loved the way he nibbled at my bottom lip, gently trapping it between his teeth and pulling it when he retreated. I loved how rapidly his pulse thrummed when I swept my fingers up the column of his neck and into his hair.

And fuck, I loved the way his massive palm spanned the front of mine, exerting slight pressure on my windpipe and cupping my chin, holding me exactly where he wanted.

I especially loved it when he did that in bed while he pounded into me.

With that thought, I broke away from him with a gasp.

"That's not what we came here for," I reminded him, attempting to marshal my breathing.

"That's *always* what I come for," Owen replied, though he yielded a step and pulled me toward the door of the distillery at last.

"If you hate it...too fucking bad," I told him as we stepped inside, suddenly nervous that he *would* hate it and break up with me because I'd ruined it.

The main wall of the foyer was decorated with a large tin sign, painted white and distressed to allow some of the metal to show through. Emblazoned across its length was our brand name in a rustic, Old Western font.

"That was designed by an artist in Detroit," I told him. "And I paid a pretty penny to have it expedited so we'd have it in time for this weekend."

Owen glanced down at me, a brow raised. "Do I want to know?"

"Nope," I said brightly, leading him deeper into the building. Past the foyer—which our gift shop and bathrooms branched off—the space opened up onto the main entertainment area. Our bar dominated almost the entirety of the far wall, the bottom half constructed of matte black posts and corrugated steel sheets, the top a highly polished bird's eye maple. A massive mirror hung in the center of the wall itself, lined with glass shelves that held our branded bottles as well as an assortment of bronze, glass, and wooden trinkets. The POS system was hidden in an alcove off to the side so as to not ruin the line of sight.

The contrast of textures and materials was one of my favorite parts of the whole design scheme, and it continued into the seating arrangements.

At the bar were metal and wood stools, the seats deep brown tufted leather. And, heavily influenced by the place we'd gone in New York, I'd taken a bit of a chance for the armchairs and couches, the deep pine fabric dotting the spots between more bird's eye maple tables with chairs that matched the bar stools.

"Green?" Owen asked when he laid eyes on them.

"Green," I confirmed. "I thought they provided a nice contrast to all the more natural elements and colors while staying cohesive."

Personally, I loved the way the deep green leather, the rolled arms studded with brass buttons, popped against the rest of the furniture. Still, I held my breath as Owen turned in a slow circle, surveying everything.

"You hate it, don't you?" I asked, unable to stand it any longer.

At last, he faced me, his face softening. "Hate it? Whiskey, it's...perfect. Masculine and rustic but warm and welcoming." He scooped me up in his arms and spun me in a circle. I couldn't help the yelp of surprise that left me, though it quickly morphed into happy laughter. "It's exactly what you promised."

"So you don't hate it?" I confirmed when he returned me to my feet.

"I fucking love it," he said, eyes suddenly sparkling with mischief. "And I love you." He stepped toward me, and I retreated, my lower back connecting with the arm of one of the couches. "In fact, why don't you let me show you how much?"

Already, his hands were dropping to the fly of my jeans, and though I opened my mouth to protest, to make it clear we couldn't do that here, I quickly snapped it shut.

After all, the building was ours, and if my man wanted to give me an orgasm to christen the space, then who was I to deny him?

chapter 33
Owen

"TURN AROUND," I TOLD her when that fire sparked in her eyes, then pointed to a couch. "And bend over that arm."

"Yes, daddy," she quipped, spinning around and hinging at her waist, wiggling her ass in the air.

"Fuck, Whiskey," I said, reaching out to smack it. She yelped, the sound shaping itself into a moan when I gave the other cheek the same treatment. "Your ass is unreal."

"It's all yours."

I damn near choked on my own tongue at the implication in her words. "You mean..."

"Why not?" she said. "Go big or go home, right?"

"I—have you ever?"

Delia shook her head. "Have you?"

"No," I whispered.

Delia grinned at me over her shoulder. "It's like we're virgins again!"

I groaned. "Christ, Whiskey."

"Just trying to lighten the mood," she said. "You're fucking shaking."

I was shaking, my hands settling on her hips without having thought about it, squeezing the shit out of her flesh. But it wasn't because I was nervous. It was because I wanted to do this so badly with her, but I didn't know if this was the place.

"Are you sure?" I asked.

"Positive, QB. Fuck my ass."

Fucking hell. Those might have just become my new favorite words.

Folding myself over her, I grabbed a fistful of her hair and turned her head, giving her a messy kiss. "I'll be gentle."

"You better not," she said into my mouth.

My control was barely leashed, and it took everything in me to not tear our clothing from our bodies. Slipping my fingers beneath the waistband, I peeled her jeans down and over her ass, letting them pool at her ankles. She made no move to step out of them, and I loved that we were adding a little bondage to the moment. Then I gripped the thin strap of her panties, curled it around my fingers, and tore it from her body.

"Fuck," she breathed, her head drooping. "Add that to the list of reasons why I should wear panties more often."

"You like me feral for you, Whiskey? Like when I'm out of control?"

"I live for it," she responded. She straightened, her back pressed to my chest, and my hands came around her front, cupping her breasts through the thin material of her sweater. My thumbs brushed over the tight peaks of her nipples, and she arched against me, breath leaving her in a soft huff. She angled her head to look at me and said, "I'm the only one who gets you like this, QB. The only one who gets every version of you, and who loves each of them. You can be as unrestrained in bed as you want to be because I know outside of it, you fucking worship the ground I walk on."

"You're goddamn right," I breathed reverently, kissing her roughly before shoving her back over the arm of the couch. A moment later, my own pants and briefs were around my ankles, one hand around my rapidly hardening cock as the other swept through Delia's slit.

Already, she was fucking dripping, and I coated my fingers, then moved them to her ass. Dropping my cock, I spread her cheeks apart and settled my thumb against her hole.

"I'm gonna work you like this first," I said, awed by the way she shifted back, urging me on, her body practically begging for it. She wanted this as badly as I did.

I worked her slowly, gently massaging before she relaxed enough for me to slip the digit inside.

She moaned in response.

"Feel good?"

"God yes."

"Fuck," I cursed. "I'm going to blow apart the second I sink in here."

"What're you waiting for?"

"Don't wanna hurt you," I said absently, marveling at the grip. It was tighter than her pussy, and I honestly wasn't even sure how I'd fit.

We were about to find out, because I couldn't wait any longer, and Delia had begun shifting back and forth against my touch, making little impatient noises, asking for more.

I withdrew my thumb and once again coated my hand in her desire, swiping up to her ass then using the rest to coat my cock.

And then I gripped myself at the base and placed the head against her.

"Relax, baby," I said softly.

Delia exhaled roughly, her muscles loosening, and I pushed my head just past her rim.

"Oh!" she exclaimed.

"What?" I asked, panicking. "You okay?"

"I'm good, QB. Just...give me a sec."

I was fucking dying, but I stilled, allowing her a moment to adjust. I felt the moment she relaxed against me, and a beat later she said, "Keep going."

Slowly, I inched my way in, sweat beaded on my brow and at my temples by the time I was fully seated.

"Fuck," Delia swore.

"How does it feel?"

"So full."

"You okay if I move?"

"I think I might die if you don't."

Nearly as slowly as I pushed in, I backed out, and Delia let out a loud moan as I pumped back in on a quick stroke.

"Oh god."

"Not god, baby. Just Owen."

"Move," she gritted out.

As if I could do anything else.

With my palms settled on her cheeks, keeping them spread apart, I watched in fascination as my cock disappeared inside her.

Slowly, I increased my pace, and Delia's cries increased in volume as I did. Her legs shook as she struggled to keep herself upright, so as gently as I could while staying buried inside her, I banded an arm around her waist and lifted her, carrying us around to the front of the couch. With my cock still in her ass, she gingerly crawled onto the cushions, folding herself in half until her face rested against the cool leather.

Seeing her like that undid me, and the fucking wheels came off.

"Hold on," I said in warning before I unleashed.

I fucked her recklessly, pounding relentlessly in and out of her. And she met me thrust for thrust, her hand disappearing between her thighs, flicking against her clit.

"No," I growled, swatting her hand away. "My pussy."

"Okay, daddy," she said, moaning long and loud when I buried three fingers inside her.

I pounded into her roughly from both sides, my hips and hand moving in perfect tandem, driving her higher and higher. I'd never heard her moan like that, so loud, so unrestrained, as though I was tearing her apart from the inside and the only thing that would save her was letting her come. And as her orgasm built, my own gathered at the base of my spine, balls drawing in, preparing to unleash on her.

"You can rub your clit now, baby."

Her hand flew to that bundle of nerves, circling roughly in time with mine fucking her, and a few pumps later, she shattered, a scream tearing free from her throat, my name on her lips.

"That's it, Whiskey," I said through gritted teeth. "You let everyone know who fucks you this good."

"Come, O," she gasped.

I did as commanded, spilling hot and long inside her. My entire body shook with the force of it, the edges of my vision darkening, every thought vacating me but a single word.

"Delia!" I shouted, my movements erratic as I worked us both through it.

That orgasm—fuck, it went on forever. I swear I lived entire lifetimes in the span of the minute we blew apart and were pieced back together.

The second I returned to my body, I pulled my fingers and cock free, sitting down and gathering Delia against my chest. I peppered her face and hair with kisses.

"You okay?"

"I think I died and came back to life," she said, and I choked on a laugh. When she tilted her head to look at me, her eyes were heavily lidded, a blissed out smile playing on her lips. "I've never come that hard before."

"Me either," I agreed. "But how do you...feel?"

Delia giggled. "My ass will survive, QB. But your cock is massive so I'm going to be a little sore."

I lifted her off my lap and rose to my feet. "Let me clean you up, then we can go home."

"What about dinner?" she asked sleepily.

I raised a brow at her. "You really want to be in public after that?"

She giggled. "No."

"Exactly. So we're going home."

"But which home are we talking about?"

I returned from the bar with a wet cloth, and she shifted to let me wipe her up. The scene would've made me laugh—her ankles banded together and trapped by her jeans—if that orgasm hadn't altered my brain chemistry.

When she was once again on her feet, pants back in place, my cock tucked safely away, I answered her question with one of my own.

"Does it matter?" I said. "To me, home is wherever you are."

⁂

"You ready?" Delia asked me.

It was Saturday, and we stood in the foyer of the distillery, facing the doors. Outside, people milled around, chatting excitedly as they waited for us to welcome them in.

"As I'll ever be," I said, giving her hand a squeeze.

"It'll be great, QB. Everyone is going to love it."

"I hope you're right," I said.

I'd never been nervous before opening a business. None of them had ever meant so much. It had been a pipe dream until Delia came along and made it possible, not just with the land, her marketing expertise, and keen eye for design, but by being *her*. By giving me something to live for again, by giving me someone to share my life with.

With a final pulse of her fingers against mine, Delia pulled free and approached the door, swinging it wide and shouting, "Welcome to Unlawful Distillery!"

The crowd outside sent up a cheer and they all descended, rushing past Delia to get inside and scope the whole place out.

We'd disinfected the anal couch, though the fucking caveman

in my chest wanted to throw a sign on it commemorating what exactly happened there as I watched people move near it.

Finally, after a mass of friends swept past us, Delia's family crossed the threshold, each of her sisters wrapping us in hugs, her mom kissing my cheek, her dad enthusiastically shaking my hand.

"You did good, son. With this"—he gestured to the building—"and with her."

"I love her," I said simply.

"Good enough for me," Leon said, clapping me on the shoulder as he moved past me, following his wife toward the bar.

"How come it's good enough for him when *you* say it, but when I tell him I love Amara, it's, 'get out of my face, Ryder'?" Cal whined, and Amara and I both broke into laughter as she pulled him past me.

There were still quite a few people outside, and I blinked rapidly when I swore I recognized one of those heads. Before I could investigate further, Delia clasped my forearms and turned my back to the door.

"I have one more surprise for you," she said, "and I need you to not get mad at me for keeping it from you, just like I promise not to get mad at you for lying to me."

"What are you talking about?"

"I invited a few more guests," she said, inclining her head behind me.

"Hi, baby," my mom said when I spun and came face to face with her.

"I—what?" I glanced between her and Delia, my brain short-circuiting. "What?" I repeated.

"Your girl called us," my mom said, tucking herself into my side. "Since you didn't invite us yourself."

My eyes widened, all the blood draining from my face as I stared at Delia, a million apologetic words sitting on the tip of my tongue.

"Like I said," she told me. "I'm not going to get mad at you for lying to me."

"I love you," I told her before wrapping my arms fully around my mom and squeezing her tightly, my eyes closing as I let her familiar, soothing lavender scent wrap around me. They quickly popped open. "Wait, what do you mean 'us'?"

"Just your siblings!" my mom said happily, letting go of me as my brothers and baby sister filtered through the open door.

I was instantly engulfed in a mass of limbs, each of them wrapping themselves around some part of me, our mob morphing into my favorite—and deeply missed—group hug.

At last, they let me go, and I stared at them all in shock.

At Trey, who could've been my twin even though he was almost two years younger, his hair the same shade and damn near the same length, the Lawless Ranch hat settled backward atop it the twin to mine.

At Lane, still testing the limits of his cotton pocket tees with his ridiculous biceps and pecs that I swore got more swollen every time I saw him. Admittedly, it had been a few years since I'd seen him in the flesh, but I reached out and wrapped a hand around one.

"You gotta chill, dude," I said. "You're making me look bad."

"Not hard to do to a washed up QB," he quipped.

I chuckled, hooking my arm around his neck and ruffling his

hair.

When I let him go, my gaze strayed to the twins. Only anyone who knew them well would be able to tell them apart, though the hair helped a lot. Like Lane, Finn preferred to keep the sides shorn close in a high fade and leave the top longer. West liked his long, longer than mine and Trey's even, the sandy blond strands brushing the collar of his flannel shirt. Aside from that, they were carbon copies of each other, two sides of the same coin.

Next to them stood my littlest brother, Crew. Despite the chill outside, he wore his standard short-sleeved Henley, similar to the ones I favored. It provided a stark contrast to the tattoos engulfing his left arm, most of the ones on his forearm doing their best to cover the severe burn scars he'd sustained in a work accident a few years back.

Before I could open my mouth to officially introduce Delia to everyone, a tiny blonde girl rushed me and launched herself into my arms. In a well-practiced dance, I scooped her up and twirled her around, squeezing her tightly.

I returned her to her feet a moment later, squinting at her. Since the last time I'd seen her, my baby sister had grown a lot, losing the last of her youthful, teenage features and becoming a young woman.

"Who are you and what have you done with Aria?"

My sister rolled her eyes. "I'm twenty-two now, O."

I glanced up at Mom, feigning shock. With a delighted smile, she said, "Afraid so. Our baby isn't such a baby anymore."

"God you guys are annoying," Aria said.

"There she is," my brothers and I said in unison, and with a stomp of her foot, Aria disappeared into the crowd in the bar, mumbling about how grateful she was to be old enough to drink.

I met Delia's eyes through the crowd of my family, and as if sensing we needed a moment, my mom touched my arm and said, "We'll see you in there," before ushering my brothers away from us.

In two long strides, my hands were on Delia, crushing her to my chest.

"You did this for me?" I asked into her hair.

She shrugged. "While I'm...*annoyed* you didn't do it yourself, of course I did. They're important to you, so they're important to me. You said it wouldn't be the same without them, so I made sure they were here."

"Fuck, Whiskey," I said, pressing my mouth to hers, murmuring, "I love you," before I pulled away fully.

"Love you more," she replied. "Now what do you say we go mingle?"

Fingers laced, we proceeded onto the main floor, where our friends and family chatted happily over our custom cocktails. The two bartenders were hard at work, and Brie and Ezra had set up camp near the buffet table, where they'd collaborated on a spread of finger foods and desserts for our guests to enjoy.

In one corner, the twins had matching tumblers of an amber liquid—neat and, if I had to guess, bourbon—deep in conversation with Cal, probably pumping him for financial advice. Near the bar, unsurprisingly, Logan and Lane were talking animatedly about something, Logan gesturing wildly as he told a story, Lane clutching his side as he cackled loud enough that I could pick it out over the din of the crowd.

My eyes swept over the room, landing on my mother chatting

with Leon and Lena, the former perched on the arm of the anal couch, the same spot I'd had his daughter bent over two days before.

I quickly averted my eyes, lest he could read my thoughts from lingering too long.

We celebrated deep into the evening, probably later than we should have, both Amara and Chloe taking turns shuttling people to their various homes and hotels.

Unbeknownst to me, Delia and her family had put *my* family up in the Villa, so with them taken care of, after we bid everyone good night, Chloe dropped me and Delia off at her house on their way back to the city.

My limbs and head buzzed pleasantly from the alcohol I had consumed, and as Delia went through her nighttime routine, I shed my clothes and slipped into bed, sighing deeply when my head hit the pillow.

"I'm never leaving this bed," I told her, eyes closed as I sank deeper into the mattress.

"What's mine is yours, QB."

"Is that your way of telling me you're going to force me to take your last name when we get married?" I asked.

My girl barked out a laugh from the bathroom, her head poking around the doorframe a second later. "How much did you have to drink tonight?"

"More than I apparently thought," I giggled.

Yeah, I, a fully grown, thirty-seven-year-old man, fucking *giggled*.

Which triggered a fit of laughter from Delia and, though her face was slathered in some sort of greasy looking substance she'd previously told me was a cleansing balm, she threw herself atop me.

Face inches away from mine, she said, "When we get married, I will absolutely be taking your last name, so you don't have to worry about that."

"Delia Lawless," I drawled. "I love the sound of that."

"One day, QB," she said as she heaved herself off me and retreated to the bathroom.

"I'm ready when you are, Whiskey."

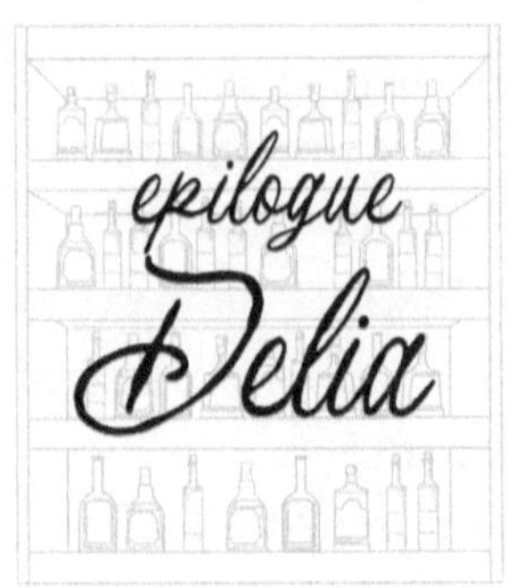

"Whiskey, if you don't get that fine ass down here right now, we're going to be late!"

"Well you won't tell me where we're going, so I don't know what to wear!"

I heard his footsteps on the stairs and a moment later, Owen appeared in the doorway of our bedroom. "You could wear a paper bag and you'd still be the hottest woman alive."

I softened a touch, though I was still frazzled, and approximately twenty-seven dresses littered our bed and the floor around it. I stood in the center of our walk-in closet, clad only in a pair of nude panties. "I love you for saying that, but I disagree."

"Actually," Owen said, stepping closer and wrapping his arms around me from behind, his large, calloused palms coming up to cup my breasts. His head bent, nuzzling my neck, placing a biting, sucking kiss over my pulse. "I think you should go just like this. It'll make it much easier to fuck you later."

I spun in his arms and swatted at him, shooing him away.

"Help me!" I pleaded, fisting my hair at my temples.

"You do realize that, by asking for my help, you're going to wear the first thing I pick out, and you're going to do it with a smile on your face."

I folded my arms over my tits and cocked a hip, glaring at him. "Or what?"

He approached, cupping my chin in his hand. "Or I'll carry you outside just like this and force you to go to dinner in nothing but this floss you call panties." He punctuated his point by slipping a finger under the flimsy material bisecting my ass cheeks, pulling and letting it go with a *snap*.

Though we weren't strangers to seeking our pleasure in semi-public places, the picture he painted wasn't exactly my idea of a good time, so I said, "Noted."

With a nod, Owen moved across the closet to the rack where all of my dresses hung, organized by length and color, sifting through the shorter ones.

I rolled my eyes, unsurprised. The man loved my legs.

Transfixed, I watched as his long, thick fingers danced over the hangers, rapidly considering and discarding each new option.

Finally, he settled on one, and turned toward me holding a little red number with a flouncy, ruffled skirt and delicate straps that crisscrossed down my back, knotting at the base of my spine.

Carefully, he removed it from the hanger and loosened the tie as I approached, steadying my hands on his shoulders to place one leg through the skirt then the other. With a gentle palm on my shoulder, he turned my back to him and adjusted the straps, his fingertips brushing distractingly against my skin as he worked his way down, tightening them before tying the little bow. He hooked his fingers in the material and pulled me back against him. My chest heaved, my desire heightened from the simple act of him dressing me.

Not entirely surprising given that everything about this man turned me on.

"Who knew putting clothes on you could be as fun as taking them off," he said into my hair.

"What happened to being late?"

"I don't know, Whiskey." Against my backside, I felt him starting to thicken, and I couldn't resist grinding my ass into his groin. "You in this dress has me thinking we should just stay home."

"No!" I shouted, shoving out of his arms and heaving a head-clearing breath as I retreated a few steps. "I've been looking forward to this."

"You don't even know what we're doing," he reminded me with a smirk.

I shrugged, moving to my shoe rack and selecting a pair of strappy, scarlet heels, sitting on the padded bench next to it to slip them on. "It's our anniversary."

Owen and I didn't have an anniversary in the traditional sense, so we'd both agreed as the day drew near that the day we first fucked would suffice.

He'd been stuck with me since then anyway, so it was as good a day as any.

That night, we were celebrating one year together, and for once, we were dressing up to go out for some fancy dinner Owen refused to give me any specifics on. All I knew was we were going somewhere in Traverse City. Instantly, I'd guessed Birdie's, being that it was the nicest restaurant in the city, but he assured me that wasn't it. I'd tried over the last couple weeks, since he first proposed this idea to me, to pump him for information. Unfortunately, the man was a vault.

"You're right," Owen said, approaching me and taking my hand, lifting it to his mouth to press a kiss to my knuckles. "It's our anniversary, and you are far too sinful in that dress just to take it right back off. We should at least let people see it."

"And you really should wear a suit more often," I told him, taking my hand back and smoothing them both down the satin lapels of his jacket. In the matching pants, the exterior seams piped with the same satin, and a crisp white shirt, he was looking particularly delicious. He'd forgone a tie, instead leaving the shirt open at the collar, his chain glinting against his skin—the zero now replaced with my first initial—and I leaned in to press a kiss to the sliver of exposed chest.

"We have to leave. Now," he said, and I giggled as he tugged me from the room, lifting me off my feet to carry me down the stairs.

About three months after we'd gotten together, Owen had sold his house on Boardman Lake and moved in with me in ABB. I'd never cohabitated with a man who wasn't my father before, so I could admit I'd been nervous to welcome him into my space.

Naturally, I'd been worried for nothing. Exactly as we'd done everything else, we settled into living together easily. Nine months down the road, it felt like he'd always lived there with me. We converted the spare bedroom on the main floor into an office for him, though he continued to beg me to let him move out to the garage with me.

I shut that suggestion down real fast. A girl still needed her own space.

We made the drive so frequently that the trip from our house to Traverse City passed quickly, mostly with me belting the words to my favorite Taylor Swift album while Owen pretended to be miserable as he silently mouthed them along with me.

Before long, we were pulling up behind Lawless, and I glanced at Owen quizzically.

"What're we doing here?" I asked, though he ignored me in favor of getting out and coming around to help me out. "I thought you said we were having dinner."

"We are," he said, not bothering to elaborate as he slipped his hand into mine and pulled me to the back door.

"Owen!" I protested, attempting to pull him to a stop, a feat I obviously didn't and could never accomplish.

Still, he didn't speak as he punched in the code on the security system keypad, and the door buzzed to admit us.

Since it was Saturday night, reasonably, the place should've been packed and loud.

It was neither of those things, and as we navigated the dark hallway that led out onto the floor, I was hit by a wave of deja vu. Instantly, I was transported back to the first time I'd come here to meet with him, how seeing it in broad daylight, void of people, had caught me off guard.

My god, it was amazing how far he and I had come in a little over a year.

The distillery survived its first winter and was at capacity day in and day out all last summer. This fall had been steady so far, and we were currently discussing the possibility of taking our product to market. In addition, all of Owen's other businesses continued to flourish, and I'd managed to land some marketing partnerships with some national and international brands I loved.

All in all, we were absolutely thriving, and we had a lot to be thankful for.

But the thing I was most thankful for was the man holding my hand, especially as we rounded the corner onto the floor of the club, and the scene unfolded in front of me.

The space typically reserved for the dance floor now held a single round table in its center, a chair on either side, the surface draped with a white cloth and sprinkled with red rose petals. More of them littered the floor, slipping underfoot as Owen led me to the table and pulled out a chair for me. A bottle of sparkling wine sat on ice, and another bottle of red was uncorked and breathing, ready to be poured into goblets and consumed. Candles glittered everywhere, supplementing the low overhead lighting.

Beyond the bucket of bubbly sat a cart, each shelf holding several domed dishes.

"Welcome to dinner," Owen said, gesturing at the cart. "Can I interest you in an appetizer?"

"*You're* waiting on me?"

Owen pursed his lips then flattened his mouth. "I wait on you all the time."

"In bed," I corrected. "Have you ever waited tables a day in your life?"

"Have *you*?" he shot back, and I reclined in my seat. He had a point. "Plus, it's not that hard. Ezra gave me strict instructions.

All I have to do is take the domes off, remove the plates from the trays, and put them on the table. Hardly rocket science."

"Ezra?" I asked, incredulous. "You made Ezra cook for us?"

"I didn't *make* him do anything. I asked, and he agreed. I also paid him a healthy sum for his services."

I shook my head, a light chuckle escaping me. My man was ridiculous.

Honestly, while the meal was delicious, every memory of the dishes Ezra had prepared for us fled my mind the moment we finished dessert and the stage suddenly illuminated.

"What is happening?" Owen only shrugged, turning his attention toward the front of the room.

All the air in my lungs and every thought in my head vacated me when a man stepped out from the wings, a guitar slung across his body, sleeves of his signature flannel rolled up to his elbows, showcasing the tattoos I'd know anywhere.

I gaped at Owen. "You didn't."

"I think I did," he said, reaching out to gently close my mouth. "You're drooling."

"That's fucking *Boston Everett*," I hissed. "Of course I'm drooling!"

"Careful, Whiskey," he said. "Lest you forget how jealous I can get."

I scoffed. "He's the biggest country artist in the world," I said. "He doesn't give a fuck about me."

"You bagged an NFL quarterback," he reminded me.

"Retired," I said, shooting his favorite quip back at him.

"Hi, Delia," Boston said into the mic. "According to your boyfriend, you're a huge fan of mine, and he asked if I'd come out and do a private show for you to celebrate your anniversary. Not gonna lie, man," he continued, directing his attention at Owen, "I about shit my pants when I got your call. I'm a *huge* fan of yours." He chuckled, shaking his head. "So anyway, here we go. This first one is called 'Rich.'"

As the opening bars of Boston's most popular love song rang through the speakers, Owen rose from his seat and extended a hand to me.

"May I have this dance?"

Still in shock that he'd done this for me, I stood on shaky legs and followed him closer to the stage, where he hooked my arms around his neck before looping his around my waist. As we swayed, Boston sang about being rich in love, and I rested my head on Owen's chest. The steady beat of his heart melted into the strings Boston picked, and I floated away, losing myself wholly in this moment.

"Whiskey," he whispered, and I lifted my head to look at him. "I have a question for you."

"If you're wondering if I love you, the answer is yes times a million." I craned my neck, and he met me for a kiss.

With a laugh, Owen shook his head. "That's not it, but hold onto that answer."

As Boston sang the final note, Owen stepped away from me...

And dropped to his knee.

"No."

"Delia..." he warned.

I slapped my palm over my mouth, holding in all the words that flooded forward.

"I performed this exact act a lot in my career," he said, gesturing to his position on the floor. "And a few times since," he added with a smirk, throwing me back to that day at Overtime when he went down on me for the first time.

Exactly a year ago.

"But it's never meant more than it does right now. You are more than I ever bargained for and everything I never knew I needed. This last year with you has been the best of my life. Pardon the football metaphor, but every day with you is a victory. I love you more with each passing second, and now I'm wondering...will you marry me and be my teammate forever?"

I didn't need to consider it. I simply dropped to the floor in front of him and whispered, "Yes, Owen Lawless. Of course I'll marry you."

He patted himself down, at last digging into his pants pocket and withdrawing a velvet jewelry box. When he popped it open, I gasped.

"It's too big."

"No such thing."

"Owen."

"Take the goddamn ring, Whiskey," he growled, withdrawing it from its cushion and sliding it onto my finger before I could protest further.

I lifted my hand, marveling at the way it sparkled. Set on a rose gold band was a large opal ringed by small diamonds. I discovered a new color in the stone with each twist and turn of my hand. It was unlike any ring I'd seen before, and it was utterly perfect.

Owen rose to his feet, pulling me with him, and I latched onto his neck as he dipped me backward and kissed me soundly.

As we straightened, applause broke out around us, and I

opened my eyes to find our families filing down the stairs from the loft.

Wide-eyed, I turned to Owen, and he grinned sheepishly.

"How do you feel about an impromptu engagement party?"

I could do nothing but laugh, drawing him in for one more kiss before I let my sisters fawn all over me.

"I love you, QB."

"Forever, Whiskey."

AS ALWAYS, THE FIRST people I have to thank are my family. My parents, who don't balk when I wax poetic about all the stories I want to write. My grandparents—particularly Granny J, who is the first person to get a signed copy of every book and always texts me her thoughts when she's finished. To my aunts, uncles, and cousins, who are the most supportive, whether it's asking how writing is going, or buying, reading, and recommending my books to other family and friends. I couldn't do this without y'all.

Yeah, I purposely left out my sister because she deserves her own paragraph. Sissy: thank you for beta reading this one, and for always being the one to catch any weird typos and grammatical errors I make, and catching all the tiny plot holes. For letting me babble endlessly about my books and how badly I just want to be writing full time. And for pretending someone else wrote them when you read the spicy scenes ;)

Mer. What can I say that I haven't already? There's nothing

I could put here that I wouldn't—and haven't—said to your face. Dedicating this one to you started as a joke, but the cheeky little "thanks for always believing in me ;)" line is a woefully inadequate way to show my gratitude. I know trying to keep me in line is a thankless job, but I love you for doing it anyway.

Hannah. My dear girl. In the last three books, you have gone from street team member to last second beta reader to alpha reader, and you've slipped into each new role with ease. Thank you for your endless love of and enthusiasm for my stories, for catching every time I say "my" when I meant to say "me," and asking ALL the questions—even when you think they're silly.

Rachel. Your feedback on this story was invaluable, and it wouldn't be the book it is without your comments and talking over plot adjustments with me. Not to mention, your unhinged comments, particularly in chapters 25-33, gave me LIFE. I'm so thankful you came into my life, agreed to read this one, and are such a great friend.

To the rest of my alpha/beta team, Mel, Ray, Michaela, and Chelsea: I couldn't have done this without you! Especially to Ray, Michaela, and Chelsea, who were always there to bounce ideas off in text and generally rooted me on while I worked on this book. I am so grateful to y'all.

To ALL of my author friends—there are truly too many of you to name—who have given me a place to land when I felt like I was spinning out of control. The constant support and encouragement kept me going on bad brain days, and I'll never be able to thank every single one of you enough.

To Lemmy at Luna Literary Management, who agreed to work with me at the last second and showed nothing but excitement for this story from the beginning. I have so loved working with you, and I can't wait for all the success our partnership has in store!

To Samantha, for once again reaching inside my head and plucking out the most perfect and gorgeous cover I could've imagined. I appreciate you more than you know.

To Meg Jones, the creator of the "dicktionary," for letting me include one in the back of this book, and to Hailey Dickert for the "spread your" pages wording. Appreciate you both so much!

And lastly, to my readers. I couldn't keep doing it without your support. Every page read, every post, every reel, DM, and recommendation to a friend—it all makes a difference, and it's the difference between me not doing this and me being one step closer to my dream of making writing my full-time gig. There aren't words for how grateful I am for each one of you, whether you've read one page of one of my books, or all six of them cover to cover. THANK YOU.

AMANDA CHAPERON REALIZED HER passion for books, and for writing, at a young age. Growing up, she was rarely found without a book in her hands, a hobby she carried into adulthood. After joining bookstagram in 2020, she felt the pull to try her hand at novel writing. She writes what she loves to read: messy, relatable characters, lots of steam, and always a happily ever after.

She currently lives in Michigan's Upper Peninsula with Gryffin, her Golden Retriever. She loves all things romance, fantasy, young adult, and thrillers that keep her up at night. You can follow her on Instagram, Threads, and TikTok at @achaperonwrites.

Dicktionary

My dear sweet reader, please use this guide to avoid (or seek out) the spicy scenes, which can be found in the following chapters:

Chapter 25
Chapter 26
Chapter 27
Chapter 28
Chapter 29
Chapter 30
Chapter 33

Spread those pages, my friend.